Double Karma

DOUBLE
KARMA

A NOVEL BY

DANIEL
GAWTHROP

Cormorant Books

We acknowledge financial support for our publishing activities: the Government
of Canada, through the Canada Book Fund and The Canada Council for the
Arts; the Government of Ontario, through the Ontario Arts Council, Ontario
Creates, and the Ontario Book Publishing Tax Credit. We acknowledge
additional funding provided by the Government of Ontario and the Ontario Arts
Council to address the adverse effects of the novel coronavirus pandemic.

LIBRARY AND ARCHIVES CANADA CATALOGUING IN PUBLICATION

Title: Double karma / a novel by Daniel Gawthrop.
Names: Gawthrop, Daniel, author.
Identifiers: Canadiana (print) 20230140963 | Canadiana (ebook) 2023014098X
| ISBN 9781770866836 (softcover) | ISBN 9781770866843 (HTML)
Classification: LCC PS8613.A9813 D68 2023 | DDC C813/.6—dc23

United States Library of Congress Control Number: 2023930238

Cover design: Angel Guerra / Archetype
Cover art: Aung Htwe Nyunt Saw
Interior text design: Marijke Friesen
Manufactured by Friesens in Altona, Manitoba in March, 2023.

Printed using paper from a responsible and sustainable resource,
including a mix of virgin fibres and recycled materials.

Printed and bound in Canada.

CORMORANT BOOKS INC.
260 ISHPADINAA (SPADINA) AVENUE, SUITE 502,
TKARONTO (TORONTO), ON M5T 2E4
www.cormorantbooks.com

For Saw Aung Htwe Nyunt Lay
and the people of Burma

In memory of Paul Cresswell Gawthrop (1927–2018)

Action is a disease of thought, a cancer of the imagination. To act is to exile oneself. Every action is incomplete and imperfect.
— Fernando Pessoa, *The Book of Disquiet*

My actions are my only true belongings. I cannot escape their consequences. My actions are the ground on which I stand.
— Thich Nhat Hanh, *The Heart of the Buddha's Teaching*

PART ONE

1

Rangoon, Burma
March 1989

My first day in another man's identity began with a flash: the blinding glare of a ceiling light the moment I opened my eyes. I tried to speak but couldn't, and if I could, my voice would have been muffled by the bandages wrapped around my head. I tried to turn over, but my whole body throbbed with pain. My head was clouded — I felt like I'd been brought back from the dead — and I hadn't a clue what could have brought me to this state. What had happened? I recalled only the heat of flames, loud voices I didn't recognize, and being picked up and dragged away. Where was I now? Lying on a bed somewhere, in a room with a window.

Within moments of my regaining consciousness, the room filled with people. A man in a white coat asked in Burmese if I knew my name. When I could not speak it, he spoke a name I didn't recognize. Other white coats who came in called me the same name and "sir" or "captain." They asked about people I did not know, places I hadn't been, things I could not recall. I responded with a blank stare until one of them shook his head, saying, "Ah, poor Aung Win. The bump on your head has damaged your memory. Don't worry, it will all come back." For the next few hours, people came in with food, Buddhist pendants, garlands of jasmine, and giant chunks of jade, which they presented with great ceremony. These visitors were uniformed soldiers of the Tatmadaw, the national army. When I noticed that the white coats addressed each other by rank, it dawned on me: I'm in a military hospital. When I speak my first words, they'd better not be in English.

On the morning of my second day of consciousness, a nurse told me a special visitor was on his way. Minutes later, the clopping of army boots down the corridor signalled his arrival. The door opened. A Tatmadaw private stepped in, followed by a second man wearing tinted aviator glasses and an officer's cap. I recognized him at once: Khin Nyunt, chief of Military Intelligence for the State Law and Order Restoration Council. The SLORC. Burma's military dictatorship. A brutal regime that had stomped on the pro-democracy uprising the previous summer, squashing it like a bug. The junta I had fought in the Karen State jungle, when last conscious, beside student and ethnic rebels. An army whose soldiers I had shot at and killed using Thai-funded weapons.

My mouth dried up. I lost my breath for a moment. For I knew what no one else in that room did: I was not a Burmese national but an American citizen of Burmese heritage. A Western meddler. A foreign menace. Now here I was, facing one of the regime's most dreaded figures. Since the crackdown in September, countless students and dissidents had been arrested and jailed before being tortured, executed, or disappeared under Khin Nyunt's ruthless, beady-eyed watch. But the private, who didn't have a clue what I was hiding, proudly introduced me to this monster as Captain Aung Win, a national hero. That's when I remembered my own name and understood what was happening: I am Min Lin. They think I'm Aung Win. The other guy.

The private nudged me, reminding me to salute the spy chief. It took some effort to respond. I painfully and slowly lifted my right arm — still attached to an IV drip — in Khin Nyunt's direction. The senior SLORC officer answered my salute with his own before scolding the private: surely, I needed more time to recover, he said, before my instincts could be a hundred per cent. Then he gestured to the door, inviting in a group of reporters and photographers I didn't recognize. All were state journalists, some appointed after the coup. Flooding into the room, they surrounded my bed. Khin Nyunt stood next to me and placed an arm around my pillow. Then, he turned to the journalists. The flashbulbs started popping as he began to speak.

"Captain Aung Win's bravery on the field of battle," he said, pointing at me, "has been well-established from the moment he joined the Tatmadaw as a young cadet." He went on to describe me as a true patriot and proud Bamar soldier who, in the most recent battle at Maw Pokay, had done the dangerous reconnaissance work necessary for my battalion to overtake the enemy's headquarters and capture a key strategic base of the KNLA. I had risked my own life to save the lives of fellow soldiers, said Khin Nyunt. For this I had suffered a serious head injury.

Khin Nyunt turned to the private, who handed him what looked like a cigar box. The SLORC officer opened it and pulled out a circular bronze medal, its centre bearing an engraving of the Burmese *chinthe*, the lion symbol, inside a star. The medal was attached to a large red ribbon with a green stripe in the centre.

Khin Nyunt continued addressing the journalists. The government had asked enough of Aung Win on the battlefield, he said, so today I was being presented with the nation's highest honour for gallantry, the Thiha Thura Medal. As of this moment, I was also being retired from active duty. Khin Nyunt then reached for my hand and shook it, congratulating me as more flashbulbs popped off.

I thanked him, stammering in Burmese that I did not expect such an honour. He did a double take at the sound of my voice. For an instant — not long enough for anyone else in the room to notice — his eyes narrowed as if sizing me up. Then, with the fake smile returning to his face, he carefully draped the medal around my neck, took my right hand and shook it again. More flashbulbs went off. A staff reporter for *The Working People's Daily*, addressing the senior SLORC officer as if I weren't in the room, asked what I would be doing once released from the hospital. Khin Nyunt squeezed my shoulder as he replied. Aung Win would not have to worry about his future, he assured the reporter, looking at me again, as a special assignment had been arranged for me to serve my country in a non-combat role.

An older reporter interjected, noting that Aung Win was only promoted to captain a few months ago, a rare distinction for a soldier so young. Surely, I should be returning to the field as soon as I recover, no? Khin Nyunt paused a moment to glare at the reporter. "For a man of Aung Win's talents," he said, "there are many ways to serve the Union beyond the battlefield, and he has earned the right to explore them." Then, citing my need for rest, he ended the press conference and wished me a speedy recovery. I would receive my instructions soon enough, he said, pausing a moment before looking me in the eye and telling me not to worry — everything would be fine. I would be fine. Then he left.

I hadn't been asked to speak and, apart from that polite thank you for the medal, hadn't said a word. Now I'd been left alone with my thoughts. My first thought was that I must be going insane. How could my doppelgänger have appeared on a battlefield in Burma, from completely out of nowhere? I didn't have a twin brother. Why did we look so alike? And how could our brief encounter have happened without a single witness before my look-alike vanished? There hadn't been enough time to find out, and all those soldiers who'd spent most of their waking hours with this Aung Win — men who knew his every detail — had mistaken me for their beloved comrade. This mistake had also made it past the country's senior intelligence officer who, inexplicably, had shown up to preside over Aung Win's medal presentation. Why not the soldier's battalion leader or some other lower-ranking Tatmadaw officer? The orderly visiting my room shrugged at my surprise. "U Khin Nyunt must crave the publicity," he said.

Later, an Army private visiting from his Rangoon barracks told me that the rescue operation to take Aung Win out of Maw Pokay had taken twenty minutes. From the moment I was mistaken for him, I assumed, the urgency to save the captain's life must have precluded a proper search for ID. After finding me unconscious, two soldiers put me on a stretcher and prepared my evacuation while the rest of the battalion chased the rebels into the jungle. I was then airlifted by helicopter to the Tatmadaw base at Hpa-an before being transferred by plane to Rangoon. It seems I had fooled everyone without the inconvenience of being awake. But, even with the real soldier now unable to speak for himself, how long would it take for the error to be exposed?

The next day, an excited nurse came in carrying a fresh copy of *The Working People's Daily*. Handing it to me with a big smile, she pointed at my image on the front page. The lead story carried a large photo of a heavily bandaged Aung Win — me — sitting up in my hospital bed, Khin Nyunt shaking my hand after giving me Aung Win's Thiha Thura Medal. The accompanying article, "Maw

Pokay hero awarded for gallantry," appeared from my reading of Burmese to include the verbatim text of Khin Nyunt's speech, along with the part about giving the young captain a non-combat role in a yet-to-be-determined office. Scanning the rest of page one, I spotted a headline in English just below the fold: "US photographer missing, feared dead in Burma." An Associated Press wire story from yesterday, it had been photocopied from an English newspaper and reproduced for the state journal, complete with grainy photo of the blown-up KNLA headquarters at Maw Pokay:

BANGKOK, March 28 — A US photographer has been reported missing and is feared dead in Burma's Karen State after being caught in a fierce battle between Burmese Army forces and the Karen National Liberation Army (KNLA), sources close to the situation say.

Min Lin, 26, landed in Burma last year. A Hollywood-based lensman known more for his work in entertainment and fashion than in conflict zones, Lin was said to have been covering the student pro-democracy movement for a long-term project when he joined insurgents in the Karen State jungle following the military coup on September 18.

When reached by Associated Press, a spokesman for the All Burma Students' Democratic Front (ABSDF) confirmed that Lin had been at the scene of an intense battle between government soldiers and KNLA rebels that concluded yesterday with the rebels' defeat. Anti-government forces fighting the military junta include members of the ABSDF, a student guerrilla organization.

> *"Min Lin was with us in a part of Karen State formerly held by rebel forces," said an* ABSDF *representative, speaking on condition of anonymity. "The Army overwhelmed us, and Min did not make it out of the area. The Tatmadaw [Army] did not take many prisoners, so we fear he is dead."*

The nurse, still going on about the other story, gushed about me being a hero.

The fact that *The Working People's Daily* had run a photo of the wrecked rebel HQ, instead of a headshot of me, to accompany the AP story about my death was a relief: photos of the same man in both stories would have meant serious trouble. As it happened, there wasn't a single image of me circulating on the newswires back then. I was like most photojournalists, preferring to remain behind the lens. The truth was further concealed by the fact I wasn't fully recognizable from the photo in the other story, which showed a highly sedated hospital patient with his head wrapped in bandages. But surely the SLORC would come across my passport and put two and two together, wouldn't they? Perhaps not. I had been using a fake passport with a different name for all but my first week in Burma, the previous year, and had destroyed both passports before going to Maw Pokay. Besides which, a foreign news report of Min Lin's likely death had rendered me a person no longer of interest to the Burmese state. Thanks to those convenient facts, my identity as Aung Win was not in doubt — at least, not among the higher-ups in the SLORC. The Tatmadaw rank and file were another matter.

Over the next week, as I regained my strength, more soldier comrades of Aung Win dropped by the hospital to pay their respects. Most were not satisfied that a simple bump on the head could have produced the degree of amnesia from which I claimed to be suffering, nor explain the accent that was suddenly so different from Aung Win's. All were disappointed that I could not remember them. One who claimed to be Aung Win's best friend was especially troubled by my obtuseness. For ten minutes he interrogated me about where I had been at certain times, the names of my unit mates, and details about my hometown. I shrugged helplessly.

He frowned, saying I was not Aung Win, before spitting on the floor and walking out.

Later, I learned that this aggrieved soldier filed a complaint with his superior officer and demanded an investigation into Aung Win's disappearance. Instead of taking the complaint seriously, his Tatmadaw commander transferred him to a new posting in Kachin State, from which he would never be heard again. Perhaps the military brass thought that Aung Win's best friend was nuts. More likely, his search for the truth was seen as unhelpful to the SLORC's promotion of patriotic narratives, which call for popular captains to lead their units with uncommon valour as they conquer a final stronghold of rebel forces while under heavy fire. Due to such compulsory storylines and a few serendipitous factors — the Tatmadaw's failure to identify the actual Aung Win's remains at the scene, the rushed medevac of me, his look-alike, and the fact no family members had spoken up on the dead man's behalf — it became conventional wisdom that I, the person carried off the battlefield in Maw Pokay on March 27, 1989, was, in fact, Aung Win.

2

Los Angeles, California
November 2012

For many aware of its existence, the land once known as Burma and today known as Myanmar seems more of an idea than an actual country. It's a place that, as a U2 song once put it, turns the old you-need-to-see-it-to-believe-it cliché on its head. "Believing" it to "see" it means that Burma strains credulity as both an object of amazement for its many wonders and a source of deep disappointment for the long suffering of its people. One must therefore believe — by paying attention to its geopolitics, its kaleidoscope of ethnicities, its history of colonial conquest, and its army's hegemonic power — before one can see the causes of its tragically failed potential.

My own relationship to Burma is complicated. My father was born and raised there, but I am Burmese American and grew up without ever setting foot in the old country. As a child, I believed everything Dad told me about the Golden Land. Burma, he said, was postcard beautiful, rich in natural resources and cultural traditions, and blessed with the friendliest of people. But since the 1962 coup, it had been a mystery to the rest of the world, cut off and isolated by the fortress of military dictatorship. In recent years it was easier for foreigners to visit, if only on a seven-day visa. But Dad — who told me he became an American citizen after immigrating to Los Angeles in the late fifties — had no interest in going back. By 1988, when I was in my mid-twenties, it had become a life mission to visit his native land. Having run out of patience waiting for him to change his mind so we could go together, I decided to go by myself.

Despite the seven-day visa restriction, my plan was to find a way to stay in Rangoon for a couple of months and accumulate enough photos to publish and exhibit back home. For a young photographer beginning his career, Burma was a land of opportunity, a holder of secrets waiting to be revealed. Thanks to Dad's Burmese language lessons from my earliest years, I was confident I could make my way around Rangoon and blend in like a local — and there was much appeal in doing so: for the first time in my life, I would be taking a vacation from all the drive-by bigotry, the random and semi-literate taunts of "chink," "gook," "slope" or "slant eyes" thrown my way in the United States. I would be spending every day in a city, a country, where most people looked like me. In Burma, in Rangoon, I would be just like everyone else.

Rangoon
March 1988

Within minutes of landing, I was enveloped by the sopping humidity of the hot season tropics. Stepping outside the airport terminal, I felt my shirt stick to my back, my long hair matted down by sweat. My taxi was not air-conditioned; when I rolled down the window to catch a breeze, my nostrils were assaulted by a strange mixture of exhaust, rubber trees, and fish sauce. During the forty-minute drive into town, we passed scene after scene of local life I presumed typical of Southeast Asia. Weather-beaten men driving cyclos that resembled pre-World War II relics — and possibly were. Groups of women at roadside noodle stalls tending to steaming pans of cheap dinner fare. Shirtless children playing soccer, using a tin can for the ball. My father's people, I thought. Mine too. Entering the city, my taxi snaked its way along the north bank of the Rangoon River until we reached the Strand Hotel.

I had chosen The Strand for pretentious reasons: I thought it would be cool to share the same lodgings once enjoyed by Kipling, Maugham, Orwell, and other titans of the literature I was taught. The Strand, a three-storey Victorian structure with palatial columns and high ceilings, fine antique furniture, and interiors of teakwood and marble, was once among the most luxurious hotels in the British Empire, right up there with Singapore's Raffles and a few others like it, its unchanging presence implying the permanence of The Realm. Now The Strand seemed a little run down — the marble floors were scratched, the mahogany furniture faded and dusty, and some of the paint stripped — but then, under the dictatorship, I didn't imagine there was a lot of money to spend on maintenance and renovations. At least the original handcrafted lacquer ceiling fan in my room still worked.

Exhausted from the flight, I flopped onto the king-size bed looking forward to a deep sleep. But jet lag had taken over; I was too excited by my adventure. After tossing and turning for an hour, I got up to go for a walk. As I left the hotel and headed for Strand Road, I squinted from the setting sun's reflection off the Rangoon River. Along the stroll into the city, giant banyan trees formed a canopy above my head, their elephantine roots sprouting up through the pavement and lifting sidewalks here and there. After a few blocks, my eyes teared up from the smoke of burning leaves blanketing the area with an eerie golden haze. As the sun went down, the shopkeepers closed for the night. All was quiet except for the humming of cicadas and crickets, their chorus broken only by the occasional barking street dog. *I should have brought the camera*, I thought, enchanted by the dreamy, sepia tone ambience of Rangoon at dusk.

My passion for photography began in my teen years. I was good with cameras and enjoyed taking pictures. Photography is one of those activities for which, relying on instinct, you can control the outcome. For me, photography was relaxing; whether it was people, animals, or landscapes in my lens I could fully embrace my subject, pursuing its inner truth while forgetting about the fears that prevented me from facing my own. In my youth I was self-conscious when out in public with my camera, hyper aware of cultural stereotypes and how white America essentialized Asian Americans by noting our affinity for high-tech gadgetry. To this way of thinking, the camera was an extension of my Asianness, the expensive equipment marking me as more exotic. Back when I still cared what other people thought, I made a special effort to appear more sophisticated than a Japanese tourist, hipper than a Hong Kong actor, when out on a shoot. Eventually, I was able to simply enjoy what I was doing. Photography was a way of losing myself in what John Berger called the eternal present of immediate expectation: that endless series of distractions that help us forget. The camera is not about memory, after all; it's about the here and now. But here and now on my first night in Rangoon, I had forgotten to bring the camera. The photos could wait until morning.

In Bandula Park, a public green space opposite Sule Pagoda, I was drawn to a towering obelisk: the Independence Monument. A small group of young people were gathered at its base, one of them clutching a transistor radio. Cries of righteous anger rose from them every few seconds. As I drew nearer, I could see they were students — three girls and two boys, well-groomed and neatly dressed in white shirts and different coloured *longyis*. All middle-class kids, they would have been the picture of carefree innocence but for the distress on their faces, an anguish that seemed too adult for their age. Speaking Burmese, I asked what was wrong. One of the boys, about twenty, stepped away from the group to speak with me. His long black hair was messed up, and his face streaked with tears. His shirt hung loosely over his *longyi*.

Didn't I know what had happened? he asked, his eyes red with grief. When I told him I had only arrived in the country that day and was American, he expressed further surprise and welcomed me to his country. It seemed I had landed in a Burma in crisis. Over the past four days, this young man told me, university students had been protesting government corruption with a series of demonstrations to which the regime had responded with esca-lating violence. On the first day, one student was killed and four others seriously wounded, one later dying of his injuries after being refused medical treatment. This had further outraged the general public and the students, leading to that afternoon's tragic events. A few hours earlier, he said, a group of students from Rangoon Arts and Sciences University, in response to the military's raid on the Rangoon Institute of Technology campus three days earlier, had begun a march that was to end at the Hlaing University campus. When they arrived at Prome Road, on the west bank of Inya Lake, they were met by an army barricade and barbed-wire fencing. The Army did nothing, but a Bren machine gun was pointed at the students. They could not pass.

According to witnesses who managed to escape, the young man said, the Lon Htein riot police snuck up from behind, trapping the students. Some tried to escape by climbing over a tall fence outside the houses on Prome Road. Many who couldn't make it over the fence were beaten to death. Others ran toward the lake and tried to swim away, but the riot police chased them into the water; some they clubbed to death with truncheons, others they drowned by pushing their heads under water. Some girls they raped. The young man, beginning to weep, apologized for taking his leave; he and his friends had to disperse soon or face arrest for the mere act of gathering. I bid him farewell and left the park. Cutting the walk short, I returned to The Strand and called it a night.

I had only been in Burma for a few hours and was already getting a hard dose of reality. The thought of all this killing happening on the first day of my visit, less than thirty minutes' drive from where I stood with those students, shook my confidence in my adventure before it had begun. In my second attempt at sleep, I tried to forget the story I had just been told, an event that came to be known as the White Bridge Massacre. It would be a few more years before journalists and historians uncovered what happened once the killing was over, Prome Road littered with bodies in pools of blood. How empty lorries arrived to collect the dead and take the injured to jail; how fire trucks rolled in to hose down the street, the small white bridge across the culvert — later removed because of its association with that event — and the staircase to the Inya Lake promenade, leaving the area nice and clean as if nothing had happened there; how the dead were incinerated at a top-secret location; and how the grieving parents were left with no answers, the regime saying nothing to account for their children's disappearance.

The next morning, after coffee and a hotel breakfast of *mohinga*, the national dish of rice noodle and fish soup, I began my day with a shopping trip at Rangoon's biggest public market. The first order of business for blending in was to look like the locals, so I spent a while searching for a nice *longyi*. Everywhere I looked, locals of both genders wore this garment. Similar to the dress-like *sarong* in India, Thailand, or Malaysia, the *longyi* is a six-and-a-half-foot by two-and-a-half-foot piece of cloth, usually cotton, sewn into a cylindrical shape. You step into it and pull it up around your waist until the bottom hangs just above your feet, then hold it in place by folding the fabric instead of knotting it. I tried on a blue one. I liked the soft fabric and it fit nicely, so I bought it and a white silk shirt. Then I boarded a bus to Shwedagon Pagoda.

During my late teens, my father and I used to enjoy driving out to La Puente, twenty miles east of LA, to visit the Burma Buddhist Monastery. Until it opened in 1980, my religious upbringing had been limited to occasional supper lessons at home about the Buddhist precepts. Now we had an actual place of prayer to make the precepts come alive, our public participation in Buddhist rites creating a shared sense of community. The temple grounds at the monastery included a large courtyard where local Burmese held social events, a meditation hall where Buddhist scholars came to teach, and a gold-festooned shrine to the Buddha. For Burmese American Buddhists in Southern California, it was a big deal at the time. But this monastery and its humble features bore no comparison to the palatial wonder I was about to discover halfway around the world.

Dad often spoke of the many gatherings he had attended as a youth at Shwedagon Pagoda, where serving as a novice monk was a religious rite of passage for most Burmese males. The country's most famous temple was more than a religious setting, he said, it was civic space that occupied a central part of Rangoon's public sphere, embodying the national psyche itself. Within moments of arriving on Singuttara Hill, I could see what he meant. Spotted from the bus a few blocks away, Shwedagon's glittering spire of gold shone like a beacon from the city's arid, dusty landscape. After entering the temple's north gate and passing between its two white marble *chinthes*, I took off my sandals and began the long climb up the *naga* staircase. Even after stopping halfway up to buy flowers and candles from one of the vendors lining the ascent, I was winded by the time I reached the summit and stepped into Naung Daw Gyi Pagoda.

Inside the temple, the bustle of the city receded into silence. A soft, sandalwood-scented breeze hung in the air. Closing my eyes, I embraced the stillness and inhaled a sweet whiff of the incense; then I calmly proceeded around the terrace, my bare feet baking on the smooth marble tiles. After locating the Buddha's footprint, I passed by one image after another of the ancient historical and Buddha figures I'd read about as a child. Dhammazedi, most enlightened ruler of the Hanthawaddy kings. Kakusandha, said to have lived for four thousand years. Padashin, known for his supernatural powers. Bo Bo Aung, the wizard of Sagaing, whose spirit some of the early independence activists had invoked as a powerful force of resistance against the British colonial occupiers. Given my prior knowledge of these mythical figures, seeing their golden icons imbued them with more power, so I pulled out the Nikon and began to shoot.

At the planetary post for Thursday, the weekday I was born, a handful of locals were lighting candles and laying chrysanthemums. I put down the camera and joined them. "*Thadu, thadu, thadu,*" murmured a middle-aged monk sitting nearby, acknowledging my observance of local custom. For all my determination to blend in, the camera was an obvious clue of my foreign status. I showed my respect with a folded-hand greeting. The monk smiled warmly, his eyes glistening. I wished I could have left our encounter with his photo but that would have cheapened the moment: with the

simplest of gestures and fewest of words, the monk had communicated so much. They say the Buddha is all about *metta*, or loving
kindness. The monk's presence — his appreciation of my offering at his country's most famous shrine — seemed the essence of
metta, the heart of Buddhism itself. Continuing along the terrace,
I found myself thinking about Dad and his peculiar disconnection
from the land of his birth, a country of which he had once been so
proud. When I was a child, he enthralled me with epic tales from
the Golden Land: from pre-colonial history — all the great royal
dynasties, the Bagan Period, the imperial conquests of Siam — to
the modern era with the first independence movement and that
blush of optimism after World War II, a fleeting moment when
independence and democracy seemed compatible. Why was my
father so reluctant to return to his native land?

Distracted by these thoughts, I found myself far away from the
tourists. Having wandered into Shwedagon's southwest corner,
I came upon a towering slab of stone. About ten feet high, the
obelisk was framed with a classic Burmese floral pattern, each
side inscribed with names and a brief introduction in Burmese,
Russian, French, or English. In the middle of a religious shrine, I
had stumbled upon a monument that was entirely political:

This is the place where the first eleven students of Rangoon
College met and affirmed on oath to boycott the Rangoon
University Act 1920 on 3rd December 1920. The names of
the first eleven students are as follows–:–

1. Ba Khin
2. Po Kun
3. Ba U
4. Aung Din

5. *Tun Win*
6. *Pe Thein*
7. *Ba Shin (Sandoway)*
8. *Ba Shin (Tavoy)*
9. *K. Ngyi Peik*
10. *Hla Tin*
11. *Mg E*

Back on the bus after leaving Shwedagon, I sat for a while with no destination in mind, enjoying the passing scenes of Rangoon street life. Then we came upon a large demonstration where, overwhelmed by the crowd, the bus lurched to a stop. Thousands of young people were gathered outside a grim-looking building. Stepping off the bus, I made my way through the masses until I spotted the words "Kyandaw Crematorium" near the building's entrance. I took photos of people shouting slogans, a speaker with a megaphone, and a young woman passing out leaflets. Dressed in a bright green *longyi* and a beige blouse, the woman was about six inches shorter than me, brawny and muscular, with thick black hair that stood from her scalp like a wire brush. She wore no makeup and wasn't pretty in a classically feminine sense but was more boyishly handsome, with dark and pronounced eyebrows. I was drawn to her at once.

When I asked her what the rally was about, she said it was supposed to be a funeral for Ko Phone Maw, the twenty-three-year-old student whose killing by police four days earlier had sparked the protests that led to yesterday's massacre at Inya Lake. But just before the funeral was to begin, she said, organizers were told that Phone Maw's remains had been secretly cremated across town in Tamwe district — a deliberate move to prevent public mourning for a victim of the regime. When I asked her about the leaflets, she handed me one. It was to promote a special meeting to establish the Rangoon Arts and Sciences University (RASU) Students' Union, taking place on campus in a couple of hours. She asked if I wanted to attend. I said yes. When I introduced myself, she said her name was Thandar Aye.

3

Rangoon
March 2013

Thandar:

He was an odd one, that Min Lin. When he first approached me outside the Phone Maw memorial, I could tell he wasn't local. Outgoing and polite, as Burmese men often are when meeting a woman for the first time, he spoke our language well but with a funny accent, very formal, as if he'd learned it from a book. And he had these peculiar gestures — the way he cocked his head when asking a question, the use of his hands to express himself — I had never seen in a man. He was also very pretty, with piercing eyes and a thick, black mane. Such a head of hair! In the moment we chatted before I had to leave, Min said he was a professional photographer from Los Angeles. He was visiting Burma for the first time, but his father was from here. I told him I was a nursing student at Rangoon General Hospital and one of the organizers for the movement. That is why I was handing out leaflets for our big meeting.

When he accepted my invitation to join us, I was pleased by his interest but thought nothing more of it. I didn't expect to see him again and was focused on the task at hand. This meeting was an important milestone in the political history of our country. We were about to launch the first major challenge to the regime in many years, forming a brand new student union that would better position us to build a much larger, national uprising for democracy. I don't think Min realized it at the time, but I had invited him to participate in a critical moment in our movement that, to my knowledge, no other foreigner would witness.

More than two thousand students filled the hall for that convention. There was a great buzz in the air when we called the meeting to order, but as conversations subsided and the last of the creaky wooden chairs settled into place, all that could be heard was the whir of ceiling fans. Sitting onstage with my fellow student leaders, I led us through the agenda completely focused on our mission: to strengthen the movement locally so we could start building student networks across the country. At one point I was distracted by the sight of the Burmese American guy I'd invited to the meeting. Min Lin was taking photos of every student who spoke out against our dictator, Ne Win. I could see he was asking for permission first, but the photos would become a problem if they fell into the wrong hands, so I made a mental note to warn him about this later.

Halfway through the meeting, the back doors opened. In walked the university official who had approved the event, clearly in distress. He had assured us we'd be safe if we remained inside the hall. But now, he said, the Lon Htein riot police had arrived on campus, along with commandos from the Tatmadaw's elite forces. They wanted us out. As he spoke, the official was interrupted by the sharp, tinny broadcast of a loudspeaker coming from the campus lawns: *This meeting is in violation of state security laws. Come out now and you will not be harmed.* Nervous murmurs arose from the crowd; students began shuffling in their seats. I turned to my comrades at the head table, but no one knew what to do. The loudspeaker repeated: *Leave the meeting now, and you will not be harmed.* We knew this was a set-up, but what choice did we have? I turned to my closest comrade, Thida, with a plan: I told her I would lead the students out from the back of the auditorium. But as I rose from my seat, she grabbed my arm and pulled me back down. "No," she said. "I'll go. You stay here and try to maintain order for as long as you can while people start to leave. Just tell them to go quietly, and I'll lead them out."

I did as she said, instructing students to begin filing out from the back. Everyone followed Thida, who led the first few rows outside. As this was happening, a third announcement came over the loudspeakers: *End this meeting at once. If you come outside now, you will not be harmed. You have two minutes.* At this, the remaining crowd erupted in a panic, for we could not possibly empty the hall in two minutes. With a repeat of the White Bridge Massacre on everyone's minds, students began storming the exits. I took the microphone and urged my student comrades to remain calm, to take care of each other.

Outside we were met by columns of army commandos in red scarves, along with Lon Htein forces, all carrying rifles or batons. The Lon Htein officers were throwing tear gas canisters into the crowds of students. There must have been several hundred of these brutes. Bren Gun Carriers and fire engines were parked inside the gates, and there were a lot of police vans. I couldn't find Thida through the haze of tear gas. I figured she must have been hustled into one of those little vans as soon as she stepped outside, for that seemed to be the fate of many students rounded up that afternoon — the police grabbed everyone they could and shoved them into the vans. To avoid this trap, I ran along the side of the auditorium as fast as I could. On my way to the campus gates, almost clear of danger, I ran into Min Lin, who was taking photos of all the mayhem. Without thinking, I grabbed him by the arm and led him to a tree so we could hide.

"Come on," I told him. "We'd better get out of here. You wouldn't want to end up at Insein Prison, where all those police vans are going."

I pointed at the vans, which were being filled with students. These vehicles weren't meant to hold more than twenty or twenty-five people, but it seemed like the police were cramming in four or five times that number. We said nothing more as we slipped away from the tree and ran through the campus gates unnoticed. Once we were safe, I asked Min where he was staying. When he said The Strand, I told him to go straight there and not show up at any more of these rallies. We were lucky not to have been arrested with all the others, which would have been bad for Min. He dismissed my concern, telling me not to worry, then asked if he could see me again. I told him he could, some time, when things settled down. But really, I thought nothing more of it. Min was a foreigner whose one-week visa would expire in a few days — long before anything settled down in my country. I would forget about him. He seemed like an interesting guy — attractive and earnest with a bold sense of adventure. But after Phone Maw, the White Bridge Massacre, and now this campus raid at RASU, I didn't have time for romance. I was consumed by our national struggle, by the fight for democracy. And our troubles were only beginning.

The next day, March 18, 1988, came to be known as Bloody Friday. The day started out well enough when thousands of students marched to Sule Pagoda and were cheered by the thousands of onlookers who joined us. But then the Lon Htein showed up again, once more with the Army's assistance: the Tatmadaw called in its 22nd, 66th, and 77th Light Infantry Divisions to terrorize us. They must have killed a hundred people that day, maybe more, while arresting thousands. By nightfall, an eerie silence fell over the city. Government vehicles mounted with loudspeakers circulated throughout Rangoon, warning people to stay home or face the full wrath of Ne Win. So we did. Meanwhile, schools and universities were closed. Our dictator had made it clear: be peaceful and obey. Or die.

I was worried about Thida, my nursing school comrade who'd led everyone out of the RASU auditorium during the raid. More than a thousand students — half the crowd at that meeting — had been arrested, and more than a few had not been heard from since. Including Thida. I talked to one of the students who was released after being held overnight, a freshman who'd been thrown into one of the police vans. He told me the drive to Insein Prison from the RASU campus had taken much longer than it should have: the driver, trying to avoid public scrutiny along the main streets, had taken another route using back roads. There were maybe a hundred students inside that van, he told me. Already suffocating from the heat, they found it harder to breathe the longer the drive went on.

Once the van arrived at Insein, the driver got out and left it in the scorching heat for another couple of hours. When the doors finally opened, forty-one students were dead. Some had been trampled, but most had succumbed to heat exhaustion, tear gas inhalation, or compressed lungs, squeezed of all air by the desperate crush of bodies packed like sardines. And yes, he confirmed, Thida's had been among the dead bodies dragged out of the van, all of them taken to the Tamwe crematorium, just like Phone Maw's and those of the other murdered students. All because Thida had taken my place in leading everyone out of the auditorium. It should have been me in that police van; it should have been me in the Tamwe incinerator.

25

Over the next week, I stayed close to home and spoke with only a few friends by pay phone. Eventually I accepted an invitation to join some students for dinner in Chinatown. When I arrived to meet them, I recognized someone sitting by himself at another restaurant across the lane from us. The American photographer! He was still there when my friends and I finished our meal, so after bidding them good night I joined him at his table. After reintroducing ourselves, I told Min how surprised I was to see him still in Rangoon.

"Oh, I did leave when my week was up," he said, referring to his expired tourist visa. "But I'm back now!" He smiled and raised his cup of tea at me.

"But how did you get back in?" I looked around to make sure there were no spies within earshot. "The government doesn't often renew seven-day tourist visas, and you couldn't have come back as a journalist."

Min smiled and told me his story. While in Bangkok, he had gone to the bars on Sukhumvit Road and chatted people up about Burma. There he met some Thai and Chinese nationals who helped him, the kind of men who can pass for Burmese and had been to our country many times. The kind who profit from selling Burmese drugs, Buddhas, and gold necklaces on the black market. They told Min not to bother wasting his time on a visa.

"So, what did you do, then?" I asked. Min slapped a Burmese passport onto the table between us. Discretely, I picked it up. In it was a photo of Min with someone else's name and Mandalay as his birthplace.

"It's a fake!" I gasped, looking around again to make sure no one heard me.

Min laughed again. He said he had the passport made at Khao San Road, which I gathered was a place in Bangkok where all sorts of fraud happened right under police noses. I shook my head, incredulous. Wasn't he worried about being caught and arrested? Not at all, he said. The exit stamp from Burma seemed authentic enough at the airport, and when the customs official asked what he did for a living, he said he was a farmer. His long hair was convincing. When I asked him what he did with his real passport, he said he had kept it but was hiding it somewhere. But what if he had been searched at the airport and the authorities found it? Min laughed, saying they hadn't searched him, had they?

I was speechless, shocked by Min's reckless but successful attempt to circumvent my country's military regime. Surely, he wasn't back at The Strand while posing as a Mandalay farmer? Oh no, he laughed, he was laying low this time, staying at a cheap guest house in Chinatown, not far from this restaurant. Min must have sensed my discomfort with his story, for he changed the subject. How is it, he asked, that only a few days after all these brutal police and army actions, my people could simply get on with our lives and behave as if everything was normal? Why was everything so orderly and disciplined, and why were the streets so clean in Rangoon? He wanted to understand how we could be so stoic, given the constant threat of midnight raids, jail, or death for the simple act of speaking out. Weren't we afraid?

I paused to take a sip of my tea, trying not to be too annoyed by this facile Western observation. I told Min not to romanticize the Burmese people. Of course we were afraid, but we had been living this way for twenty-six years — longer than I'd been alive. We had no choice but to go about our routines as usual and not allow the regime to intimidate us. I asked Min if he had noticed how quiet it was in Rangoon most of the time. In most other cities in the world, I said, that would be a peaceful kind of quiet. But not here. Rangoon's was the silence of enforced compliance, I said.

There was a reason Min couldn't see any police or army in the streets: they had done their jobs and didn't need to be there. The police and the army were always in our heads, you see — that is how they controlled us. We were living in a surveillance society. I didn't bother telling him about Thida, still too gutted by her death to talk about it.

Min nodded thoughtfully, letting my words sink in. If he was going to be staying in my country for a while, I continued, he needed to understand the differences between our cultures. We were not the same, although Min had Burmese blood. Then I asked him what he really wanted to achieve here and why he had come to Burma. He said he had always wanted to see his father's native land. It bothered him that his father had never explained why he left Burma and refused to return. Min had been pestering him for years to come back but with no luck. So here he was, experiencing my country for the first time on his own. By seeing Burma through Burmese eyes — by meeting and photographing as many of my people as he could — Min's ultimate hope was to learn more about himself. He was also tired of "celebrity chasing," a meaningless competition for the best photos of the hottest personalities in Hollywood, where he lived and worked. He was seeking more meaningful subject matter in ordinary people who lived in extraordinary circumstances, people whose choices were limited by circumstance. That's what made Burma so appealing, he said: it offered him a chance to capture human portraits seldom taken by other American photographers.

I appreciated his honesty. Min had come to my country to bear witness to our people and our culture. Based on his impressions through captured images, his aim was to show Burma to the rest of the world. I hadn't met many foreigners like Min Lin. The few I had met — all white European, Australian, or American students who knew much less about Burma than Min did — I had not allowed to get close enough to trust. But Min was persuasive. His Burmese heritage and facility with our language, combined with his Buddhist perspective, carried a lot of weight. And I must confess to a degree of opportunism on my part: his photography, however profitable for him, might also prove useful to The Cause, to our growing democracy movement.

That is why, when he asked me to help him find subjects, I agreed. Despite my activist commitments, I found time over the next few weeks to buzz around the city on a motorbike with Min, showing off Rangoon while convincing taxi drivers, merchants, food vendors, street artists, monks, and other average citizens to let him take their photograph. Min was interested in everything and everyone, so no corner of the city was left unexplored in his attempts to capture what he called "the Burmese moment." In Bogyoke Aung San Market, two young women out shopping, their cheeks dabbed with *thanaka* paste. In a Tamwe tea house, a trio of old men playing cards, their laughter exposing betel nut–stained teeth. At Insein Township, a group of teenage boys enjoying a game of *chinlone*, the Circular Train passing behind them as they deftly foot-tossed the tiny rattan caneball between them.

Min was a real professional. He knew how to make his subjects relax, how to capture them in their most natural state. But during the shoots he also tried interviewing many of them. He wanted to know more about their lives, and what it was like to live under the Ne Win regime. I advised him to keep the conversations light; nobody wanted to be turned in by their next-door neighbour for saying the wrong thing to a foreigner. But Min surprised me again, gaining his subjects' trust after only a few minutes of conversation. Fascinated by the chance to become acquainted with an American — and, no less, a Burmese American who could pass for a local

— most people he photographed were happy to share their opinions about the Ne Win regime and the sorry state of Burma's economy. We all have opinions, they told Min, we just want to be free to express them, like you are in America.

4

Min:

Entering Burma with a fake passport was a stupid thing to do. I knew it was risky but did not feel the consequences until Thandar confessed, three weeks after my return to Rangoon, why she hadn't yet introduced me to her family: it seems her parents weren't thrilled by the optics of hosting an American photojournalist with a fake passport posing as a Mandalay farmer. When at last she invited me for supper at the family's three-storey mansion in Mayangone Township, it was only after convincing her mother and father that she and her two brothers would tell no one of my visit. Humbled, I was determined to leave a good impression.

Both civil servants born and raised in Rangoon, Mr. and Mrs. Aye were the cream of the Burman Buddhist crop — society people of impeccable breeding who were warm and generous in their welcome despite the security risk I posed. When I showed up at the family home, they greeted me at the front door formally dressed in the finest of silk *longyis*, magnificently coloured and radiant. Mr. Aye directed me to the living room, where I sat on a silk cushion on the polished teakwood floor. Mrs. Aye asked Thandar to help present the traditional Burmese feast she had prepared for the occasion — tea leaves, pulses and beans, an assortment of curried meats, and steamed vegetables with jasmine rice, all of it served from shiny metal boxes on a silk cloth that Thandar carefully spread out on the floor in front of me.

Thandar's brothers, both history majors at RASU, arrived as the meal began. Also formally dressed in fine silk shirts and *longyis*, Aye Maung and Hla Min were polite but said little during the meal, observing in fascinated silence as I dropped food and struggled not to fall over while sitting cross-legged on the floor. I had never eaten with my hands this way and didn't recognize many of the dishes. Burmese food did exist in California, but I had been raised on an all-American diet, so I only ever sampled this exotic cuisine at the annual Thingyan festivals, where everyone sat at tables using cutlery. It was a sobering revelation that all my advance training — the language lessons, the monastery visits, the history books from Dad — was hardly adequate preparation for the culture in which I was now immersing myself. Despite a rapidly improving Rangoon accent, I hadn't convinced anyone at that dinner that I could pass for a local. But I was a good sport, laughing with Thandar's family at my clumsy Burmese manners as I reached over the deep-fried insects and hard beans and helped myself to the green tomato salad.

After the visit, Thandar and I began seeing each other every day. The more time we spent together, the more she seemed to forget about my potential security risk as an American. She clearly took delight in showing me the Rangoon that she knew. When we weren't arranging photo shoots, we wandered aimlessly through downtown streets, stopping now and then to browse in a bookstore, catch a film at the cinema, or enjoy an hour of people watching from the tea houses near Sule Pagoda. One day she took me on the Circular Railway for a train ride that tracked the circumference of the city, giving me a glimpse of peasant life on the margins of Rangoon. These were neighbourhoods where people lived on next to nothing but enjoyed the richness of community. All around the route, whether at the trackside markets or in front of the corrugated tin shacks of family homes, I took photos of people who met every day and looked out for each other. Kids playing games. Mothers hanging the house laundry. Vendors selling produce, rice, and betel nut, all of it carried in large bags on their heads before being poured onto wicker trays for market display.

Thandar also accompanied me on a second visit to Shwedagon, pointing out things I might have missed the first time. That chorus line of young women I noticed sweeping dust from the temple's polished marble floors? They were volunteering their time to make merit, she said; during the monsoons, they swept out the rainwater. That reminded her of other public displays of the faith, such as those colourful parades of Buddhist drummers that pass through residential neighbourhoods. I had taken several photos at one of these processions, delighted by the way it brightened an otherwise dull afternoon. Visiting foreigners are always impressed, said Thandar, but these parades lose their charm once you realize their purpose as donation magnets for the temple, to which even the poorest of Rangoon residents contribute. At one point during our Shwedagon visit, we found ourselves standing in front of the student monument I had seen the first time I went, the one with the list of eleven names of the first student activists. I was surprised, I told Thandar, that a regime so threatened by the student movement would allow such a tribute in the country's main temple. But Burmese history, religion, and politics were more complicated than that, she assured me.

The purpose of the 1920 boycott of Rangoon University, she said, was to protest the British colonial education system. The university's administration and curriculum were seen as elitist because they excluded the Burmese people. Colonial-era law only permitted students from the privileged schools, the minority elite, to attend RU. Because the Rangoon College students had used this spot at Shwedagon to plan the strike, their gathering was regarded as the first heroic act on the road to Burmese independence. So, when Ne Win created this monument in 1970 to mark the fiftieth anniversary of the protest, said Thandar, he was honouring those students as great patriots. Today's students were great patriots, too, but there was a difference. The students of 1920 wanted an independent Burma, which they achieved. Today's students wanted a free Burma — and yes, it was Ne Win who stood in their way.

Taking a stroll on the Kandawgyi Lake boardwalk, we competed for bench space with teenage couples — young people with raging hormones who, having escaped the prying eyes of their families but with nowhere else to go for privacy, huddled beneath umbrellas to feel each other up. When they weren't sneaking out with their boyfriends this way, I learned, most Burmese girls and young women were chaperoned by brothers or other male relatives when out on dates. But Aye Maung and Hla Min had left Thandar and me alone. Perhaps they thought she was old enough to take care of herself. Perhaps they saw me as less of a threat than other young men who had bid for her affections. Or perhaps they regarded their sister as impervious to the attentions of men in general. Whatever the case, they saw no need to accompany us during the Thingyan festival in mid-April. Part of me wishes they had.

Back home, Burmese New Year was little more than a traditional dinner for overseas Burmese — a dry event, in every sense of the word. But in its country of origin, the Thingyan tradition was to toss a cup of water at your neighbour as a friendly bit of harmless fun and community-building during the hot season. In recent years, that little cup has been replaced by firehoses and water cannons. The Thingyan festival is now an annual occasion for sanctioned, if temporary public sensuality, an unspoken licence for Burma's youth to get drunk and celebrate the body in what amounts to a five-day-long, communal wet T-shirt contest.

It wasn't quite like that in '88, but it was festive for sure. On the day we attended, Thandar and I spent a couple of hours getting soaked while dancing among hundreds of revellers on Kabar Aye Pagoda Road. At one point, I turned my back on her just as the mass of bodies began squeezing us closer together. Forcefully pulling me towards her, she held on tight, her breasts pressing against my naked back through her wet blouse as she wrapped her muscular arms around my chest. Out in the open, away from this crowd, I'd have had trouble concealing what began rising beneath my *longyi*. But in this mass of intoxicated youth, not even Thandar was aware of my erection.

Our chaste romance continued for months. Toward the end of May, we took the bus north to Mandalay, where Thandar was helping organize students. Spending a few days in the former capital, we slept in separate dorms on the Mandalay University campus where Thandar did her activist work. She could sense my impatience to spend more time together, so one afternoon she left a meeting early and dropped by my dorm. Joining her on the back of a rented motorbike, I wrapped my arms around her waist as she sped us away from the downtown centre, past the moated grounds of the imperial palace toward Mandalay Hill. We parked at the bottom, then spent a while exploring Kuthodaw Pagoda. Inhaling the jasmine-like scent of the starflower trees, we wandered through the maze of shrines containing the "world's largest book": seven hundred and thirty marble tablets etched with the script comprising the entire Buddhist canon. Then we followed a meandering footpath up to the summit.

The sun was about to set when we arrived at Su Taung Pyae (literally "wish-fulfilling") Pagoda and passed through one of the decorative archways to the terrace. Squinting from the glitter-ing iridescence of the temple's gold-festooned pillars in the day's remaining light, we crossed the polished marble tile toward the patio's edge and leaned over the railing to look down on the city beneath us. Saying nothing, we held hands and gazed at a shim-mering strip of water in the distance, the setting sun's reflection off the Irrawaddy River.

Thandar broke the silence. The two months I was planning to stay in Burma were almost up, she said. How much longer did I intend to stay? I had to think about it. Two months seemed hardly long enough, and only now was I seeing the country beyond Rangoon. I told Thandar I had barely scratched the surface of Burma, with so much more to see and do, and besides, I liked her so very much. She said she felt the same about me, but that we had to be realistic. I was an American. There were people waiting for me back home, where I had responsibilities. If I stayed in Burma much longer, I would have to find a way to make a living, and my fake identity would become harder to hide from the authorities. I said I could make enough money selling photos overseas, and no one would discover my identity.

Then she got to the point. The Burmese people were headed toward a confrontation with the Ne Win regime, she said. Life was about to become a lot more dangerous. Things could get out of control and sooner than I might think. So, she needed to know how committed I was to the movement.

What a question! I told her I was committed.

She wanted to know if she could count on me if there was to be more violence from the Tatmadaw or the Lon Htein, something bigger than in March. Could I make that promise? Would I stand up for her?

I laughed: "Don't be silly, Thandar. Of course, I will."

At that moment, a passing European tourist carrying the same camera as mine stopped to compliment me on my good taste. Then he pointed at my Nikon, offering to take our photo. Handing it to him, I sat on the ledge beside Thandar. She draped one arm around my shoulder and goosed me from behind with the other, just as he pressed the shutter.

Universities reopened in June. The protests resumed as if nothing had stopped them, with students back on the streets seeking justice for the bloodbath in March. Thandar was at the forefront. One day, she produced a leaflet urging all students to join the struggle — *Never forget Bloody Friday. Free Burma!* — and enlisted volunteers to help distribute copies on every campus. At one school, a first-year student told her that no one was taking the leaflets; people were too afraid to challenge the regime. In response, Thandar called together the volunteers and collected their leaflets, stuffing them all into a giant bag. Then she led everyone upstairs to the fourth floor where, opening a hallway window, she dumped the entire bag into the square below. The leaflets rained down like confetti on surprised passersby. "There," she said. "Problem solved. An hour from now, you won't find anyone who hasn't read it."

The generals responded with a twelve-hour curfew and a ban on public gatherings. The students then called for a general strike, scheduled to begin at 8:08 a.m. on the eighth day of the eighth month of the year 1988: auspicious timing, according to numerologists. A few days before the big event, Thandar called me at the hotel, telling me to bring my camera to 54 University Avenue. There was someone I had to meet. Taking the bus to a winding, tree-lined street at the south end of Inya Lake, I was allowed through the property's gated entrance, then walked down the driveway until I arrived at a simple white villa, a remnant of the colonial era, facing the lake. The first thing I noticed in the foyer was a framed black and white portrait of slain Burmese independence leader Aung San. The General was handsome but expressionless in this image, exuding a Buddha-like calm in his immaculate features, dressed in a military overcoat and officer's cap that seemed too big. Taken in the last year of his life, when he was only thirty-two, the photo suggested a proud and defiant patriot staring confidently into a future he would not live to see.

As I was studying this portrait, another door opened. Thandar emerged, followed by a tall, elegant woman in her early forties, dressed in a purple silk *longyi* and a white cotton blouse. Her long black hair was tied up in a bun, neatly adorned with a white orchid. She had the delicate features and bearing of a princess. Thandar introduced me to Aung San Suu Kyi, the great man's daughter. Surprising me with flawless English and an upper-class British accent, she welcomed me to Burma saying it was a pleasure to meet me and that she hoped I would find what I was looking for here. That last comment was a perfectly innocuous bit of small talk — and not the first time a Burmese national had said such a thing to me. But in the moment — and given The Lady's importance — I found it oddly unsettling, as if intended to put me in my place. For Suu Kyi, told in advance that I was American, had marked me unequivocally as a foreigner, instantly destroying the fantasy I had embraced since being accepted into Thandar's inner circle. *Wasn't I Burmese too? Weren't we all looking for the same thing?*

I said nothing but nodded politely in response. Then I switched to Burmese to give Suu Kyi instructions while preparing to take her portrait, seating my VIP subject in the foyer against a plain white background. Without prompting, she folded her hands on her knee exactly as I would have suggested — she was a natural, the camera loved her — then sat through several frames before excusing herself and leaving us alone. Thandar said that Suu Kyi lived in Oxford with her British husband and their two sons. After flying back to Burma a few months ago to look after her ailing mother, she had been staying at the family home and was keeping an eye on national affairs. In recent weeks, she had invited democracy activists to hold meetings here. Now the pressure was on for Aung San's daughter to follow in the great man's footsteps.

On July 23, Ne Win announced his retirement as Supreme Leader, ending his twenty-six-year reign as Burma's strongman. The regime was losing its grip. Transition to democracy seemed inevitable, possibly weeks away. Everything was coming together beautifully. I was living a life of adventure. I had met a person I wanted to be with all the time. And Burma's future was looking bright after so many years of darkness. How could love and justice not prevail? As general strike day approached, we knew August 8 would be all-consuming. Thandar and I would not see much of each other, given her duties at different rallies all day. But when I phoned her on the night of August 7, I insisted we meet for breakfast at a tea shop in Lanmadaw Township, before her first big rally. She said no. We would be too busy to take time for ourselves. But I insisted on a meeting. This was something I could not share over the phone.

At eight minutes past eight o'clock the next morning, shipyard workers walked off the job on schedule to begin the general strike. Thandar and I were sitting down in the *lat-pei-yey-saing*, a Burmese tea house, to order breakfast. When the server left us alone, I pulled a small box out of my pocket and gave it to Thandar. The moment she opened it and set her eyes on the modest, fourteen-karat gold ring, I asked her to marry me. She gasped. We had known each other less than five months, but she had become my universe. I loved everything about her and marrying her seemed the right thing to do. My father would not only approve, he would get off my back. Thandar and I could figure out the sex thing later.

Staring at the ring, she paused a moment and then laughed as she wiped away a tear. "Yes, you silly fool," she said, looking searchingly into my eyes. "I will marry you."

5

Thandar:

I still can't believe he did that — nor that I said yes. How serious could he have been, proposing to me on general strike day? At the time, I thought really serious. Min was awkward but sincere about his feelings when he found a way to express them. The longer we were together, the more it seemed he had no intention of returning to the US but wanted to forge a life with me in Burma. Min said he was deeply attracted to me. The feeling was mutual, but he was hard to figure out: he never tried making an advance on me, like other men did. When it came to his work as a photographer, or expressing opinions about art and politics, he was as confident and forthright as anyone I'd met. But when it came to dating, he was passive and shy; it was as if he didn't understand his role, as the man, to take the lead. So when he proposed, I didn't hesitate to say yes. Not only had he taken initiative at last, but in recent weeks he had begun taking more liberties by holding my hand, kissing my cheek, or stealing the odd peck on the lips. And it worked. A hopeless romantic, I fell for him.

Min wanted to tie the knot right away. I said there was plenty of time and insisted on waiting until the national struggle was over. I did want to marry him, but I thought we should wait until

democracy came to Burma; until the Army got out of politics and
civilian rule became the law of the land. Because I wanted us to
take that personal step in a free society, I thought we should keep
our engagement a secret until final victory was won. If the uprising
failed and the government threw everyone in jail, they would find
out I was engaged to an American, and there would be trouble for
the two of us and my family. I insisted we tell no one, including
my parents, until the struggle was over. Only when the regime was
toppled, free elections were held, and a democratic people's party
took government would we formalize our commitment.

When August 8, 1988 began, such a fate seemed inevitable.
Throughout the country, people stopped working to observe the
general strike. In Rangoon streets, masses numbered in the hundreds
of thousands. Soldiers abandoned their posts to join us rather than
acting against their fellow citizens. It was exhilarating, this sense
that people power was truly prevailing after twenty-six years of
dictatorship. The historic events surrounding us only heightened
our euphoria in the wake of our breakfast engagement. How could
I not have said yes to Min when every big rally, every shouted
slogan, every smiling face among the thousands we saw that day
was like a giant "yes" to our collective and personal futures?

The euphoric feeling lasted until just before midnight, when
Tatmadaw forces came out of the shadows and began spraying
civilians with automatic gunfire. From that moment on, there was
no future to talk about — only the present. Our lives were now
at risk. Two more days of violence followed. Troops opened fire
at Rangoon General Hospital, killing medical staff as they tried
to protect patients. One of the dead was a mentor in my nursing
program, a good friend and one of the most selfless people I had
ever met. In the weeks that followed, more of civil society joined the
demonstrations. Rallies were held in cities and towns throughout

the country. Meanwhile, Ne Win's replacement resigned after eighteen days.

On August 26, Aung San Suu Kyi formally began her political career with a speech at Shwedagon Pagoda that drew half a million people. She condemned all violence, calling for a people's consultative committee to act as an intermediary between students and government. The resistance soon expanded to include civil servants, lawyers, writers, actors, and singers. Former prime minister U Nu — deposed as Burma's last democratic leader in 1962 — proclaimed a parallel government with himself as prime minister. And, as expected, student activists formed the All Burma Federation of Student Unions, making ours a truly national movement. For a few weeks, it seemed, the popular uprising was gaining critical momentum; this was our finest hour as citizens, with so many people courageously standing up to this morally bankrupt regime.

But I can't say I was proud of everything, and there were troubling signs that the People's final victory might prove elusive. Several weeks of violent clashes between protesters and district authorities led to the collapse of municipal government; neighbourhood committees took over local administration. Prisoners staged riots, including at Insein, where nine thousand inmates, including hardened criminals, either escaped or were released by the government. Meanwhile, in our zeal to punish an evil regime, some of us played judge and jury of anyone deemed to have colluded with it. One day, spy agents from the state's Directorate of Defence Services Intelligence were exposed after infiltrating the protest movement in Rangoon. Activists responded by arresting these people and chopping off their heads. In North Okkalapa Township, outraged citizens beheaded four police officers with an ancient sword. Elsewhere, suspected informants were similarly decapitated, the offender's head impaled on a stick and displayed in a public square as a warning to would-be traitors.

A sense of chaos began to take hold. The government refused to budge on our demands, ignoring our threats of an indefinite strike. By mid-September, our actions had failed to move the country any closer toward representative government. How would it end? The answer came on September 18 with a grim announcement over state radio: the Tatmadaw had launched a coup against the sitting regime. The Burma Socialist Program Party was disbanded, the cabinet replaced with a new military junta called the State Law and Order Restoration Council, or SLORC. Soldiers were deployed throughout the country, their orders to dismantle strike centres and blockades wherever they found them. Resisters were to be shot on sight. This was a military coup against a military regime. Could things possibly get worse?

With precious little time to act before we'd all be arrested, the students' federation called a series of emergency meetings. At the one I attended with Min, a group of self-appointed martyrs proposed that we continue marching in the streets. The rest of us knew this plan was suicidal. None of us could forget the White Bridge Massacre, the RASU campus raid, Black Friday, or Ne Win's warning the day he retired as dictator, that when the Tatmadaw shoots, it doesn't shoot up in the air, it aims for its target. Hadn't the SLORC just given shoot-to-kill orders? And yet, because our power as a movement had grown since March, there were more than a few dreamers still among our ranks, students who believed that continued acts of civil disobedience would be met with nothing more than a prison term. How sadly delusional!

There was a second option, I told everyone, raising my voice above the chatter: we could leave the capital, dissolve the ABFSU, and regroup in the jungle as a revolutionary movement.

The moment I said it, conversations stopped. People turned to face me, some with fear in their eyes, others shaking their heads in dismay. Min clutched my hand to get my attention. We hadn't discussed this idea in private, so my bringing it up here came as a shock to him. Truth be told, I shocked even myself. Until Thida's death, I still believed the Tatmadaw had at least a shred of basic decency. When all those soldiers came to our side, I thought there was still a chance that the generals would hand back power to the people. But then they started killing protesters by the dozen and slaughtering medical staff at RGH. A government that murders health care workers and other civilians is not interested in sharing power. Many of us would die for democracy, so why not go down fighting? Several comrades, I reminded everyone, had already left for the jungle while we sat here in Rangoon, twiddling our thumbs.

One of the martyrs was unconvinced. He said it was impossible to join the insurrection from Rangoon. I repeated myself: Some of our brothers and sisters had already joined the Karen National Liberation Army and other ethnic rebels near the border. These rebels had weapons and could train us to become battle-ready. It might take a while, but if we combined our resources, we could build the capacity to fight back and overthrow the SLORC. The room fell silent. Some of my comrades, if not surprised that a woman was calling for violent insurrection, seemed alarmed that I had raised the possibility so openly. This only made me wonder about the more weak-kneed among them, those who might not have disagreed with revolution in principle but, if arrested, might feel compelled to reveal its strongest advocates. Scanning the room, I was no longer sure who I could trust. But my concern was moot for the moment. A vote was held; we would continue marching in the streets, with a rally scheduled for the next day.

Min:

Thandar scared the hell out of me at that meeting. I had no idea she was capable of armed struggle; she had given no clue in all our time together. My fiancée was a nursing student, a future health care provider, not a killer. So her intervention at that meeting of the All Burma Federation of Student Unions came as a shock. Since the end of May, our relationship had deepened to the point where all I could think about was how we would spend the rest of our lives together. It didn't matter where. I could easily imagine us building a future in California or staying here in the new democratic Burma. But how long would this New Burma take to become reality? And would it ever happen if armed struggle was the way to get there? I worshipped the ground Thandar walked on, so I had to trust her. But I had a funny feeling that our commitment to marriage had just become a theory to be shelved indefinitely.

Was she saying she'd be willing to go into the jungle and join the rebels herself? I asked, confronting her after the meeting. She was surprised by the question. Of course she would. And I would join her there, right? She looked at me earnestly, no doubt recalling my promise in Mandalay. I thought of her family, of how devastated her parents would be if she joined the rebels. I felt sick. But yes, I replied, of course I would join her there.

I had come to Burma to take pictures, not wage war. The notion of killing for democracy seemed hypocritical and self-defeating, a contradiction. Mine was the wrong temperament for armed combat. I detested the patriotic machismo of US gun culture, from the obsession with defending private property to the nauseating legacy of proxy wars in Southeast Asia and Central America. I had contempt for the gun culture's narcissistic freedom fetish, its demonization of any man who refuses on principle to own a gun. This was a culture steeped in white supremacy that enabled all sorts of knuckle-dragging bigotries. Forced at eighteen to register for Selective Service, I had vowed never to report if Uncle Sam came calling, which luckily didn't happen. I thought I had avoided guns for good. But now here I was in Burma, engaged to a future health care worker who suddenly wanted me to channel my inner Rambo.

As it happened, Thandar was outvoted at the meeting so the question of joining the rebels was put off. Instead, she would join a group of students for another rally the next day. I would be there with my camera. But from the moment I arrived downtown late that afternoon, I knew the rally was doomed. The jubilation of recent weeks had been replaced by a deep sense of foreboding, of inevitable carnage. In the days before the coup, the Tatmadaw's presence had been limited to Rangoon's periphery; now the soldiers were everywhere, with Army units deployed throughout the city. Making my way to the rally on foot, I had just reached the corner of Sule Pagoda and Bogyoke Aung San roads when a Tatmadaw Jeep pulled up to the curb behind me. Four soldiers jumped out, each carrying a Kalashnikov rifle. All skinny recruits barely out of their teens, wearing uniforms far too big for them, they carried weapons that seemed bigger than their bodies. They ran past me, toward Sule Pagoda, with a crazed look in their eyes — a combination of deer-in-the-headlights fear and steely, single-minded intent.

I followed behind them from a good distance. Within a block of the Buddhist shrine, I saw what was happening: the four soldiers were joining a couple dozen others who had spilled out from the alleyways onto both sides of the street, each unit falling into formation with a larger group in the centre under the barked commands of a bullhorn. I had arrived, a few minutes late, on the wrong side of the street; a mass of soldiers blocked my view of the front. But this was where Thandar and I had agreed to meet, so it must have been the nursing students the Tatmadaw were confronting. The soldiers took no notice of me; I turned around and snuck up an alley, circling back until I came out to the area where the students were. From the sidewalk, I searched desperately for Thandar but couldn't find her in the front row, which was composed entirely of nursing students chanting "Democracy now!"

Where the hell was Thandar? The protesters kept chanting slogans. The commanding officer shouted his orders into a bullhorn. The soldiers knelt on the ground and aimed at the crowd. The chanting stopped. For a moment there wasn't a sound but the safety clicks of a hundred rifles echoing off the buildings around us. And that's when I spotted Thandar in the front row, leading her group. The commanding officer gave the order. Between the first report of gunfire and the second, I thought I saw a red splotch appear on the front of my fiancée's white blouse. But it wasn't Thandar whose body went limp and fell to the ground; it was the student standing next to her. Four others dropped like rag dolls while she remained standing. The crack of gunfire was soon accompanied by ear-piercing shrieks as people realized what was happening and began to scatter. When I saw Thandar turn to run, I began chasing her. At one point I tripped over a boy crossing my path. When I looked up, my fiancée was gone.

For some time afterward, I would second-guess my response after the shooting began. Instead of hanging on with the deep current of humanity flowing down Sule Pagoda Road, why hadn't I fought against the crowd to look for Thandar? Why had I assumed, after scanning the pavement for bodies, that she had dodged the bullets and escaped down a side street? But I was too hard on myself. After losing her, I could not have ignored the soldiers shooting in my direction. I had to go with the crowd. Pulling out my camera, I clicked away as I ran. Within a few minutes, dead bodies were everywhere. I took pictures of it all: of the dead and injured being lifted onto rickshaws, pickup trucks, or the backs of bicycles, and of people risking their own lives to provide water, tourniquets, or medicine to those struggling for theirs. Eventually I put the camera down to help out, spending several hours into the evening assisting with transports to the hospital. Then, exhausted, my clothes soaked with the blood of Burmese students, I returned to my low-budget hotel in Chinatown.

The man at the reception desk turned away at the sight of me, not wanting to witness anything he might have to report to his employer — or the police. Safe in my room, I took a long shower before sitting down to guzzle a couple of Tiger beers. Then I fell asleep until a crowing rooster awoke me at dawn. After putting on a clean cotton shirt and a pair of jeans, I stuffed my bloody clothes into a bag for the trash bin, grabbed my camera, and left the hotel. Wandering the empty streets, I looked for signs of the slaughter I had seen a few hours earlier. As with the White Bridge Massacre, the city had been cleansed of most evidence of atrocity. But there was at least one telling detail. An image that, despite its lack of human subject, told the story: a blood-spattered curb, the crimson pool beside it having drained into a sewage hole next to a swept-up pile of abandoned flip-flops. My last photo in Rangoon.

I hailed a taxi. As the car made its way toward Mayangone Township, my mind kept returning to a young student I had tried to keep warm as he lay dying in the street, the blood gurgling from his mouth as his guts fell out. I was haunted by the bewilderment in this boy's eyes, his disbelief and despair that his short life was already coming to an end. At Thandar's house, Mr. Aye met me at the front door and directed me to the living room where his wife was waiting. The floor was covered with shattered glass and books pulled from their shelves. Antique British sofas had been torn open with knives. Mrs. Aye directed me to one of them before joining her husband on another. There was no sign of Thandar or her brothers.

"The Tatmadaw raided our home at three in the morning," explained Mr. Aye. "They took Thandar to Insein and her brothers to the police station. Aye Maung and Hla Min will be released in a few hours," he added, "but Thandar is likely to receive a long prison sentence. And you have been in the thick of it, Min. You should leave the country at once."

But I had to tell Mr. Aye that Thandar and I were engaged to be married.

He sighed. He told me that one day I would make a fine son-in-law. But I would not be much help to Thandar, or to the family, from a jail cell. The uprising was over. I had to leave.

Mrs. Aye, wiping away a tear, nodded silently as her husband spoke.

I never saw them again.

6

Mr. Aye was right: I should have fled the country as soon as our conversation ended. There would have been no shame in flying home. I could have had my photos published, raising awareness of the situation in Burma in real time. I could have lobbied for Thandar's release. For a few hours, I did consider leaving. But hopping on a plane at the first sign of trouble seemed the easy way out. Choosing that moment to return to my life of safety and privilege in the United States felt wrong when all the new friends I'd made in Burma were stuck, living through the fresh hell of a SLORC dictatorship. And Thandar, my fiancée, in the worst hell of all at Insein.

Thandar had called on her fellow students to go into the jungle and fight. I opposed violence for political ends, but I had come to Burma to gain new experience and perspective. The more I thought about it, the relentless brutality of the SLORC made the notion of joining an armed insurrection defensible. A reckless bid for democracy through guerilla warfare might seem counterintuitive, but who was to say that joining the rebels meant I had to embrace a combat role myself? There was plenty one could do that didn't involve fighting, and I could still be useful to the revolution with my camera. So there it was: in the time it took me to gulp down a few nervous shots of Mekhong whisky in my hotel room, I decided to join the rebels.

There was not a lot of time to act. If I was arrested in Rangoon, the SLORC would eventually match my photo with their records from March, find my real name, and uncover my fake identity as a farmer from Mandalay. Tracking my movements over the previous months, they could also identify me as a foreign enabler of pro-democracy student radicals, establishing a connection to Thandar that would endanger her family while making her own situation worse. So if I wasn't getting on a plane to go home, I needed to leave the city right away.

A few hours after my visit with Thandar's parents, I went looking for students in the only place they would still be safe in Rangoon: Shwedagon Pagoda. Around the corner from the student monument, I recognized a young man in disguise, with a shaved head and dressed in the Full Saffron — Kyaw Zwar, a student leader I'd met at a few meetings with Thandar, an engineering major at the Rangoon Institute of Technology who had joined the protests in June. I liked Kyaw Zwar. He was earnest and friendly, well-informed and inquisitive, interested in learning more about the world beyond Burma. Each time we met, he had peppered me with questions about life and politics in the United States. Fascinated by our system of government and how our constitution guarantees freedom of speech, he was more eager to explore our similarities than our differences. And he knew a lot about how democracy had worked in Burma before 1962.

Now disguised as a monk, Kyaw Zwar spotted me as I approached him from the terrace. Taking me by the hand, he led me to a hidden corner near a stupa, his bright orange robe flowing behind him. Why was I still in Rangoon? he wanted to know. When I told him I wanted to leave and was looking for a way out, he said he was fleeing the city later that night with a few comrades, heading to the border. I asked if I could join him. He agreed to let me accompany his group, but I wasn't to breathe a word to anyone. Just pack a few things and meet him at three a.m. behind the clothing factory in the South Dagon industrial park. I wasn't to be late!

Our journey to the Karen rebel compound at Manerplaw, not far from the Thai border, took us a couple of days. To make our way there, we depended on the kindness of strangers. From South Dagon Township northeast to Pegu, we rode in the back of a chicken farmer's truck. From there to Kyaikto, a produce van. To the Karen State capital of Hpa-an, a semi-trailer with industrial parts. Into the jungle towards Kawkareik, a straw-filled ox cart. For the final stretch, a Karen rebel army truck. Along the way, I became better acquainted with my travel mates. Kyaw Zwar was the youngest at twenty-three. The rest were twenty-five-year-old graduates, all history majors and arts students who had survived the White Bridge Massacre. I was struck by how events had aged these young men. Barely into adulthood, they carried themselves with the world-weary heaviness of battle-scarred war veterans. And yet, far from being discouraged by defeat in the streets of Rangoon, their sense of purpose had hardened. Back home, most educated guys their age I knew were preoccupied with girlfriends, cars, or finding a good job after graduation. But Kyaw Zwar and his friends cared most about democracy, freedom, and representative government. In a country like Burma, ideals were the only escape from despair.

Manerplaw, a village nestled along the Moei River about a hundred miles north of the Thai border town of Mae Sot, means "victory field" in the Karen language. Founded in the early seventies by Bo Mya, a pro-Western chairman of the Karen National Union,

Manerplaw lay at the heart of an ethnic insurgent–controlled liberation zone known as Kaw Thoo Lei, the proposed capital of an independent state the rebels hoped would one day be governed by the Karen people. Bo Mya was one of those charismatic rebels for which Burma was becoming infamous — like Khun Sa, the Shan State drug lord and leader of the Shan United Revolutionary Army, who embraced his own legend as a renegade and outlaw — and had the press clippings to show for it.

In recent years, Manerplaw had become a gathering place for anti-Rangoon forces. In the wake of the coup, the crowded field of Burman and ethnic opponents of the SLORC could fill a small football stadium. It was hard to tell the players without a program. There was the Democratic Party for a New Society, the National Democratic Front, and several other groups, including one loyal to former prime minister U Nu. Shortly before the September coup, at the age of eighty-one, U Nu had declared himself head of an interim government. This after leading an armed resistance group, some years earlier, that tried to defeat Ne Win from the border. U Nu was something of a Buddhist weather vane, switching from peaceful non-violence to armed insurrection as circumstance saw fit. Some praised him as the country's first democratic leader, but history has not been as kind given his decision to make Buddhism the state religion.

Within a few months of our arrival, Manerplaw would see the birth of a new coalition. The Democratic Alliance of Burma would include the Karen National Liberation Army and more than a dozen other opposition groups like the All Burma Students' Democratic Front — the guerrilla army whose birth Thandar predicted before her arrest. Enthusiasm for the Alliance would be short-lived, but in early 1989 it was a big deal: never before had so many Burman activists accepted ethnic minority leadership in their bid to overthrow the dictators. On our first day in Manerplaw, Kyaw Zwar's group and I reported to the teakwood mansion head-quarters of the Karen National Liberation Army. I insisted on doing nothing more than photography. Apart from my feelings about guns, I made a good case for non-military status: I had no more experience handling a firearm than the urban middle-class Burmese students who had recently signed up for the rebellion. "Fair enough," said the KNLA recruitment officer; I would not be forced to fight. But I wouldn't be of much use in Manerplaw if I was only taking photos, either. Instead, he suggested I continue down the road and cross the border to Mae La, where there was more than enough work to do supporting refugees.

Mae La, a former base for KNLA rebels on the Thai side of the border, had recently been converted to a giant reception centre for more than a thousand refugees from Karen State, people whose homes and villages the Tatmadaw had burned to the ground. East of Manerplaw, it was the safest place for SLORC opponents to hide and still be within spitting distance of the revolution: thanks to the pro-rebel sympathies of its residents, Mae La was a convenient shelter for students on the run who weren't quite prepared to pick up arms but wanted to help the resistance. The camp, spread across the town's muddy hillside, was a crowded cluster of bamboo shacks on stilts, each structure separated by a few trees.

Reporting to a KNU organizer at the camp, I agreed to serve as an interpreter while assisting medical staff. As long as the NGOs kept providing health care, food, and clothing for displaced Karen villagers, almost none of whom spoke English, there would be no shortage of things to do when not taking photos. The daily sight of malnourished children dressed in rags was hard to take, but my heart melted with every smile on those kids' faces after a meal. Once I was directing a Karen girl of about twelve toward the medical tent when I happened to touch her shoulder. She recoiled, backing away from me.

"You'll need to keep some distance," a Karen medic told me. "This girl thinks you're native Burman. She's not a big fan of Burmans, having been raped by Tatmadaw soldiers."

Turning to the girl, the medic apologized on my behalf, telling her I was American; she gradually relaxed in the remaining few weeks that I served her family.

Also humbling were the thanks from refugees grateful for the NGO-provided clothes I gave them. One middle-aged farmer wept as I handed him his bundle: he and his three teenage sons had been wearing the same clothes since escaping their village a month earlier. Most gratifying was the reunion of a five-year-old boy with his parents. Separated after the Tatmadaw destroyed their village, his mother and father assumed the boy was dead. But when I checked a manifest of recently arrived orphans, his name and village were on it. After locating him and confirming his identity, I sent him running into the arms of his overjoyed parents.

I was beginning to feel like I was making a difference when I was confronted by an inconvenient truth. The more I learned about these Karen families, many of whom had fled their burning villages with nothing but the clothes on their backs, the less convincing were my arguments for avoiding combat. By this point I hated the SLORC with a passion, and the Tatmadaw were its military expression — the storm-trooping front men for the junta. After a couple of months of meeting so many people in trauma after barely escaping Burma with their lives, after all the senseless slaughter I had witnessed committed by the SLORC and by the Ne Win regime in its final gasp, I made my peace with war. Abandoning the pacifist, non-violent political stance I had once thought inviolable, I signed up for basic training.

Back in Manerplaw, the Karen squadron leaders put me and my fellow trainees through the paces with relentless workouts three times a day, with repeated cycles of push-ups and pull-ups, sit-ups and crunches, squats and lunges, running races, and strength tests like tug-of-war. After four and a half months of this, I felt like a new person. Before joining the rebels, I was indifferent to physical fitness: a shiftless bohemian, soft and lacking definition. Now I was lean, muscular, alert. A quarter could bounce off my abdominals. I had sinewy arms and legs, and the cardiovascular fitness of a long-distance runner. I had a mind whipped into shape with tunnel-vision purpose thanks to the military training which included hand-to-hand combat, knife-fighting skills, ambush techniques, and lectures on strategy, including how to gain territorial advantage regardless of terrain. I also grew familiar with the Karen rebels' arsenal of weaponry: from machine guns and hand grenades to rocket-propelled grenades and mortars, flame-throwers, surface-to-air missiles, and rocket launchers. Once deemed ready for combat, I was assigned to an ABSDF squadron joining Karen forces on a mission heading northwest.

Before leaving Manerplaw, I gathered all the film canisters from my time in Burma. Then I paid a KNLA recruiter traveling to Chiang Mai to courier the package to the Associated Press bureau chief in Los Angeles. I included a note giving AP the rights to all my photos until I returned — or died. Then I destroyed my passports, ripping out every page and watching them burn in a fire barrel. I was surrendering my identity to the whims of fate: Min Lin and the Mandalay farmer no longer existed. The camera, too, had become excess baggage: having chosen combat over journalism, I was now a rebel responsible for his own rifle, ammunition, and other heavy equipment. Leaving behind the Nikon was hard, but I reluctantly let it go, handing the camera and all its accessories to the KNLA recruiter who would be stopping by Mae La on his way to Chiang Mai. At my request, he gave it to a refugee camp organizer — a welcome replacement for an older, inferior Pentax his NGO had been using to document camp life.

High up in the rolling hills of a mosquito-infested mountain range straddling the Thai border lay a critical strategic base for the KNLA, a village called Maw Pokay. Its location along the Moei River marked a key point on the line of defence for thousands of rebel troops dedicated to establishing the independent Karen republic of Kaw Thoo Lei. The Tatmadaw had been pounding Maw Pokay for the past five years. Field reports said they were close to capturing it, so the KNLA were sending in our squadron as reinforcements. When we arrived around mid-March, we spent a few days fortifying the camp and preparing for battle. Our HQ, located at the end of a grassy field beside a deep forest of rubber trees, was a simple bamboo shack, its only notable feature the flag on its thatched roof bearing the KNLA's blazing-sun-and-star logo. But it lay on coveted ground: once the Burmese Army captured it, they'd be able to cut off key supply routes for the rebel forces. That's why they had spent so much time in this area, engaging the KNLA every now and then in a cat-and-mouse game of "who controls the river."

When Tatmadaw forces began shelling Maw Pokay late on the afternoon of March 25, I feared for my life. This was not the fear of September streets in Rangoon — the adrenaline rush of avoiding gunfire as random targets at a demonstration — but something of a much deeper, more existential sort. The fear that comes from suddenly realizing you're part of a sustained military engagement where there's no turning back; the fear of knowing that, as rebels going head-to-head against a massive national army, we were stuck in a numbers game where the odds of getting killed were far greater for us than for our opponent. On March 25, it was this kind of fear that gripped me as the first bombs exploded around me and the first bullets zinged past my head, inches from killing me. Dropping to the ground I crawled into a trench, my heart pounding so fast and so hard I thought it might explode. My skin broke out in a cold, nervous sweat. In that moment, I thought about Dad, of how he'd tried to stop me from going to Burma. And I thought about Thandar, rotting away at Insein for inciting the very action I was now taking on her behalf. *Well, here we go,* I thought. *I guess this is it. Let's see how long I last.*

By clearing the landscape in front of HQ, we had left advancing Tatmadaw forces exposed, allowing us to attack them with mortar fire. The minefield we had planted was picking off Burmese soldiers by the handful but not enough to make a difference in our overall fortunes. And how could it? The combined KNLA/student rebel force was only five hundred soldiers strong, no match for a Burmese Army brigade of five battalions — or six times the manpower, at three thousand soldiers. On day two, I was standing next to Kyaw Zwar, my student buddy who had brought me along with his friends on the long trek from Rangoon, when he was hit by a mortar. Bleeding out from a nearly severed torso as he lay in the weeds beside me, he gathered what little strength he had left to lift an arm and reach for me. I held his hand and tried to comfort him as he took his final breath.

After three days of fighting, several scores of KNLA and student rebels lay dead. But we had killed more than our share of Burmese soldiers, and I had done my part. Over the first two days, I lost count of the Tatmadaw soldiers I had shot dead or blown apart with grenades tossed from the trenches. I felt sick about it. I had signed up for war after adopting Thandar's cause, putting aside all reservations about violence for political ends. But having been through the actual fighting and dealt with the primal fear of combat during days one and two, I was numbed to the shock and horror of it all by day three. With the end now in sight, and my own death a foregone conclusion, I thought nothing of walking into the line of fire. Acceptance of my doom had infused me with the hollow courage of fatalistic indifference.

Our HQ was now within reach of the Tatmadaw. KNLA command was growing desperate. There was little choice now but to retreat or face annihilation. During a mid-day pause in the fighting, the rebel commander called us together. We needed a decoy, he said. Then he pointed at me. I was one of the few good Burmans he had left. He commanded me to approach him. He handed me a pile of folded clothing I recognized from the green fabric: a Tatmadaw uniform. This one bore captain's chevrons but no nameplate. The plan was to abandon the trenches on the hill overlooking the Moei River, basically inviting the Tatmadaw to climb up and swoop right in on us. Everyone except for me would be hiding in the jungle behind HQ. My orders were to stand in front of it, posing as a Burmese Army captain, then wait for the advancing Tatmadaw forces to crest the hill and cross over the trench. I was to beckon the first few of those soldiers toward me until they were close enough for my comrades to launch an ambush.

The success of this strategy depended on the illusion that I was an actual Burmese Army regular who had somehow arrived here ahead of his unit. It was a low-percentage strategy, and everyone knew it, but I was in too deep now to refuse — and, as it happened, the uniform fit perfectly. I was about to leave the building when the commander stopped me. I couldn't possibly step into the field with such long hair, he said; the enemy would know right away that I was not real Tatmadaw. So he ordered a private to cut it off. All of it. When the hack job was done, the commander gave me a pocket mirror. A few comrades gathered around, breathing down my neck as I regarded my own reflection, whistling like a bunch of idiots at a go-go bar. Desperate to find humour in anything. Yes, I was a handsome Burman cover boy, all right: the epitome of a Tatmadaw captain. But what difference did it make? I was going to die out there. We all knew it.

By mid-afternoon, radio reports indicated that Tatmadaw forces had begun their advance up the hill and were only a few hundred yards away. The compound grew silent — we knew what was coming — and I reviewed my assignment. With KNLA and student rebels hiding in the jungle behind me, I was to walk no further than twenty paces in front of HQ and wait. When the first of the Burmese soldiers reached the top of the hill, I would call out a signal as if I were one of them, then draw them close enough for my comrades to step out of the jungle and fire away. A knot grew in my stomach. Was this how I was to die? On some shitty little mountain range in Southeast Asia, fighting someone else's battle? Without Dad ever finding out where I was? What would my father think of me now, dying for democracy as a killer-hero? Would this make me a man in his eyes? And what about Thandar? Would my death on a blood-soaked battlefield in Karen State convince her of my commitment to The Cause?

At three o'clock, the commander gave his signal for me to leave the building from the front. Taking my rifle, I obeyed while he and the rest of my comrades walked out the back and headed into the forest. Stepping outside, I felt the sun's burning heat on my face and shoulders. There wasn't a sound but my own breathing and footsteps, my boots crunching through bone-dry weeds. I had only stepped a few paces before I spotted a Tatmadaw soldier about thirty feet away, standing still. I hadn't prepared for an early arrival. I was supposed to be alone outside HQ, anticipating the sight of Tatmadaw troops clearing the edge of the hill, more than a hundred feet away. How had this guy managed to get so close to HQ without any of us noticing? And why was he alone? I had no idea what to do since it was no longer necessary to beckon him over. I froze as he kept walking toward me. When he was within fifteen feet, he froze as well.

Holy shit. How on earth could this be possible?

The guy looked exactly like me. Ethnic Burmese of the same height and build, he had the same dimpled chin, the same pronounced lips and high cheekbones, the same pencil-thin brows over matching brown eyes. Every detail of the man's face and figure was completely identical to mine: eyes, nose, mouth, jawline. The works. If I hadn't just been shorn of my long black mane minutes earlier, that would have been the only difference between us. But as it happened, our jet-black hair was cut exactly the same way on our identically shaped heads. For a few seconds, all we could do was stand there in wonder, staring at each other and twitching our faces this way and that, as if doing so would result in simultaneous identical motions. I'm sure he was hoping — as I was — that he had merely stumbled upon a giant looking glass in the middle of a forest. Why were we both here? What should be done about this mind-blowing coincidence?

My double, an actual Tatmadaw soldier, was here to conquer the Karen rebel HQ. With the rest of his comrades sure to join him at any moment, he had bumped into me, his doppelgänger — the only thing standing between him and his prize. After a few seconds, he seemed to realize that my presence was a trick by the enemy, a ruse intended to throw off the Burmese Army and set up an ambush. I could see from his eyes that he'd figured out our trap. Since his mission was to take our headquarters by force, his only option now was to fire the first shot of the afternoon at the rebel who happened to be defending it. From the moment we set eyes on each other, our hands were shaking as we gripped our rifles. But now, stepping forward while I remained frozen, my double calmed himself. Lifting his rifle, he was about to squeeze the trigger when he hesitated. Then his eyes opened wider, and he glared at me, taking aim again.

"*Yut! Ma-lotpar net!*" I shouted, telling him to stop and not shoot. I had raised my arms and dropped my rifle — not so much to plead for my life but only to convince him to talk. But the real Burmese Army captain said nothing as he took one more step toward me … and then the explosion.

I was on the ground. Stunned but okay, apart from the sharp sting of shrapnel grazing my right shin. My uniform was spattered with blood. His. My double had stepped on a land mine, the last explosive device we'd planted in front of HQ, detonating it before he could shoot me. The blast, which had thrown him several feet, had torn off his left leg at the knee. Still conscious, he sat up and regarded his gushing wound, eyes bulging and mouth agape. Then he looked over at me. We kept eye contact for a few seconds as I crawled over to reach for his gun. It seemed as if he was on the verge of saying something, of speaking to me at last, when a rocket-propelled grenade fired from the bushes behind us whistled past my ear and blew his head clean off. His decapitated torso rested briefly in an upright position before sagging to the ground like an overturned sack of rice. I bent over and began vomiting.

Moments after launching the RPG, my comrades spilled out of the forest to begin the ambush. But they were too early: the dozens of Burmese soldiers who followed their now-dead captain up that faraway hill had only just crested it and begun charging in our direction. By spotting their enemy from a distance, they had foiled our ambush plan and were now in position to return fire at no disadvantage. Back on our side, my comrades had little choice now but to unleash a thundering fusillade — all at once, every bullet and missile we had left. Too dazed to join them, I was still adjusting to the shock of first meeting my look-alike and then witnessing his gruesome obliteration when Tatmadaw shells began landing all around us. One scored a direct hit on the headless corpse of my double, the explosion cratering the ground where it lay while blasting it apart, reducing it to scattered pieces of anonymous DNA.

My comrades kept shooting at the advancing Army troops as I rolled around at their feet, covering my ears from the deafening roar. As Tatmadaw forces continued powering their way toward us and my rebel comrades continued dropping dead or retreating into the forest, I stood up to face the inevitable. The last thing I recall was the hissing arc of a mortar shell grow louder as it drew nearer. I do not recall the projectile's impact when it hit HQ, nor the moment I was thrown back by the explosion and knocked out when my head hit the ground.

7

Twenty-four hours later, I woke up in that military hospital bed, mistaken for my dead double, expected to act, feel, and be exactly like him. After taking a full week to recover from my injuries, I informed my caregivers that I was ready to learn about my future as Aung Win — about the "non-combat role" I was expected to fulfill as a national hero. A few hours later, I received a visit from the junior SLORC official tasked with bringing me this news. I would not be working for the Tatmadaw, he said, but for the larger state apparatus. Instead of being trotted out for parades and school assemblies to extol the virtues of army service, I would be tucked away in an office writing news releases for the Ministry of Information. In Burmese. Uh-oh. Not good. Although I had learned how to read and write in basic Burmese as a child, I was woefully out of practice and nowhere near as good a writer as I was a speaker of the language. It would show.

Thinking quickly, I apologized and told the SLORC official I must decline the assignment. Having suffered nerve damage in the fingers of my right hand from a previous war injury that had neither been diagnosed nor reported, I was incapable of using a typewriter as efficiently as before and my handwriting competence was severely diminished. As a writer, I would only become a burden to the Ministry, whereas I didn't need my right-hand fingers so critically to hold a camera, as that was my shooting hand. Could I be assigned as a state photographer instead? My request was granted. Soon, another puff piece about Aung Win appeared in *The Working People's Daily*, this time praising the national hero's hidden talent.

The new job came with a brand-new Nikon. I missed the one I'd left behind in Manerplaw, the one I had donated to the refugee camp in Mae La before heading to Maw Pokay. Having a brand-new replacement, and so quickly, was great. But my delight was dampened by the fact I'd be using this camera as a propaganda tool for the SLORC. I would be misrepresenting the actual state of the country with endless photo ops featuring loathsome junta officials. Or, out in the field, images of smiling Burmans getting along famously with ethnic border peoples. There might be some novelty to this insider's view of the dictatorship for the first few weeks. But after that? I shuddered to think. Clearly, I needed an exit strategy for this life as Aung Win.

Before my discharge from the military hospital, I received new clothes and a personal identity card bearing my photo, a new address, and Aung Win's birthdate: January 4, 1962. Wow. Independence Day. Was he really born on that date? Or was he an orphan, merely assigned that date because his real birth details were unknown? This was a common practice, my father had told me, with babies given up for adoption who had no records. The desk clerk giving me the card saw me regard it carefully and smiled: "Lucky you, Captain! Not only are you a national hero, but you also have a hero's birthday!" He then apologized for the joke: someone had told him that Aung Win's original birth certificate had gone missing after he was born. With no other copies available, and no parents to vouch for him, he automatically became a January 4 baby.

A young corporal, after directing me to a military Jeep, drove me to my new home. As we passed through the downtown area, I noticed dramatic changes to the city's landscape since my escape to the border in September. The double brick wall surrounding the Defence Ministry on Signal Pagoda Road, with bunkers facing the city's main entrances; the conversion of Prome Road from a tree-shaded avenue to a four-lane concrete highway completely stripped of its trees; and the bulldozing of entire neighbourhoods regarded as hotbeds of radical activity. Downtown Rangoon was now a military fortress, its public sphere reduced to a grim arena of defensive architecture.

As we entered the leafy district surrounding Inya Lake, I suddenly realized I was being given special treatment. Instead of the usual military lodgings of cement-block row housing at one of the city's Tatmadaw bases, I was being taken to an exclusive neigh-bourhood on the tonier side of town. On the west side of the lake, a few minutes from Aung San Suu Kyi's villa — and less than a mile from where the White Bridge Massacre took place — we turned into an asphalt driveway and proceeded through a thick forest of bamboo. Where the greenery ended, the skies opened up to reveal a waterfront property the likes of which I'd never seen. The house, which stood at the edge of an oval roundabout, was a three-storey Beaux-Arts mansion built in the French neoclassical style. It had marble pillars, arched windows, and a flat roof crowned with deep cornices. On the lakeside, mangrove trees flanked a boardwalk running along the property's edge. At the roundabout in front of the house, a marble fountain shot vertical blasts of water. The Jeep pulled up beside the fountain, next to a cement pathway leading to the house.

"You've got to be kidding," I told the driver. This was where I'd be living? No joke, he replied. As a national hero, I might have ended up at the Kandawgyi Palace Hotel. Nice bungalows but not very spacious. Luckily for me, the house had become available a few days earlier when its previous occupant, a once-respected colonel, was charged with theft. Such disgrace, I later learned, was a typical fate for those who lost the senior general's confidence. The colonel was convicted and sentenced to seven years at Insein. Out with the old, in with the new.

Stepping inside, I gazed up the teakwood spiral staircase that led to the top floor and stared at the foyer's thirty-foot ceiling. Then I turned into the kitchen. Despite a cooking island in the middle, there seemed enough floor space to host a dance competition. A hired chef, assigned to the house 24/7, introduced himself and asked what I'd like for dinner. Embarrassed, I asked him to surprise me. Upstairs in the master's chamber, I took a long cold shower before putting on a silk robe and flopping onto the mattress of my king-size, four-poster bed. After gazing out the window at a postcard view of Inya Lake, I fell asleep. Later, I spent a while wandering through the house and marvelling at its jade sculptures, its rock fountains, and its sculpted teakwood banisters. When I passed by the kitchen again, the chef let slip that he was preparing roast beef with Yorkshire pudding and whipped mashed potatoes for dinner. A Western meal! The butler asked if I'd like some red wine with that. Then he led me to the basement, where he showed off the mansion's temperature-controlled wine cellar. The racks, seven feet high and ten feet long, were fully stocked with international wines of various vintage. The butler dusted off a well-aged French red from Château Cheval Blanc: a Premier Grand Cru Classé, Saint-Émilion, 1982. The last bottle of it, he told me, saved by the house's previous occupant. How a colonel in the Burmese Army would have known of such a vintage, much less obtained it, was beyond me. I hadn't been within a whiff of such a wine, one of the world's finest Bordeaux. I was thrilled by the prospect of washing down a gourmet meal with it.

I drank lustfully as I drained the first glass. But with every sip of Saint-Émilion, every tender, mouth-watering morsel of beef that passed my lips, my mood began to shift. At first there was contentment. After so many months of near brushes with death, I was now in the lap of luxury, enjoying world-class cuisine and the finest of grape. *I've earned this*, I thought. A few sips and bites later came the guilt. It was only my predicament as an imposter that had granted me access to such undeserved bliss, a decadence most people in Burma could not experience and which I was enjoying at the expense of a fallen colonel who happened to be locked up in the same prison as my fiancée, a few miles away from where I sat gorging myself. I was savouring this meal in a mansion owned by the state, with its spectacular view of Inya Lake, while being served by a five-star chef and butler, Burmese nationals impeccably mannered and deferential toward me because of my supposed position, as a Tatmadaw captain, in Burmese society.

As I shoved the last piece of beef into my mouth and drunkenly shook the last drop of Château Cheval Blanc into my glass, there came a deep sadness. All at once, the recent traumas — the battle for Maw Pokay, Thandar's arrest, the crackdown in Rangoon — came flooding back in a wave of emotion. When I thought about all the students massacred by the SLORC; about the deaths of rebel comrades like Kyaw Zwar, with whom I had travelled from Rangoon and come to know over months of training before witnessing his horrible end in the jungle; about the Burmese soldiers I had riddled with bullets, most of them younger than me; and about my double, the man who would be sitting here in my place if he hadn't been blown to pieces, the tears kept flowing. I thought about Thandar and the other political prisoners languishing at Insein. What would they be eating for dinner right now? I knew I'd become a blubbering mess when, slumped over the table with a silk napkin on my lap, I turned around to see the butler and the chef, who had stepped out of the kitchen at the sound of my sobbing. Seeing the concern on their faces, I apologized for my unseemly display — battle trauma, I pleaded — thanked them for the excellent meal, and retired for the night.

I still had trouble accepting that I had bumped into a total stranger who looked exactly like me. There had to be an explanation for Aung Win's existence but finding one would be a solitary pursuit. Part of me wondered if I had imagined the whole thing. Perhaps it was the fog of war, the result of a severely concussed brain from my battlefield injury, messing with my mind. It all happened so fast, our encounter, that maybe it was a trick of the light, and we were not so identical, Aung Win and I, not carbon copies at all. Perhaps it was merely a coping mechanism, a way of pushing the horrible memories of combat out of my mind by focusing on a bizarre coincidence. But if that were the case, why did so many people think I was him?

So far I had fooled almost everyone about my true identity, and now I possessed that most critical of documents: a Burmese ID card declaring that I was Aung Win. Having come this far, I would rely on my Burmese roots and improving accent to continue fooling everyone with my performance as a Burman Buddhist patriot adored by the masses. Meanwhile, there was no shortage of reasons to be paranoid about possible exposure. When I first woke up in the hospital to my new reality, I was confident there were no images of me circulating in the media back home, nothing the SLORC could dig up through the wire services that would blow my cover.

But then I recalled an image that would have shown up in the film cannisters that were forwarded to the AP bureau chief in LA, just before I left Manerplaw: that photo of Thandar and me, taken by a tourist on the summit of Mandalay Hill. Without having developed the film, I'd never know how well that picture turned out nor how recognizable I might be. But the worst part was knowing that the AP, who had my permission to publish any photo they wished, must have gone through those film rolls trying to find an image of me to run with stories about my disappearance. For the rest of my time in Burma, I lost more than a few hours of sleep over this.

Then there was the mystery of the dead captain I was impersonating. Who was this Aung Win? Without a doubt, I would need to be discreet when seeking information about the man I was pretending to be. Asking government clerical staff for Aung Win's file would draw instant suspicion — especially if I offered a bribe. Thanks to stories I'd heard in Manerplaw from former soldiers who had joined the rebels, I knew just enough about the Tatmadaw to understand that no soldier would ever ask to see his own file. It's not that he wouldn't dare, it's that the thought would not occur to him. But extracting information from Aung Win's friends and colleagues would be riskier still. I had already raised eyebrows with my excuse of amnesia, an unlikely explanation for my complete ignorance about the man's life. So many of Aung Win's friends visiting me at the hospital had expressed concern about my change of character that the notion of going out on the town with these people seemed foolhardy. How could we pick up where we'd left off before the actual man's death? Would I not, inevitably, behave in a manner completely at odds with the real Aung Win? I wondered and worried about the peculiarities of his personality that I did not possess, how obvious my lack of them would be, and the likelihood of exposure for this fact. I might have kept fooling everyone Aung

Win was meeting for the first time, but what would I say to those who knew the real Aung Win?

The best strategy, I concluded, was to play the damaged recluse: to use the post-traumatic stress of Aung Win's Maw Pokay experience to claim the need for privacy. A cruel but necessary strategy. I would cut off his old friends and relatives, as discretely as possible making new friends with people who had not known the real Aung Win. This would buy me some time until after the multi-party national elections, set for the following year, which the SLORC had announced soon after I left the hospital. That would be the best opportunity for escape. If all went as planned, Aung San Suu Kyi and the National League for Democracy would easily win, and all would be well. Soldiers would return to their barracks. Thandar and all political prisoners would be released. Student exiles would be granted amnesty. Ceasefire agreements with the Karen and all other ethnic armed groups would be signed. Freedom of the press, of assembly, and of association would become law. Burma would be free at last, and, in this liberated environment, I would reveal myself as Min Lin, American citizen. Under the new NLD government, there would be amnesty for someone in my uniquely unfortunate position. All I had to do was wait for twelve months to pass. It wouldn't be easy, spending an entire year as Aung Win. But I had to do it, so I would.

For my new job, I would be working from the Ministers' Office building, a colonial-era complex that occupied an entire block in downtown Rangoon. My father used to tell stories about this building, formerly known as the Secretariat. Constructed by the British toward the end of the nineteenth century, it had served as the administrative seat of government for the nearly one hundred years spanning British rule, Japanese occupation during World War II, the post-independence era up to Ne Win, and the dictatorships. The Secretariat was also the scene of one of Burma's darkest moments. On July 19, 1947, General Aung San and most of his cabinet were slaughtered in one of its upstairs meeting rooms. Since the 1962 coup, the building had been allowed to rot. The decay was evident from my first day at work, when my driver dropped me off at security. Gazing up at the patchwork of moss and fern sprouting from the crumbling red brick, I thought of all these colonial remnants that had faded through the years. The ghosts of Old Britain could be found in every corner of Rangoon, from offices and storefronts to the upper-class homes that sprung up after the final conquest of 1885. As with The Strand, they had lost their former lustre; the country was so poor from Ne Win's looting of the treasury that there was no money for basic maintenance, never mind renovation, of these heritage buildings.

Inside the lobby, I was led to the Information Ministry to meet the office staff. My immediate superior, Kyaw Sann, was the government's official spokesman. Kyaw Sann told me my job was important because the future of Burma was at stake. We were waging war against radical elements and external forces bent on destroying the nation, he said. It would be my responsibility to capture glorious images that show the world what a great force for good the SLORC really was. Kyaw Sann added that his superiors were surprised that I wanted the photographer's job because I was such an excellent writer. But then, what the regime needed most was people with strong moral character and nationalist principles — good, courageous patriots like me, Aung Win — to set the right tone for communications. I could still provide that service, he supposed, by taking pictures. His spiel exhausted me, his every utterance like something out of Mao's *Little Red Book*.

At one point, a secretary brought in a Coronamatic typewriter and plunked it onto the desk of a communications officer. The young man, named Soe Moe, beamed as if he'd just won the lottery. I stifled a snicker. I had never owned a typewriter, but just before coming to Burma had been using an Apple Macintosh II computer, which replaced a Commodore 64. Kyaw Sann left the room briefly, returning with a pile of books he then dropped on Saw Moe's desk. On top was the Printers and Publishers Registration Act of 1962. He said, reciting from its pages, that all publishers were required to register each new book and to provide copies to the Press Scrutiny Board. There were incentives for good behaviour, such as national prizes. Bad behaviour would result in rejected manuscripts or magazines with missing pages or words covered in silver ink. Then, turning to Saw Moe, he told him to memorize every word in the Act.

This reminded me of a time when I was fourteen and my father took me into his study, the proud history professor showing off several tomes about the old country. Dad's library contained an original Burmese edition of Dr. Maung Maung's effusive 1969 hagiography of Ne Win — who knows how he obtained that? — a British academic's account of the coup, and several novels. Now that I was old enough to learn about Burma in all its complexity, he said, why didn't I start with this? He handed me a faded Penguin paperback of George Orwell's *Burmese Days*. I gobbled it up in a couple of sittings. Then, getting a head start on my junior high classmates, I read *Animal Farm* and *Nineteen Eighty-Four*, as well. Once I'd finished all three, Dad gave me a free undergraduate tutorial on Orwell's damning portrait of a failing British empire in the first novel and the allegorical and literal workings of totalitarianism in the other two. *Burmese Days* is a critique of British colonialism, so it is freely available in Burma, he told me. Whereas the characters in *Animal Farm* and *Nineteen Eighty-Four* inhabit dystopian, nightmarish worlds that could easily be compared to Burma today, so those two books are banned there. As I grew older, and the longer Burma remained shut off from the rest of the world, the more curious I became about it. How did one of Asia's most literate societies cope with total censorship? Speaking with exiles, I had learned that many people in Rangoon hoarded old copies of forbidden books, clandestinely trading or stuffing them away in mouldy hiding places where, through the years after the coup, they continued to be read despite falling into disrepair. Magazines as old as two or three years were still valued as news. Burmese writers trying to reach their audiences with politically subversive messages learned how to write in code, couching their ideas in elaborate metaphors. All to avoid the scrutiny of men like Kyaw Sann.

On May 26, 1989, I arrived at the office to find Saw Moe flipping through a pile of documents on his desk. "Look at this," he complained, throwing each one on the floor. He had worked on all of these papers last week! A press release on Tatmadaw activity in Arakan State. A new draft of the censorship law. A speech for Saw Maung about rebel activity in Karen State. Briefing notes, memos, and other reports. It all must be redrafted! I began picking up each document off the floor as Saw Moe dropped it. A flood of red ink appeared on every page, with words scribbled out and corrections inserted. Each instance of "Burma," "Rangoon," "Irrawaddy," and "Prome Road" had been replaced with "Myanmar," "Yangon," "Ayeyarwady," and "Pyay Road," respectively. Each Karen State had become "Kayin," the Karenni people "Kayah," Burman culture "Bamar," Arakan State "Rakhine," and the Tenasserim region "Tanintharyi."

Kyaw Sann told us that the country would henceforth be known as "Myanmar." Several other locations, including the capital city, would have new names as well. An hour later, at a press conference attended by three state reporters, a SLORC official I didn't recognize took the lectern and began spouting the regime's message. My camera still slung around my neck, I looked toward Kyaw Sann and shrugged. He nodded toward the podium, signalling me to get to work and snap away at the nameless SLORC official. This government hack said the country's name was being changed because "Burma" in English corresponded to "Bama," which referred to the majority Burman ethnic group. "Myanmar," he said, included all ethnic groups. This, I knew, was a lie: "Myanmar" was, in fact, a specific reference to the Burman majority. As he spoke, state bureaucrats were amending the Adaptation of Expressions Law to convert all English names for Burmese people and places. These included states, divisions, townships and their zones, towns, wards, villages and their tracts, rivers, streams, forests, mountains, and islands. Crazy.

In September I was named chief photographer at the state's main propaganda vehicle, *The Working People's Daily*. The new job gave me a key role in the junta's self-promotional efforts. There would be countless ribbon-cutting ceremonies, stage-managed photo ops and other good news shoots featuring Saw Maung and other junta bigwigs, and state visits by the leaders of countries like China, North Korea, and Iran. I would take photos of smiling farmers, visit industrial plants to show off the flourishing economy, and create the impression through my images that there wasn't a rocket launcher, a flame-thrower, or a battalion of soldier-rapists jacked up on amphetamines to be found anywhere in the Golden Land.

8

Thandar:

The moment those soldiers on Sule Pagoda Road began shooting, I thought I'd be dead for sure. On the outside, I was defiant: holding my ground, standing tall with my sister nursing students, staring down the throat of the Tatmadaw beast. Inside, I was saying my prayers. Convinced the entire front row of us would be slaughtered, I froze and awaited my turn. But only a few of us went down in that first volley, selected for death as if by lottery. One of the unlucky, my fourth-year classmate Pyone, was standing right next to me shouting slogans, her spittle brushing my neck until a gun blast threw her to the ground. I am still haunted by the sight of dear Pyone, lying motionless in the street with a gaping hole in her chest. I ran away as fast as I could.

Once beyond the line of fire, I began looking for Min. I'd spotted him before the shooting began, approaching from the side with his camera. But he didn't see me waving and couldn't hear my calls through the crowd. When the bullets started flying, I had to look out for myself. That's when I lost Min and had to make my way out of the downtown area. When I arrived back home, my parents ran out to greet me, enfolding me in a long embrace. I felt badly for them, and guilty too. They both had good jobs with the government, and I knew they had been harassed with many awkward questions about my role as a student activist. So now they would be in very big trouble. When my father approached, I was afraid he would beat me for having brought this trouble to the family. But from his embrace — he did not show his feelings often, but this time he held on for a long time — I was reassured. My safety was all that mattered to him.

My parents had heard radio reports of the "disturbances" — the SLORC's word for protests requiring brutal suppression — so they knew there had been bloodshed. Aye Maung and Hla Min had arrived safely an hour before me, so my parents were relieved. Our family was intact. When my father asked about Min, I burst into tears. I explained that I had lost him downtown. But Papa reassured me that Min knew what to do and would be fine. At moments like this, I loved my father so much. I had put the family at great risk, but he was willing to delay serious conversation — including discipline — until morning.

But morning did not come. In the middle of the night, the sound of barking dogs down the street signalled a Tatmadaw invasion. Minutes later, soldiers were pounding on our front door. When my mother, still drowsy in her night clothes, opened it, they violently barged in and tore the place apart. Calling me a "Communist whore," they arrested me and my brothers, giving us five minutes to gather our personal belongings before tying our hands with bamboo cords and throwing us into a truck. All I was able to bring was a single change of clothes, a hairbrush, a bar of soap, a container of *thanaka* powder, and a notepad and pen. My brothers brought nothing; they were being taken to the police station first and, after a few hours of interrogation, would be freed. The SLORC had other plans for me.

When the police van arrived at Insein, it backed up against the prison's main gates so I could be brought in directly from the vehicle through a smaller door built into one of the gates. A female guard took me into a storeroom to body search me. Then, avoiding my eyes, she took my bag and emptied it. Sorting through all the items, she grabbed the notepad and pen and left the room without returning; the guards who replaced her did not return those items. I knew political prisoners weren't allowed to read, so I didn't bring books. But depriving me of writing tools was cruel and unnecessary. Our ability to think was the reason we ended up here, so I guess our jailers didn't want us producing manifestos from our cells. After a while, when I wanted to write, I used whatever sharp instrument I could find — sometimes a spike from my hairbrush — to scratch my thoughts on the wall or the floor. You have to be resourceful at Insein.

After admission, a guard brought me into the prison's panopticon maze. Past a pair of red brick buildings that led to the women's section, my destination was a large hall with barred French windows on either side, the block divided into ten open cells in two rows of five. When the guard left, the doors of the main hall clanged shut behind him with a boom. I was left alone in a nine-by-seven-foot cell, but not for long. Within seconds of my arrival, I heard my name being called. Women from other parts of the ward approached my cell. Many of them I knew, and they all greeted me with a hug. I was so glad to see my student federation sisters! One offered me her wooden sleeping platform — a sign of deep respect, as I would come to learn. At four inches high, these little platforms were a luxury item at Insein; most inmates endured the concrete floors with bedbug-ridden bamboo mats. Moved by her gesture, I thanked my sister for her kindness but declined. She had been at Insein since March and needed it more than I did. I was fine with sleeping on a mat for now.

At the time of my arrest, I had no idea the regime would lock me up for so long. As a female political prisoner, I thought I would be sentenced to no more than three years for organizing students and speaking at rallies, distributing leaflets, and calling for democratic rule. But just before the trial, my lawyer informed me that the expected charges of "causing a disturbance" and "political activity" came with two additional counts of treason we hadn't anticipated. Those charges, which called for much stiffer sentencing, were for "collusion with terrorists" and alleged membership in the Burma Communist Party. I thought both charges were ludicrous and should have been thrown out; however, as has been the case in my country, they did not come out of thin air. There was a grain of truth to them both. In Burma, that is enough to convict.

The first charge was related to my advocacy of armed struggle. "Terrorism" was the SLORC's word for any form of armed opposition to the regime. In my case, the junta was referring to the All Burma Students' Democratic Front. But there was one little problem with this allegation: there could have been no record of my contact with the Front because it didn't exist at the time of my arrest. Nor had I made any contact with future members, ordered weapons, participated in espionage, or led counter-revolutionary military surveillance and reconnaissance missions. Nor, obviously, had I ordered summary executions of Tatmadaw or SLORC personnel. But during the late-night interrogations before I was formally charged, I was accused of having committed, aided, or abetted all of the above. The only way I could have been charged with terrorism — the only way for the SLORC to draw up such a case against me — was if one or more of my comrades who attended that final student union meeting had snitched on me; if, after being arrested and interrogated themselves, they had cracked under pressure and told military intelligence that I had called on my fellow students to join the ethnic rebel armies in Karen State. That much was true so, by the SLORC's definition, I was indeed a terrorist.

The second charge, membership in the Burma Communist Party, required much more creativity from my prosecutors. They must have dug deep to find out that, at eight years of age in 1974, I had handed out leaflets about the U Thant funeral on the RASU campus. I recalled this. As a child at the time, I did not appreciate the danger of handing out leaflets; I was volunteering for an older cousin who had asked me to do it. How was I to know that student activists had stolen the coffin of the deceased former UN secretary-general, triggering a confrontation with the regime by demanding proper burial and a state funeral? When I came home and showed my parents a copy of the leaflet, my father spanked me. Then he phoned my uncle, his brother, telling him to scold my cousin for giving me the leaflets, which bore the Burma Communist Party logo. That's where the "Thandar the Red" charge came from.

Needless to say, I was not at age eight — nor at any time afterward — a member of the BCP. I was too bourgeois for the Marxist-Leninists; they were too dour and extreme for me. But the leaflet story must have had legs, for it had followed me all the way to 1988, its basic facts proof enough to the SLORC that I was a Maoist apparatchik. A revolutionary true believer. (Weren't those two years I spent as a Buddhist nun my father's punishment for my youthful political activism?) During the trial, the chief prosecutor noted my "unladylike" behaviour and "aggressive, masculine" characteristics, a personal attack that implied I was some sort of sexual invert: the Stalinist lesbian bitch, sadistically whipping her compliant cadres into shape. This fanciful portrait, this cartoon caricature by the state prosecutor, attributed far more influence to my role in the democracy movement than I actually had.

In the end, the charges stuck, and I was convicted on all counts. Far too late, I wished I hadn't spoken up at that final meeting of the ABFSU. I should have known I would pay dearly for the indiscretion, that my support of armed struggle would land me the maximum sentence. During my first night at Insein, a couple of weeks before the trial, I had no clue of the inner strength I would need to survive imprisonment. But when I returned to my cell after the trial, the words "twenty-five years" ringing in my ears, I broke down in a fit of loud sobbing that no amount of comforting by my cell block sisters could stop. Over the years, I would learn to hold my head high and not despair. For the sake of the movement, we student activists from the '88 Generation were expected to put up a courageous front as prisoners of conscience. And so, through all this time at Insein, I have tried my best to maintain some degree of dignity, despite the terrible injustice of my sentence. It's the Buddhist way. All life is suffering. My desire for democracy had caused my suffering. I must let go of desire. And I must meditate my way out of suffering to achieve wisdom. Four Noble Truths, indeed!

Apart from the bedbugs, the smelly squat toilets, and the hospital-like food — salted rice, bland lentil soup, and pickled mango day after day — the worst thing about life at Insein is the constant lighting. To discourage us from trying to escape or otherwise engage in inappropriate behaviour at night, senior administrators insist the lights remain on. The glare is in my eyes, even when I'm trying to sleep, which at night is harder to do without mosquito nets. Thanks to the five a.m. wake up call, sleepless nights are frequent and leave the average inmate exhausted for most of the day. But that is exactly the condition our jailers wish for us

during interrogation. In the early days of an Insein term, those intimate sharing sessions are a routine part of a political prisoner's life.
Perhaps I was one of the lucky ones; Military Intelligence allowed
me two full days of acclimatization before throwing a blue cotton
hood over my head and shuffling me off to receive the third degree.

In one sense, those MI folks knew what they were doing. The
blue hoods were to prevent other prisoners from seeing who was
being interrogated, while preventing the hooded from being able
to identify our inquisitors or the route to the MI compound. After
some of their questions, I could understand why they would not
want to be seen. Their approach to these encounters, their whole
line of argument, was a joke. When they asked why I joined the
Burma Communist Party, I said I hadn't joined the party, which
they knew was true. When they asked where I hid my weapons, I
said didn't hide them, they were all out in the open. What does that
mean? Intelligence and critical thinking are my weapons, I said.
When they asked why I was trying to destroy the country, I said
I was trying to save it. The sessions went on like this for hours:
one stupid question after another, followed by a cheeky rebuttal
in which I reframed their incriminatory storyline to suit my own
purposes.

Now and then, my jailers sent in a more skilled interrogator
who knew my personal history. This MI type, focusing more on my
personal network with the Federation of Student Unions, would try
to figure out which of my comrades might be leaving Rangoon to
join the rebellion. But no matter how long or how hard they grilled
me — at least three times a week during the first month, always
in the middle of the night — I never gave up a single name. After
a few sessions, it should have been clear that I would not betray
my sisters and brothers from the student movement. But this only
seemed to puzzle them, since I was likely sold out by someone who

attended that final meeting of the ABFSU. Didn't personal interest trump solidarity? Weren't we all just in it for ourselves? Wouldn't we snitch on each other at the first offer of jail privileges? Didn't I want revenge on those who had turned me in? They also tried to play my family against me. My brothers, they said, had told them I was planning to leave Rangoon with three members of the Burma Communist Party. Who were they? Nice try, I'd respond, Aye Maung and Hla Min would never give up information about me, and I did not make such plans. Those of us in that room had voted, as a collective, to keep demonstrating in the streets.

The one person my interrogators failed to ask me about was Min Lin. Even with the fake passport and different name, it seemed incredible that my fiancé had eluded the SLORC. Min and I had been together since at least April, and he had been everywhere taking photos, from before the general strike all the way up to the September 18 coup. No one knew about our engagement, but someone from the SLORC must have gone after him for the camera, no matter who he claimed to be. And yet no one at Insein ever mentioned his name, nor that of a farmer from Mandalay who happened to have an expensive Nikon and spent all his time with student radicals in Rangoon. Min had somehow escaped Military Intelligence's notice. It seemed strange. How could he have remained at the centre of the uprising without being spotted? Was it simply his talent for blending in? Despite his status as an American who had not been to Burma until 1988, Min's assimilation into Burmese society had taken only a few months. For this reason, I tried my best not to worry about him too much.

9

November 1989
Rangoon

Min:

Late one afternoon I was alone in the darkroom, running some prints through the chemical bath, when the office phone rang. Some *kalar* was here to see me, the private at reception informed me. Says he's an old friend. *Not good*, I thought. Such an impromptu visit from an Aung Win acquaintance was bound to happen, but I hadn't prepared for such a surprise at work. And my first visitor was from the Indian race; this would raise eyebrows among my peers, all of whom were ethnic Burmans who shared the private's casual, unexamined racism. So I told him to pass on my apologies and say I was busy. Then I hung up. Moments later, the phone rang again. His name is Sayed Hosin, the private informed me. He insisted I would want to see him. I instructed him to send the man through. What the hell else was I going to do?

My office door opened, and the stranger walked in. Sayed Hosin's presence was instantly disarming. He was quite young — seventeen or eighteen, I guessed — and a few inches shorter than me. Lean and well-groomed, wearing slacks and a silk shirt, he was not merely handsome but astonishingly so. He had great bone structure, a perfect set of sparkling white teeth, and a curly black mop of hair that shone as if the sun followed him everywhere. How did this kid know Aung Win? I welcomed him by name, perhaps a little too heartily, for the disappointment registered immediately in the dark brown pools of his matinee-idol eyes. Sayed Hosin said he was fine, but that I seemed different. Then, brushing aside the pleasantries, he asked what time I would be finished work. Five o'clock, I said. Could I leave early? I looked at the clock — it read four thirty — and told him to wait a few minutes while I cleaned up and turned off the lights. Then he led me outside onto Strand Road. We headed east on foot.

When I asked where we were going, he shook his head in disbelief. "We've gone there many times before," he said. "You know it well." Then he gestured toward the promenade along the Rangoon River, noting how lucky I was to find a job so close to it. We used to take a bus here, he told me. Trying to think of something convincing to say, I apologized for my foggy memory, which hadn't been the same since the injury. He frowned. He knew that already, he said. Then, pointing at the river again, he directed me toward Botahtaung Pagoda. We continued walking in silence as we reached the gates, entered the temple grounds, and made our way down the road past the shrine until we reached the river's edge. I began to feel awkward. Why would Aung Win have come here, several times, with this minority kid? There was nothing down here, nothing to see or do. Was Aung Win into drugs, and Sayed Hosin was his dealer?

He led me down a ramp onto the dock and then to a rusty, abandoned fishing boat. We stopped where the boat was tied up, then he climbed a short ladder onto its portside deck, entering the cabin through a hatch. Reaching for my hand, he told me to climb up quickly before anyone noticed. *What the hell?* I thought, obeying. Once I joined him in the darkness, the boy abruptly pulled my face to his own and planted his tongue in my mouth. Startled, I pulled away.

What was the matter? he wanted to know, confused. Didn't I love him anymore?

Ah, so this was it. Of course, I told him. It was only that —

He pulled my face towards his and kissed me again. This time I went along with it, surprised but alert, my tongue wrapping around his. My first instinct was to keep performing. Strategic and task-oriented, focused only on doing whatever I thought Aung Win would do under the circumstances — something, I now realized, he must have done countless times with this enchanting young man. But soon I felt something else: the unmistakable stirrings of desire, prompted by the unexpected thrill of a first sexual encounter. As a teenager I had fantasized about boys I wanted to kiss but pushed away such thoughts, persuaded by daily reminders from popular culture and my father's traditional ways that man-on-man love was wrong. Later, as the horrors of AIDS unfolded in the media and in homophobic society everywhere, I fought against gay feelings until convinced I had stamped them out.

Once in Burma and in thrall to Thandar's charisma, I fooled myself into thinking I could marry a woman. But at twenty-six and still a virgin, I hadn't gone further with my fiancée than an earnest peck on the lips; nor, since her arrest, had I enjoyed an erotic moment with anyone else — not even at the rebel base in Manerplaw, a cauldron of male hormones with no shortage of blue balls among the many attractive young trainees sleeping beside me. Now here I was at twenty-seven, sharing a deep French kiss with another guy, some stranger from an ethnic minority — a most unlikely candidate for sex, one would think, given my lack of exposure to his people. I felt like I'd come home at last, and Sayed Hosin was my one-man welcoming committee. His probing tongue behaved as if its owner knew every inch of me already — lucky Aung Win! — his full lips drawing me in with a tickle from the downy peach fuzz above them.

The revelation of our coupling was beautiful and sad all at once, for I now understood the pleasure of a human need I had denied myself for more than a decade. Until that moment, sex had seemed impossible; now I knew that this version of it was what I had always wanted. All these years later, I still get goosebumps recalling the moment I accepted that knowledge. I marvelled at Sayed Hosin's ability to communicate so much without saying a word, at how fervently he desired Aung Win! The transgressive nature of our encounter — the seedy public setting, the fear of being caught — only added to my excitement as our tongues kept mingling.

As we kissed and caressed each other, I was clutching his buttocks when I noticed something in his right back pocket. Slipping my left hand into it, I found what felt like a credit card. For no reason but playfulness, I guess, I pulled it out and tucked it into the back of my *longyi* without Sayed appearing to notice. When we pulled apart, he looked at me longingly, evidently convinced that I was the Aung Win he remembered. Then he dropped to his knees and went straight for my *longyi*, tugging it from the top and sliding it down my legs without seeing what I had taken from him. But suddenly, with my loins fully exposed, he recoiled.

He was alarmed and demanded to know who I was.

I did not understand what he meant.

He shook his head and shuffled backward, moving further away. I was missing a scar.

"My scar?"

"Yes, your scar! Aung Win has a big, long scar," he said, pointing just above my pubic hair. He told me it was from a battle injury, when Aung Win fell against a bamboo spear in a booby trap. A big, brown scar. I had nothing on my skin. No sign, no trace.

The heat of moments earlier, the electricity between us, was gone. Within seconds, the promise of ecstasy with this beautiful boy was withdrawn. I looked down at the unblemished part of my body he was pointing to. I could not possibly be Aung Win, he said. He demanded to know who I was. I pulled up the *longyi*, tied it in a knot, and looked away. After living successfully as an imposter for eight months, I hadn't been directly challenged this way since that one soldier at the hospital in April, the one who filed a complaint after visiting me. Since then, not a single person had raised any doubts about my identity so directly. Now this Sayed Hosin, alarmed by the discovery I was not his lover, was confused and angry.

I asked him for a cigarette, playing for time. He pulled out a pack of Red Ruby from his shirt pocket, took out a smoke, and threw it at me. When I caught it, he grudgingly dug out a match and lit it. I cupped both my hands to his left one as he took the match to the cigarette, an intimate gesture now ruined by my exposure. Apologizing for the shock, I told him I had no idea who I was. All I knew was that I'd woken up in a hospital bed not remembering anything, and that I had been told I was Aung Win. I still could not recall anything from before the hospital and had been trying to cope with this fact ever since. Sayed Hosin absorbed my words, his delicate features tightening into a frown. I prayed he would believe me, but he didn't.

It made no sense to Sayed that I looked like Aung Win in every other way. He repeated his demand to know who I was. I took another drag from the cigarette before dropping it on the boat's dusty floor and stubbing it out. Just someone who's trying to keep his head above water in the New Myanmar, I said. His reply was direct: he could report me. He should report me. People at the Ministry, and others who knew Aung Win, would be angry to learn that I was not him.

I had run out of moves. I could not think my way out of this. Then I noticed something on the floor: the card I had taken from the boy, undetected, while our lips were locked. Picking it up before he could grab it, I held it up to examine it. "Hey!" he shouted. "That's my ID card!" The laminated white card bore a faded, black and white mug shot of a younger Sayed Hosin, with his vital stats. Birthplace: Akyab, Arakan State. Ethnicity: Bengali. He must have taken it out to show security at *The Working People's Daily* and forgotten to return it to his wallet. "Give it back," he said, his anxiety growing. At that time, I don't think I'd ever heard the word "Rohingya," but I had some sense that, as a "Bengali" — a term the government had long adopted for his people, marking them as foreign — Sayed Hosin did not belong to one of Burma's officially recognized minorities. And his white card was all that allowed him to stay in the country. It was his lifeline. There was no way he could leave this place without it, and soon he was begging for its return.

I looked him in the eye. "Are you going to report me?" He seemed self-confident enough to do such a thing, although — as a member of a reviled minority with no citizenship status — his word might not be worth as much as the fake Aung Win's.

Then he promised not to reveal my secret. How good was his promise?

He stepped forward and brought his face back to mine. The kiss, which lasted almost half a minute, said this: *You may not be Aung Win, and I don't like you for tricking me, but you're still pretty hot, and in better circumstances we might be lovers. So no, I'm not going to rat you out.*

"I promise," he said, pulling away again.

I handed him the card. He turned toward the door.

"Wait," I said. "If you're not going to report me, can we see each other again?"

He shook his head. He was sorry, but this was all too much. I was not Aung Win, and I could never replace him in his heart. And with that, he walked through the door and left me — to my everlasting regret — alone on that rusty old fishing boat.

10

There was no question of escape before the 1990 elections. With so many Ministry staff watching my every move, I was afraid to do anything that might suggest Aung Win had plans other than loyally serving his country. Office colleagues were frequently taking me out to dinner and golf games, angling for invites to the Inya Lake mansion, or inviting me to their homes. All complained that I was such a loner. Constantly on everyone's radar, I could not imagine finding time alone for myself, even for a few hours. Escape meant stealing a car and racing for the border without being caught. Living under the microscope as I was, I knew that any dereliction of duty would be noticed at once, lowering my odds for escape. That's how I rationalized it while still under the bubble. I would make a run for it only when the time was right.

This paranoid mindset — only reinforced by the incident with Sayed Hosin — convinced me that casual wanderings through the streets of Rangoon, the luxury of spontaneity I had enjoyed before the September coup, were now part of my past. Before the SLORC, my sense of entitlement as a foreign visitor — including one who posed as a Mandalay farmer — had allowed me to explore the city completely at liberty. But the pleasures of an evening stroll at Kandawgyi Lake or a morning browse in the downtown markets became less feasible after Thandar's arrest and all but impossible after I woke up in that hospital bed as Aung Win. In my new role on behalf of the Burmese state, posing as a national hero, I had no choice but to self-monitor my every public appearance. There could be no more missteps. If I wanted to avoid another Sayed Hosin–like incident, I would have to check my behaviour and body language whenever out in the city. To minimize the risk of exposure, I spent as much time as possible indoors at the office or at home.

Had I been forced to endure such wilful imprisonment of my identity for much longer, I would have gone insane. But I knew that wouldn't happen — not with elections scheduled for May 27, 1990 and the National League for Democracy expected to win. In such an event, I was confident I could safely leave the country soon afterward. Until then, my only justification for remaining in Burma — the only way to endure the guilt-inducing stress of working for the SLORC — would be to regard the whole experience as a kind of absurdist research project. An American spy by default only, I wasn't in Burma on anyone's agenda but my own. In my unique position, I was able to see first-hand how a dictatorship works. By probing the authoritarian mindset through observation, I would come to some understanding of how total power can turn some of us into monsters.

The Burmese people had been living under military rule for twenty-six years when the Tatmadaw launched the second major coup in '88. They already knew the generals couldn't govern their way out of a paper bag. The rot had set in not long after the first coup when Ne Win fired, arrested, or forced into exile all the great minds that could have run the civil service and national treasury. By 1987, the senior general's solution for national prosperity was to devalue bank notes and reorder the national currency to be divisible by his favourite number, nine. His fellow generals, instead of dismissing the idea as despotic lunacy that would ruin the economy, lauded Ne Win as a visionary genius. Now, under the SLORC, things appeared to be getting worse. Like an ambulance-chasing journalist with the scoop of the century, I happened to have a front-row seat to this train wreck of a country now calling itself Myanmar.

One of my first assignments was the opening of a new military museum in Rangoon. The SLORC were spending millions on these monuments to themselves, which were being built in cities throughout the country. Like the Uncle Ho museums in Vietnam, aimed at distracting the public from Communist government atrocities by ramping up the cult of personality around the people's dearly departed visionary leader, the SLORC-sponsored military museums aimed to distract the Burmese public from Tatmadaw atrocities by celebrating the Army's role in Burmese history as defender of the Union. At the opening, I found myself barking orders at some of the junta's worst offenders as I herded them like cats for a group photo. The regime's top three — Senior General Saw Maung, Military Intelligence chief Khin Nyunt, and General Maung Aye — were there, along with half a dozen other decorated officers. They all laughed and chortled away about various banalities, a macho mutual admiration society, while I arranged their positions in front of the museum entrance. Peering through my lens before pressing the shutter, I took a moment to regard this ghoulish collection of mostly overweight, post-middle-aged military men, their uniform breasts bursting with unearned medals that gleamed in the sun. For all I knew, their underlings were engaged at that moment in "clearance operations" in ethnic minority villages, raping and killing peasants at will.

"Come on, Captain," said Saw Maung. "We haven't got all day ..." *Oh, what I wouldn't give for this Nikon to turn into a Kalashnikov right about now ...*

Around the same time, the SLORC presented its "Exhibition on Historical Records of the State," an attempt to justify Tatmadaw atrocities by claiming that Burma had been the victim of multiple conspiracies. The Army had little choice, this logic went, but to save the country by "maintaining law and order" and "preventing anarchy." I wasn't assigned to cover this dreary exercise in SLORC propaganda, to which state employees and children were subjected. But I did take a photo of some graffiti a bold dissenter had spray-painted outside the exhibition hall: *Come, everyone, and witness Khin Nyunt's magic show!* The chief spy was not amused.

The SLORC's promotion of the Tatmadaw had no other purpose than the swelling of its ranks. Between 1988 and 2000, the number of military personnel in Burma would more than double, from 180,000 to 400,000. All this while the regime was squandering the country's intellectual capital, crushing the dreams of its youth and destroying their potential by keeping universities closed. The push to army up was well under way in that first year while I was there, and my bosses made sure I wasted no opportunity to promote it by visiting recruitment centres with my camera. But taking photos of new draftees was a real chore: most of these boys, fresh out of high school, were miserable about their situation. It showed on their faces, and I felt their pain as I took these photos. By journalistic standards they were good images that told a real story, for they captured the hopelessness of Burma's press-ganged youth under the junta. Much later, I would use these photos in a context far removed from this moment. But the editor of *The Working People's Daily*, my superior, was outraged when I showed him the prints.

"How can we possibly use these?" he spat at me. "Those boys have to be smiling. Go back and do another shoot."

I explained I could not force them to smile.

The editor sighed, shaking his head before disappearing into the next room for a few minutes. He returned with a box filled with sweets, cinema tickets, and a small wad of cash, telling me to dish it out to every new soldier willing to be photographed. So yes, the generals got their recruitment photos.

Soon after I began working for the SLORC, I learned that the Burma Communist Party had collapsed after decades of defeat and a recent outbreak of acrimonious infighting that had led to a mutiny. The SLORC's top generals celebrated this news as a great victory. Their glee was understandable, since the greatest military force arising from the BCP's ashes, the United Wa State Army, would end up replacing an ideological threat with an empire-building opportunity: a ceasefire agreement with the SLORC that would allow the UWSA, with the Tatmadaw's assistance, to expand its narcotic drug trafficking operations to neighbouring Thailand and Laos. A win-win for the Tatmadaw and the ethnic army, both of whom reaped the rewards of a booming trade in opium and, sometime later, methamphetamines.

The UWSA was one of five armies that reached ceasefire agreements with the SLORC after the collapse of the BCP. It was my job to attend the signing ceremonies for each of these ceasefires and to take photos of SLORC/Tatmadaw bigwigs posing with rebel army chiefs. After one of these ceremonies, the festivities continued with a dinner. Everyone got so drunk that I was told to put away the camera. It's hard to remember much of what happened next because I, too, was drunk. I do recall the rebel chief tearfully confessing, as we sidled up to the bar for another round of cheap whisky: "We've sold our souls to the devil with this fucking deal. My people will never forgive me."

By early 1990, reports from the border areas were confirming, with devastating clarity, the futility of challenging the Burmese army on the battlefield. In mid-February, a Tatmadaw force of more than a thousand soldiers overran the small town of Three Pagodas Pass near the Thai border. Dozens of rebels were killed, including ABSDF fighters who'd been sent in as reinforcements. The Tatmadaw added insult to injury by seizing large amounts of timber and logging equipment, arms, and battlefield communications gear from the rebels. In late March, the Tatmadaw destroyed a joint force of Mon and student rebels that had launched a major attack on the town of Ye, in southern Mon State. The disastrous ambush resulted in the loss of forty rebels, several of them killed under bombardment by the Burmese Air Force.

On hearing these reports, my Ministry colleagues celebrated with loud triumphalist cheering and idiotic drinking games. They were delighted. But I was reminded of Maw Pokay. How stunning it had been, how dumbfounding, to come face to face with the full force of the Tatmadaw juggernaut, with its giant battalions launching wave after wave of deadly assault! I was deeply depressed by the news of these crushing defeats for the All Burma Students' Democratic Front, among whose ranks I had belonged only months earlier. Such overwhelming battle losses only reinforced my initial doubts about the wisdom of trying to defeat this regime through armed combat. When civil war breaks out in a country ruled by military dictatorship, the generals are in it for the long haul; completely invested in their self-preservation, clutching to power at all costs, they're in it to win it. The Tatmadaw, having built up the largest arsenal of weaponry and manpower that side of China, spared no expense in crushing its enemies. Domestic insurgency, without the full support of large foreign corporations, governments, or both, was a suicide wish.

The longer I stayed in Burma, the more compromised I felt. Each day after work, my driver would take me back to Inya Lake where I'd sit in the living room with a confiscated novel — Ian Fleming, who knew? — while the butler, unsolicited, served me one gin and tonic after another. Bored and impatient as 1989 gave way to 1990, I couldn't wait for the elections. During the final weeks before the vote, I noticed the same little red flag flying from cars, shops, and restaurant windows everywhere in downtown Rangoon: the "fighting peacock" of the NLD's party insignia, the traditional symbol of Burmese nationalism. The flag looked a bit like Communist Vietnam's, but the star was white rather than yellow and flushed left rather than centred, as if chased to the margins by the yellow peacock scampering from the lower right corner. The pride of the people, keeping the army in its place?

After the elections were held on May 27, it took another two weeks for the results to be announced. But the news was as good as it gets: a massive majority — more than 7.9 million people or 60 per cent — had cast their votes for the National League for Democracy. Thanks to the first-past-the-post system, the party of Aung San Suu Kyi, who heard the results over radio from the privacy of house arrest, won a larger percentage of the parliamentary seats, taking 392 of the 447 contested. I was so thrilled that I began forming my plan for escape.

I would do nothing rash, I decided, but wait until the new NLD administration was sworn in. Then I would hire a lawyer to conduct negotiations with the government. As Aung Win, I had gained access to classified material; the new regime would first want to clear me as a security risk before letting me go. Burma's new leader — Suu Kyi, though the SLORC had forbidden her from running for office — would be all too aware of the junta's intimidating methods and thus rule that my recruitment due to mistaken identity made my sixteen months of fraud a forgivable offence. I would then be granted full amnesty and pardoned, likely on condition of deportation. Suu Kyi would arrange for Foreign Affairs to contact the US Embassy and send me a new passport. Shortly after that, the new Information Minister would call a press conference to reveal my identity and confirm the death of Aung Win. Then I'd be free.

My next priority would be a brief reunion with Thandar, certain to be freed along with every other political prisoner. Our first meeting since the night after the coup would be painful, our engagement called off by mutual consent once I confessed what I'd been up to all this time. I would also attribute my misguided marriage proposal to the fanciful whims of a tourist caught up in the euphoric springtime of a nascent democracy movement — leaving out the part about sexual contact with an underage Rohingya male more than a year after Thandar's jailing. Then I would fly home. How long would this take? Hard to say, but I figured no more than a month.

Before the election, SLORC dictator Saw Maung had promised to hand over power to the winning party. With the NLD clearly the winner, I estimated that it might take a couple of weeks for Suu Kyi to assemble her transition team and swear in her cabinet, then perhaps another week for me to hire the lawyer and prepare my documents. In a perfect world, I'd be home in LA by mid-July. Alas, it was not a perfect world. After the election results were announced, the NLD took Saw Maung at his word and put off its public call for Parliament to convene. The people were too ecstatic and the public mood too euphoric to bother pressing the issue of governing right away. But as each day gave way to the next, I began to see a lot fewer of those NLD flags. No transition appeared on the horizon. As the days turned into weeks, I began to wonder, like everyone else, *What's the big delay?* There had been no reports of ballot box tampering, and the SLORC had not contested the numbers. But still, nothing happened.

Another month passed with no more news about the election. Then, on July 27 — exactly two months after the vote — I arrived at the office to find Soe Moe stretching back in his chair, a bottle of whisky on his desk and a smirk on his face. He handed me the press release he had just written. The candidates elected on May 27, it said, were not actually MPs-elect and the election was not about forming a new government; it was about launching a process to rewrite the constitution so that one day there could be a democratic transition. A small number of NLD MPs would be invited to join the SLORC's hand-picked group of Army officers to draw up the new constitution.

I didn't get it, I told Soe Moe. Did this mean there would be no transition?

He coolly replied that I was right, eyeing me carefully. Business as usual.

So, there it was: the generals had been playing for time until they could squash the people's hopes forever. Having promised an election, they were deluded enough to think their party could actually win it. When they lost, they were shocked, so they changed their minds — stubbornly refusing to honour their promise. I felt like an idiot. Having spent the past sixteen months observing these men, how could I have thought for a moment that the SLORC would simply hand over power like the keys to a factory for the next crew's shift? Instead of allowing elected NLD members of parliament to take office as the new government — or follow through on that invite to help them draw up a new constitution — the SLORC began arresting them. The party was outlawed and public display of NLD images prohibited; party offices were closed throughout the country and Suu Kyi's house arrest was extended. Hundreds of NLD activists went into hiding or fled to Thailand to form a government-in-exile.

With the SLORC refusing to give up power, the dream of democracy was over. The bad old days were here to stay. That was my cue to get the hell out of Burma. Escape through the Thai border was my only option but running away this time would be trickier than two years earlier; I was no longer the anonymous Mandalay farmer with freedom of movement but someone whose presence in Rangoon too many people knew about. I was a minor SLORC official whose whereabouts were monitored. Then there was Thandar to think about. I had promised myself I wouldn't leave the country until I had done everything possible to spring her loose from Insein. Now, sixteen months after returning from the jungle, I had done nothing on her behalf. What was worse, I had discovered Thandar's name on a list of political prisoners given twenty-five-year sentences — a term indicating that the regime saw my fiancée as one of the country's most dangerous political activists. I couldn't show anyone how much this news upset me. A jail sentence of this length, devastating enough for Thandar, would be a terrible blow to her family. Her added notoriety would only make things worse for her parents.

After learning of Thandar's jail term, I wished there was some way I could comfort her or offer encouragement about the future. Even though I no longer had any intention of marrying her, I also wanted to see her. But it was hopeless, and I knew I couldn't. Only immediate family were allowed contact with political prisoners; a minor SLORC official trying to visit an inmate at Insein without permission could be locked up for insubordination. Visiting her parents wouldn't work either; apart from the risk of exposure if I encountered their neighbours, they might well have already suffered terrible consequences for Thandar's criminal conviction and were no longer reachable. Since the coup, about three thousand Rangoon residents had been forcibly evicted from their homes and relocated in satellite shanty towns on the northern and eastern outskirts of the city, some eight hundred of their homes demolished. Were Mr. and Mrs. Aye among this unfortunate group? Surely, they would have contacted me by now, as Aung Win was well-known and his resemblance too much of a coincidence for them not to have noticed. But when I checked city records for their house in Mayangone Township, it was still there.

I had run out of excuses not to try reaching Thandar directly. So, on July 28, I wrote her a letter in my best Burmese, taking care not to include anything incriminating. I started by acknowledging what a shock it would be for her to hear from me at all, since she had probably received word of my death more than a year ago. It was too long and complicated a story to explain how and why I was reported as missing and presumed dead, but I wanted her to know that I was still in Burma and yes, very much alive. I could not imagine how dreadful it must have been for her to be stuck in that place, the horrors she and her fellow inmates must have been suffering. I assured her that I missed her, that I hoped she would forgive me for not having communicated sooner and that my letter would reach her somehow. I closed off by reassuring her that she had the inner strength to persevere through her long sentence, that I dreamt of the day we would be together once again, and that I would hold her in my heart until that moment. Signing off as her fiancé, I stuffed the letter into an envelope and sealed it.

For some time afterward, I felt like I should have crumpled up the letter and started over, removing certain notes of affection bound to be misleading. For months now our engagement had felt stale-dated, as if the statute of limitations on my fiancé status had expired the moment I shared that second kiss with Sayed

Hosin. I shouldn't have used words like "dearest" and "darling" or spoken of missing her, though of course I did. Now I missed her as I would a favourite sister. In the wake of that brief and furtive moment in a rusty old fishing boat on the Rangoon River, I found myself revisiting every moment I'd spent with the woman I had planned to marry. Two years later, it was hard to fathom my hasty proposal, given the platonic nature of our relations. At some point in my liberated future, I would explain the move as a desperate avoidance of my true nature, a bid to satisfy my father's wishes for grandchildren. While in no way diminishing my love for Thandar as a comrade and soulmate, the encounter with Sayed Hosin had driven a wedge between us, suggesting incompatibility. That, and the fact I was still in Burma because I was working for the junta, would have broken her heart had I told her.

After choosing a hiding place near the family home, I stashed the letter. Then I looked up the number of a friend of Thandar's brothers who hadn't met me. Reaching him from a post office phone, I identified myself only as a schoolmate of Thandar and asked for a favour, telling him where I'd left the letter. The next day, I returned to the hiding place; the letter was gone. I trusted that my courier would pass it along to Aye Maung or Hla Min who, in turn, would find a way to smuggle it past the guards at Insein so it reached their sister. Having no idea where I was, nor how to reach me, she could not respond. But at least she would know I was thinking about her.

The next day, I woke up at five o'clock. After packing some clothes and a few belongings, I took one last look out the bedroom window at my favourite view of Inya Lake. I was about to walk out the door when I noticed the Thiha Thura Medal still hanging on the wall. I pulled it off by the ribbon and looked at it closely, running my thumb over the edges of its golden star in the centre.

I was tempted to take it with me — what a conversation piece it would have made! — but changed my mind. If I were apprehended before reaching the border with a military medal for gallantry in my possession, that would be the end of my escape plan. Instead, I quietly placed it on the bedside table and tiptoed downstairs. The domestic staff hadn't begun work yet, so I slipped out of the mansion unnoticed and made my way downtown.

It took me a while to find a parked car with its key in the ignition. Once I did, I stole the car and drove it a few blocks before turning into an alley where I found five or six other parked cars. I stopped to switch plates with one of them, then drove it out of the city and didn't look back until I was clear of Pegu, north of Rangoon. When I arrived in Karen State and reached Myaing Ka Lay — a small village on the banks of the Thanlwin River, not far from Hpa-an — I parked in an alley, abandoned the car, and began wandering around town looking for someone I could trust. Stopping at a beer bar, I chatted up a chicken farmer who said he was going to Mae Sot. I offered him a hundred thousand *kyats* for a lift, and he agreed.

When I lifted the tarpaulin covering the back of his truck before hopping in, I was overcome by the stench of chicken manure. Lying in the cargo bed between two sets of cages were two other men, a woman, and a couple of young boys. I climbed in and joined them, pulling the tarp back into place. The farmer turned on the ignition, setting the truck on its way. Soon I heard the humming and felt the vibration of its tires going over a bridge. The truck slowed down as it approached the checkpoint. As it came to a halt, I heard a soldier approach. I held my breath as the farmer stepped out of his truck to join him for a cigarette, the two men making small talk as they stepped around the back.

"Pretty routine work these days?" the farmer was asking.

"Mostly," the soldier replied. "Except for the alert from Yangon about some staffer from the Ministry of Information who failed to report for work. Wait a minute …" The soldier went off to his booth, returning a few moments later. "Have you seen anyone who looks like this?" he asked. I gulped. The soldier was showing the farmer my official SLORC photo. I watched the others lying with me in the truck bed, the adults regarding me warily. The woman and one of the men covered the two little boys' mouths to keep them quiet.

The farmer said he hadn't, taking the right amount of time to study the image before replying. The soldier slapped the edge of the tailgate, prompting nervous clucking from a couple of chickens. "Right, then — off you go," he said. The six of us in the back exhaled. After we passed Myawaddy, the farmer used part of the fees we had paid him to buy off the Thai border guards so they wouldn't search the truck. I took a deep breath, by now accustomed to the stench — including that of the two young boys, who had wet themselves on the journey — and waited for the truck to be waved through. Sure enough, the border guards lifted only the front of the tarpaulin to see the chicken cages, then let us go. Moments later, we were free.

In Mae Sot, the farmer stopped the truck and let us all out. After bidding my fellow escapees farewell, I began wandering through town. My only possessions were a small bag of clothes and some leftover Burmese currency. With no identification, I was free but anonymous — an American without proof who spoke no Thai and whose Burmese would be of little help beyond Mae Sot. After renting a room in a cheap guest house, I showered off the chicken shit and changed into fresh clothes. Then I went downstairs to the guest house beer bar and began chatting people up in English. Within an hour, I met a Singha Beer truck driver who said he was driving to Chiang Mai the next morning. For a small fee, he would give me a lift.

It would take the better part of a day to reach Chiang Mai. When we arrived, the Singha Beer man dropped me off at Tha Phae Gate, a corner of the moated city popular with foreign backpackers, hill tribe trekkers, and other tourists and expats. I spent the next week decompressing from my sixteen months posing as a dead man's imposter. Renting a motorbike, I explored the city: hanging out in beer bars, browsing in the markets, and gorging myself on Thai food. I needed time to adjust to reality outside the paranoid bubble of dictatorship. I needed to find out for myself to what extent I had succumbed to Stockholm Syndrome while working for the junta and, thus, how difficult it might be to reintegrate into free society, into my old life. Then there were practical concerns. How could I possibly return to the United States with no passport, and what would I say to my father, and everyone else, once I was home?

On August 8, 1990 — two years to the day after the general strike and my engagement to Thandar — I found myself sitting at the US embassy in Bangkok.

11

Thandar:

Not long before the trial, I received a care package from home. My favourite sweater, a blanket, and a package of tea leaves. Putting on the sweater, I noticed an elbow patch that hadn't been there before. Ripping it off, I found a handwritten note my mother had cleverly sewn inside the patch. Opening it when the guards weren't looking, I recognized Mama's elegant hand. She told me that "M." had come by the house the morning after my arrest. He told her and my father that we were engaged. Mama congratulated me, expressing her hope that my fiancé and I would one day be reunited and enjoy much happiness together. But she and Papa had advised "M." to leave Burma until the situation improves, and he was very reluctant to do so. She closed by encouraging me not to give up hope.

After reading the note, I shredded it and stuffed the tiny pieces of paper in my mouth, taking minutes to chew and swallow them. I was surprised that Min had told my parents of our plans. We had agreed not to share the news of our engagement until final victory for the people. Ha! Our naïveté now seems quaint — pathetic, really, given how the years would unfold under the SLORC. Had we stuck to our promise, we'd probably have kept that secret forever. I could hardly blame Min for breaking it. My parents probably told him to go back to the US and lobby for my release, but I could not see Min doing that any more than I could see him joining my comrades in the jungle. I knew how much he wanted to stay in Burma, but I also knew how terrified he was by the idea of armed resistance.

That final meeting of the All Burma Federation of Student Unions was the moment that Min woke up to the reality of our struggle, when a little light bulb went off in his head. It's when he realized that the world as he understood it growing up in the West, the confidence in his own personal security, no longer existed. Despite the police raid at RASU, and the Bloody Friday and August crackdowns — most of which he had experienced directly — he seemed to regard our national struggle as something apart from himself; something that, while exciting and risky at times, would neither take over his own life nor require engagement to a degree that meant sacrificing everything. The selfless commitment and raw courage required for the violence of armed resistance seemed beyond his capacity. But then came that meeting, where the stakes could not have been clearer, followed by my arrest. Could he have changed his mind about the revolution? If not, and he was still in Burma, then what on earth was he doing?

I fretted for six months after receiving that note, wondering why I hadn't heard from Min, when another of Mama's packages arrived containing another sweater with an elbow patch. This time, her note began with the news that she and Dad had lost their jobs with the government a couple of months earlier. After my twenty-five-year sentence, they were both ostracized by their colleagues to the point of complete isolation, making it impossible to work. *Set up to fail*, I thought, reading Mama's note, *thanks to their political activist daughter*. And yet they did not blame me. After selling the family home, they had moved up north to Taungoo and started a small retail business. Money was tight, and my brothers were in no position to help. Cleared of any involvement with the democracy protests, Aye Maung and Hla Min had been co-opted: drafted by the Tatmadaw, they could only visit on special leaves.

I turned over the page to find more news. A friend of the family who also knew English had read a foreign news report in *The Working People's Daily* about some American photographer who had gone missing in Karen State and was feared dead. The photographer was identified as Min Lin. Was this your future son-in-law? the friend had asked Mama. The note concluded with an apology. Mama and Papa had agonized over how to tell me the news. She wished there was some way to comfort me ... My God. Min had kept his word: he had joined my comrades in Karen State. My heart sank. I had called on him to support The Cause. But not once did I expect that my coddled, urban, Western fiancé would actually immerse himself in the rugged, hyper-masculine world of a jungle-based, armed insurrection.

How could my Min — such a fish out of water, a man so far removed from his easy American life — have survived a single day, never mind months, in the KNLA's company? If he had ended up in one of those battles in the mountains, I was certain, there was no way he could have survived it. The newspaper story must have been true. I tore up Mama's note, this time dropping it in the toilet rather than trying to swallow it, flushing away the evidence with small bowlfuls of water. Tears rolled down my cheeks. Such a sweet spirit, that strange man I had agreed to marry! How easily he had charmed his way into my life! I had said "yes" to Min's hand in marriage without considering the implications, so persuasive in his ardour he had been. And yet we had not been intimate. Not once. Did he want me to move back to the US with him one day, or was he willing to stay here in Burma? I would never know.

Min was dead, and I felt partly responsible. I had killed him, in a sense, by inspiring romantic visions of our national dream; by pushing him further toward revolutionary consciousness than he would have moved on his own. Standing with me on Mandalay Hill, he had pledged to support my nation's struggle to be free. Later, when I committed to joining the resistance movement and asked him to do the same, he agreed. I wasn't entirely convinced by his promise, given my doubts about his courage. But I turned out to be wrong: it was he who ended up in the jungle, not me. And now he was gone. After mourning him for several weeks, I struggled to recover from the guilt of having led him astray.

By 1990, the last hope for democracy lay with the national elections. By that point I felt like political prisoners were the only skeptics left in Burma, the only people who weren't pinning all our hopes on Aung San Suu Kyi and her gospel of non-violence. We knew the generals too well; we knew how they thought and schemed, and we knew there was no way they would hand over the country to the politicians because they had lost a vote. Should anyone have been surprised that they lied? From what I heard, the masses had been holding their collective breath waiting for Daw Suu to form government and were shocked when power was stolen from her. Fools! At Insein, a healthy dose of skepticism kept one from going crazy. But then, a few weeks after the SLORC announced that Parliament would not convene — about the same time they began arresting the NLD's victorious candidates — something else began to challenge my sanity.

It was another package from home. This one came from my brothers who, as Tatmadaw soldiers, took a risk every time they sent me anything. Hidden inside was a note whose awkward

Burmese scrawl I recognized at once as Min's handwriting. It was dated July 28th, 1990 — a few days earlier. *I am very much alive,* it said. *I am still inside Burma.* There were no details. This was more than a year after Min was supposed to have died, and it had taken me that long to let go of my fiancé after mourning him. And now he was alive? Part of me wanted to rejoice, but another part was deeply disturbed. This news tore another hole in my heart.

Why was Min still in Burma? What had he been doing all this time? I spent weeks wondering about his complicated situation; perhaps he was working on a scheme to reduce my term. But as the weeks turned into months, then years, with no more word, I moved from fear for his safety to despair at not hearing from him that was followed by sadness, and ultimately resentment at the possibility he had simply abandoned me. During my first year at Insein I asked every newly arrived inmate, even if she hadn't known Min, whether she had seen him around Rangoon. One sister who'd been to a few of the meetings Min had attended said she thought she might have seen him one day, at a tea shop near Sule Pagoda. But despite an eerie resemblance, the man she saw could not have been Min. He was wearing Tatmadaw green, was well-built with a military haircut, and sat with a shady-looking group of SLORC types. I agreed: my fiancé was capable of a lot of things but selling out to the regime was not one of them.

For a few years, I went back and forth between thinking he had gone back into hiding or returned to Karen State, and assuming he had given up on us. Perhaps he was incapacitated and couldn't reach me. Or perhaps he had been killed for real this time. But the more I doubted it, the more I began second-guessing our engagement. How much did I really know about the man I had agreed to marry, and during such a brief and optimistic moment in Burma's history, when everything seemed possible? When every knowing smile, every secret kept, every shared act of intimacy or solidarity seemed imbued with emotional significance out of all proportion to life in Burma since 1962? Min's promise to me in Mandalay was not unsolicited. I had challenged him to commit to our movement, and he had agreed because he wanted us to be together. Later, when I called for armed struggle, he seemed to hesitate. Americans talk a good line about freedom and democracy, but have they ever had to fight for it with everything at stake? At least Min had joined the rebels, which proved he was willing to sacrifice himself. He may have done nothing more than take photographs, but he deserved credit for that, at least.

But after sending me that one note, he simply vanished. During all the time I waited to hear from him again, my mind kept returning to his motivations for coming to Burma. He had often spoken of his father's ties to our country, of how family history had led him here like a compass. I understood that. I also respected his professional work, knowing his photos could do some good by raising international awareness and putting more pressure on the SLORC. But there was no avoiding the fact that Min had come to my country to serve his own ambition and build his reputation. There was nothing wrong with that — and he was hardly the first Westerner to use my country as a career stepping stone — but it did make me wonder if his loyalty was skin deep. I had known him for only five months when I pledged my heart to him. What made me think he truly loved me, when the only chance to prove it lay somewhere in the abstract future? My trust in him was not earned. For such a guileless leap of faith, I had only myself to blame.

I heard nothing more from Min, or about him, after 1990. It would take five more years to give up on ever hearing from him again, another five before I stopped thinking about him. It has often been said by my sister political prisoners that the good people in

your life are the ones who don't stop fighting for you, but sometimes it's the ones you rely on the most who end up disappointing
you, the ones you least expect to wash their hands of you and
move on. At the time I received Min's letter, still clinging to belief
in our relationship, I found it impossible to accept that he was still
alive and not doing everything in his power to have my sentence
reduced. Given the jungle's rough conditions, and the dangers he
would have faced by resurfacing, it seemed unlikely that he was still
with the rebels and had written that letter from Karen State. Nor
could I believe that he had gone missing again. So where was he?

The longer I waited, the more I believed he had gone back
home to start his life over again, as I had assumed he would the
first time we talked about his future. How many hours did I spend
wondering what he was up to back in the US? How long seething
in resentment as I imagined him living it up in California while
boasting of his adventures in exotic Burma? How long trying not to
think about what a great career move it must have been, coming to
my country and taking photos that would earn him a great deal of
money? He had probably met someone else, too, no doubt settling
down to start a family and live a wonderful life while I sat here
in this prison cell, swatting away the cockroaches while counting
the years. Yes, he was a challenge to my Buddhism, that Min Lin.
But eventually I came to regard him as merely another example
of the impermanence of life, a part of the suffering we must all
experience on the road to wisdom. In my best moments at Insein,
I would thank him for giving me that wisdom.

One day, about five years into my sentence, Aye Maung and
Hla Min paid me a rare visit while on leave from their base in the
north. I was overjoyed to see my brothers, even in their uniforms.
Like so many other young men who hated the Army, but whose
politics were stifled after being forced into service by the Tatmadaw,

they took their humiliation in stride. We were good examples for each other; they might not have been in a jail cell but they, too, had become prisoners of the regime. As good Buddhists, the three of us had little choice but to endure our respective sufferings with humility and grace. During our visit, we sat across a table from each other, Aye Maung holding my left hand and Hla Min my right. We all cried when we spoke of our parents, who had fallen on hard times up north and needed every *kyat* they could find.

At one point I pulled off my engagement ring and placed it in Aye Maung's hand. "Go sell it," I told him, "and give the money to Mama and Papa." After that, I began to let go of Min Lin. Before long, my missing fiancé was reduced to a ghostly presence, a man whose light had shone so brightly and briefly in my life before so sadly, and mysteriously, flickering out.

PART TWO

12

Los Angeles
March 1989

The morning sun blazed through the bedroom window, waking up
the history professor and triggering his daily ritual. Putting on a
bathrobe, Ko Lin Tun shuffled down the hall to the kitchen where
he made a pot of coffee. As he did so, he found himself staring
once again at shadows on the wall cast through the sliding glass
doors from the patio garden. A thicket of bamboo trees dividing
the sun's golden rays with dark vertical lines, the effect reminding
him of jail cell bars, thanks to the country that had swallowed
up his son. Ko Lin Tun hadn't heard a word from Min since he'd
flown to Rangoon a year ago. Months later, Burma had imploded
with protest and violence, with thousands dead and thousands
more in jail. Was his son among either group? He had contacted
the Secretary of State's office and the US ambassador in Rangoon
but to no avail. Min had gone silent for a year now, and the
uncertainty of his whereabouts had been Ko Lin Tun's private
agony ever since.

When the coffee finished brewing, Ko Lin Tun poured himself
a cup and sat down with it. Then the telephone rang: it was the

Associated Press, calling to inform him that his son had gone missing in Burma.

"I could have told you that," he replied rudely, interrupting the AP desk staffer. "He hasn't called or written once in the whole year he's been gone."

The AP staffer continued. "I'm sorry to hear that, Mr. Tun, but what I'm saying is that your son has officially been reported missing and is presumed dead. A few months ago, he left Rangoon to go to Karen State and join the student and ethnic rebels. We learned of his disappearance from one of our stringers in Southeast Asia who was covering the insurgency. What we know is that Min was last seen near the Thai-Burma border with rebel forces, but he wasn't among the group that escaped an attack by the Burmese Army. I am so sorry."

The AP staffer added that Min had sent a bunch of film to AP before leaving the rebel base camp. The wire service would be happy to arrange for its delivery, or he could pick it up any time. Ko Lin Tun thanked the man and hung up, gutted. He had been right after all, in a way he did not want to be. Despite his warnings that Burma was too dangerous, Min had gone anyway, walking straight into the danger. Now he was dead. He must be. Ko Lin Tun, fighting tears, took a gulp of coffee and went to his son's old bedroom.

The room had gone unused since Min moved out to attend college. It was full of things he had probably forgotten, but not his father: high school photo albums, an unused football, the boy's first Nikon. There was another item, not one of Min's, that he had placed in the room's closet after his son flew to Burma, something previously hidden in the attic. Going to the closet, he pulled out a dusty leather suitcase and brought it to the living room. There he placed it on a coffee table and, using both thumbs to undo the locks, opened it. With great care he pulled out a folded green garment, using his bathrobe sleeve to wipe off the gold nameplate on its chest: *Maj. Gen. Lin Tun.* Raising the uniform to his face, he breathed in its musty scent and fondled its buttons. How proud he once was to serve his country while wearing it. How quickly he'd been deemed unworthy of it for expressing an opinion. How ashamed he now was of the dishonour it represented in the eyes of the world. And yet how right it felt to have kept it all these years.

Ko Lin Tun put the uniform back in the suitcase and returned it to Min's bedroom. Then he went to his study and sat at his desk, sighing. He was a proud and dedicated history professor, loved by his students and fulfilled by his work; he lived for the joy of reaching young minds with the lessons of a changing world over centuries and across continents, cultures, creeds, and ideologies. Over the decades he had spent in the United States, this work had expanded his consciousness, as much as anything could, from that of the land and times in which he was raised. But at sixty-four, he had one more year of teaching before retirement. Then what?

After that phone call from the Associated Press, his mind was filled with thoughts of Min, of Burma, and of things he had not shared with anyone. He had regrets about the things he had left unsaid to his son. Now, taking out a pen and a brand-new journal bought for this very purpose, he felt the need to unburden himself of secrets. Long ago, when he first thought of drafting his memoirs, he imagined he would render them in the objective voice that typified so many of his carefully crafted essays. But in the fog of his grief, he found himself adopting the epistolary form, addressing his dead son directly.

My dear boy, he began. It is most unfortunate that it has taken the occasion of your death, my learning of it just now, to provide me an opportunity to write down certain truths I have kept to myself for so long. It pains me to do this, for these are truths

I should have shared with you before you boarded that plane; I fear that, in having failed to do so, I failed you as a father. For how could you have understood yourself, how could you ever have really known yourself, without knowing the man who raised you from birth? And so I must begin by disabusing you of certain things, of essential information I had encouraged you all your life to accept as fact.

I did not tell you that your birth mother died. I did not tell you that Chia Yong was actually your stepmother, that you were not my only son, and that you were not born in Bangkok. Nor did I tell you that I did not leave Burma in 1958, nor that I was more than a history teacher when I did. It is true, as I told you, that I was born and raised in Mandalay. It is also true that I attended Rangoon Arts and Sciences University, obtaining my bachelor's and master's degrees in history while serving in the Tatmadaw. What I didn't tell you was that in 1951, when I was twenty-six, I was promoted to a junior officer's rank. My job was to provide field reports on ethnic army activities in the border areas. It was not my ambition to lead in the Tatmadaw, but I rose steadily through the ranks over the next seven years.

In 1958, Ne Win staged a minor coup and reached a deal with Prime Minister U Nu: the Tatmadaw would rule for the next two years as a "caretaker" government, then elections would be held. During this period, I became, at the age of thirty-three, the youngest man promoted to a major general's rank. I also served as Deputy Minister of the Interior. In February 1960, U Nu's party won the elections and Ne Win returned the reins of power, as promised. But two years later, things were not going well. U Nu's government was reeling from some major challenges: insurgencies by the Burma Communist Party and the People's Volunteer Organization (the latter a paramilitary outfit founded by Aung San that lost control after his death), uprisings from several ethnic guerrilla armies fighting for independence, and the incursion of Kuomintang troops which, having lost the battle for China in 1949, had crossed into northern Burma with CIA-funded weapons and logistical support.

What was worse, in Ne Win's view: U Nu was dancing with the ethnics, entertaining their bids for independence. When the prime minister decided to meet with Shan and Karenni leaders to formally discuss the idea of replacing Burma's unitary constitution with a federal one — and this after planning to grant statehood to Mon and Arakan — Ne Win was outraged. Ever since the Panglong Agreement in 1947, Shan leaders had shown threatening signs of exercising what they believed was their right to secede from the Union; these latest developments, in Ne Win's mind, only confirmed U Nu's weakness. Thus, on February 27, 1962, he called a final meeting of senior advisors and Army command to prepare us for a coup. The time had come, he said, to replace parliamentary democracy with military rule. This time, there would be no turning back.

During the meeting, as Ne Win outlined his plan for the coup, most officers were quick to endorse it — some literally applauding his diagnosis of Burma's political situation. I said nothing. Having known the senior general for years, I was not the kind of officer to curry favour by kissing his bottom. But now I was angry. You see, Min, I was a true democrat. When I served in the caretaker military cabinet for those two years after 1958, I did so on the understanding that such arrangements should only be temporary. Ne Win himself had once insisted that the Army should never be involved in politics, so perhaps he enjoyed those two years a little too much. For now, it seemed, he had changed his tune. And herein lay my dilemma: I saw the coup as a treasonous betrayal of everything we had celebrated fifteen years earlier when Aung San went to London to secure Burma's independence. A military coup would put an end to representative government — a dream for which, once achieving it, Aung San would pay with his life only six months after that trip to London. I could not possibly go along with this plan, but here was my other dilemma: as one officer after another voiced support for the coup, the notion of opposing it became increasingly dangerous.

I stared at Ne Win, trying to guess his next move. The senior general could be ruthless: an open display of dissent could result in a court martial or worse. I said nothing. When the meeting was over, I approached him and asked to speak privately. When he agreed, I told him, with utmost respect, that a military coup was premature under the current conditions. He frowned, asking me why. I then shared my argument for allowing parliament to continue, at this point still believing that I could reason with the senior general. It is true that there are many problems in our country, I told him, and unrest in the border areas. But turning the Tatmadaw into an overlord, treating the people like unruly children in need of a whipping, was no solution.

I was not sure how he might respond to such frankness, but I knew he'd appreciate my keeping this intervention private, sparing him the indignity of losing face in front of colleagues. Having known him for so long, I knew that discretion was important to Ne Win. And I was certain he had confidence in my judgement: it was he, after all, who had appointed me major general. On many occasions we had played golf, a sport I did not enjoy but tolerated because it relaxed the senior general. Golf had a way of lubricating social environments for uptight military men, allowing someone like Ne Win to be more casual with subordinates. I had shared my opinions during these golf games. Ne Win had not only been receptive but had acted on some of my advice. Once I told him we should withdraw troops from certain areas in Karen State where the Tatmadaw had sufficiently pacified the population; another massacre would turn the Karen people against us forever. And with good reason: when Burma Independence Army forces entered the country from Thailand near the end of World War II, they took revenge on the Karen for supporting the British by killing more than 1,800 people and wiping out four villages in one district. Ne Win agreed with me that time, saving hundreds of lives.

But we were not on a golf course this time, and the senior general was in no mood to consider new ideas, especially since he had been planning the coup for several weeks, if not months. As I made my case for allowing parliament to serve out its term, I could see that my intervention was not going over well. Ne Win's eyes narrowed. His lips tightened into a frown. The more I spoke, the more the blood seemed to drain from his disturbingly cherubic face. He would take my concerns under advisement, he coolly replied, addressing me by rank instead of by name. Then he dismissed me with a perfunctory salute. I went home that night wondering if I had signed my own death warrant.

Nothing happened for the next couple of days. The suspense was unnerving, and with no indication of what my act of dissent might cost me, I found it hard to sleep. Meanwhile, your mother, Nu Nu — a beautiful woman I had met in Mandalay during my undergrad years — was eight-and-a-half months pregnant with you, our second child. The timing for premature delivery could not have been worse but, sure enough, she was practically bursting at six o'clock on the evening of March 1. At that moment I was sitting in my office when the telephone rang. It was your big brother, seven-year-old Than Tun. He was excited. "Mummy's going to have the baby!" he said. "Please come home!"

I tried to calm him down. "Listen," I said. "You need to get someone to bring your mother to the hospital. It will be the

American Hospital. You should go with her and wait. I can't come yet. There's an officer's meeting I must attend. So call someone now!"

At seven o'clock I reported to the officer's meeting, but no one was there. After waiting awhile, I had a sinking feeling that I had been duped; that, far from being a future member of cabinet, I was to become one of the coup's first casualties. I didn't know what to do, but I wanted to be by my wife's side when she gave birth to you, so I headed straight to the hospital. Than Tun met me in the lobby, in a panic. The doctors had put Nu Nu to sleep. She was in a ward down the hall from us, he explained, but we couldn't go in because her room was being kept under guard. I told your brother to wait while I spoke with the soldier in charge.

When I arrived at the maternity ward, I was met by a junior Tatmadaw recruit I recognized, a real keener who had completed officer's training despite being only twenty-two. I could not recall this lieutenant's name but addressed him with a nickname one of his teachers had given him *Kyi-gan myat see*, Little Crow Eye, this in reference to his apparent talent for noticing certain details. He struck me as an overly earnest ladder climber, so his sudden appearance at the hospital, blocking access to my wife and new child, was disturbing. I dreaded the prospect of being arrested by someone several bars below my rank.

Addressing *Kgyi-gan myat see* as my inferior, I demanded to know what he was doing. Saluting me and adjusting his eyeglasses, he asked me to follow him. I was desperate to ignore him and turn straight into the maternity ward, but his urgency convinced me otherwise. He led me into a linen closet and, turning on the light, informed me that I was in grave danger, as was my family. We would have to leave the country that night. When I asked him why, he shook his head sadly, indicating that he knew everything:

that I had told the senior general, in his words, that I opposed "the liberation of Burma." Ne Win had now issued a warrant for my arrest, and soldiers would be coming to our home at midnight ... Perhaps I should not have been surprised, dear Min, but *Kgyi-gan myat see*'s words stung. How did he know this? I asked him. Never mind, he said. He had arranged with hospital staff to release my wife within the hour. The labour hadn't gone well, and the doctor had to deliver the baby by Caesarean section. Nu Nu was waking up at that moment but was very weak. Once she was ready, I would have to bring her, the baby, and Than Tun home immediately. We were to pack our things and drive out of the city well before midnight, said *Kgyi-gan myat see*. And I was not to tell Nu Nu or Than Tun anything — just get them in the car and leave immediately.

Things were happening so fast. *Kgyi-gan myat see* had thought of everything. But how had such a junior soldier learned that Nu Nu was in the hospital having a baby? And why would he go there, instead of first tracking me down at the office? These questions have haunted me ever since. I thanked *Kgyi-gan myat see* for his assistance, telling him that he was taking a great risk by helping my family. But how did I know I could trust him? I asked. He grimaced, insisting that I take my chances. He said he respected me and did not wish to see me become the first victim of what he called The Big Event. But I was a fugitive now, so we could not be seen to be talking. After saluting me, *Kgyi-gan myat see* turned to leave.

Halfway down the hall, he turned around and congratulated me on the birth of my new son. Had we chosen a name yet? "Yes," I replied, delighted to confirm it was a boy. "It is Min Lin." *Kgyi-gan myat see* smiled awkwardly and, adjusting his glasses again, saluted once more before leaving. I entered the delivery room to find your mother awake, sitting up and exhausted, with you on her chest. "He's beautiful," I told Nu Nu, wiping the perspiration off her forehead before kissing it. "Yes," she sighed. "Our little Min." Your mother, pale and weak, could barely embrace you. I had no idea how I could bring her, you, and your seven-year-old brother out of the city and safely across the border in a few hours. Nu Nu was in great pain when I had a wheelchair brought in. The nurses were weeping as they placed her in it, apologizing for allowing her to leave the hospital so soon after a difficult birth. But the young soldier had ignored their protests and insisted your mother be discharged because of a greater danger to the family.

We did as we were told. I said nothing as I drove us all home and packed some bags with Than Tun. We returned to the car with you and your ailing mother. Nu Nu was in no condition for a long drive, so I lay her down in the back seat with a blanket and a pillow while Than Tun sat up front with me, cradling you in his arms. Just before sunrise, when we arrived in Hpa-an, I stopped the car to see how your mother was doing. She was still in great pain, and begging for water, so I handed her a Thermos. When I reached around her to pull more of the blanket over her, it was soaking wet. Then I realized it was blood. I said nothing but returned to the driver's seat and encouraged Than Tun to get some sleep. Meanwhile I prayed that your mother would have the strength to make it to Myawaddy, where a hospital awaited across the border.

When your brother and I awoke to your cries a few hours later, I turned around to discover that Nu Nu was dead. Than Tun screamed. I said nothing but turned on the ignition and continued us on our way, driving until we reached the outskirts of Myawaddy where I turned off the main highway onto a dirt road, driving deep into the forest until we reached a small clearing. There we found a ditch, and I buried your mother in it. After pausing to say a prayer with Than Tun, we proceeded to Myawaddy, where we abandoned the car about a mile from the checkpoint and walked across the border. Than Tun held you in a blanket while I carried a couple of suitcases, one containing a bundle of cash.

I had lost the only woman I had ever loved. And I was an exile, stuck with a seven-year-old son out of his mind with grief and an infant son screaming for the breast of his dead mother. About a week after we arrived in Mae Sot, your older brother became seriously ill. A few days earlier Than Tun had awoken with a fever, so I gave him some medicine and told him to rest. But by the seventh day he was drenched in sweat and had a bad case of the shakes, his torso riddled with mosquito bite rash. After scratching himself all over his body he had begun to hyperventilate, so I brought him to the same health clinic where I'd brought you the first day for more formula. After four hours, a doctor approached. In English, he told me that Than Tun's was one of the worst cases of malaria he had ever seen, a rapid and progressive attack on all the body's defences. Your brother had gone into cardiac arrest shortly after being admitted. The doctors were unable to save him.

I don't recall much else about our time in Thailand after that. I know we spent several weeks in Mae Sot before I took you down to Bangkok. I spent several more weeks wandering around in a daze while Thai nannies took care of you. Once I was ready to visit the US embassy and seek political asylum, I must have been a sight to behold: a high-ranking Burmese Army officer in exile, carrying an infant son. Where was my wife? She's dead, I replied. Died after giving birth to this child. When and where did this birth take place? I thought for a moment, before replying: March 20th in Bangkok. My wife died two days later. I had no proof of either event, but the embassy processed our papers anyway. Our family now had a new story.

13

Ko Lin Tun received his test results from the doctor. Blood pressure and cholesterol levels? Good. Heartbeat? Normal. Body fat index? Perfect. Yes, he was in great shape for a man of sixty-four, his virtuous diet and exercise regime guaranteeing him a long life. But for what? Since Chia Yong's death he hadn't bothered seeking a third wife, and the relationships he did have with women didn't last more than a few dates. Since Min's departure to Burma, he had been completely alone, with no one to talk to apart from colleagues he met occasionally for lunch. Now he spent most of his time at home, wallowing in regrets about how he had raised his son. How he had pressured Min to show more interest in manly things; how he had tried to set him up for dates with the daughters of colleagues because the boy never seemed to have a girlfriend; and how he had dismissed photography as a career choice because of Min's chosen medium and subject matter. He wasn't doing hard-news journalism, Ko Lin Tun had complained, but taking pictures of clothing designers and ballet dancers!

Ko Lin Tun had done his best to compensate for Min's lost Burmese life by teaching him the language and culture he had grown up with in Mandalay; by regaling him with stories of Burman Buddhist culture and history, chock full of masculine role models. But Ko Lin Tun had wanted it both ways for his son: he wanted him to be proud of his Burmese heritage but to avoid the country itself since, in his view, Burma's best qualities had vanished since 1962. Now he felt guilty that Min had gone there as a young adult deprived of the knowledge of his family background and his father's critical position with the Tatmadaw. There was much for Ko Lin Tun to be ashamed about in these omissions.

While Chia Yong was alive, he had made sure that the woman Min believed to be his mother remained a peripheral figure in the boy's life. He didn't want her telling Min anything that might reveal she was his stepmother. All Min ever knew about Chia Yong was that she was a Chinese Burmese immigrant who had left Burma a year before his father, on a scholarship, and that she and Ko Lin Tun met soon afterward. What he didn't know was that the scholarship was to study broadcasting, that Chia Yong had previously met another man, became pregnant by him and miscarried, and that the man had dumped her soon afterward. Too ashamed to return to Burma, she had abandoned her studies and begun working as a housekeeper around the time she met Ko Lin Tun at a supermarket. They made small talk. After bumping into each other a week later at the same supermarket, he asked her out. Intrigued by this widower with an infant son, Chia Yong married Ko Lin Tun and put the miscarriage behind her, raising Min as her own child. For the first dozen years of the boy's life, she quietly provided for him while saying little about herself. She wanted to forge a new life. That meant keeping her own secrets.

Every day when Ko Lin Tun returned home from work and Min from school, Chia Yong would prepare dinner while the men folk sat in the living room to do Burmese lessons. Ko Lin Tun patiently led his son through language exercises that helped the boy progress from basic conversation to more complex linguistic phrasing.

Although the boy was unlikely to ever need it, he also taught Min the Burmese script — helping him become familiar enough with it that, by the age of six, he was fluently bilingual and, to some extent, could read and write in Burmese.

Min was not the only person Ko Kin Tun kept in the dark about his past. None of his fellow Burmese expatriates in LA knew about it either. At Burmese community events in Southern California, including the Thingyan New Year festivals in mid-April, everyone believed him when he said he was an ex-history professor from RASU. At such events he introduced Min to other immigrants, including Burmese Americans who self-identified as passport holders or sojourners rather than as exiles or refugees. More than a few of these folks grimaced when others mistook them for asylum-seekers, or they changed the subject whenever the words "dictatorship" or "dissident" came up. These people tended to be the wealthiest Burmese at such events, the men dressed in tailored suits and their wives wearing far too much makeup and oversized jewellery. They were also the immigrants least critical of Ne Win.

At one of these Thingyan dinners in the early eighties, Ko Lin Tun recalled, Min had complained when he caught his father making small talk with a regime apologist. Later, on the sidelines, Ko Lin Tun instructed his son: It is important to keep up appearances with overseas Burmese, regardless of loyalties. You never know if there might be a mole or a spy — a stooge — among them. Min had shrugged this off, abandoning his father to join the dissidents. The boy clearly preferred the company of exiles, who made no effort to hide their hatred of Ne Win. When dinner was served, these Burmese sat as far away from the business folk as possible. Ko Lin Tun lamented the irony: at a seasonal community event and cultural ritual aimed at bringing all Burmese together, two groups divided by mutual distrust and loathing managed to participate while completely avoiding each other.

When did things start going wrong with Min? Ko Lin Tun wasn't sure. He had hopes of a serious career, like law or medicine, for his son. He felt that Min's chosen career path was too bohemian, not serious at all. For a while he tried talking him out of photography, but failed. As with the long hair, or the reluctance to sign up for Selective Service, Min seemed determined to defy his father's wishes. One day in the spring of 1985, while completing his arts degree with honours at UCLA, the boy brought his student portfolio to the Associated Press. He didn't hear back, so he kept pestering them with more submissions. After several weeks of persistent calls and unannounced visits, they gave him his first assignment: doing publicity stills for Mikhail Baryshnikov, who had recently appeared in the film *White Nights*. Min's career took off after that. Ko Lin Tun, while relieved that his son appeared to be gaining financial independence, feared that his own influence over the boy was slipping away.

In the twenty-seven years since he'd fled Burma, the idea of returning there had not once occurred to Ko Lin Tun. Now that his son was dead, he hated the place more than ever. Since 1962, the rest of his family had either died or fled the country, and he hadn't known anyone else there in decades. Now that Min was gone, he was certain that he would never return. But he still felt guilty about his life of privilege in the United States, and that feeling sent him back to his journal. Writing this extended letter to Min in the afterlife, as morbid as it seemed, was therapeutic for Ko Lin Tun. It helped him to clarify the issues that troubled him.

To my dear and most unfortunate son: The recent news of your death has caused me to rethink everything about March 2, 1962. On that day, I had no doubt that leaving Burma was the right thing to do. We might not have survived had we stayed; at best, facing the wrath of Ne Win would have meant my going to jail and depriving you of a bright future. Your mother and Than Tun would have survived, yes, and you would have grown up knowing and loving them. But what kind of life would that have been, without a father and under the yoke of dictatorship? Things would have been much worse for you in Burma. And yet, I can't help but wonder: when I abandoned the car in Myawaddy, crossing the border with you and Than Tun, was I doing the right thing? If he and your mother had survived, would that have justified my desertion?

In the years that followed, I would learn through overseas mail what had become of those closest to me. My mother and father, your grandparents, were interrogated in Mandalay on March 2. They didn't know what had happened or where I was; calling them to say goodbye would have implicated them. They were kept in jail for a week before their release. Your grandfather had a fatal heart attack in 1963. Your grandmother followed him to the grave a year later. In 1966, I reached your maternal grandparents and uncle in Mandalay with a letter. A neighbour who was caring for them responded. My in-laws had wondered what became of us, so they were devastated to learn of their daughter's death. But they insisted I not blame myself for this misfortune. Their only son, Nu Nu's brother, was still alive, but locked up at Insein.

In 1970, my brother Ko Maw, a teacher in Pegu detained at the same time as my parents, died of liver disease after taking to drink soon after the coup. I had tried sending him a letter in 1966 but, like those to my mother and father which went unanswered, it likely never reached him. In 1970, I heard from his wife who had left him years earlier. She said your uncle never recovered from Ne Win's decision to drive out foreigners, shut down the free press, and censor literature. Before she left him, she said, he kept repeating the same complaint while drunk: "They are trying to turn us all into idiots!"

Those are only our relatives, Min. I cannot begin to count all the friends and colleagues I left behind who also suffered terribly under Ne Win while I enjoyed a new life of freedom in the US; people who were punished for no other reason than not being able to leave Burma. In July of 1962, two former cadets I had trained who were RASU students took part in campus protests against the coup. Both were inside the student union building when it was blown up, killed with several other students. Their history professor, a good friend of mine, sent a letter to the Ministry of the Interior calling for the firing and immediate arrest of Sein Lwin, who had ordered the dynamiting of the student union building. Instead, the professor was arrested, charged with sedition, and sentenced to four years at Insein. In 1976, many other good men who had served the Tatmadaw with distinction — men it was my honour to count as colleagues — were executed or received lengthy jail terms for their role in a plot to kill Ne Win. Theirs was a courageous endeavour, no less honourable for we Burmese people than Operation Valkyrie had been for courageous Germans in 1944. When I think of the quiet desperation those men and their families must have endured after 1962, living in a police state, I cannot imagine suffering fourteen years of that, never mind the twenty-seven it has now been! How differently our lives would have turned out had I simply shut my mouth and said nothing to Ne Win; had I waited for March 2 to arrive, followed my orders, and allowed myself to be cowed into silence.

What kind of man would I have been by 1976? I am certain I would have hated Ne Win like everyone else. But would I have had the courage to join my colleagues in an assassination plot against him? And when it failed, would I have faced the firing squad like a good patriot, knowing I'd be leaving behind a grieving wife and two sons? The question haunts me to this day, Min, for I cannot be certain the answer is "yes." As grateful as I am for our life in the United States, I shudder to contemplate the possibility of my own cowardice under those circumstances. Every day I wonder why I deserve this life more than anyone else and cannot come up with an answer.

When we first arrived in Los Angeles, I had no idea how to support us. All I had was a master's degree and some teaching experience while performing military duties. History was a competitive field at the university level, so I was happy to land my first US job at a high school before I met your stepmother. After that, it wasn't hard to fool the neighbours about you and Chia Yong. Some people may have had their suspicions about the lack of resemblance, but I doubt it. This was before the Hart-Celler Act of 1965, which opened the United States to Asian immigrants. In those days, apart from Hollywood, Southern California was an innocent place; Americans, being self-centred, were superficially friendly. Unlike we Burmese, who closely observe every human interaction, Americans did not probe too deeply into other people's lives because their own individual liberty was all that mattered. White neighbors, if they knew any Asians at all, wouldn't have known the difference between Burman and Han Chinese ethnicity. So, if I told them that a Chinese Burmese woman was your mother, they were okay with that. And if I said I was a history professor who left Burma in 1958, that I had lived in different US towns before landing where we did in 1962, then that story held up as well.

If everyone else could believe the family story as I presented it, then I was certain I would be able to move on with my life, raise you in a healthy environment, and forget the trauma we had left behind at the Thai-Burmese border. Over the years, thanks to my *gravitas* as a model immigrant, my story began to carry the weight of received wisdom. If I felt no need to change that story for friends and colleagues, then why change it for my own son? So, you see, Min, I did not intend to lie about our family but only wanted you to live a normal life. Perhaps I spoiled you by providing all those material comforts you desired. Perhaps I should have been harder on you. My one worry about raising you in the United States was that everything came too easily for you here. As a child, you knew nothing of the living conditions of those less fortunate than yourself, especially in the country of your birth. And so, my son, if there is any consolation from your death in Burma, it lies in the hope that you eventually had a chance to see, with your own eyes, how the other side lives.

14

US Embassy, Bangkok
August 1990

Min:

When I first stepped off the overnight train from Chiang Mai at Hua Lamphong Station, I was in no rush to return home and wasn't ready to contemplate boarding a plane. After a week in northern Thailand, I was still trying to figure out how to account for the past sixteen months of my life. So I spent my first few days in Bangkok hanging around the beer bars at Khao San Road and getting lazily drunk on Singha beer, alternately watching far-too-loud Hollywood action movies on guest house pub TV screens and scribbling notes about my ordeal. Then I gathered up the nerve to visit the Embassy.

Things didn't get off to a good start. The receptionist gave me attitude for having no identification. I told her my story was complicated, and I'd be happy to tell it, but in the meantime the embassy should contact my father and let him know I was still alive. He would confirm my identity so that a new passport could be issued. The receptionist agreed but said I would also need to speak with Embassy staff: the US government would want to know what I'd been doing since March 1988, and the Thai government would expect payment for an overstay. Directing me to the waiting area, she then picked up the phone and continued working. Nearly an hour passed before another staff person arrived and led me down a hall to a windowless meeting room, where two large white men in navy blue suits were waiting.

Both State Department officials, they were built like linebackers and had the kind of bad haircuts that suggested born-again Christianity, CIA status, or both. They wore matching US flag pins on their lapels.

"Welcome back, Mr. Lin," said the blond one, offering his hand. "We thought we'd lost you."

"Thank you," I said, shaking his massive hand and attempting a smile. I was a bit rattled. These men were friendly but physically intimidating. How much did they know? Surely their most recent information would be the AP wire story about my disappearance. The brunette closed his folder and looked directly into my eyes. It's not every day, he said, that someone who's gone missing in a combat zone and is presumed dead turns up alive sixteen months later, completely healthy, and presents himself from out of the blue. Especially if there hasn't been a single tip on his whereabouts. So I could appreciate their curiosity, right?

"Yes, I certainly do," I nodded politely. I understood completely.

Could I tell them what happened on March 27 of last year, and where I'd been since then? Now they were both looking me directly in the eye, their expressions neutral.

Well, I said, they probably knew I'd gone to the border area as a journalist accompanying a group of student activists who were joining the KNLA to battle the Burmese Army —

I hesitated a moment before proceeding. I needed to be satisfied, in my own mind, that a combat role in fighting the Burmese dictatorship, not being counter to US interests, was unlikely to classify me as a terrorist in the eyes of my own government.

— but I was convinced to join the rebel forces in a combat role after meeting so many refugee families who had been terrorized by the Burmese Army. As they knew, there was a lot of rape and murder going on during the Army's clearance operations to root out revolutionaries.

"Yes," said the blond. "We are aware of that."

I said we were caught in a fierce battle that went on for three days and that, when the Burmese Army drew closer, I was separated from the rebels.

"We know that too," said the brunette. "So, what happened?"

I had no intention of telling the US government about my double, about being rescued by the Tatmadaw and spending sixteen months promoting the SLORC's many good works. Instead, I went with the version I'd been working on since Chiang Mai: that we all fled into the forest and later fanned out into the village. And then ... and then ...

I began to stammer. Putting it all together on the spot, without my notes, was difficult. But my interrogators misread my struggle as emotional distress. The brunette turned to his colleague and whispered something in his ear. Then he turned back to me, suggesting that I gather my thoughts and put them all down on paper. I could take as much time as I needed, and then we could talk. Oh, and they didn't have a lot of information about my time in Burma before I disappeared, so I should start from the beginning, from my arrival in Rangoon. He then pulled out a pen and notepad from his briefcase, pushing them across the table at me. Take all the time you need, he repeated, then call reception with the phone when you're done. Then he and the blond left the room.

I picked up the pen and, recalling everything about that first year in Burma, began scribbling away about my relationship with Thandar, the demonstrations, her arrest — everything leading up to Maw Pokay. All of it true until that final day. What follows became the official record of my life between March 27, 1989, and August 8, 1990:

We fled into the forest. As the last defender of HQ, I was well behind my comrades by the time I reached the trees. Once I got through the trees, there was no sign of them. The Tatmadaw were still bombarding our positions and continuing their advance toward the village, so I had little choice but to run as fast as my flip-flops could carry me. The only real escape route was south-east, where I could circle back toward the river about a mile away. The Army had abandoned that spot. Along the way, I noticed one or two villagers cowering in their homes as I ran past but none of my comrades. By the time I reached the water's edge and was still alone, I knew I would survive so I jumped into the river and swam across. On the other side, I stepped out of the water in Thailand.

There were many mountains to climb and forest trails to follow before I would find anything resembling civilization. Night was falling. I needed a warm and dry resting place, so I found shelter under a tree surrounded by bushes and lay down on a bed of leaves. For the next few minutes, I could hear the distant thunder of exploding bombshells gradually fade into silence. Then I fell asleep. The next morning, I awoke to absolute stillness, the silence broken only by the occasional squawking of a megapode or a barking deer. Arising from my forest bed, I continued through the jungle for another two days, heading southeast. Along the way, I passed through a wildlife sanctuary where I crossed a river and was almost dragged into rapids. I competed with monkeys for berries and fruit, and, on the second night, slept in a stalactite-filled cave riddled with bats before being tickled awake by salamanders.

When I arrived in Tak it was late afternoon, so I wandered around awhile, looking for a guest house. I still had some money in a waterproof billfold, my only possession on the final day of combat. But I was going to be conspicuous wearing the filthy and tattered uniform of a KNLA rebel. So, before throwing it out I stopped at a market to buy some new clothes. Safely attired, I then stepped into a local beer bar. I didn't speak Thai, so I looked around for Westerners who might be able to help. The bar was filled with expats. I met one who said he was an NGO worker from San Francisco; I introduced myself as "Ben." Thinking he wouldn't believe me if I told him the truth, I pretended I was a stupid American tourist who had grown bored of the Chiang Mai club scene and gone to Mae Sot in search of adventure. After getting drunk and into a fight one night, I told him, I discovered that my ID had been stolen. I had tried hitching a ride back to Chiang Mai from the border, I said, but received no ride offers after Tak.

I was pretty sure this story would fly — knowing there were plenty of Americans who came to Thailand and got into exactly this kind of trouble — and it did; the NGO worker sympathized. He told me not to worry, that this sort of thing happened all the time, and he could easily take me back to Chiang Mai. He said he spoke some Thai and knew a couple of local farmers who sold produce in the North's largest city. One of them was leaving the next day, he said, a farmer who seldom took stowaways in his truck but would if I paid him generously. It took all the next day and most of the night to reach Chiang Mai, and the farmer dropped me off at Tha Phae Gate. I knew that I'd run out of money in a few days, so I went straight to the Night Bazaar and, in broken English, told everyone I was a migrant worker. One of the bars hired me, paying me under the table like thousands of other Burmese illegals living in Thailand.

The Night Bazaar pub job meant that I could live in my employer's building and, when I was off work, explore the old Lanna Kingdom. I was in no hurry to return home, still needing to get my mind off the horrors of Maw Pokay and happy to be on my own for a while. For the first few months I divided my time between bar shifts and hitting the road on a rented motorbike. Everywhere I went gave me a contact high. Southwest of the city, I hiked through a forest and climbed Doi Inthanon, Thailand's tallest mountain. North of the city, I swam between waterfalls at a national park near Mae Rim, rode on the backs of elephants, and stopped at an orchid farm to savor the deep fragrance of the national flower. Back in town near the university, I took a *songthaew* bus up the winding road to the hilltop temple at Wat Phra That Doi Suthep, where, on a terrace overlooking the city, I rang the temple bells for good luck. Once, I rode all the way to Chiang Rai, rented a guest house room, and spent a few days exploring the Golden Triangle. I had seldom enjoyed such freedom, not even in the US: alone on a motorbike with the wind in my hair, discovering the countryside, stopping now and then for crossing herds of water buffalo, sampling all the fresh food markets. I also did a lot of trekking among the hill tribes, including near Mae Hong Son.

High up in the hills, with temples that seemed to sprout from the mountainside, Mae Hong Son seemed like a place lost in time. Shan and Hmong hill tribes coexisted with other ethnic groups, and the only foreigners were educated professionals assisting with local development projects. I'd been living in Chiang Mai for eight months when I decided to move to Mae Hong Son — easy enough to do with no possessions, having earned enough at the pub to afford a few months without having to work. On my second night there, I wandered through the tented stalls of the night market, by now familiar with the North's regional edition of the Thai market-place. Mae Hong Son's night market had its own abundance of ethnic clothing and hill tribe crafts, baskets, lanterns and lacquer-ware, cheap trinkets, expensive jewelry, and teak furniture of all sorts.

That night at the market, I was passing through one of those fenced-off little beer gardens with the red neon lighting and fake palm trees when I noticed a young white woman with short brown hair in a tie-dye shirt and blue jeans. She was sitting alone, nurs-ing a Singha with three empties in front of her. Taking the liberty to join her, I greeted this attractive young woman with the usual *sawatdee krub*. She was wary at first, assuming I was some local Thai guy hitting on her. But when I switched to English and told her I was American, she relaxed. Her name was Miranda Barron. She was Canadian, working in Mae Hong Son with one of the big NGOS — Oxfam, Médecins Sans Frontières, I can't recall which — after completing a master's degree in anthropology at one of the universities in Vancouver, where she lived. I told Miranda the truth about my background, about Thandar and the rebels, and why I'd escaped from Burma. I said there was nothing I could do to get Thandar out of prison but that, once home, I would lobby for her release. Miranda said her post in Thailand would be over in eight months.

For my part, I was in no hurry to return to the US. My father must have been worried, but I wasn't ready to face him yet. We had problems, and I guess I wanted him to suffer awhile before I resurfaced. Miranda said she could find me a bar job in Mae Hong Son, but only if I agreed to accept migrant-worker wages despite being a Westerner; that was the only way not to blow my cover. She said she could help if I needed more cash. I agreed and ended up staying with her for the next eight months — her last — in Thailand. We became lovers. After a while it became hard to contemplate leaving. Each time I awoke to another Mae Hong Son morning in the arms of Miranda, the sweet scent of frangipani blossoms outside her bedroom window blending with her green tea perfume and the musky residue of our lovemaking — a kind of ambrosia I won't soon forget — I'd put off a decision about the future for one more day. I had never known such bliss. But once she had to leave for her next assignment — Bangladesh or Cambodia, I can't recall exactly, Miranda didn't say much about her work — the fun was over. I returned to Chiang Mai for a few days before flying down to Bangkok this week and reporting to you here at the Embassy. I am now ready to return to LA, face the music with my father, and resume my rights and responsibilities as a US citizen. Sincerely, Min Lin.

The two consular officials took their time reviewing my statement, the brunette having a harder time believing it. Could I provide evidence to place me in those locations at the times I claimed? Could they reach my boss in Chiang Mai or confirm that Miranda Barron existed? Before I could respond the blond jumped in. Well sure, they could speak to my boss, but it would be hard to receive accurate information from a Chiang Mai bar owner: the Thai employ all sorts of Burmese illegals, and they do it off the books to avoid the law. The bar owner might not remember Min Lin after eight months, there are so many of these migrant workers. In any case, blondie added, they did reach the owner of the last guest house where I stayed, and he said I speak excellent Burmese and could easily pass for a Myanmar national. So it's quite conceivable that I could have been employed in this way. As for Miranda Barron: haven't we all enjoyed a romance with someone whose full story we didn't know before they exited stage right?

"Usually not for eight months," the brunette deadpanned.

"Besides which," blondie added, "Mr. Lin has no priors. No criminal record, no suspicious political activity. In fact, he's squeaky clean. It does seem odd that, after escaping from Maw Pokay, he would drop his career for a year and a half. But remember: the last place he saw in Burma was a Karen State battlefield, and we know what conditions are like there. I think what we have here is one traumatized individual who needed a time out from the real world, time to put himself back together. And he's done that."

Well, well. I had a cheerleader. Bless him. I must admit, I impressed even myself with the Miranda story, which established my hetero bona fides with blondie. I did go a bit overboard with all that "Mae Hong Son morning" and "kind of ambrosia" nonsense, but it seemed to work. There were no more questions from my government about those sixteen lost months.

The next day, when my father's lawyer faxed several pages of documentation confirming my identity, Embassy staff told me to have my photo taken for a new passport.

15

Los Angeles International Airport
August 15, 1990

Outside International Arrivals, Ko Lin Tun pushed his way through the crowd of well-wishers for a better view from the front. As the first Bangkok passengers made their way through the glass doors, he scanned the procession of weary travelers hauling their bags behind them. After a few minutes, he spotted a lone Asian fellow, young and short-haired, dressed in a formal suit and tie — too conservative a look for his son, thought Ko Lin Tun, darting his eyes back to other travellers. But as the young man drew nearer, that familiar walk and shy grin, those big brown eyes, confirmed at last: yes, his son was alive. Min approached Ko Lin Tun, his arms outstretched. The two men enfolded each other in a long, teary embrace.

As they left the airport, Ko Lin Tun felt there was an edge about Min he hadn't seen before. The boy's deliberate movements, his confidence in moving through crowds, his lack of hesitation in hailing a taxi, suggested a quiet maturity that wasn't there before. But the drive home was awkward. The old man struggled to make eye contact and conversation, and Min said very little, spending most of the taxi ride staring out the window. When he'd called from Bangkok after visiting the Embassy, he told his father nothing about what had happened to him, and Ko Lin Tun didn't ask. Having recently been through some sort of trauma, the boy wasn't going to be an open book. But whatever happened must have been bad enough to make a man of him. *Yes, trauma can be good for you*, thought Ko Lin Tun. *Builds character*. His own escape from Burma in 1962 was no picnic, and, unlike him, Min hadn't lost a wife and son on his way out.

For the first night of their reunion, they said very little to each other. Ko Lin Tun prepared a stir-fry dinner, which they ate together in silence before Min excused himself and went to bed. The next morning, Ko Lin Tun woke up first and prepared coffee. Two hours later, when a jet-lagged Min shuffled into the kitchen, he served him breakfast. Then, having waited long enough for the boy to speak, he went to the counter and picked up his journal, bringing it to the table and placing it in front of his son. "Please read this."

Min opened it and started reading.

Min:
Asleep on the plane home, I had a nightmare about my impending arrival. Despite those State Department officials at the Embassy believing my story, events had conspired to ensure maximum exposure of my scandalous time in Burma. Before I'd boarded the plane at Don Mueang, word got out about my Lazarus-like return from the dead. An investigative reporter from the *Bangkok Post*, learning of my sixteen months embedded with the SLORC, broke the story of my work as a spy, editorializing his own sense of wonder that I could sleep at night after working for such an evil regime ...

Then I woke up, still on the plane. At LAX, I sighed once I realized there was no media scrum at Arrivals but only my father — a bit greyer, with deeper worry lines on his face, after two and a half years of wondering what the hell had happened to me. We didn't say much that first night. The next morning when we sat down for breakfast, he did something to guarantee that we wouldn't say a lot more, not about anything important, for a long time. We had barely finished eating when he handed me a journal he'd written. He seemed anxious for me to read it, so I did.

Then my world fell apart.

My father ... a major fucking general in the Tatmadaw. Golf buddies with Ne Win. This was too much to believe, almost ridiculous after what I'd been through. When I burst into laughter, I couldn't help it. It turns out I'd been an army brat all my life but didn't know it, and the army from which my father had earned his living was the same army I had fought in Karen State before defending it, by implication, as a SLORC employee. Dad had kept this secret from me since I was born, concealing even his Tatmadaw uniform which my childish curiosity had somehow failed to sniff out in the attic. I had endured sixteen months as an imposter in Burma, only to find out that Dad was the original imposter. The ultimate poser.

The revelation made me sick, but that wasn't the end of it. As I read on, there were more discoveries about the person I really was. The mother I'd lost and mourned at age twelve not being my real mother, the real one being lost right after my birth. A much older brother dying along with her, revealing that I was not an only child but a surviving sibling. And why would my mother have travelled with Dad to a conference in Bangkok, right after the coup in Burma, to give birth to me? I should have known that was bullshit. I should have known that my 1988 flight to Rangoon was, in fact, a return — not a first visit. The fact my father had escaped on the night of the coup, carrying me as his newborn son, might explain why he did not want to go back. But it didn't explain why he had deprived me of this knowledge for so long, despite knowing that curiosity was bound to lead me there one day as an adult.

My mind raced as I thought about how long I had lived in the dark about our family history. Would I have still wanted to go to Burma in '88, had my father told me the truth? Probably more than I did without knowing the truth. But how much richer would my experience of the country have been, how much better my decisions, had I known the truth? Would being fully informed about my father's life have made a difference in my choices? Would I have taken the same risks? Who knows? By keeping those secrets for all those years, my father had revealed himself as a masterful liar, a fraud to his own son. And look at me now: a virtuoso of deceit after pulling off the most artfully dangerous fraud imaginable. Yes, a chip off the old block I was, the irony hardly reassuring. I couldn't help turning on him.

"A father in the Tatmadaw. A mother and brother I never knew. A midnight escape after the coup. You know, Dad, if you had told me all this before I went to Burma, I might have been angry you'd kept the secret so long, but I would have recovered. But not to tell me at all, when you knew I was going? It seems —"

"I'm sorry, son. I didn't know how to tell you. But read more of this later, and you will understand. In the meantime, why don't you tell me your story? What was it like for you in Burma? What really happened when you disappeared?"

"Oh, you're going to change the subject, are you? Moving right along, are we? Really?"

"Please, Min! I understand your feelings. I know it will take a long time to forgive me, but you need to think about this for a while. There's no point having an argument now. So please, do tell me about your experience."

I looked him straight in the eye, this stranger I'd known all my life. Was he guilty of atrocities too? Had he done something before escaping Burma that he was ashamed of but couldn't bring himself to mention in his letters to me? He seemed troubled by the journal's impact. But the ease with which he could flip a switch and turn the attention on me was annoying. During the flight home, when I wasn't having nightmares about media exposure, I considered telling Dad the truth about my time with the SLORC. But now I was angry, and not only from the shock of the revelations. I felt like I had nearly been killed in Burma because of his negligence. And now he wanted me to spill about my adventures? Well, fuck him.

"Here," I said, reaching into my bag, "Now I have something for you to read."

Pulling out the photocopy of my statement to the US Embassy in Bangkok, I tossed it on the table. Then I watched as my father made his way through it.

Ko Lin Tun eagerly grabbed his son's statement to the Embassy and began reading. For the first few pages, about Min's early days in Rangoon, he was impressed by the boy's derring-do: the skill with which he had infiltrated Burmese society, the contacts he'd made around the city, the historic events he'd witnessed, and the important photos he had taken — the latter reminding him to tell his son that the AP had returned his film. The story of Thandar was uplifting at first, providing Ko Lin Tun a glimmer of hope that a grandchild might be in his future. But then he reached the part about her arrest after the SLORC's bloody crackdown, and his heart sank. His son's account of his time with the rebels was surprising, a glimpse of a courageous Min he hadn't seen before. But the part about crossing the border after being reported missing, and the year and a half spent in Thailand without telling his father he was still alive — because they "had problems" — was upsetting. All this for some Canadian do-gooder the boy would never see again.

"You didn't call me. Not once," he said, looking up from Min's statement. "And what are these 'problems' between us?" Min said nothing, turning away.

Ko Lin Tun knew his letters would upset his son — that was understandable. But as he looked at the boy now, he was mystified. Who was this young man? What had happened to Min? And what "problems" could he have meant without yet knowing the family story? Had he not given the boy everything he could possibly want in life? Where was the gratitude?

Ko Lin Tun thought his letters would be a revelation for them both, building a new trust that would put an end to the secrets and avoidance once and for all. But Min was guarded about his time in Southeast Asia — especially the Thailand part — and would not bring it up after sharing his Embassy statement. Something else was bothering Ko Lin Tun: Min's continuing status, at age twenty-eight, as a bachelor. This Miranda Barron from Canada was easy enough to dismiss — a meaningless fling that went on for too long, an excuse for his son to avoid responsibility and keep the real world at bay. She hardly seemed worth the time and was not the reliable sort, flitting about the globe from one trendy human rights cause to another. No, the Canadian do-gooder hussy was only in it for the good times. Not the right woman for Min.

But Thandar, this courageous young Burmese student, appeared to have won Min's heart before sacrificing herself for the cause of democracy. She was another story altogether. But in his written statement, Min seemed to speak of his fiancée in the past tense. While her prospects for freedom were indeed grim under the SLORC dictatorship, Ko Lin Tun had the impression his son had given up too easily and allowed her to slip away from his affections. Now, as Min's father, he found himself mourning a daughter-in-law he would never have, a woman still alive but whom circumstance — and his son's quixotic whims — had prevented him from ever meeting. This drove another wedge between father and son, for Ko Lin Tun could not possibly share these feelings with Min without risking further alienation. He had only recently reunited with his son and didn't want to lose him again, this time to estrangement. But failing to confront the issue would not help matters, as the silence allowed Min to draw a curtain around his private life.

Sure enough, as Min settled back into American ways and resumed his former career, he did draw the curtain. That old awkwardness between the two of them — the mutual avoidance of difficult subjects as path of least resistance, the let-sleeping-dogs-lie approach to peacemaking, which they'd followed for years — took hold once again. Before long, Min moved out and rented his own studio apartment, putting more distance between them. After that, each time the boy came by for a visit, Ko Lin Tun would drop hints about suitable young women or offer to introduce him to yet another daughter of a friend. Min would dismiss these appeals with a silly laugh, only fuelling his father's fears that he would never have grandchildren.

Well into adulthood and comfortably resettled in the US, Min was stubbornly determined to defy his father — this time with fancy clothing, modern hairstyles, and an overabundance of dandified, bohemian male friends. Such presentation, and the fact he was once again running around taking pictures of fashion models, dancers, and actors instead of finding a real job, only proved to Ko Lin Tun that the boy lacked discipline, that he wasn't serious. Everything was about entertainment and escapism, and everything came too easily. Min understood nothing about the hard work and, yes, conformity required to succeed in America. Or anywhere. *You have to present yourself in a serious, professional way to make it in this world,* thought Ko Lin Tun. *Sometimes you must also sacrifice your desires.* He knew this all too well, having put aside his academic career to serve his country all those years ago.

Meanwhile, Min was hiding something from him, something essential about himself. This only increased the distance between them, further straining their relations at a time when all the older man wanted was clarity. If confronted about his own views, Ko Lin Tun would insist he was no bigot. As a middle-class history professor in Southern California, he was too well versed in American liberalism to descend to the vulgar homophobia of religious zealots or gay-bashing thugs. But in the comfort of his convictions, he was also a hypocrite, the unreconstructed product of traditional Burmese mores who in fact was deeply conflicted about sex and gender. The possibility of having a homo son was too painful to contemplate. Ko Lin Tun was convinced he had done everything possible to make sure his own child would not become one of those people. Had he not raised Min to be a man? Chia Yong, the boy's stepmother, had employed a passive hand in his upbringing; after her death, Min's exclusive adult influence was his father. In Ko Lin Tun's mind, the only way Min could have ended up homosexual was corruption by Western culture — the same Western culture that he himself had embraced in so many ways, celebrating it every Fourth of July as a proud American. For Min's blithe dismissal of the perfectly suitable Thandar as a potential life mate, this was an explanation he could live with.

16

Min:

It was hard living with Dad during those first few months back home when I could not afford my own place. After sharing our stories, we barely spoke and for the most part avoided each other until mealtimes, when one of us would cook. I'd only been back a few days when the Associated Press called to tell me that a short article about my reappearance was running the next day across the AP newswire. The story, which a desk staffer read to me over the phone, was faithful to the version I'd shared with Embassy staff in Bangkok. When I asked if they'd be running a photo with it, he said no, this was standard wire distribution for updating purposes, so there was no need for a pic. To my relief, he then confirmed that the only film AP had developed before returning everything to Dad the previous year were a couple of rolls from August '88. The rest were unopened. He then asked if I'd be interested in doing an interview about my experience for a follow-up story. I declined, saying I wasn't quite ready yet. But I did look forward to meeting him and other colleagues over a few beers.

As triumphant returns go, the AP staff reunion was an awkward affair. Colleagues and old acquaintances seemed glad to see me, but our encounters were brief and superficial — a handshake or a hug, a welcome back, and encouraging words about rebooting my career. Then they'd each move on. It seemed like everyone was walking on eggshells around me.

It was about the Thailand thing, my old boss told me. A lot of people didn't understand how I could drop off the map for that long, despite knowing what I'd been through in Karen State. At my age, most photographers would want to jump right back into work.

So, how about now? I asked him. He shook his head and politely turned me down: unless I happened to have met Khun Sa while motorbiking through the Golden Triangle, and he invited me for tea with his fellow drug warlords and mercenaries — and I happened to take photos of them — then I would have some convincing to do to receive another gig from AP any time soon.

I understood. Meanwhile, there was almost no media follow-up from the AP wire story. What news value could there be in the confessions of a shell-shocked lensman who, rather than returning to the battlefield after going missing — which would have been the sexiest angle — or resurfacing immediately back home in the US after a daring escape, chose to sit out the real world for a year and a half while pursuing a dissolute life of skirt-chasing vagabondage in northern Thailand? But one mainstream daily newspaper did follow up on the AP story: the *L.A. Times*. After turning down AP, I changed my mind about doing an interview, telling the *Times* that I would give them an exclusive if they agreed to run one or more of my Burma photos — rather than a photo of me — with the story. They agreed. When the reporter, a city desk veteran, showed up, I steered her away from the subject of Thailand. Focusing only on Burma, I told her of my plans to lobby our government in the hopes of securing Thandar's release.

There was not much time to act, she replied. Had I not heard that the United States was closing its embassy in Rangoon at the end of September? Well, yes, I knew that. But had the US government taken up the case already or shown any interest in doing so at this late stage?

She had me there. All I could tell her — and she ended up reporting it — was that our embassy was still in contact with the Burmese government, so Thandar's file was still active. But I was mistaken in assuming that engagement to an American would count for anything. While Thandar's status as my fiancée was no longer a true reflection of our relationship, I was trying to use it nevertheless as a bargaining chip for diplomacy, a way of convincing the US to lobby for her release. But the *Times* reporter was right: after twenty-six years of Ne Win and two years of the SLORC, the United States was closing up shop and getting the hell out of Burma.

When I next received word from the ambassador's office in Rangoon, Burton Levin was clearing out his desk and not answering calls. Had he been taking on new cases, Thandar's would not have been among them. She was neither an American citizen nor legally married to one, so she was not a person of interest to the United States. Period. End of story. Short of an attempted jail break — the very notion was suicidal — there wasn't a lot more anyone could do for Thandar. As well as exhausting diplomatic channels, I had convinced Amnesty International to add her name to its growing list of political prisoners in Burma. But with the US government washing its hands of her, I knew her cause was lost. I had done all I could.

Meanwhile, there was my own life to live. Like my old AP boss had implied, my best-before date as a young hotshot photographer had expired. Unless you become famous early and your work's recognizable, falling off the map for two and a half years can be a career-killing move for a young pro. It takes lots of time and hard work to re-establish contacts, line up gigs, and get noticed. But thanks to the *L.A. Times* story — I came off sounding pretty good as a witness to Burma's national struggle, and the article ran with five of my photos from '88 — I received a few offers. The best came from a gallery that signed me up for a solo exhibition. *Burma: Portraits* featured photos I'd taken while exploring Rangoon with Thandar, along with images from the protests, the violent army crackdown, the rebel base at Manerplaw, and the refugee camp at Mae La. The show, dedicated to Thandar with partial proceeds going to Amnesty International, ran for a whole month. It received lots of good reviews and sold many prints.

At the opening, I noticed a tall, lean, and handsome white guy about my age. Dressed in black, he was clean-shaven with a big mop of brown hair. Standing next to a series of photos I'd taken at a temple outside Rangoon, he seemed fascinated with one image in particular: a large blow-up of two young monks bathing each other in an outdoor shower at dusk, their saffron robes clinging to their smooth wet skin as their exposed flesh gleamed in the sunset. An innocent moment rendered disturbingly erotic. The stranger turned when he saw me approach. "If you're looking for representation," he shouted over the crowd's noise, "we should talk!" He handed me his card: *Robert Malcolm, Art Dealer.* "Thanks!" I said, putting a cute smile on his face as I tucked away his phone number for future reference.

By early 1991 *Burma: Portraits* had given my flagging career a much-needed boost. Thanks to the good reviews and sales from that show, the gigs in fashion and advertising started coming in. By mid-March, I had enough money to rent a small studio in Century City and start my own business, Karma Communications. The name was a private joke no one else was in on: it nicely captured the irony of how Dad had kept a secret for twenty-six years, and now I was turning the tables on him. To Dad, my friends, and everyone else, I explained away Karma Communications as a reflection of the Buddhism with which I'd been raised. Yes, the sum of our actions in one life or previous state of existence can, indeed, decide our fate in another, future life. It seemed to have done so for me, and I wasn't even dead yet.

My goal for Karma Communications was to develop an instantly recognizable oeuvre: a camera eye that captures its subjects in their most honest moments but without exploiting vulnerability. Most of my commercial work was in colour, but I did a lot of portraits in black and white. I was going for a style, a look, as distinct as that of Richard Avedon, Annie Leibovitz, Herb Ritts, or Bruce Weber. Of course, I'd have a long way to go before I was that good, and much of the work to improve my self-confidence would involve sorting out my personal life. Performing as hetero for so long had been a failure; I'd landed home in the late summer of 1990 as a twenty-eight-year-old virgin. But thanks to that single, awakening moment in Rangoon nine months earlier, at least I knew what I wanted.

There was nothing to hold me back now. No SLORC to imprison my identity, no obligation to a woman I should not have proposed to, and no sense of filial obligation to a father who had lied to me my whole life. Emboldened by my escape from Burma, by this second chance at life, I began pursuing sexual liberation within days of landing back home. For the first few months, when I couldn't afford my own place, logistics were a problem: bringing someone home to Dad's was out of the question. But after visiting the gay village, I soon met more than enough men who were willing to take me anywhere: their apartment, a bathhouse, a public park, a shopping mall toilet.

At first I was intent on finding someone who reminded me of Sayed Hosin. I wanted to reclaim that magic moment on the fishing boat with a reasonable facsimile of Sayed, right here in the City of Angels halfway around the world and a seeming eternity from that glorious awakening. But in 1990 West Hollywood, this was a tall order: South Asian Muslims in the US were far more restricted by cultural taboo than I was as a Burmese American Buddhist, so there weren't many of these men to be found cruising the streets or looking remotely available. But no matter, I would simply develop tastes for all kinds of men while working my way around the protocols of safe sex. Having conveniently missed the first decade of AIDS, I'd landed on the playing field fully briefed on the methods of virus transmission, so I had no worries. Safe sex would be a lot better than no sex.

My first discovery was that there were more than enough men who wanted me. My second was that chatting up cute guys of every race between the ages of eighteen and thirty was a winning strategy. I got picked up everywhere — pubs, discos, restaurants, and bus stops — by every kind of guy. For a while I was a bit wary of the white dudes. I'd be in a bar somewhere, chatting up some cute blond twink for several minutes, when I'd happen to put the moves on him — stroking his back or his ass, suggesting we go somewhere quiet — and he'd recoil, muttering, "Oh, I'm sorry. I don't date Asians," then walk away as if I had the plague, blanking me for the rest of his time in the bar as if we hadn't met. I found the same sort of bigotry with certain men's wish lists in the classified ads section of the gay press: "No fats, fems, or Asians."

Other white guys liked me but were put off by my forwardness, as if I were breaching some sort of neo-colonial erotic code by making the first move. These guys preferred their Asians passive and submissive. Weren't we all bottoms? They also tended to essentialize Asians, but fetishistically. However, with one or two creepy exceptions — the overly aggressive top, the Asian sampler who says "Oh, I've never had a Burmese before" — being considered hot for my ethnicity was preferable to being untouchable because of it. In any case, anti-Asian racism on the dating scene was much more disappointing than Yellow Fever. The gay community owed its existence to political oppression, and yet racist assholes were everywhere — and were by no means exclusively white either. There were Japanese who wouldn't fuck Chinese and vice versa, and other gay men who, despite being racialized themselves, regarded darker skin among their own folk as a sign of lower caste. I wouldn't claim to be more enlightened than anyone else with an open mind, but being a Benetton slut sure got me laid often during those first six months.

By the spring of 1991, my erotic apprenticeship had run its course, and I was longing for a boyfriend. To remedy the situation, I threw a launch party for the new studio. While putting together the invite list, I found the business card of that handsome stranger from the *Burma: Portraits* opening: Robert Malcolm, Art Dealer. The drinks were flowing, hired waiters were circulating with canapés, and sixty people were crowding the studio when I met Robert at the door, Madonna's "Vogue" blasting from the stereo. Stepping inside, he presented me with a bottle of wine and a miniature replica of a nude by Matisse: a seated male figure, reclining with his arms behind his head. Rather bold of Mr. Malcolm, I thought, given our bare acquaintance. How did he know I would like it, based on nothing more than an *L.A. Times* profile that wasn't particularly revealing and a single photo exhibition completely concerned with Southeast Asia, not exactly a hotbed of French Post-Impressionism? Fortunately, he had guessed right. I happened to love Matisse, so I was charmed by the gift.

Robert made himself at home as I continued circulating among the guests, discretely waiting until everyone else had left and the last of the hired waiters had finished cleaning up before taking my hand and slow dancing me to "Wicked Game."

I invited him upstairs to the loft. The next morning, suitably impressed, I made him breakfast. I wasn't interested in hiring him to represent me. But we started dating and didn't really stop.

17

A lot was going on in my life. I was readjusting to the United States after two and a half trauma-filled years in Burma. I was coming to terms with the fact that my life story — the family narrative before 1988 — had been a fraud. Alienated from my father because of it, I had further distanced myself by lying to him about how I'd spent the better part of my time in Burma and then, safely home, pursuing an active gay life he knew nothing about — a life which, given his conservative ways, I had no intention of revealing to him. Now I had a boyfriend for the first time, which was great, but there was a new problem I couldn't share with him, Dad, or anyone else: I was suddenly having nightmares about Burma.

They came on slowly, infrequently at first. Dreams of horrific memories from Rangoon and Karen State. Moments like the Tatmadaw crackdown after the coup and the kid who died in my arms on Sule Pagoda Road. The faces of Kyaw Zwar and other comrades in Maw Pokay as they lay dying. The Tatmadaw soldiers I had killed. Sometimes I dreamed of Thandar, imagining her in a prison cell. But mostly the nightmares were about Aung Win, my double. Those dreams were always the same, like a tape loop that goes on forever: the sense of panic in his eyes the moment we meet, the fear and confusion mirroring my own as he glares at me from a face exactly like mine. In every instance, I woke up screaming just before Aung Win steps on the land mine. In the aftermath of the actual events, I had tried to push the memories out of my mind. Once back home, I tucked them away in the deep subconscious. Now they were back.

Before my one and only meeting with Aung Win, I thought I'd seen everything. At some point in life, we lose the capacity for surprise. Experience tells us there's nothing new under the sun, that what seems miraculous to a child should be commonplace to an adult, and that rational explanation can account for what seem to be supernatural phenomena. I thought I had reached that degree of certainty by my mid-to-late twenties. But then I came face to face with the ultimate mystery — an existential crisis, really — on that blood-soaked battlefield in Karen State. For what rational explanation could there have been for the sudden appearance of my doppelgänger from out of nowhere? Nothing in life prepares one for such a coincidence. When I found myself locking eyes with Aung Win, all my instincts — all my prior faculties for logical deduction — failed me. Perhaps because I could not solve the mystery, it was inevitable that Aung Win would eventually haunt my dreams, even interrupting wet dreams about Sayed Hosin, as if jealously policing from the beyond my every erotic thought about his lover.

Was there some deeper meaning to our encounter in Maw Pokay, some hidden explanation for Aung Win's existence? Obviously a first meeting would have lasted longer had it not taken place in a war zone. Had that been the case, what would the two of us have learned about each other? Would we have exploited the miracle of our sameness to mutual benefit? Or would we have become dark rivals, like the teacher and the actor in Saramago's *The Double*, taking selfish advantage of our likeness with a mutually destructive campaign of opportunistic one-upmanship? Would we have competed for Sayed Hosin's affections? Or would one of us have surrendered? In my dreams of them both, often within seconds of each other but not with both together, I am not provided with an answer.

The thought has occurred to me, more than once, that I might have imagined the whole thing. I had wondered about this in the first weeks and months after my "rescue" by the Tatmadaw. Perhaps Aung Win was not really my double, but we were similar enough that I managed to convince everyone who knew him, once I woke up in Rangoon, that I was him. Whatever the case, I couldn't get him out of my mind. What was Aung Win's purpose as a presence in my life? Was he a subconscious proxy for something else — the wish for a brother, thanks to the loss of Than Tun so soon after my birth? Or was he a symbolic mirror, a spirit trying to tell me something about my presence in Burma? Of course, I could not discuss any of this with my father, nor with Robert. Especially not with Robert, as we had only recently begun dating, and I didn't want him to think I was nuts. But I was waking up screaming in bed beside him, so I had to say something. I told him the dreams were all about those first two days of battle in Maw Pokay. This explanation was not a complete lie, so I could live with it.

But it also occurred to me that I would not be able to keep my secrets forever. I needed to talk to someone — a perfect stranger, ideally a professional — who would understand. I needed to unburden myself about leaving Thandar behind, about working for the SLORC, about Dad's lies and my own, and about what it was like to pursue the sex life I found so liberating but couldn't shout about from the rooftops because I didn't want Dad to find out. I needed to discover what kind of person I really was and whether there was any redemption for me as a human being after what I'd done in

Burma. And that is how I found myself horizontal one morning, box of tissues by my side, on the Beverley Hills couch of one Julius Cottler, psychiatrist to the stars.

Dr. Jules, as he was known around West Hollywood, was straight out of central casting. The shrink as mensch, completely reliable in his intellectual paternalism. As with the favourite Jewish uncle who spouts all the correct liberal views, reads all the right books, and donates to the worthiest of causes, I could easily imagine Sydney Pollack or Judd Hirsch playing him in the film version of my life, though he reminded me more of the former with his wire-rim glasses, curly hair and slower, more ruminative speech. From the first session, he was determined to find out more about my dreams and why I was having them, so we covered much ground.

Dr. Jules knew how to convince his patients to talk, and I talked a lot. I told him about my first year in Burma, filling in details I'd left out of my statement to the Embassy in Bangkok. At the battle for Maw Pokay, I stopped for a moment because I needed Dr. Jules to confirm the obvious: that our sessions were governed by industry standards of doctor-patient confidentiality, his own professional reputation depending on it. Thus assured, I spilled the beans about Aung Win, about his gruesome death, and about those sixteen months I spent working for a military dictatorship. Dr. Jules kept circling back to the question of why I hadn't tried to escape earlier. He didn't get it: if I was not a military-minded person, then why did I stay with the Burmese military for so long?

I told him he was mixing things up, that I didn't stay with the "military" as such — that was the Tatmadaw, the actual army — but with the SLORC, the leadership council that ran the government. But what was the difference? he asked. Working for the SLORC was supporting the military dictatorship — it was the military, wasn't it? I had to take some time to explain a key distinction to Dr. Jules:

the Tatmadaw, as the army, was a tool of the SLORC, the council's main device for carrying out its policies. Whereas the SLORC was the nerve centre from which army operations were directed. Administration and planning, the bureaucracy.

"I had a desk job, in an office where everyone worked closely together," I said. "All day long. Unless I was on assignment taking photos, where I was also accompanied by Ministry staff."

"I see. So, what you're saying is that if you had stayed in the military as a soldier out in the field, it might have been easier to escape than it was as a government worker?"

"Exactly. Reporting to an office, you are never out of sight. In terms of escape, I had to choose the right moment after the elections. I mean, those people in the SLORC are scary. Ever heard of Khin Nyunt?"

"No, can't say I have."

"Picture a Burmese Allen Dulles. Or Henry Kissinger. Not as intelligent, but every bit as creepy and Machiavellian. And working internally rather than overseas, with a free hand to arrest, torture, or kill civilians deemed enemies of the state. That's who pinned a medal on me the day after I woke up in a military hospital. You don't escape so easily from that."

"No, I guess you don't."

The reason I kept working with the SLORC for so long, I told my psychiatrist, was self-preservation. If the generals found out who I was, they wouldn't have thrown me in jail, I said; they would have tortured and killed me and taken their sweet time doing it. I told Dr. Jules that he wouldn't believe what those jailers at Insein were capable of doing, and I didn't just mean electric shock or waterboarding, either. I meant that the SLORC engaged in the most primitive forms of abuse the human body can endure. Forcing prisoners to carry giant rocks while crawling on broken glass. Putting them on the rack, stretching their arms and legs until they break off. Hanging them from meat hooks …

"Holy shit."

"And students and ethnics are not their only targets. One day, a guy in our office was exposed as a spy for the Karen National Liberation Army. He was caught stealing Tatmadaw weapons and sending them to the border to replenish the KNLA arsenal. A week after his arrest, his wife received an anonymous call telling her to meet her husband at the hospital. When she arrived, they directed her to the morgue where her husband's corpse was splayed out on a gurney. His organs had been removed."

After the first session, Dr. Jules concluded that I was having the nightmares because I had spent too much energy trying to suppress bad memories from Burma. Having no one to talk to about them, I should have known they'd resurface through dreams one day. But now I needed help to stop them. When I showed up for our second session, I told Dr. Jules I needed some pills to end the insomnia. To his credit, he was not one of those shrinks who has a drug for every problem. Refusing to indulge my desperate demands for medication, he instead suggested meditation through something called audio-assisted relaxation.

A therapeutic medium based on patient-generated visual imaging, AAR used the reinforcement of peaceful images to help patients relax enough to unlock their subconscious minds. The aim was to remove whatever blockages or barriers prevented them from enjoying the freedom of expression that guarantees restful sleep. Shrink mumbo-jumbo, I thought, for what sounded like hypnosis. Dr. Jules's preferred AAR method was to have the patient lie on a matted floor while listening to gentle affirmations on cassette. It all sounded a bit too New Age, Southern California flake-o-rama for my liking. But eventually he convinced me to try it.

The tape he played featured a soothing woman's voice encouraging the listener to imagine being somewhere idyllic and calm: a leafy meadow in the summertime, near a waterfall and a gently babbling brook. Moments later, the recorded sounds of such a place filled the room, accompanying her voice. From there, her gentle commands focused on relaxing every muscle of the body, from the face to the shoulders and arms, the chest and stomach, and then the calves, thighs, and buttocks. Having obeyed her commands to tighten and release all my muscles, I was soon calm enough to concentrate only on breathing. Once I had reached an acceptable degree of chilled-out bliss, Dr. Jules stopped the tape. When I opened my eyes, he was kneeling on the floor beside me, bent over, his face only inches from mine.

"Keep your eyes shut, Min. I want you to return to that moment you crossed the border into Thailand."

I obeyed.

"Now tell me: how do you feel about leaving Burma?"

"Like part of me died there, and the rest should have. I felt like Aung Win was trying to tell me something just before he stepped on that land mine, that something was wrong about my presence in his country."

"Okay, now before you open your eyes, I want you to leave it behind. All of it. All those things you feel guilty about, those facts you can't change. One day you'll have a new understanding, a new perspective, about your time in Burma. But for now, you need to leave it all behind. Let it go. Let it go …"

Dr. Jules was good. At our next session, I talked about my sex life since returning home, and how my awakening had been triggered by Sayed Hosin. At first, I was reluctant to share details with a middle-aged Jewish intellectual who appeared to be straight. But Julius Cottler had heard it all. Nothing shocked him, so I began describing what he called my "obsession" with the memory of that fleeting acquaintance. The encounter with Sayed Hosin hadn't lasted much longer than the one with Aung Win, but I had built up its importance to become a big part of my experience in Burma. When he asked me why, I told him that it clarified things. It set me on the road to becoming more honest, at least with myself.

Yes, he acknowledged, but I had been with many men since then. I had experienced sex at a much deeper and, he assumed, more satisfying level. Shouldn't this Sayed fellow have begun to fade in my memory, or at least gone down a few notches, by now?

I could see his point — and he certainly had me pegged, in terms of sexual appetite — but I told him it wasn't that simple. My encounter with Sayed Hosin had happened in Burma. Despite my American nationality, I was Burman by ethnicity — part of the majority culture — and Sayed was a South Asian Muslim. A non-citizen, part of a racial and religious minority with no status in the country. Rohingya, I believed they called themselves. The fact that Sayed managed to have a relationship with Aung Win, to be with him at all, when Aung Win was a member of the Burmese army, was incredible. They must have loved each other a great deal to have kept on meeting, when doing so put them both at great risk. The Burman Buddhists, who had been persecuting Sayed's people for years, discourage relations between Muslim men and Buddhist women. Imagine their views, I told Dr. Jules, about a gay Muslim getting it on with a Burmese army captain. How did he think that would go over with most Burmans?

"And so you felt the love he had for Aung Win when he kissed you."

"Exactly. And I won't forget it."

Dr. Jules paused awhile, letting that sink in. Then he changed the subject, asking me how work was going. Was I getting lots of gigs? What type of shoots was I doing? I told him things were going well, that I was finding more clients. Mostly in advertising and fashion. He wasn't satisfied with that answer, telling me this field wasn't my true passion and that I should get back to my real work. But wasn't this "real work"? No, he said, my real work was telling stories. The *Burma: Portraits* exhibit was fabulous, he said. Didn't I want to keep that going? I told him he was confusing me: that he had just finished saying I should leave it all behind in Burma, so this suggestion seemed counterproductive. Besides, there was only so much more I could say about Burma and my experience there, only so many more photos I had yet to publish or display. Dr. Jules interrupted me to explain himself: he didn't mean keep Burma going, he said, but my storytelling in general.

He said my exhibition work was outstanding and that I should consider developing new themes. For example, I could go out and find subjects, then take photos, along the theme of nation and race, presenting them as another exhibition. The story I had shared with him about Sayed Hosin was about two lovers, limited by circumstances beyond their control in the ways they can express their love. Limited by stupid unspoken rules of race and religion, culture and ethnicity, sexual orientation. Rules applied arbitrarily for the purpose of social control.

Dr. Jules was onto something. Why hadn't I thought of this? I was Burmese by birth and ethnicity but American by citizenship, upbringing, and a commitment to certain values. In Sayed Hosin's story, I had discovered the limits of nationality as defined by race and religion.

And so began my next big project: a photo exhibition exploring the differences, the margins, between race and nationality. At first it was an exclusively gay project. Trolling the bars, restaurants, and gym clubs of West Hollywood, I met guys from various ethnic groups who had been born and raised in the USA or were immigrants. Each had a story to tell about his own race and ethnicity, and each shared his thoughts on the meaning of nation. All identified as American, some more patriotic than others, and those who were immigrants still felt ties to their native lands. All agreed to be photographed at their homes, around their neighbourhoods, alone or with family and friends, and a few had permission to be filmed at work. As word got around, though, it occurred to me that I had ghettoized my subject by targeting only gay models.

Within a few weeks of a new ad launch promoting the photo shoots, dozens of women, straight men, and elderly Angelenos joined the young gay men lining up for their portraits. I launched the show, titled *From Near and Far: Between Race and Nationality*, a full year after *Burma: Portraits*. Every photo said something about race and nationality that went far beyond skin colour; from zip code and occupation to fashion sense, home decor, and personal accoutrements, the markings of class and culture that transcended race and nationality. Like the first exhibition, this show drew lots of good reviews — and this time a feature, in Andy Warhol's *Interview*, that put me on the map as a serious photographer.

Karma Communications was coming into its own.

18

Robert Malcolm turned out to be a good catch. My first and only steady boyfriend checked off all the boxes: kind, intelligent, good-looking, and much better off than me. Physically, he was nothing like Sayed Hosin. Tall, white, and skinny, Robert had ocean-blue eyes, a prominent chin, and a baritone voice made for late-night FM radio. Well-groomed, clean-shaven, and fashionably dressed, he was more socially outgoing than me and I was no wallflower. He was also more of a leader, often taking the initiative to get things done when no one else would. This may have been the result of having never been in the closet: Robert had come out during puberty, immediately alienating his uptight, Protestant fundamentalist parents and younger brother, who wasn't particularly devout but lacked the spine to challenge their mother and father. Leaving home at sixteen, Robert did not contact his family again. Becoming streetwise in a hurry, he made his way to the top of the art world on wits alone. Uneducated but self-taught, he could out-talk any tenured academic on art history or contemporary theory.

Within a few months of our first date, I decided to keep the studio but move in with Robert, both of us confident the arrangement could work. Before long, it was hard for us to imagine having ever been apart. Mutually attracted as opposites often are, we were turned on as much by complementary difference — he the practical realist, I the creative dreamer — as by similarity — we were both gourmands who loved bike riding and tennis but not team sports. As a lover, Robert was generous and attentive; he'd had a few Asian sex partners before me but had also been around the world and enjoyed men of every kind. An equal opportunity lover, like me. We both happened to be ready to settle down at the same time.

One of our biggest differences was family. Robert was at peace with his decision to abandon his, which I found shocking. Abandoning relatives requires a coldness I could not fathom. I may have been estranged from Dad, but I could not imagine cutting him off completely. We still met once a month for lunch or dinner, but only the two of us; I wasn't ready to introduce Robert, to share that part of my life with Dad. But Robert made things more difficult by asking to meet him. He was rather insistent, bringing it up repeatedly because I'd told him so much about Ko Lin Tun. This hardly seemed fair since Robert had made it quite clear that I would never meet his parents. They were a lost cause, he said, so why would I want to? There was no redemption from homosexuality in the eyes of a fundamentalist Christian, Robert insisted, so I would not be regarded as family by his mother and father. They would see me only as a Chinese sodomite, not knowing the difference between Asian races and frankly not caring in the least. Robert had no interest in subjecting me to their stupidity and judgement, and in his view, they were not worth my time. Whereas Dad, by comparison, was well worth meeting. Far more interesting.

"He's an enigma," said Robert. "You don't actually know how he really feels about your queerness because it's never come up directly. I suspect he's more capable of accepting it because his religion is Buddhism, not Christianity."

"Well, don't idealize Buddhism. It's not exactly pro-queer. According to the precepts, homos can't achieve nirvana. For Theravada Buddhists, we gay men are the object of pity, at best."

"That may be so, but I'm sure your love is more important to your dad than whether he has a grandchild. And when we meet, he'll have no choice but to embrace me. What's not to like?"

Robert did have a point there. My boyfriend was exceedingly suave, charming, and winsome. With all his practice wooing artists and curators of various backgrounds from around the world, he knew a thing or two about drawing out the best in people, and I was sure he could find my father's sweet spot. But I wasn't ready for a meeting yet. I still had some anger to work through. This must have been in 1993, when I was still seeing Dr. Jules five or six times a year. I recall making another appointment specifically to address my relationship with Dad.

"Part of me still hasn't forgiven him for lying to me all those years," I told my shrink, within moments of flopping on the couch.

"Why do you think that is?"

"Because I know what Burmese army culture is like. And I bet it hasn't changed all that much since 1962. I grew up without knowing that my father was a high-ranking military officer. He must have done a good job of faking it with me, because once it's in you, the culture never leaves. And that's what bugs me: the likelihood that Dad's worst qualities — his obsession with rules, his stubborn conservatism, his resistance to anything that smells of counterculture — are the result of Tatmadaw brainwashing. And that's not the worst of it. Because he's so good at keeping secrets, I won't ever learn what he really did while he was a major general."

"It's only a title."

"No, it's much more than that. It's power. Did I not tell you that he sat around a table with Ne Win, who became the Supreme Leader?"

"Yes, and you told me he spoke out against the coup. A very brave thing to do."

"That's his version of the story."

"You don't believe it?"

"I don't know what to believe about Dad. It's human nature to be selective when confessing things we're not proud of. I can't help wondering if there's something about his service in the army that he still hasn't told me. Also, the reason I still haven't told him about me and Robert is that he's homophobic but can't admit it. I fear his reaction once I tell him. At the same time, I know he misses me because he keeps asking why we only meet once a month. I suppose he loves me in his own awkward way, and that must count for something."

"Yes, you're right, it does."

Dr. Jules said no more, waiting for me to continue. When my next thought came, I didn't share it. But I knew right away that I had to find a new project and start working on it. Once it was ready, I'd make sure to give Dad a private showing before the opening.

By the fall of 1993, Ko Lin Tun was sixty-eight and no closer to being a grandfather. He had given up on that dream the previous year when Min turned thirty, no closer to being married than on the day of Thandar Aye's arrest. Since Min had moved out on his own, father and son had barely seen each other. Only monthly meals at restaurants where Min talked about work but not his personal life. At these meetings, Min would embarrass his father by handing him another envelope with a check to supplement his pension. Min was a good son, but Ko Lin Tun felt cut off from the boy's life and too afraid to invite himself in — less out of fear of rejection than wariness of what he'd find there. Then, at one of their regular lunches, Min invited him to a private showing of a new exhibition he was calling *Fathers and Sons*.

Ko Lin Tun arrived at the studio, its neon Karma Communications logo flashing above the front entrance. A smiling and confident Min greeted him at the door, taking his coat and hat before pouring him a glass of white wine. Then he led his father to the exhibition space. Start from where it says "Birth," he instructed. There's an order to all this, just like in life. Then, turning to his office, he left Ko Lin Tun alone to look at the photos, all large frames hung at or just below eye level. The pictures were black and white, which annoyed Ko Lin Tun. He saw this choice as pretentious, not particularly helpful to the viewer, and preferred to see colour. But he kept that thought to himself as he began viewing the photos one by one.

The first series featured several young men with their infant sons. For each family pair, the display featured candid shots taken at home — father and son playing on the floor, father feeding son, father dressing son, no mother present — and then one formal portrait, taken in this studio, of each father staring into the camera while carrying his baby boy. Ko Lin Tun was intrigued. Seeing the pride and joy in the eyes of every dad, the trust and adoration in the eyes of every little son, he recalled his own joy at the birth of Than Tun and his devastation at the death of his first son. Then he recalled his joy at Min's birth, how it was compromised by the distraction of having to escape the country a few hours later.

The next section, called "Youth," featured images of fathers appearing with their teenage sons. Ko Lin Tun slowly walked through a series of photos of a white father posing with his son who has won a baseball championship, another one of an African American father consoling his son after losing a football game, and another one showing a Latino father helping his son with his homework. Then he stopped at a series of photos showing a

Chinese man with his son. The boy wore earrings, facial make-up, and clothes that made him look like a girl. The boy was clearly a homosexual. Ko Lin Tun's stomach churned. Looking around to see if Min was nearby — he wasn't — he began examining the images more closely. In one photo, the man was shopping at a cosmetics counter with his girly-boy son; he didn't seem at all bashful. Another showed the two of them together at a Pride parade, the father holding one end of a banner that read: *Parents and Friends of Lesbians and Gays*. Another captured them at a restaurant in a candid moment of riotous mutual laughter. The final image, taken in Min's studio, showed the father standing behind the boy, who was sitting on a stool as they both faced the camera. The father had his arms wrapped around his son's chest. Both wore radiant, ear-to-ear smiles.

Ko Lin Tun felt a wave of conflicting emotions. The first was irritation: had Min invited him here to rub his politics in his face? He couldn't help thinking his son had staged the shoot with the Chinese father and son for propagandistic reasons. "You see, Dad? Asians can be homos too!" But then he studied the images again. The father's sincerity and earnestness came through; the bond with his son was undeniable. It then occurred to Ko Lin Tun that he was wrong not to have taken Min's profession seriously. He regretted having missed the boy's previous exhibition, for it was clear to him from these images and the ones from Burma that Min had enormous talent as a photographer. Such fine depth of vision and excellent instincts. How on earth had he managed to get so near his subjects and capture them in complete authenticity, including in the posed shots? He thought again about the Chinese man, who looked respectable and clean-living, a man who clearly loved his homo son. There was no mistaking it in their proximity, their body language, their obvious pleasure in each other's company. The girly-boy son seemed happy, self-assured in the knowledge that his father loved him. So much happier, it seemed, than his own son. Or himself.

Ko Lin Tun was stewing in this thought as he passed through the "Mid-Life" section, which featured different sets of fathers and adult sons doing things together on a more equal basis. Fathers and sons attending the opera, sharing cooking duties, completing their respective tax returns from the same dining-room table. Still distracted by those final pictures in "Youth," he walked past most of these photos, then a few of the images in the "Late Life" section, before stopping at a photo of a middle-aged Black man visiting his father in the hospital, holding his hand as the father sits up in bed, eyes moist with tears as he gazes upon his son. For the studio portrait of the two men together, Min shot them in the same pose as the Chinese father and son from "Youth" but in reverse position: the Black son in "Late Life" stood behind his father, who sat on the stool holding a cane, with his arms wrapped around his father's chest. In the curatorial notes, Min said the father died a week later. These photos were the final testament to their love.

Ko Lin Tun's eyes teared up. There were no words to describe what a beautiful thing Min had done by documenting the relationships between these two generations of men. Through such fine photography, his own son had made a powerful statement about the unbreakable bond between fathers and sons — including, he could not deny, fathers and their homo sons. He was proud of Min for producing such quality work but struggled to find a way to tell him so, since he also suspected an agenda, a message Min was trying to send about himself. Despite his initial defensiveness about the exhibition, Ko Lin Tun could hardly begrudge his son for that.

Min stepped out of the studio office carrying his own glass of white wine. He walked up to his father and clinked his glass, from which Ko Lin Tun had taken barely a sip.

"So, Dad, what do you think?"

"I don't know what to say, son. These are amazing pictures. I have clearly underestimated you, and that was foolish of me. You are a fine photographer, Min."

"Thanks, Dad. You know, I —"

"Another thing, son. I really want you to know ... I have been wrong about many things. I did not apologize properly for not telling you the true story about our family in Burma. I should not have kept those secrets for so long into your adulthood ... I really ... I should have told you before you went to Burma. I understand why you were angry, why you felt you had to stay in Thailand all that time. Perhaps I might have done the same."

Tears filled Min's eyes. The two men hadn't hugged since his return to the US three years earlier. Now the son folded his arms around his father and, awkwardly spilling his wine on the floor as they embraced, wept like a child.

A few days later, Ko Lin Tun arrived at Melrose Station to meet his son for dinner and to be introduced to a "special friend." Min was already there waiting for him, sitting in a booth beside an attractive white man of about the same age. At the booth, both men rose to greet Ko Lin Tun and introductions were made. Suave and sophisticated, Robert Malcolm was dressed in a fine black Armani suit and a pressed white shirt with gold cufflinks. Ko Lin Tun, noting his firm handshake and deferential bow, spent a while observing him. What could this man with the cufflinks possibly want from his son? Ko Lin Tun dismissed the thought. No judgement!

After taking their seats, the three men exchanged brief glances before Robert Malcolm dispensed with the formalities. Begging Ko Lin Tun's forgiveness, he said he shouldn't have come because he didn't feel he should be part of such an intimate conversation at their first meeting. This was really a private matter between Ko Lin Tun and his son, he said, before Min interrupted.

"But I wanted you to be here with me. Dad, Robert's not being entirely honest. It was he who insisted that we have this conversation. I told him that I wouldn't do it unless —"

"— Unless I came along," said Robert.

Oh, my goodness, thought Ko Lin Tun, *they finish each other's sentences. What else do they do together?* He already knew the reason for this introduction, so he wanted his son to get to the point.

"Dad, Robert is my partner."

Well, well, thought Ko Lin Tun. I won't let him off the hook so easily. "What kind of partner, exactly? Your business partner?"

"No, Dad. My boyfriend. My lover. My partner in life." Ko Lin Tun said nothing, staring at both men for a few moments.

"Well? Say something, Dad! Please don't tell me you're surprised."

"No, I can't say that I am. I've had an inkling for a while now. How long has it been?"

"Two and a half years."

Ko Lin Tun raised an eyebrow. "Two and a half years together? Or two and a half that you've known you are … you know …"

"Gay. No, Dad, I mean two and a half years together."

"He's been living with me for almost that long, yes," Robert chimed in. "I've been trying to convince him to turn his loft into more studio space instead of a bedroom, but he won't do it. And that's fine, but I don't like how he 'straightens up the house' every time you come over to visit the studio. He has pictures of us everywhere, but he hides them all and kicks me out every time before you arrive. Then he puts them all back after you've left."

Ko Lin Tun grimaced. "Min, is this true?" Min said nothing. Robert spoke up.

"Look, I'm going to step outside for a cigarette so you two can talk."

A few days later, Ko Lin Tun accepted an invitation to Robert's home for dinner. The host prepared a roasted free-range chicken and stir-fried vegetables with jasmine rice. After the meal, Ko Lin Tun and Robert discussed art history and US politics while Min cleaned up. Ko Lin Tun decided that he liked this Robert fellow. If he was as good to the boy as he appeared to be, then why resist? Why not embrace this new reality, like the Chinese father in Min's photo exhibit?

Within a few meetings, but without actually saying so, Ko Lin Tun welcomed Robert Malcolm to the family.

19

Min:

Toward the end of the nineties, California's Domestic Partnership Registry Act granted legal status, analogous to marriage, to same-sex couples. Robert and I took advantage. In making him my spouse, I adopted his surname and changed my first name to Benjamin. This wasn't about being a "banana" so much as recognizing my cultural duality: having gone by "Min" for the first thirty-six years of my life, I wanted a first name where I could have it both ways. "Benjamin" was a perfect solution to all the teasing from my art world friends who kept calling me "Benja." It's true that "Ben Malcolm" had a WASP-ish ring to it, but I was okay with that. I could still answer to "Min" as easily as "Ben," and going Anglo certainly wouldn't hurt my career. Dad wasn't crazy about the idea but, having accepted everything else about me, didn't argue.

Around the same time, I decided to wrap up my therapy with Julius Cottler. Our sessions had been helpful, especially in the early years when he helped me to navigate some of the challenges posed by the secret life I had been living. I still had dreams about Burma but seldom now, and the nightmares had all but faded away. Having reduced my visits with Dr. Jules to a couple of times a year, we both knew our final session would be more of a personal call to thank him than an opportunity for more therapy. And yet I found myself, once again, bringing up Aung Win. Although I'd recovered from the trauma of our encounter and the guilt of impersonating him, I still hadn't shaken the nagging obsession with discovering his origins.

Perhaps there was a way to help me make peace with that reality, Dr. Jules replied, suggesting I do an exhibition on identical twins. If I put my mind to that subject for an entire show, he explained, I might gain new insight into my double. Or at least find a more positive association with his memory by exploring the phenomenon of twinship. As usual, my shrink was way ahead of me. Later, when I told Robert I was contemplating a new exhibition about identical twins from Greater Los Angeles, I didn't tell him my real reason for doing it, only that I hoped to gain new understanding about the nature of identity, of identical likeness, by focusing on this genetic rarity. "Sounds cool," was all my hubby said, giving me his blessing. The next day I put out a call for identical twins to pose as models for an exhibition to be called, simply, *Twins*. As with my previous shows, I placed classified ads in all the LA papers and sent out emails on my arts listserv.

In the end I found sixteen pairs: male and female, old and young, white, Black, Hispanic, and Asian, both self-identified straight or both gay, and those of opposite or undisclosed sexual orientation or gender identity. Only three of the pairs had been raised apart but, in adulthood, rediscovered each other. Satisfied with that grouping, I booked all the shoots for the studio and devoted half a day to each couple, scheduling all the shoots over two months. For each of the sessions, I arranged for the twins to wear identical outfits as well as different clothing. I captured them in serious and playful situations, candid or posed. And I made sure to end every session with a spontaneous round of frames in which the twins could behave however they wished, their poses completely voluntary. Without exception, I found every session fascinating. So did my subjects.

Despite my obsession with Aung Win, I hadn't really given much thought to identical twins and how they relate to each other, not being a twin myself. Now I gobbled up all the literature I could find on the subject: revisiting Shakespeare's *Twelfth Night* and *The Comedy of Errors*, probing deeper into the mythology of Artemis and Apollo, and Romulus and Remus. As the project evolved, I began to see consistent patterns of behaviour between my subjects. I was struck by their instinctive responses to each other's speech and physical movement, by their mutual sense of protectiveness, the little ways that twins reveal how nothing and no one can come between them, that no one can violate their shared privacy or break the bond they so treasure, and that any attempt to do so is deeply offensive.

Not knowing the whole picture — that there can be pitfalls and anxiety to being a twin — many people express envy of the twin relationship and wish they could have been born one of the lucky few. The more pairs I met and photographed, the more I felt as though I, too, had missed out on something. Believing myself to have been an only child for the first twenty-eight years of my life was an obvious reason. Since 1990, I had been regretting the loss of an older brother I never knew, someone who would have been thirty-five if he were still alive then. What would Than Tun have been like as a sibling, had he survived our escape from Burma in 1962? How different would my life have been with an older brother to look up to? But twins were something else. Regarding these couples and their instinctive interactions, their knowing smiles, their enjoyment of private jokes no one else was in on, I felt envy too.

The Taiwanese brothers were the most interesting pair of the group. Aged twenty, they were athletes who spent a lot of time in the gym. During the pre-shoot interview — standard practice in getting to know the models, helping them relax before they position themselves in front of the camera — the brothers got into a playful argument while sitting next to each other. Slapping and lightly punching each other, laughing all along, they stood up at one point and tripped each other, landing on the floor. From this I came up with the idea of shooting them, stripped to their undies, in formal poses of Greco-Roman wrestling. The resulting photos were full of tension, not least for the hint of incestuous homoeroticism implied by these apparently straight boys' fumblings. Once on the floor, the twins required no direction as they began wrestling. They knew what they were doing, being familiar with Greco-Roman technique.

In the beginning, I took several frames from the tripod to maintain distance. Then I switched to manual shooting, moving in closer for different angles. At one point I told the brothers to freeze, then I clicked. Okay, keep going and freeze ... Click ... Keep going and freeze ... Click. Then I let them continue to the finish, eager for some unposed action frames. Later in the dark room, as I watched the images develop, those playful smiles with which the boys had begun their struggle for dominance gradually turned into hard grimaces, their eyes glaring from their respective efforts to come out on top. By the time I had told them to stop, one had hurt the other's left leg while pinning him down. The hurt twin yelped and, with all the adrenaline he had left, turned his brother onto his back and sat on his chest to end the "match."

The injured twin, still angry despite his victory as they caught their breath, wouldn't let his brother off the hook. My camera captured his expression as he looked down upon his mirror image, alarmed at the reckless manner with which his closest relative had risked serious injury to him by twisting his leg that way. In the darkroom, the details of his face sharpened: his eyes were filled with indignation and shock at what had occurred, as if his brother's careless act had been a violation of the bond between them.

The exhibition drew big crowds, great reviews, and more lucrative gigs for Karma Communications. Once again, I had Dr. Jules to thank for his inspiration in suggesting this subject, for *Twins* did bring me some peace of mind as he had predicted. I still had the occasional dream of Aung Win, but now it was more surreal, less trauma-centred: fantastical episodes that took my double out of Burma and placed him right beside me in Los Angeles, as if he had always been here with me. Instead of that repeated cycle of the moments leading up to his gruesome death, these dreams took the form of wistful fantasies in which Aung Win and I lived and hung out together, like real brothers, competing for the affections of Ko Lin Tun who, being a good father, wanted only the best for his two surviving sons.

Yes, for all my blessings — a loving partner, a forgiving father, a successful career, and the private satisfaction of knowing what I really survived in Burma — my only wish now was that I actually did have a twin brother. A twin brother with whom I could have grown up and shared all my secrets, his uniquely empathic perspective helping me make sense of our crazy world. A twin brother who would have accepted me in every way, so that I would not have had to hide my true self. With a twin brother, I sure as hell wouldn't have boarded a plane and travelled alone to Burma in 1988. He would have been with me all the way.

PART THREE

20

November 2012

It has now been nearly twenty-five years since I travelled to Burma, more than twenty-two since I left. I would like to think I was successful, long ago, in confronting the demons of my past; that, once I returned home, I took full advantage of psychotherapy to deal with the wreckage from my time in that country and leave it all behind. Robert agrees. On several occasions over the years, my hubby has mentioned how my work in the mid-nineties with Julius Cottler, one of the best shrinks in Hollywood, was a major factor not only in helping me face those demons and end the nightmares, but quite possibly in saving our relationship as well. Which is why, sitting in the living room together just now, discussing options for our annual New Year's vacation, he's not quite prepared for the curveball I throw at him.

"I've been thinking of going back to Burma."

"Huh? What brought this on?"

"I don't know, hon. I've been paying a lot more attention lately to what's going on there. And that only makes me wonder: have I really left it all behind?"

These days, I cannot help but pay attention to Burma. The country keeps showing up in the news every few months, it seems. It all began in the summer and fall of 2007, with the Saffron Revolution: those courageous monks who led the first demonstrations against the dictatorship in nearly twenty years. Things hadn't changed much since '88. There was a new dictator, Than Shwe having replaced Saw Maung, removed from office in 1992 after going insane. There was a new name for the regime, State Peace and Development Council replacing the equally doublethink State Law and Order Restoration Council. But the response to civil disobedience was identical: like the student-led uprising in '88, the monk-led demonstrations of 2007 were brutally crushed. Meet the new junta: same as the old junta.

Seven months later came the tragedy of Cyclone Nargis, the worst natural disaster in Burma's modern history, claiming nearly 140,000 lives and leaving 3 million people homeless in the Irrawaddy Delta. Nargis and its harrowing aftermath highlighted the callous inhumanity of the generals, who for weeks refused to accept international aid while at the same time insisting on holding a national referendum on the new constitution. This was a document that, once passed, would formally entrench the Army's institutional power; it would forever immunize the generals from prosecution, at least domestically, for their lengthy record of human rights abuses. Given the regime's reputation around the world, you could see why they might consider that a priority over the messy work of finding housing and food for millions of disaster victims.

After that, no one was fooled when Than Shwe announced that he would step down and dissolve the dictatorship after 2010, paving the way for the first parliamentary elections in two decades. The new constitution bearing Than Shwe's fingerprints guaranteed twenty-five per cent of parliamentary seats to unelected Tatmadaw officials. With the National League for Democracy boycotting the vote as a sham, the pro-Tatmadaw Union Solidarity and Development Party (USDP) predictably won the elections and a former general, Thein Sein, became the first president of a quasi-civilian government. The country's new leader raised eyebrows by releasing Aung San Suu Kyi from house arrest a week after the elections. But when Thein Sein began introducing one surprising reform after another and releasing political prisoners, recent history seemed to have come full circle. And that is why, I tell Robert, I've been paying more attention to Burma lately. After decades of inertia, the promise of real change has renewed my interest in the country.

That renewed interest has also sent me back to my personal archives. I'm curious to go into my files and dig through material I haven't seen for years — if ever. In my storage locker, for example, there's a box containing several large envelopes with photos from '88. Shortly after the battle for Maw Pokay, the Associated Press had returned all my undeveloped film rolls, along with the prints they had published, to my father. Once back home, I developed only the photos I needed for the *Burma: Portraits* show and left all the other film rolls intact, passing them on to Robert to arrange for development elsewhere. Determined to move on from Burma after the exhibition, avoiding all thoughts of the country after recovering from the nightmares, and focusing on rebooting my life and career, I simply forgot that prints of these photos actually existed. Now, decades later, I can't wait to see them.

Opening an envelope marked "Mandalay," I flip through a series of images from my trip to the old capital with Thandar. There are photos from the student meetings at the university, the dorm where we stayed, the Royal Palace, and several other Kodak moments. Then my heart stops at an image I knew existed and had once feared AP might publish with their reports of my disappearance. They did not, as luck would have it, because I had marked the film roll it came from as "Temples" — thus allowing a desk staffer tasked with finding an image for the story to assume there were no photos of me, inadvertently saving my life from across the Pacific Ocean. It's the picture of me and Thandar, taken on the summit of Mandalay Hill at the edge of that temple terrace where I pledged my support to the Cause. The only photo ever taken of us together. Not once had I bothered to look for it, perhaps out of guilt for my having abandoned Thandar — or out of fear of what truths it might reveal.

Like my own memory of the moment, the print has faded with time. But despite the sunset glow that fills its frame, the lighting, focus, and contrast are clear enough that Thandar and I appear in full detail. It is exciting to see my former fiancée's face for the first time since 1988: shimmering with the brightness of youth, all the strength and vigour I recall from our time together. Positioned beside me on the ledge, one hand hidden behind my back, she is tall and proud with a mischievous grin. Clearly the one in charge, completely at ease in her own skin. Confident but harbouring no illusions about what history has in store for us. As for me? I've forgotten how earnest and confused I was in '88: leaning into Thandar, I am all skinny arms and legs, trying to look cool as I slouch on the railing, affecting a James Dean–like pose while Thandar is goosing me. Eagerly embracing my Burmese adventure in this photo, I haven't a clue of the disaster awaiting us and am utterly unprepared for its consequences. Full of hubris and false hope about a future that's about to be taken away from us. For all it reveals about Thandar and me at the time, the photo seems a remarkable portrait of doomed courtship.

Lingering on the image, I cannot deny Thandar's impact on me. To reduce our awkward romance to an unfortunate chapter on the long road to self-knowledge would do her a disservice, for my erstwhile fiancée was a critical presence when I needed someone like her the most. Thandar changed me for the better. She opened my eyes to harsher realities, giving me the courage to make choices I would not have contemplated back home or had we never met. Now, after barely thinking about her for twenty-three years, I feel an urgent need to tell her so; like a debt collector knocking at the door, her claim to my conscience has become impossible to ignore, a reckoning long overdue. If she's still alive, she is likely still at Insein Prison but not for much longer. The closer she gets to her release, the stronger my desire to see her again.

On Facebook, a headline pops out from my laptop screen: "Rohingya villages burned, dozens massacred." The story describes a Rwanda-like frenzy of blood lust and murder in Burma's Arakan State. Out in the open in broad daylight, local police stand by on the sidelines or join in as Rakhine Buddhist mobs swarm Rohingya Muslims in the streets. In the ensuing rampage, Rohingya men, women, children, and the elderly fall victim to tribal justice. Brutal thrashing or arbitrary execution by bullet, machete, or baseball bat. Women and girls raped, homes looted and torched, and thousands left homeless. This is the second round of violence in Arakan since last June, and the hostilities seem far from over.

Robert and I talk about it. What the hell is going on? I don't recall Burman Buddhist ethno-nationalism — or anti-Muslim bigotry on such a scale — being a thing back in '88. But it's all the rage now, quite literally. Has there always been a dark racist underbelly in Burma that, as a foreigner, I simply didn't notice while I was there? Whatever the case, there's no denying that the country's recent opening up has produced negative effects that undermine its efforts to join the global community — a one step forward, two steps back sort of progress, with a major assist from social media. Millions of citizens enjoy access to the Internet that was unavailable a few years ago, and many are taking advantage of it to air tribal grievances. Facebook is especially culpable in recirculating the toxic propaganda of nationalist monks and their ardent followers.

Since when did Buddhist monks, the gatekeepers of a peaceful religion based on *metta*, or loving kindness, become the standard-bearers for fascist racism? The Thein Sein government's legalization of non-state media — the new press freedom laws — appears to have lifted the lid off some long-held resentments only now seeing the light of day. And the anything-goes, free speech ethos of Facebook, far from empowering citizens by prioritizing the broadest promotion of international human rights standards possible, has instead unleashed a torrent of anti-Muslim hatred, poisoning public discourse by enabling the most violent impulses of ethno-nationalism. One might think the new government would be defensive about all the negative headlines in the international media, concerned that Western governments might change their minds about lifting sanctions. But no. Despite the usual hand-wringing by diplomats and NGOs, President Thein Sein is doing nothing to quell the violence. On the contrary, USDP government messaging reinforces conventional Tatmadaw wisdom that "Bengalis" are not part of Myanmar.

Then there's Burma's Nobel laureate. Aung San Suu Kyi won the Peace Prize in 1991 as an exemplar in the fight for dignity and human rights. Back then, The Lady had stood up to the generals in defiance of military dictatorship. But now, as a free citizen, Suu

Kyi has nothing to say about the Rohingyas, a Muslim minority not included among Burma's one hundred and thirty-five recognized ethnic groups. Their name does not pass her lips. Suu Kyi's Western supporters, still embracing her iconic status, hold out hope that she is simply biding her time: two and a half years from now, the NLD — a party she should still be leading, twenty-five years after its landslide election win — will contest the 2015 elections and win them. She should then become Burma's de facto leader, if not its president, and take a firm stand for justice to save the Rohingyas from annihilation.

"But she's the Opposition leader right now," Robert protests. "Opposing bad government policy is the essence of parliamentary opposition. The time to take a principled stance would be now, wouldn't it?"

"Yes, it would," I reply. But the more I think about it, the harder it is to imagine Suu Kyi taking a position on the Rohingyas that's any different from the Tatmadaw's. She simply can't.

Despite all the recent good news — more freedoms, the lifting of sanctions, new trade and investment opportunities, a revitalized tourist economy — Burma's transition to parliamentary democracy is not going well. Apart from the carnage in Arakan State, ongoing problems include border wars in Kachin and Shan States, cronyism and corruption, out-of-control development with environmental destruction and land-grabbing, and a still-booming illicit drug trade. But it's the Rohingya issue, above all else, that's giving the New Myanmar a black eye in global opinion. Attempting to erase an entire Muslim group from existence is no way to gain legitimacy in the global community of nations. Is Burma truly satisfied to cast its lot with China, Russia, and other authoritarian regimes who share the Tatmadaw's indifference to human rights?

After half a century of authoritarian rule, Burma's transition to so-called "discipline-flourishing democracy" is proceeding without any members of the former military junta suffering consequences for their countless atrocities: no legal prosecutions, no war crimes tribunals, no truth and reconciliation commissions, nor any accountability of the sort that helps people recover from the traumas of dictatorship. The main culprit is the 2008 constitution, which empowers the Tatmadaw to do as it pleases. The former generals still running the country, in business suits instead of military uniforms, say it's the Buddhist way to forgive and forget. And The Lady herself — Aung San Suu Kyi, a good sport despite her own suffering at their hands — says it's not the Buddhist way to seek retribution for past misdeeds. But no one has asked the ethnic minorities, most of them non-Buddhist, what they think of the forgive-and-forget ethos.

Robert has good reason to be worried about my renewed interest in Burma: he knows I wouldn't be returning as a tourist but would want to take photos. He is afraid I would put myself in harm's way to capture these images, and he may be right. But, by early in the new year, there is no talking me out of this plan. I know there is something I can do to make a difference for people in Burma, and this time I won't have my head in the clouds. For all the stories in the news about anti-Rohingya violence, there are few glimpses of the people themselves and what their lives look like in 2013. Photos of Rohingya men, women, and children and their current living conditions would have an impact on global opinion. And being one of the few photographers to take them might help compensate for my time as Aung Win. Spending sixteen months as a SLORC photographer may not have been a crime against humanity in itself, but nothing about my job — or anything else I did while I was in the country — helped to make Burma a better place, either. Stuck inside the bubble as a regime insider, I was wilfully blind to the worst of its excesses — all of which happened out of sight. Since coming home and dealing with the nightmares, I have buried that chapter of my life. But thinking about Burma now makes me queasy: all these years later, it's harder to stomach the fact that I spent nearly a year and a half collecting a paycheck from a regime responsible for so much human misery.

More than sixty years before I landed, another Westerner left Burma feeling utter shame about his time there. Eric Blair — later known as George Orwell — never quite shook off his guilt over having colluded, as a young man, with the dark forces of imperialism that oppressed the Burmese people. His was a crisis of conscience that led to a cathartic final break with mainstream public opinion back home about the British Empire. He felt deep remorse about his own participation, as an officer of the Crown with the Indian Imperial Police, in the triumphalist racism and violence that defined the colonialist project. This was something he had witnessed first-hand, as a privileged member of an occupying power, during the five years he spent in Rangoon, Mandalay, Moulmein, and more remote parts of the country.

I have only sixteen months to feel guilty about. But unlike Orwell's period of service in colonial Burma, the time I spent in independent Burma was in the service of a government that brutalized its own people, a military regime condemned around the world as a human rights disaster; a pariah state most Westerners avoided like the plague. What's more, Orwell was transparent about his time in Burma and what he had learned from his experience there, mining that period of his life for future material. His struggle to shake off the colonial mindset that diminishes us as human beings became a source of inspiration for the writing that would one day make his name. Whereas I have selectively censored my time in

Burma, limiting it to a sentimental, black-and-white episode defined by my love for Thandar and devotion to the student resistance and pro-democracy movement. An easy sell for family and friends. My guilt is not merely over what I did for the SLORC but over the fraud I have perpetuated all these years, my failure to reveal the truth to my loved ones and take ownership of it publicly.

In all the years since my return to the US, I have had free access to mainstream international and exiled independent media, academic research, and other credible source material from the Internet. Within seconds at a computer keyboard, all of these sources can reveal a multitude of SLORC/SPDC horrors from 1988 right through to 2010. There are too many atrocities to count, including of the truly sickening variety. One example perfectly illustrates the SLORC/SPDC mindset. In May 1998, Senior General Than Shwe received a phone call from navy officers in the south. Fifty-nine impoverished villagers had been caught foraging for wood and bamboo on Christie Island in the Mergui Archipelago, a place zoned for military use and off-limits to civilians. When asked what to do with these villagers — men, women, and children who appeared to be living on the island — Than Shwe reportedly paused briefly over his lunch before replying: "Shoot them all and bury them on site." A few days later, when a Thai fishing boat strayed too close to Christie Island, the twenty-two fishermen on board — all foreign nationals — were captured, shot, and buried beside the villagers. Like a Roman emperor at gladiatorial games, Than Shwe could give a thumbs up or thumbs down on a massacre without interrupting a meal. For the SLORC/SPDC, human life was that expendable.

Over the years I have tried to avoid knowledge of stories like these, knowing that such horrors unfolded while I was in the country impersonating Aung Win. But since 2007, when friends and colleagues began asking about Burma or passing along the latest article they'd read, there has been no avoiding the grisly details of widespread rape, murder, torture, and sundry other atrocities with which the Tatmadaw "pacified" villages in the ethnic border zones; no denying the Army's stake in the illicit drug trade, nor the strip-mining of natural resources to line generals' pockets while local populations starved. All of which occurred while I was still living in Burma on the SLORC's dime. Going back now and photographing the Rohingya people, documenting their lives and struggle, might go some way to improve my karmic balance sheet. Along with seeing Thandar for the first time since '88 and coming clean with her, this return visit might help me achieve closure — both with the woman I was once to marry and with Burma itself.

21

Insein Prison
March 2013

Thandar:
"Gather your belongings," the warden told us before bedtime last
night, our final sleep as prisoners. Of course, he was being sarcastic.
After a quarter century here, I have nothing to show for it but a
single change of clothing and a hairbrush. Much the same is true
for the twenty-four others being released with me. When it comes to
the material-free life, the monks have nothing on an Insein prisoner
... well, except for the ones who have joined us here.

Perhaps I should be grateful for having won my release seven
months short of serving my full term. But since I have given up
more than half of my life serving this sentence, "early" seems a
cruelly unnecessary qualifier. Most of the '88 Generation activists
still in prison were freed last year in President Thein Sein's first
general amnesty. For whatever reason, I was made an exception.
Was it the Communist rap? My bad attitude? Doesn't matter. I am
leaving Insein today and will be happy to be free once again. But
this latest round of amnesty seems hollow: despite my own release
and that of twenty-four other inmates, the state continues to jail

people for public protests. It's as if nothing has changed since '88. I suspect the president's lifting of media censorship will turn out to be conditional, too: some of the more enterprising journalists, unleashed by the new laws and enabled to properly investigate, research, and develop sources, are sure to be jailed for doing too good a job of demonstrating their press freedom.

The worst thing about serving such a long sentence was not being able to marry, have children, or become a nurse. That and the fact I did not see my parents again before they died. Of course, a long sentence can be rough on a prisoner's health, but apart from gastroenteritis, decaying teeth, and arthritis in the knees and elbows, I haven't done too badly. Things could have been much worse health-wise, so I guess I should be grateful for that. Not everything is bad at Insein, and women do okay here compared to the men. We are seldom raped, and only once do I recall female prisoners being beaten: a couple of years into my sentence, after an inmate strike to protest prison conditions. The women who took part in the strike were roughed up and transferred to another prison, then beaten again on their way there. For some reason, I was spared a prison transfer. I guess they saw me as a permanent resident here.

Most female inmates from the '88 Generation were "A" category political prisoners, which meant they served a maximum of three years with hard labour. Association with the Communist Party could net you a longer sentence, rebel activities on the border even more, so I guess that's why they made an example of me. My reputation as a plain talker might be another reason. In Burmese culture, bluntness is not a virtue; it is considered rude to be forthright, so plain talkers are often banished from polite society. My father was very forgiving of this flaw, but my mother warned it could prove my undoing one day. There were certainly no clever witticisms coming from my mouth on the day I learned I was being sentenced to twenty-five years. With that single phrase, a judge confirmed that my life had just been ruined. My first challenge was maintaining my composure. The ability to keep one's dignity in the face of severe injustice is not only good Buddhism, it's also the best revenge, a very un-Buddhist concept, on our captors.

Over the years, the challenge for me became less about maintaining dignity than holding on to my sanity. The secret to not losing my marbles at Insein was finding ways to keep myself occupied, especially for work detail. When I wasn't in the garden, I spent most of my time with a group of women who worked the sewing machines. We made everything from simple cotton blouses to cloth flowers, which were then sold at social welfare retail outlets in Rangoon. I also cooked a nice soup now and then to supplement our boring daily menu. Other women working with me in the garden shared some of their pickings for the soup, including bits of lemon grass and okra they picked near the halls. On a few occasions, I was chosen to lead morning prayers before breakfast. I tried to set a good Buddhist example for my sister inmates, sometimes making merit by donating food from my brothers' packages to a cellmate who was depressed. Sliced fried sausages or fresh noodles are sure to bring a smile to a sad sister's face.

In the evenings, we passed the time by telling stories and singing songs. We were all good storytellers, sharing memories of favourite books or movies. We weren't all great singers, but one cellmate, a sister who joined us not long after I arrived at Insein, really stood out. Hearing her soft angelic phrasing, the beauty of her voice as she sang a favourite ballad, it was easy to forget that this young woman was here because, in a fit of rage, she had beheaded another woman accused of being an informant. Contemplating such things kept me awake some nights. Often when I couldn't sleep, I followed the path of a gecko scampering across the wall, waiting for its tick-tock cry. According to Burmese myth, the cry of the gecko is a sign of good news to come. With countless of these little creatures at Insein, there must have been millions of their little cries since 1988. But as far as I know, no good news ever came from all that squawking.

For years, it was hard to live without reading. Books weren't allowed until late 2003, and only in Burmese. After that, anything foreign had to be smuggled in by the page. At some point it occurred to me that my English skills had become rusty from non-use, so I decided to catch up. With ten years remaining in my term, I began practising with a guard I befriended who was as fluent as I had once been. He started smuggling in pages from English magazines, so I read them over and over, memorizing every word. But then I had to promise him I would "eat after reading," to hide the evidence from less trustworthy guards. Now, at the end of my sentence, my English has returned to its previous fluency thanks to those smuggled pages and conversations I enjoyed with the guard and a few of the newer, younger inmates who were all fluent.

I probably could have secured my own early release much sooner than this. Given the many important people who knew of my case, and other activists who had lobbied for amnesty during my final decade at Insein, I had the connections to make it happen. But I could not have done that. Early release usually involves some sort of compromise with the government; I would also have felt disgrace for using my privilege to abandon sister inmates who enjoyed no such connections on the outside. So here I sit, awaiting my turn.

There's an old superstition at Insein, one that every inmate learns before leaving: don't turn to look behind you once you've walked out the front gates, or one day you'll be back here for good. I keep this in mind on the morning of my release, as two guards escort me through the entrance. But I needn't have worried: it's impossible to look anywhere but straight ahead. A large crowd of supporters and media are there to greet me, including a man who has spent the past thirteen years lobbying for my release. Khine Kyaw was a chemistry student at RASU during the '88 uprising. He fled to Mae Sot after the coup and had been living on the Thai side of the border ever since. In 2000, he joined a newly formed non-governmental organization called the Assistance Association for Political Prisoners. That same year, he wrote me his first letter.

Inspired by former jailed dissidents living in exile, the AAPP lobbies for the release of prisoners of conscience, helps us and our families during incarceration, and then, after release, helps us find jobs, education, health care, and other services. One of its founding organizers, Khine Kyaw lost his family to the cause when his Burmese wife of ten years ran away to Bangkok with a Thai man, taking their two young children with her. For the first decade of our acquaintance, our only connection was through letters. But Khine Kyaw seemed to understand what was going on in my head. Though he hadn't been a prisoner himself, his advocacy work helped him appreciate what life was like for long-term inmates. He was grateful to us, knowing he'd been spared a similar fate by fleeing the country — "You are all serving my sentence," he would say — and he empathized with our daily struggle to find meaning in life.

Khine Kyaw's letters lifted my spirits. If he wasn't making me laugh with offbeat philosophizing about our insignificant place in the universe, he was consoling me in my darkest moments — such as in 2003, when my parents died within months of each other after I hadn't seen them in fifteen years. In 2011, thanks to a general amnesty, student-activist exiles and other dissidents began returning to the country. The following year, Khine Kyaw came back when the AAPP opened its Rangoon office and began working there. The government then decided to allow visits to Insein by Association members. When I first set eyes on him, I was reassured; Khine Kyaw was solid and manly, not too attractive but with a face you could trust. I had already fallen in love with him, sight unseen. But now that we've met, I have begun to imagine a life together. I laugh at the memory of my promise to Min. Instead of waiting for marriage until democracy came to Burma, I ended up waiting through a quarter-century prison term before the possibility of wedded bliss presented itself with someone else.

Khine Kyaw is the first to greet me as I pass through the front gates, holding my hand as I take my first breath of freedom in twenty-five years. Those familiar Rangoon-street smells of exhaust, noodle soup, and barbecued chicken fill my nostrils, bringing tears to my eyes. I begin to laugh at my own weeping, and Khine Kyaw laughs as well, for my freedom is being delayed once again, this time by a large crowd of well-wishers who have shown up to celebrate my release and that of two dozen other political prisoners. It takes us half an hour to make our way through the mass of bodies, my attention divided between reporters' questions, greetings from strangers who have held a candle for us since our arrests, and tearful reunions with people I haven't seen since '88. Among them is a favourite mentor from the nursing program at Rangoon General Hospital. She is in her mid-seventies now but has the same beauty and elegance I recall from my student days. She tells me there are plans to grant me my nursing degree, which I was so close to completing when I was arrested. I thank and hug her.

By the time we've made our way through this crowd, I think I've promised media interviews, lunch dates, or personal visits to at least thirty people. After the last of these encounters, we climb into a taxi and make our way to Kamayut Township, where Khine Kyaw lives in a one-bedroom apartment. We will soon be joined there by my two brothers, who have arrived from Mandalay but wanted no part of the festivities outside the Insein front gates. I love Aye Maung and Hla Min, of course, but in recent years our sibling relationship has become more complicated. On the night we were arrested, my brothers held the same contempt for the Tatmadaw that I did. But after I was locked away at Insein, they were drafted into service against their will. Gradually they became accustomed to Army life and, by their late twenties and early thirties, had begun to adopt military ways of thinking. Eventually they embraced the Tatmadaw mentality around discipline, law and order, nation, and patriotism. Having both served in Kachin, Shan, and Karen State border wars, rising through the ranks to become lieutenants and colonels, Aye Maung and Hla Min are now the patriarchs of their own military families; the husbands of women dedicated to their positions in society and the parents of teenagers they constantly monitor for any sign of subversive behaviour or thought.

Unlike them, I feel no different about the Tatmadaw today than I did in '88, and this has made for some awkward family visits. Aye Maung and Hla Min, knowing my feelings, made a point of wearing civilian clothing when they came to see me at Insein. During our visits, we avoided all discussion of national affairs, policing, the border wars, or politics of any sort. Instead, we talked about art and music. We talked about the natural beauty of our country, of places I hadn't been but had always wanted to see. Places my brothers had been and enjoyed, thanks to their military service. Today my brothers will be here with their wives and children — three daughters for Aye Maung, two sons and a daughter for Hla Min. The kids will be on their best behaviour as they meet their radical auntie and her divorced boyfriend for the first time.

While we wait for them to arrive, I look around the apartment. Khine Kyaw checks his emails. As much as I've tried to keep up with the outside world from my prison cell, email is an alien concept. The Internet did not yet exist when I was arrested, and no one in Burma had computers. Now, my boyfriend tells me, everyone seems to have one kind of device or another, all connected to the online world. Khine Kyaw, saying he has some news, calls me over to his computer. It's an email, in English, forwarded by the AAPP office assistant. The sender is karmacomms@yahoo.com, the subject heading "Back in Burma":

Dear Thandar,

Congratulations on your release! I hope you are in good health and spirits after being granted your long-awaited freedom.

I have returned to Burma — I still can't call it "Myanmar" — on a brief visit and would like to see you. There is so much to tell, and I am sure you will have questions for me. Please let me know if we can meet. I will be happy to see you anywhere in Rangoon at your convenience.

Fondest regards,
Your long-lost fiancé, Min

Well, well, Min Lin, from out of nowhere, is back. Like a weed I thought had been pulled from its roots, only to resurface after the monsoon rains, my long-lost fiancé is back in Burma. Joining the countless Western correspondents, businesspeople, and tourists who, during the Great Opening Up, have come back to recapture the glory days; the exotic Burma they recall from their youthful first glimpse of our country. Perhaps Min is here for professional reasons again. Khine Kyaw, reading over my shoulder, pinches me and frowns.

Fiancé? Since when was I engaged to be married? he wants to know. And is he the last to find out? I sigh, telling him to relax. My brief moment with Min was a very long time ago, and I never heard from him again after 1990, so why would I bother talking about him? But then I do. I tell my boyfriend everything. He says nothing for a while and then asks if I want to see Min Lin again.

I have to pause for a moment. I think so, I tell him. And then, yes, I absolutely do.

22

Min:

When I inform Robert of my decision — that I am following through on my plan to return to Burma — it leads to our first big fight. I still can't bring myself to tell him the real reason I'm going: the overwhelming guilt I have buried for so long about my life with the SLORC, a secret I have shared with Julius Cottler but no one else. Robert thinks my only motivation for returning to Burma is guilt about Thandar and some sort of misguided altruism about the Rohingyas. Not knowing the whole story, he can't possibly make sense of my reasons.

I am being foolish, he tells me. Thandar has probably forgotten me. And even if she hasn't, she must have recovered from my having abandoned her. So this is nothing more than vanity. I am doing this for myself, not her, Robert insists. How will I be able to see her if she's still in prison? And if I am allowed to see her, what makes me think she'll want to see me again? And I have to admit, it's entirely possible that my sudden appearance will go over like a lead balloon. But I need to do it, I tell my spouse. It's all about unfinished business. I need to clear my conscience and show Thandar what became of me. Does she not deserve to know the truth?

Robert objects. But why this Rohingya project? Why do I have to be the hero? And what do I actually know about conditions in Arakan State and what I'll be up against? Sure, the government is opening up the country, everyone knows that. But I of all people should know that the Army is still in charge. Besides, he says, I am fifty-one now and not exactly a seasoned war correspondent. So I should think about what I might be facing there.

"The only time you've been in a conflict zone is when you nearly got your ass blown off at age twenty-seven," he concludes. "That's a very long time ago."

"Don't worry, my dear. Unlike in '88, this time I'll have the assistance of local and international NGOs and their 'fixers,' people who can assist me in finding subjects and getting around. I will not be alone."

"But who appointed you saviour of the Rohingyas?"

"No one, honey. I only want to do some good, that's all. We both know my photos can have an impact, but I wasn't able to make a difference in '88. Maybe this time I can."

But Robert says my father will be deeply upset if I follow through on this plan, and he's right. I know Dad will disapprove, and he does when I tell him. He tries to stop me from going, reminding me that I should feel fortunate to have escaped the first time. Like Robert, he insists that I don't know what I'm getting into, that things in Burma are unpredictable right now. He begs me not to go. He nearly lost me once, he says. He doesn't want to lose me for real this time. Like Robert, Dad has no idea why I feel such a sense of obligation to a country which, as far as they know, I fled in early 1989. Knowing I won't convince him about the Rohingya project, I appeal to my father's sentimental side: I tell him that the main reason I'm going to Burma is to arrange a meeting with Thandar, apologize to her and tell her how my life turned out. But that idea backfires. "You are gay," he says. "She thought you would marry her. This will only upset her ..." Dad also shares his concern that the Rohingya project will be dangerous. As in 1988, however, his arguments do not sway me. In the final days before I leave, he reluctantly joins Robert in accepting that the family's Burma story will have a third chapter.

To prepare for my first visit to Rangoon since fleeing the city in 1990, I clear my schedule for the next three months. After working out a freelance arrangement with the Associated Press I apply for a journalist's visa. The visa is approved, no questions asked, so there's no reason to fear arrest once I land. My passport says "Benjamin Malcolm," not "Min Lin," and I look nothing like the twenty-eight-year-old "captain" who abandoned the country while posing as Aung Win. A far cry from the slim and pretty youth who once turned heads both male and female, I have filled out in middle age with puffier cheeks, bags under the eyes, and traces of grey hair. Assuming I might still be recognizable, there must be a statute of limitations for offences committed against the SLORC regime. So I anticipate no problems securing entry permissions and NGO escorts for Arakan State. No problem flying to Sittwe, the state capital, to bear witness to injustice.

As for Thandar? I cannot imagine apologizing to her without confessing to everything for which I need to apologize. And that, I am certain, will not go over well.

The road into Rangoon from the airport in Mingaladon looks much like it did twenty-three years ago. When I close my eyes and open them again, the tropical greenery and scenes of Burmese country life easily convince me it's 1990. But the illusion is shattered the moment I arrive downtown. Where blocks of tea shops and family-run noodle stands once dotted the landscape, air-conditioned shopping malls and fancy hotels have sprung up in their place. Busloads of tourists compete for road space with local commuters, the traffic gridlock worse than ever. Another change is with my hotel: I have decided to splurge on accommodation by revisiting The Strand, which, since undergoing major refurbishing in the early nineties, has been restored to the glory and grandeur of its colonial heyday.

As a footloose, twenty-something freelancer back in '88, I could not have afforded to stay at this version of The Strand. Rangoon's oldest hotel is now a heritage site that's been renovated to attract wealthier guests and has the daily room rates to prove it. Entering the majestic grand lobby, with its enormous chandeliers and black-lacquer ceiling fans, its high-backed rattan chairs and polished marble floors, I do recall being in this place in '88, but it feels different this time, as if I've been transported to its original state. I can easily imagine bumping into the Prince of Wales, the future King Edward VIII, arriving with his entourage. In The Strand's bar, I settle into a cozy padded chair and admire the wooden interiors while enjoying a tropical-themed cocktail and gobbling assorted nuts. Here I can envision Somerset Maugham in his prime, stealing glances at the waiters between sips of his Strand Sour. Yes, everything old is new again, and The Strand has clearly benefited from its long overdue facelift. I wonder if the same can be said of the political facelift the country's been receiving under quasi-civilian rule.

During a walk downtown, I am overwhelmed by signs of progress everywhere. At sidewalk vendors, posters and t-shirts bearing Aung San Suu Kyi's image sell like rock star merchandise. *The Irrawaddy*, once banned as subversive, is prominently displayed at newsstands. At Bogyoke Aung San Market, I have to push my way through the tourists. The New Myanmar is indeed booming,

but there are remnants of the bad old days too. On Prome Road —
now called Pyay Road — I come across a faded billboard from the
SLORC/SPDC era, a piece of propaganda that for some reason has
been left intact for all the world to see. It's the "People's Desire," a
short list of the military regime's wishes for a compliant citizenry,
presented in English:

*Oppose those relying on external elements, acting as stooges,
or holding negative views.*

*Oppose those trying to jeopardize the stability of the State
and progress of the nation.*

*Oppose foreign nations interfering in the internal affairs
of the State.*

*Crush all internal and external destructive elements as the
common enemy.*

The billboard is crudely amateurish, almost childish, the text
splattered in hand-painted white lettering on a stark, Tatmadaw-
green background. To the Western eye, it seems like postmodern
satire. Why has such nakedly ideological police-state messaging not
been scrubbed from the public sphere since 2010? Does its being
left there imply some sort of nostalgia for the old way of governing? Perhaps. No doubt there are current members of parliament
— those sitting in the sizable Tatmadaw section of the Hluttaw —
who see continuing relevance in these billboards, which I'm told
still appear in cities and towns throughout Burma.

As I'm standing there, pondering the peculiar ironies of
authoritarian public relations, a group of six or seven American

backpackers approaches me on the sidewalk. All young men in their early twenties, fresh off the college campus on their first overseas adventure, they are full of swagger and giddy tourist laughter. Sweating from overexertion under the hot season sun of the tropics, these boys in their testosterone-fuelled parade — complete with shorts that expose their smooth muscular legs and sleeveless shirts that show off their abs — are equally alluring and repulsive. Stopping when they notice the billboard, each of them takes a turn reading a "desire" out loud, mocking it with stilted, military cadences, emphasizing the totalitarian kitsch of it all.

"What a bunch of bozos!" says one.

"Careful, dude," says another, sizing me up. "We may have a local here. Wouldn't want to cause offence."

"Don't worry," says a third, "he probably doesn't speak English. Right, Mister?" I shrug and give them a dumb smile, throwing up my hands. They look at me in silence, waiting until I walk past before erupting in laughter.

Leaving that scene behind, I think of all the ghosts of atrocities past that haunt this city, the locations of protest that ended in bloodshed. Like the multiple massacres near Sule Pagoda in 1988 and 2007, including the spot outside Traders Hotel where Japanese photojournalist Kenji Nagai was gunned down while trying to cover the Saffron Revolution. Like Kyaikkasan Playground in Tamwe, site of the U Thant riots of 1974 that led to a student massacre at Rangoon Arts and Sciences University. Or the White Bridge Massacre on the west bank of Inya Lake, which happened on the day I first landed in Burma. For countries emerging from military dictatorship or other brutal forms of autocratic rule, one measure of good democratic health and civil society is the extent to which government is willing to acknowledge historic wrongs through public commemoration of events with traumatic public impacts. The more visible the gesture, the thinking goes, the easier it is for a country and its citizens to come to terms with the dark legacies of a violent and oppressive past. The notion of the state taking public ownership of shameful misdeeds from the past is based on the civic ethic of truth and reconciliation, a form of accountability designed to encourage healing among the citizenry. By ensuring that the misdeed is remembered, the state demonstrates that it has learned from historic mistakes. Such acknowledgement, at the scene of the crime, can be as understated as a bronze plaque or as large-scale as a museum. Post-Nazi Germany and post-Khmer Rouge Cambodia are two obvious exemplars: the former has more than two dozen Holocaust memorials, while the latter recognizes Pol Pot's genocidal legacy with multiple Killing Fields exhibits and monuments.

In Burma, the notion of truth and reconciliation seems almost utopian. There are simply too many atrocities to count; you'd have to put a plaque on every street corner, a museum in every district. Another barrier is politics. Burma's current leaders would prefer to memorialize historic wrongs by the British colonial occupiers, or the Japanese invaders of World War II, than acknowledge any injustice committed by the Tatmadaw in the years since independence, especially with so many human rights lawyers licking their chops at the prospect of bringing the generals to trial for crimes against humanity. Public monuments to Tatmadaw horrors would only shame the perpetrators, some of whom are not only still alive but have traded in their military uniforms for business suits and are now sitting in the Hluttaw.

Another thing I can't avoid during my wanderings about town, seemingly everywhere but around fancy hotels like The Strand, is the residue of a cancerous national habit. Somehow, the local addiction to betel nut escaped my notice as a young man here in 1988.

Perhaps the distractions of the pro-democracy movement and the SLORC's violent crackdown, then the daily paranoia of my existence as Aung Win, were too great for such a thing to have registered. But today in Rangoon, there is no escaping the ugly dark mess of betel nut spittings, their crimson expulsions sullying much of the public sphere. The projectile red splash is ubiquitous, staining the streets, sidewalks, and stairwells of Rangoon like the bloodstains of fallen protesters. Every patch of it I see spattered on the ground reminds me of the state brutality I witnessed so long ago, that sticky red discharge like a silent protest all its own, the wished-for blood of someone who has wronged the spitter, his family, or his friends.

On day three, my email inbox is filled with messages from Robert, friends, and colleagues who all want to know if I've heard the exciting news: twenty-five political prisoners, including Thandar Aye, have been released from Insein. At first, I laugh at the irony: I was only moments away from visiting *The Irrawaddy*'s website, where I would have read this announcement, but my loved ones have beaten me to it from across the ocean. The reality fills my stomach with butterflies. For the first time in nearly twenty-five years, Thandar and I will both be circulating in Rangoon at the same time, both as free citizens. Instead of having to seek approval to visit her in prison, I can now meet her on the outside with no restrictions. We can finally have our reunion. Thrilled beyond belief, I compose a quick message. The email will reach her via the Assistance Association for Political Prisoners.

The next day, I'm back at The Strand after my return visit to Shwedagon Pagoda when I open up Thandar's reply to my email. I wrote to her in English, and she has replied in kind. These are her first words to me since September 19, 1988:

Double Karma

Dear Min,

Thank you for your note, which came to me through the
AAPP. *Good to hear from you after all these years. I am
indeed happy to be free at last, and I agree there is much to
discuss. I can meet you for coffee at Junction Square next
Wednesday afternoon at 3 p.m. Please advise if this works
for you.*

Yours,
T.

Wow. Formally polite. Barely available. No surprise I guess, given
all she's been through. In the days before our meeting, Thandar
does several media interviews in which she recalls the many
injustices political prisoners have suffered since 1988: primitive
cell conditions, lack of access to medical care, and no means of
support for family members, to name a few. She also holds forth
with several opinions, advising politicians, activists, and average
citizens how they ought to be building a better country. Clearly,
imprisonment has not killed her spirit. She is grateful not to have
been placed in solitary confinement, but in a ward where women
lifted each other's spirits with poetry and song. And she has no
regrets about the political activity that cost her the prime of her
life, telling reporters she would do it again. She also knocks the
politicians who have just freed her. Thein Sein's reforms do not go
far enough, she says; as long as political prisoners exist, the shift
toward quasi-civilian rule is but a sham. Mere window dressing.

That's my Thandar: always telling it like it is.

23

I arrive at Junction Square. Looking up from the escalator, I see a woman sitting in the second-floor café where Thandar and I have agreed to meet. Can it be her? I draw nearer. It is her, but the confirmation is devastating, for the sight of her reveals what all those years in prison can do to a person. The thick mass of short black hair that once defined Thandar's look is now a coarse and lifeless, wiry mop of grey. The silky complexion of her twenty-two-year-old features has, at age forty-seven, shriveled into a patchwork of wrinkles and blemishes. When she smiles at a worker cleaning her table, her teeth are chipped and black. It is hard to reconcile this weather-beaten ex-convict with the shine and vigour that was Thandar in '88. While happy she is free, I am also racked with guilt about the gulf between us, her physical decay a stark reminder of our contrasting fortunes. I'm hardly an oil painting at fifty-one — my gut flab and jowly features go some way to conceal the Min Lin of yesteryear — but the stress lines on Thandar's face are frightening to behold. Four years younger, she has eclipsed me by several years. It is sad.

On my way here, I was excited to see her again, but now that I've spotted her, I fear what's to come. What can I say that will make her feel any better about what happened so long ago? And why have I decided to tell her about my time with the SLORC when I know the revelation will hurt her much more than it would Dad or Robert? I begin to wonder if I am as ready for this meeting as I thought I'd be. Hesitating to approach her table, I have to work up the nerve not to run away. After a few minutes, I take a deep breath and move toward her ...

Thandar:
Ah, here he is at last: Min Lin, my once apparent knight in shining armour. My suitor. The man who wanted to marry me, who promised to support me but faded away after a single letter. He's looking good. A little chunkier than I recall but with the same beautiful eyes. And he still has his hair! I can't wait to learn what he has to say for himself. When I stand up to greet him, he walks right up to me with a big, goofy smile. I'm afraid he's going to try to hug me in that awkward, overly familiar American way, so I sit down before he can do that. He stands before me, folding his hands instead.

"It's so good to see you at last," he says warmly, before sitting down opposite me.

He looks a bit nervous. Maybe afraid. Good. He ought to be. But I try to put him at ease. We start with small talk, sharing our impressions of how much Rangoon has changed since '88. He tells me about his arrival in the city and where he's staying — how nice for him, to be able to afford The Strand! — and I tell him about my last few days at Insein. I tell him how it feels to be out of prison after so long and what the adjustment to freedom has been like. Min is still fluent in Burmese, which is impressive. But soon I tire of the pleasantries and get straight to the point: what happened to him after my arrest? How did he end up joining the rebels in Karen State?

And he tells me. He gives me the whole story: how he came to our house and spoke with my parents the morning after my arrest, how he joined a group of students for the long trip to the border, and how he agonized over his decision to put down the camera and fight before joining the rebels in Maw Pokay. He tells me about the horrors of battle, of his sadness at the deaths of comrades, and most strangely, of a confrontation with his virtual double that ended with the man's complete obliteration. Then he assures me that, if I seek out any surviving KNLA or student rebels who were in Maw Pokay in 1989, they will remember — they will confirm everything about his combat activity except for that final encounter, because he'd been left alone to defend the rebel headquarters.

As he shares all this — and I can't help but believe him — the reality sinks in. I first learned of Min's time in Karen State early in my prison term, from a newspaper report about his disappearance. Convinced at the time that his only activity on the battlefield would have been taking photos, I had not once considered that my fiancé might be capable of anything more heroic. Now I learn that he not only picked up arms but, near the end of the battle, took on what amounted to a suicide mission for the KNLA. I tell him that's one of the most selfless acts anyone could have committed for the Cause. It sounds like he really proved himself there.

"Yes, well, thanks," he replies, looking at me warily. "But that's only the beginning."

Then he informs me that the rest of his story is something he hasn't even told his father. It's too incredible to believe, he says, and, once you do, too difficult to accept compassionately. He wants me to be the first to know — well, the second as he has also told a psychiatrist — because he owes me this; he thinks I deserve to know as his former fiancée, as someone who served a long sentence on behalf of everyone who ever dreamed of a free Burma. He has carried the burden of guilt for what he did almost as much as, perhaps more than, his guilt for having abandoned me. After twenty-four years, he needs to unburden himself. This is quite the buildup. But as he begins his confession, I can see why he found it necessary. The more he tells me, the deeper my heart sinks.

After the man he's described as his double was blown to pieces, Min says, he woke up in a Tatmadaw hospital bed back in Rangoon, where he received — and accepted — a medal from Khin Nyunt. He stops to apologize for that, knowing how deplorable it sounds, before explaining that, from the moment he awoke, everyone thought he was the dead guy. He goes on to describe his job with the Ministry of Information, how the SLORC gave him a mansion at Inya Lake, and how he rubbed shoulders with Tatmadaw generals at photo shoots. It all seems too much to believe, but when I look into his eyes I know it's as true as his combat memories. Gradually, with each revelation, a bit of the old anger and resentment I had long forgotten rises to the surface once again. I am finding his confession hard to take, and I tell him so.

I start by saying how amazing it is that he could pull off an act like that for sixteen months. How it demonstrated, once again, his incredible capacity for survival. But he can hear the sarcasm in my voice, so I get to the point. I tell him it's hard to imagine myself in his position, making the decisions he did to survive. Was it worth it, I ask, all those falsehoods, all that fraud to fool the SLORC?

He says he can't imagine having done it any other way.

I reply by asking him how he could come out of that experience and still have a conscience. He was being paid by the junta. He was doing their work.

Yes, he says, but his life was at risk. And I mustn't forget what he did at Maw Pokay. He could have been killed there. After surviving that, the last thing he wanted was to give the dictators satisfaction.

Yes, I reply, eagerly trying to understand his perspective. But there are some things in this world on which we must never compromise.

He says nothing, so I lay into him. I tell him how, sometimes at Insein, when I wondered why I hadn't heard from him after that one letter confirming he was still alive, I feared that he wasn't really the person I had made him out to be. That he was actually one of those Western opportunists I had heard about, the kind who take full advantage of their privilege in the developing world before getting out when it suits them, when the heat becomes too much.

He interrupts me, raising his voice to complain that I am being unfair. What would I have done in his position? He explains that he was in a coma for nearly twenty-four hours and woke up surrounded by Tatmadaw soldiers, men whose comrades he had just been killing the last time he was awake. They were coming into the hospital every day bearing gifts, he says, so it's not like he could have escaped from that. If they found out who he was, he would have been executed. He implores me not to forget what he did in Maw Pokay, that he really did risk his life for democracy. That political prisoners weren't the only ones who sacrificed.

That may be true, I reply, adding that his courage in Karen State is impressive. But once he survived, it seems that his courage abandoned him. I wasn't saying that he should have risen from his hospital bed and made a run for it. But he had a choice to make, and he didn't have to hang around for sixteen months and collect a salary from the SLORC either.

He sighs, telling me I'm right, and that he was foolish to believe Saw Maung when he said he would hand over power to the NLD. Min says he should have known better than to wait for that possibility and could have made his run to the border much sooner. He looks down at the table, saying nothing more, so I ease up a little.

I tell him I know there wasn't much he could have done to help me once he returned home. So what happened to him in Los Angeles? He must have met someone else, no? Did he ever marry? He reaches into his pocket, pulls out his wallet, and thumbs through it until he finds a photo. Then he hands it to me.

"This is who I married," he says. A handsome white man.

"Oh. I see."

I can't think of what else to say. I was not expecting this. But then, the more I think about it, a lot of things I didn't understand in '88 begin to make sense as I sit here, across the table from my former fiancé. Like all that time we spent together without getting physical. Like the way Min treated me more like a sister than a girlfriend and couldn't take the lead in anything. Like the way he became shy and nervous around my brothers. And like his ability to walk away from me and my country without so much as a backward glance.

Min:

After disappointing Thandar with the story of my sixteen months as a SLORC photographer, I wasn't sure how she'd handle my other surprise. The news about Robert seems to have thrown her off. I watch her while she regards his photo, noting the change in her expression. It's like her internal tape is being rewound to 1988 and, in a few seconds, reviews our time together and how I behaved then. A subtle smile forms on her lips. She expresses surprise that I can "do that sort of thing" in America now. I wait for more, but that's her only response to the news of my marriage to someone else.

Affronted, I tell her "that sort of thing" is a human right we fight for in the United States: the freedom to love, as important as the freedoms of association and assembly, the freedoms to vote and have an uncensored press — the democratic rights we fought for in 1988. But then I apologize for the indignation, telling Thandar that she must not have seen it coming — my being gay, I mean.

No, she says, she didn't. Should she have?

I ignore that, telling her my hubby's name is Robert Malcolm, that he's an art dealer I met at an exhibition of the photos I took in Burma. He is very kind, I tell Thandar. She would like him.

Yes, she replies, unsmiling. She is sure that she would.

I apologize again, telling Thandar it must have been hard to have been alone for all those years. I regret those words as soon as they leave my mouth, but Thandar has her own surprise. She hasn't been alone for the past dozen years, she tells me, but met someone through the Assistance Association for Political Prisoners, the organization I contacted to reach her.

His name is Khine Kyaw, she says. He is very kind. I would like him.

Well played. I attempt a smile while nodding at her to continue.

Khine Kyaw was a volunteer for the AAPP who was assigned to her case, she says. They began writing to each other, and then he moved back to Rangoon from Mae Sot last year, after the country opened up. He started visiting her at Insein and after that, things got serious.

I'm not sure what to say. The Assistance Association for Political Prisoners is one of the most prominent NGOs in Burma. Anyone with family or friends at Insein who's serious about freeing them would at some point establish contact with this organization. But I hadn't kept up with affairs in Burma until 2007 and hadn't known the AAPP existed. I hadn't sent a single email, picked up the phone, or otherwise made any contact with this group until I'd heard about Thandar's release. My last attempt to contact her had been a letter in 1990 that only exposed my failings as a potential spouse. But none of this matters now. Thandar gave up on me almost as long ago as I gave up on her. The confession about my time with the

SLORC now seems anti-climactic. Other than Dr. Jules, Thandar is the only person I have told about what I did, and she has reacted as I feared she might: unimpressed, offended, but not as surprised as I had hoped she would be. Her negative reaction seems entirely cerebral, completely lacking in empathy. For the Thandar who sits before me in 2013, there is no emotional investment whatsoever in my personal decisions, past or present. Indeed, I detect not a flicker of nostalgia for what we once were. Or tried to be.

She changes the subject, telling me I couldn't possibly have come all this way to see her. What else am I doing in Burma? I tell her I'm still a professional photographer. Reaching into my wallet, I pull out a business card and hand it to her. She regards my new name and Karma Communications with curiosity and then, flipping over the card to see Robert's name and phone number scribbled on the back, grimaces. Stuffing the card in her handbag, she notes that I've taken my partner's surname and changed my first name. I explain, then make a joke about how "whitening" it is but that I'm still Min Lin inside. Then she asks if I'm here to take photos again. Yes, I tell her, I'm here for a project on the Rohingyas in Arakan State.

She corrects me: I must mean the Bengalis. In Rakhine State.

No, I tell her, I mean the Rohingyas, in Arakan. Why does she call them that?

The mood darkens. Thandar frowns. "Because that other name doesn't exist. Those people don't belong here. They are not our people. They are Indians. But then I wouldn't expect you to know that, being a foreigner."

And what is that supposed to mean? I ask, now offended.

It means, she says, that I am not Burmese by birth but an American, so I have an American, black-and-white concept of right and wrong. I don't understand the complexity of our country, she says, and I probably never did.

Whoa. Where did this come from? I'm too shocked to correct her about my place of birth. I was getting around to telling her that story, too, but we've hit a roadblock here.

Do I remember Mandalay? Do I remember what I said when she asked if I'd stand up for her? That I'd said, "Don't be silly, of course I will stand up for you"?

Yes, of course I remember, I tell Thandar, adding that I failed her and will always feel guilty about that. I can't apologize enough. But what does this have to do with the Rohingyas?

I see everything through a romantic Western lens, she tells me. I did that in '88 when I was here with her, and now I'm doing it again with the Bengalis. Then she asks: I suppose you want to go into Rakhine and take pictures of people whose human rights are being violated, yes?

Of course, I say. What could possibly be wrong with that?

What's wrong, she replies, is that the Bengalis are aliens who are meddling in our national affairs. They are trying to spread their religion so they can take over Rakhine State and ban Buddhism.

I can't believe my ears. The person I thought I once knew is melting before my eyes. What on earth happened to her at Insein? I tell Thandar she sounds like that crazy fascist monk, Wirathu. She tells me I don't know what I'm talking about. Same as before.

What happened to her? I ask. What happened to the brave warrior who fought on behalf of the people? Thandar regards me coldly and shakes her head. If I think she's been hardened by her prison experience, she says, I'm wrong. She has always been Buddhist. Her country will always be Buddhist. And a good Buddhist always defends her religion. But, she adds, she wouldn't expect me to understand that, coming from the West where faith is as cheap as talk.

What? She could not be serious! Not her, of all people!

Yes, dead serious, she replies, urging me to go ahead and sign up for a junket with Oxfam, Médecins Sans Frontières, or one of those other lying foreign NGOs, as she puts it, and fly out to Rakhine to get my one side of the story, and tell it to the world. Good luck to me.

I stare into her furious eyes. Where is the Thandar I used to know? The Thandar who, the other day, told a reporter that democracy without justice is a sham? What do "democracy" and "justice" mean to her now? Back in 1989–90, I worried that I might succumb to Stockholm Syndrome if I stayed too long with the SLORC. Now I wonder if Thandar's been captured by another version of it at Insein: were she and her sister prisoners pumped up with ethno-nationalist Burman Buddhist propaganda by their jailers? How else could my former fiancée have turned into such a racist?

Rising from my seat to end our meeting, I tell Thandar that I will contact her again when I return from Arakan. Then I'll let her know if I've changed my mind.

I say nothing more but turn and walk away, leaving her alone in the café.

24

I can't wait to get out of Rangoon. My plan was to stay here for a few more days before flying to Arakan, but the nasty argument with Thandar has stiffened my resolve to board the next plane to Sittwe. Luckily, I've already arranged for guides. The day after landing in Burma, I called up Oxfam, Médecins Sans Frontières, and a few other NGOs to see who might have the resources to take a freelance photographer on a tour of the country's most dangerous state. The first to return my calls was Oxfam. After confirming my AP credentials and reviewing the Karma Communications website — I had made sure to highlight a gallery of my Burma photos from '88 — they told me to call as soon I was ready to go. When I do call, they tell me there's one seat left for the next day's flight to Sittwe. I will hardly be the first photographer to make tracks in this part of Burma — journalists from *The New York Times*, Reuters, and other media have already been there — but I count myself lucky to be signed up for an exclusive tour.

On the plane, I remind my Oxfam hosts that my project is a photo essay and that I hope to interview people as well as take their photos for an article to accompany the images. They advise me to spend as much time with ethnic Rakhine Buddhists as with Rohingyas; accusations of biased media reporting have caused

problems for NGOs working in the area. International media have
been accused of focusing too much on anti-Rohingya violence while
ignoring Buddhist perspectives on the conflict. Impartiality, or at
least the appearance of it, will help build trust with local authorities. I am more than happy to oblige, grateful to be provided with
a multilingual Oxfam guide, a local host, and a driver for the
duration of my five-day visit.

Within minutes of our leaving the airport in Sittwe, Rangoon
starts to feel very far away. You can't see a Muslim, a dark-skinned
kalar, anywhere. They've all been sent to "resettlement" camps,
forced to flee the city, or otherwise hidden away. I'm told that some
of the Kaman Muslim minority, who look a lot like the Rohingyas,
have suffered this fate as well. Among the locals, I don't see many
smiles. But I do see enough frowns to suggest how unwelcome a
camera-toting Burman from out of state ought to feel here. Sittwe
feels like a place that has recently expelled every member of an
irksome and vilified minority but doesn't want to talk about it;
the kind of place where one shouldn't express political opinions
too openly, certainly not in Burmese, if those opinions diverge
from the dominant Rakhine Buddhist line or express any degree of
empathy for the Rohingyas. On our first night there, I share these
impressions over dinner with my Oxfam hosts. They tell me I'm
not mistaken, and that I will need to be discreet.

The next morning, our tour begins in downtown Sittwe with
the ethnic Rakhine Buddhists. My first subject, a middle-aged
shopkeeper, tells us that policing is underfunded. Buddhists feel
vulnerable to attacks from Bengalis bent on revenge, he says, but
police response is inadequate: there are neither enough weapons
to defend local citizens nor enough cops to enforce the law. The
Thein Sein government, clearly regarding this as a regional problem, has allowed frontier justice — mob rule — to sort things out.

They have washed their hands of us, the man says, mimicking the gesture literally. The shopkeeper's grievance seems heartfelt. Others we meet in the city, who agree to have their photos taken, share similar views. Many Rakhine Buddhists are as angry with the Burman-dominated federal government as they are with the Rohingyas. They are also angry about the outside world's sympathy for the Rohingyas.

A woman running a coffee kiosk is dismissive of middle-class Burmans from Rangoon. She tells my Oxfam hosts and I that we seem to think the "Bengalis" are the only ones who lost their homes. If we want to see deprivation, she says, we should start with the Sat Roe Kya camp.

And so we do. Sat Roe Kya is a sad refuge for Buddhists displaced by the riots in 2012, an ugly assortment of flimsy, weather-beaten teakwood row houses with few amenities. But every family has its own quarters, with water hook-ups outside every home. People are free to come and go as they please, without fear of arrest or assault. They can also work, with enough opportunities to earn money, leave the camp, and start over. Life for displaced Arakanese Buddhists is no picnic, but how do their difficulties compare to those of the Rohingyas?

The next stop after Sat Roe Kya is the Aung Mingalar ghetto. On our way there, an Oxfam staffer describes how the streets of this old Muslim quarter used to blend in to Sittwe's overall fabric, its shops and restaurants once part of a thriving local economy. But all that has changed since the first riots. Now, he tells me, Aung Mingalar is an open-air prison for the local Rohingya population. Members of this condemned Muslim minority are confined to a few blocks of housing and deprived of health care services that local Buddhists take for granted. When we arrive at one of its gated entrances, a couple of police officers debate whether to let us in. Only when my guide returns from the van with the papers he has forgotten — government clearance for Oxfam's visit — are we admitted through the barbed-wire barricade.

Inside, a grim silence surrounds us. Far from the pulsating beat of Sittwe's urban centre, Aung Mingalar is reminiscent of black-and-white photos of 1942 Warsaw or colour photos of 1982 Beirut. Several buildings are pockmarked, their windows broken, and doors ripped off their hinges. Most storefronts are shuttered. The streets are filled with throngs of malnourished people, the mentally ill mingling with the merely tired and angry. On one dusty street, naked toddlers run around unattended while older kids, dressed in rags, play soccer with a semi-deflated ball and empty soft drink tins for the goalposts. They greet me with blank stares as I lift my camera and take their photo. In a sea of dark Muslim faces, a light-skinned Burman with a camera slung around his neck is more than a little conspicuous.

Not far from the ghetto's entrance, I spot two Rakhine police-men armed with assault rifles. They're harassing an old Rohingya man who appears to be pleading with them to allow him to leave the area. After a few minutes, and a couple of jabs from their rifle butts, he turns and walks away, giving up.

Wait! I shout in Burmese, following him. I tell him that I want to speak with him.

The man turns to look but says nothing. The Oxfam rep who speaks the local dialect catches up with us. When I ask why this man was so determined to leave the area, the Oxfam rep starts addressing the man in Chittagonian, conversing with him a few moments before turning back to me. He says the man has been working as a rickshaw driver for most of his life. Before the riots, the guy worked all around Sittwe, he explains. But since he was herded into this place with everyone else, he hasn't been able to work at all. Aung Mingalar is only a few square blocks wide. Anyone can walk it in ten minutes. So his rickshaw sits at home, unused.

The man turns away, dejected. Moments later, an elderly woman approaches and grabs my arm, crying and pleading in Chittagonian.

The Oxfam rep, pulling her hand away, tells me to pay her no heed. When I ask why not, he says she witnessed her husband being hacked to death with machetes. Four or five Buddhists, all taking turns on him. Then they burned her house down. Her children are all in Malaysia, so she had nothing left when she was forced into this ghetto. She's lucky she can stay with friends, he adds, but she's totally nuts. Completely gone. She's here all the time now, whenever we visit, but there's nothing anyone can do for her.

Pointing at my camera, I smile faintly at the woman but receive no reaction until I begin snapping photos of her. She gesticulates wildly, wailing at no one in particular. After half an hour of taking photos in these streets, I am already exhausted. The heat is bothering me, my clothes weighed down by sweat. Seeing my discomfort, my Oxfam guide takes me by the arm.

"Come on," he says. "There are some people here who want to talk to you, some of the community's leaders."

He points toward a dilapidated shack he says was once a bustling restaurant. Inside, half a dozen Rohingya men, hand-picked by Oxfam field workers familiar with their stories, are seated around a table. Told that their visitor is a sympathetic Burman American journalist, they seem eager to greet me as I sit down to join them for an Oxfam-provided meal of lamb curry and roti. Another translator is present, so I receive their stories in English.

A young man gets things started by giving me an accusatory look, saying "your people" — by which he means Buddhists — are trying to kill them all.

Please don't call them "my" people, I tell him. I don't identify with anyone who would do these kinds of things, so I don't wish to be painted with that brush.

The elder among the group, a man in a white robe with a long grey beard, winces. But am I not from the Bamar race? he asks earnestly.

I tell the group that I don't see what difference that makes. If they are judging me from my skin colour, then that is exactly what the Burman nationalists have been doing to them. And that's the whole problem, isn't it?

The Rohingya men look at each other after hearing my comments translated. One of them shrugs, others nod thoughtfully. Not quite sure what to make of me, they remain cautious. But gradually they open up, sharing stories of oppression under the national and Arakan State authorities. They speak of their poverty since the riots, of being prevented from leaving the ghetto without permission, of being cut off from food, water, and medical supplies. They speak of their houses being torn down for Buddhist firewood. More than a hundred thousand Rohingyas have lost their homes, one tells me, so it is very hard for the community to recover. Some Rohingyas were successful businessmen, says another. "Some of us were better off than the Rakhine Buddhists," he boasts. "Our fishing boats had the greatest catch, our farms the biggest harvests. The Arakanese themselves used to admit that we do the most with the very least."

All of them speak of the killings they have witnessed or barely escaped. One man, sobbing, recalls the day that a group of Buddhists came looking for his son. The boy had talked back to one of them because they had stolen his bicycle. When he came to the door, they pulled him out on the street and beat him to death in front of the man, his wife, and daughter. He was only twelve years old, and there was nothing his father could do to save him.

And he was not allowed to bury his son in the Muslim cemetery, in keeping with custom, says another man, comforting him. Like all other Rohingyas, he had to bury the boy in a mass grave behind the mosque.

Over the next hour with these men, I learn about the history of Rohingya presence in Arakan State. The recent round of violence, they tell me, is only the latest example of ethnic cleansing against their people. In 1978, Ne Win chased two hundred thousand Rohingyas into Bangladesh with "Operation Dragon King"; in 1991, the SLORC did it again, sending a quarter of a million across the border. During the mid-nineties, these men tell me, the junta launched a "model village" program aimed at increasing the Buddhist population while reducing the Muslim one. Hardened criminals serving time in Rangoon jails were offered early release in exchange for relocation to new homes located three hundred and fifty miles from Rangoon in Buthidaung, in the northernmost corner of Arakan state. There, inside a network of newly built villages, each former inmate was gifted with a house, a cow, a bit of cash, and monthly rations of cooking oil, fish paste, beans, and rice. All to encourage the propagation of Buddhism and prevent the spread of Islam. I also learn about laws to prevent intermarriage between Rohingya men and Buddhist women, and other social and legal engineering experiments aimed at denying the Rohingyas their humanity.

Eventually, the men run out of stories. There is a long silence. When I haul out the camera and prepare to take their portraits, they insist on a group shot only. When I raise my camera, they hold themselves with dignity as I press the shutter. How many of these men, I wonder, will still be alive by the time this photo is published?

The next day, my Oxfam hosts take me to camps for what the NGOs call internally displaced persons, or IDPs. If the slum-like conditions of Aung Mingalar are reminiscent of the Warsaw ghetto, I think these places are as close as it gets to concentration camps. Walking through two or three of these primitive holding pens, we find the same grim conditions: endless rows of rickety bamboo shelters, corrugated tin shacks and canvas tents, every structure overcrowded and unsanitary, each "home" a cesspool of bad hygiene unfit for human habitation. Camp residents are under guard and prevented from leaving. Our local guide tries to hurry us through them all, barely allowing enough time to stop and talk to people.

At one point I object, telling my hosts that I came to Arakan State to bear witness, not do third-world tourism. The guide apologizes: Rakhine Buddhist guards and state police are positioned all over the camps, so it's quite possible that I could jeopardize the safety of residents by making too big a deal of interviewing them. Thus, in the IDP camps near Sittwe, my work as a photographer is reduced to the voyeuristic gaze of trauma porn, the only photo opportunities quick, stolen moments of anonymous human suffering: large groups of starving Rohingya camp dwellers staring back at me from behind barbed wire, eyes bulging from blackened sockets as their skeletal frames barely keep them up. This looks a lot like a post-millennial Asian Dachau.

For day three, we take a boat ride to Myebon, the epicentre of last year's violence. Our first appointment is at a small outdoor restaurant overlooking the Myebon River, where we sit for a lunch of fresh seafood with an Arakanese Buddhist fisherman. This man, who appears to be in his mid-fifties, is well versed in the extremist rhetoric of the ethno-nationalists. The Muslims, he says, are taking over Burmese society. When I ask him how, he replies with conspiracy theory: by stealing Buddhist land, by targeting Buddhist women for marriage, conversion, and child-bearing, and by trying to prolifically outbreed the Buddhists. And they do all this, he says, with Western sympathy as so-called victims of Buddhist hate.

"Mark my words, Mr. Benjamin," he concludes. "Afghanistan, Bangladesh, Malaysia, and Indonesia all started out as Buddhist. Now look at them."

Like the shopkeeper and others in Sittwe, the Myebon fisherman sees mainstream Burmans as the enabling enemy. The Thein Sein government has not only neglected security but allowed Arakan State to become an impoverished backwater. As for the Rohingyas? They have only themselves to blame for their misfortune, he says: by refusing to speak Burmese, spend their money at Buddhist-owned businesses, or eat in non-halal restaurants, the Bengalis only further ghettoize themselves.

Day four is dedicated to more IDP camps. On the outskirts of Myebon, we stop at Taung Paw, a tent city housing more than three and a half thousand people. Local Rohingyas have been stuck here since the second round of violence in October. Walking through Taung Paw, we can see how bleak their situation is. The stench of state-sanctioned impoverishment by hostile neglect confronts us everywhere. A nauseating blend of raw sewage, garbage, wood-smoke, and barbecued fish fills the air, along with that telltale sign of overcrowding: the acrid sweat of too many bodies crammed into one place with not enough water to bathe. Several men are suffering from various ailments but toughing it out, they say, because the choice is between their own medical treatment or food for their children. A young woman tells me her first child died at birth because she couldn't receive the medicine she needed. Most people here can name at least one close relative killed by marauding Buddhists. Some can name many more.

Back at our guest house in Myebon that night, I dread the prospect of another full day of these encounters. The Rohingya people are so far from salvation that it's painful to be near them knowing there is nothing I can do to ease their suffering. The Oxfam translator had to stay behind in Sittwe, so communication without another translator is impossible. And even if I could speak the local dialect, the police would try to prevent me from talking to Bengalis. These photos I've been taking of a condemned minority — people in various states of distress, deprivation, and loss — have begun to wear me down. Over drinks at the guest house, I consider cancelling the final day and arranging for an earlier boat trip back to Sittwe. But my Oxfam hosts convince me to tough it out and complete the tour. They have found another translator, they say, and know a place where we can speak to Rohingya families. When we meet with these families, their dispiriting stories are no different from the others I've heard, with one difference: these people make a point of begging for international assistance. "They are going to kill us all someday, if they can get away with it," one man tells me.

By sundown the next day, I have left behind the soul-crushing apartheid of Arakan for the air-conditioned luxuries of Rangoon. Safe and cool back in my room at The Strand, I pour myself multiple Scotch-and-sodas from the mini-bar as I begin uploading photos to the MacBook Pro.

25

In Chinatown, at one of those street-side beer bars that replaced the tea houses where Thandar and I used to meet, I have come to chat up the locals over barbecued chicken and seafood. The people here, mostly office workers in their late twenties and early thirties, are friendly until I bring up the subject of Arakan State. As soon as they realize that the person they're speaking Burmese with is American, they clam up, change the subject, or switch into English. They don't want to discuss the issue with a foreigner. At best, they'll offer shrugs of resignation. What can we do about it? Whatever the Tatmadaw says, goes, is their best answer. At worst, they'll glare at me for being a meddlesome foreigner.

Things aren't much better across the street, at a beer bar full of expats, where I go after finishing my meal. Opinions are more progressive, but there's a cynical degree of hopelessness among these foreigners. I chat with a couple of them, both white sub editors from one of the domestic English dailies. The younger one, a South African in his late twenties named David, is just passing through. Using a newspaper gig in Burma as a stepping stone to something better — NGO work, say, or the UN. The older one, pushing fifty, is a long-term expat named Arthur who's bounced around newspaper gigs in Southeast Asia for the past couple of decades. Rootless and rudderless, he's a hedonistic libertine who — by his own, unsolicited account — appears to be into recreational drugs and serial monogamy with as many young Asian guys as he can charm. Betel nut blow jobs are all the rage now, he assures me.

Both David and Arthur complain of being looked down on by other expats. It's because they work for the racist domestic media, they say, rather than a foreign news service or a do-gooder NGO like Save the Children. And it's an unfair rap. All domestic media would lose their publishing licences if they broke ranks with the government or with the Tatmadaw, which amounts to the same thing. It's the Army that calls the shots here, so domestic media have little choice in the matter, says Arthur, by now on his sixth or seventh beer. Broadcast and print news, state-controlled and independent alike, all sing from the same Orwellian song sheet: there is no such thing as "Rohingya," "those people" must be referred to as "Bengalis," and everything bad in Arakan State (which must be called "Rakhine") is the "Bengalis'" fault.

Reporters are told not to interview Rohingyas — including off the record, for background — nor provide any space for sympathetic coverage of Rohingya concerns. Such coverage would only humanize a population the authorities have spent so long demonizing as the alien "Other"; humanizing them would run the risk of allowing public support to build for them.

"Empathy is lethal to the cause of nation and religion," Arthur sneers derisively.

"And it's not as if the Burmese majority are unaware of what's going on, either," chimes in David. "To the contrary, Burman civil society knows a bloodbath is inevitable, but most people seem prepared to let the chips fall where they may. After all, if the Bengalis are not true citizens, then why should anyone care about them?"

I let that sink in for a moment before responding. "But what about Aung San Suu Kyi? Couldn't she do something? Surely, she must have a position on the matter."

The two expats snicker, detecting my irony. "Oh, she has a position all right," says Arthur, "though she doesn't have to say much to reveal it. She refers to the Rohingyas as Bengalis, like the generals do. That should tell you all you need to know." He finishes with a loud belch.

"Thanks," I reply, "it does. I would ask The Lady myself, but her office rejected my request to meet with her." I don't tell them that this would have been my second meeting with Suu Kyi.

Other expats join the three of us, our conversation continuing for hours. The consensus among the Burman majority, I'm told, begins with the Buddhist monk leadership. Since 2007, the sangha has been infected with a small coterie of conservative nationalists led by a forty-four-year-old fascist from Mandalay named Ashin Wirathu. On one side of their mouths, Wirathu and his ilk rhapsodize about their peaceful religion: Buddhists would never hurt a fly. On the other, they describe Rohingyas — in terms more colourful than one might expect from men of the saffron cloth — as less than human. For these reactionary clerics, the Rohingyas are a convenient scapegoat for paranoid conspiracy theories about the alien "Other," a xenophobic mythology the Tatmadaw have been force-feeding Burmans for decades. The Bengalis, they say, multiply like rabbits, "steal" Buddhist women — as if Buddhist women have no self-agency — and take Buddhist jobs, hell bent on wiping out the Buddhist religion. The much-cherished principle of *metta*, loving kindness, applies to everyone in Burma, it seems, but the Rohingyas.

Staggering back to The Strand at two in the morning, I am overcome by impotent rage. Much worse seems inevitable in Arakan, but nothing is being done to prevent genocide. Memories of '88 are flooding back in the place where it all happened, and my sense of betrayal is enormous. From the argument with Thandar to the vitriol of Rakhine Buddhists and the ostrich mentality of Rangoon's Bamar middle class, I have begun to second-guess my own memory of people I thought I once knew, my understanding of events I experienced in the black and white world of 1988. When I joined that year's pro-democracy protests and later the rebellion, I assumed I was standing beside Thandar and her comrades in a project of higher calling than national identity. I assumed I was joining civil society and all of Burma's ethnic groups in the common cause of human rights. Our struggle was The People versus The SLORC. The issues of race, ethnicity, and religion were irrelevant. Had I been wearing rose-tinted glasses all this time? In the year 2013, how could it be that one group's claim to its own ethnicity and history was offensive enough to the majority for its entire population to be cancelled from the country?

It seems that people I once supported in their moment of crisis — and whose values I assumed were my own a quarter century ago — have either abandoned human rights as a universal principle or simply revealed that they never embraced the concept in the first place. When Thandar and her fellow students locked arms in front of those Tatmadaw soldiers were they really fighting only for a Bamar Buddhist Burma? During the Saffron Revolution, was religious purity the hill to die on for all those courageous monks?

Perhaps, for Suu Kyi — a political leader who has not defined what her version of democracy would actually look like, never mind how an NLD government will fight for equality or create a fairer society — human rights are situational; good for most people but not for one Muslim minority. But this is hard to fathom. After being globally revered for so many years, how could The Lady have turned out to be just another garden-variety bigot? A blue-blooded ethno-nationalist? Was her own father, martyred and sanctified before his legacy could be tainted by the hard realities of governing, any different?

To be sure, the Bamar Buddhist embrace of nationalism did not come out of thin air. The British occupation was a constant violation of Burman dignity. From the three military defeats that led to it — with the ceding of territory and the payment of millions in indemnity fees to the victors and King Thibaw's humiliating eviction from the Glass Palace in a ramshackle wooden carriage — to the British Protectorate's lust for Burma's natural resources, its establishment of governance, civil service, and education systems that excluded most Burmese from participation, and British soldiers' obnoxious habit of stomping into Buddhist temples wearing boots, the colonial period gave birth to historic grievances that have lasted a century and a half. Those grievances blamed on the British included the mass immigration of Indian labourers, which began in the 1880s and didn't let up until the early 1930s, when almost fifty per cent of Burma's urban population was Indian.

But not even all this can account for what's been going on in northern Arakan. It's true that ethnic Rakhine Buddhist resistance to Rohingya Muslims is nothing new, and problems are bound to arise when two distinct ethnic and religious groups live in close proximity without their communities interacting to a significant degree. But the Rakhine Buddhists and the Rohingyas somehow managed to live next to each other for centuries without the kind of violence that's happening now. And this is where the extremist monks are shaming the State Sangha Maha Nayaka Committee, which oversees and regulates the Buddhist clergy in Burma: for if Theravada Buddhism is such a peace-loving religion based on humility, does it not behoove the monks to make the first move toward peace? You know, hold out an olive branch of some kind, a gesture that points the way toward peaceful coexistence?

Back at The Strand, I decide it's time for a Skype call. Dad and Robert are long overdue for an update on my trip, so I've arranged via email for Robert to visit Dad with his laptop so the three of us can do a video call. When Robert's screen shows up on mine, I see the look of relief on their faces. It's clear they've been worried about me, especially Dad, who seems exhausted. This is our first contact since I flew to Burma, so they are happy to see that I'm in good shape and both visibly relax after hearing my voice. I reassure them that I'm fine, that the riskiest part of the trip is over. Then I give a brief summary of the Arakan tour before Robert interrupts.

"So, how did it go with Thandar? Have you seen her yet?"

"Yes, I have. And, well, we certainly had a full and frank discussion about a lot of things. But I don't want to go into that right now. I'll tell you more on another call. Let's just say she has some pretty shocking views about the Rohingyas. As do a lot of other Burmans."

That leads me to the sorry subject of the '88 Generation and my disappointment with mainstream Buddhist politics in contemporary Burma. When I tell them the government and Tatmadaw line, that the Rohingyas have never been considered a Burmese ethnicity — that they only crossed into Arakan during the British occupation — it's Dad's turn to interrupt.

"That is wrong, and the Army knows it. Dig deep enough, son. You will find the source. I was there in Maungdaw, on the fourth of July in 1961 — a few months before the coup — when Brigadier General Aung Gyi, the Tatmadaw vice-chief of staff, spoke of the Rohingyas."

"You're kidding." This was not among the stories Dad had told me as a child, having hidden that whole chapter of his life.

"No, I'm not kidding. I remember. Aung Gyi was presiding over a ceremony where the last of the mujahedeen had surrendered their weapons to the government. He said something to the effect that the Army not only recognized the Rohingya people as one of Burma's ethnic minorities, but also acknowledged their settlements along the border between Burma and Bangladesh. Like the Kachin, whose settlements straddled the border with China. In this way, they accepted the Rohingyas' place in the Union. So today's generals are talking a lot of garbage when they suggest otherwise. They are reinventing history for their own purposes."

Determined to find some evidence of inter-religious harmony in Burma, I am encouraged by signs of it in different parts of Rangoon. Traces of empathy between Burman Buddhists and South Asian Muslims can still be found in certain districts where Muslims live and run businesses. It's also evident near the Independence Monument downtown, where Sule Pagoda and Surti Sunni Jamah Mosque peacefully coexist across the street from each other. Such openness to diversity is typical of any metropolis, I suppose. But given what's been going on in Arakan and other parts of the country, I'm curious to find out what I might discover of the ecumenical spirit there. Spending a couple of days in the neighbourhood and hanging around Sule Pagoda Road, I visit both religious sites and chat up the merchants and shoppers. I'm happy not to need a "fixer" in Rangoon, a city that still feels familiar after so many years away from it.

On the second day, I offer an alcohol-free lunch of chicken biryani and rice to a couple of elderly gentlemen — one Buddhist, the other Muslim — who seem to know each other. At first, they are wary of an impromptu invitation by a foreign Burmese man with an undisclosed agenda. But as we tuck into our meal, they warm to me and are soon trading religious jokes they've found online. The Buddhist joke: Why don't Buddhists vacuum in the corners? Because they have no attachments. The Muslim joke: A man is talking to Allah and asks, "Allah, how long is a million years?" Allah answers, "To me, it's about a minute." Then: "Allah, how much is a million dollars?" Allah says, "To me, it's a penny." Finally, "Allah, can I have a penny?" And Allah replies, "Wait a minute." When our meeting is over I explain why I've put them together; they agree that racism and xenophobia are caused by fear of the unknown.

They have both run shops in this neighbourhood for decades, notes the Buddhist. Their children have played, gone to school, and grown up together. The Muslim adds that their wives share food and recipes, so why not be friends?

I take their photo as they shake hands and laugh, my faith in humanity restored.

Buoyed by this brief and superficial episode of religious harmony, I pay a taxi driver to take me on a long road trip north to Meiktila. The city intrigues me, partly because of its geography and history. Meiktila is located in the dry zone of the central plains, almost the exact middle of Burma. It was here that the British won the decisive battle that helped defeat the occupying Japanese forces during World War II. Today, the city provides the central command base for the national air force. But what really draws me to Meiktila right now are its thirteen mosques. With such a significant Muslim population, I wonder how things are going there under the current political climate. On the morning we depart, my driver is having second thoughts.

Two days ago, an argument broke out in a Muslim-owned jewellery shop in Meiktila. A Buddhist couple from a neighbouring village had bought a gold hairpin at the shop. The couple returned to accuse the shop owner of ripping them off, saying the hairpin was a fake. After a violent confrontation, riots broke out. The jewellery shop and neighboring Muslim businesses were torched. Since then, the violence has spread throughout the city. That should be enough information to cancel the trip, says my driver. But I am determined to go. Won't we be safe if we stay on the city's perimeter? The driver shrugs, and we go. By the time we arrive, Meiktila's an inferno. According to news reports, a state of emergency has been declared. Nearly eight hundred and thirty buildings have been destroyed, including most of those thirteen mosques.

Only now do I realize what a serious mistake it was to come here, not least because I forgot to clear it with the government and hire a local fixer, assuming that my driver could adopt the role. I met this man, a middle-aged Burman Buddhist, at the Oxfam office before the flight to Sittwe. Impressed by his knowledge of history and current affairs — and by his ecumenical stance on religion — I thought he was one of those chauffeurs who doubles as a guide and paid him accordingly. But now that we've arrived in Meiktila, his qualifications don't matter. With a violent mob not far from his taxi, we are both in danger.

He tells me firmly, as a flying projectile barely misses his car, that we must turn around right away and drive back to Yangon. I agree but remind him that we've come a long way to get here. I tell him to give me ten minutes so I can take a few pictures, and then I'll be right back so we can leave. I tell him to wait at his car.

No, he says, calling me "Mister Benjamin." Don't do it!

I step out of the taxi and walk away, barely avoiding a Molotov cocktail that crashes on the sidewalk. My driver, still gesturing for me to come back, puts his taxi in reverse to catch up with me. But he is forced to brake hard; the burning detritus of a collapsing building has ended his backward progress, its fallen debris now separating us. The last time I see him he's outside his car, parked a few metres from the burning wreckage, shouting at me to come back. As I prepare the camera, a blood-curdling scream behind me cuts through the angry crowd noise. It quickly fades away with a groan, and then, moments later, a gust of wind hits me with a sickening stench. I turn around to find its source: burning human flesh. A Muslim man has been torched alive in the street, his body flaming as a cheering Buddhist mob stands by. Security forces, doing nothing to prevent the savagery or save the man, instead encourage his killers.

Minutes later, on another street, I spot a few monks defying the blood lust by rushing a group of frightened Muslims into their temple to give them shelter. But other Buddhist men of the cloth enable the rampage. At one point I spot a few monks harassing another photographer, forcing him to give up his camera before pulling out its memory card and stomping on it. That's my cue to duck into an alley and hide. The ten minutes I promised my driver have turned into thirty. He'll be worried, but I can't make my way back to him yet; new street fights have broken out, preventing safe return in his direction. Then I hear shouting at the other end of the alley. Two young Burmans are wielding machetes as they circle and taunt an elderly Muslim man dressed in tattered shorts. Their feeble target is kneeling on his knobby knees in the dirt, begging for mercy in what are surely the final moments of his life. There is no one to rescue this poor man, and all I've done for the past half-hour is take photos of people getting killed.

"STOP!" I scream. "Leave him alone!" The ruffians turn around to face me, giving the old man just enough time to run away. Then they approach me, still clutching their machetes.

One of them sneers at me: since I'm so high and mighty, maybe I can defend myself.

"Wait! I'm a journalist," I cry. The two men stop and look at each other, sly grins on their faces. The first, handing his machete to the other, snaps his fingers to see my credentials. I pull off my backpack and dig out a passport photocopy bearing my journalist's visa and Associated Press card. He gives me a cold, hard stare.

Yes, he confirms, I am indeed a journalist. In which case, I am under arrest because I am not authorized to be in this area, and I am obstructing justice. Then he turns to his partner.

"Come on," he tells him, "let's take away this pathetic little *kalar* lover."

26

Thandar:

During those last few days at Insein I was filled with a sense of urgency, the feeling I had precious little time remaining to do the things that matter most in this life. The day after my release, I joined my boyfriend's organization, the Assistance Association for Political Prisoners. The gates at Insein had only just closed behind me and already I was on a mission: I wanted every remaining prisoner of conscience released. And why not? Every political prisoner made the same sacrifices I did, so they should all enjoy same the freedom. Thanks to my influence as an '88 Generation leader, I've been doing a lot of media interviews. Several days after my awkward reunion with Min Lin, I do another one with *The Irrawaddy*, renewing my call for the release of political prisoners. The next day, my phone rings at eight a.m. It's the Ministry of Home Affairs.

A gruff male voice at the other end of the phone barks my name and notes that I am seeking a meeting with the president. I wish to speak with him about conditions at Insein Prison and the terms of certain prisoners, do I not? Yes, I tell him.

He replies that the president will not see me about this matter, but the Home Affairs Minister is interested. Can I come to Naypyidaw tomorrow?

Tomorrow seems rather soon, I tell him. There's a pause at the other end. The caller sighs. I do want to share my concerns with the government, do I not? When I assure him that I do, he tells me to come to Naypyidaw tomorrow. Two o'clock at the Home Affairs Ministry.

When I hang up I turn to Khine Kyaw, asking if he wants to join me on the trip to Naypyidaw. He frowns and shakes his head. No, thanks, he says, last place on earth he'd want to go. But I should call him when I get there — he can't wait to hear what I think of it. When I ask him what's so bad about our new capital that he won't join me, he winks and says I'll find out.

Weird things happen when you're locked up for as long as I was. Things like finding out your country has a brand new capital city, built from the ground up in a jungle in the middle of nowhere. Naypyidaw didn't exist until the seventeenth year of my sentence, but I was hardly alone in being unaware of it. Until its construction was completed and the city officially unveiled on November 6, 2005, most of the country hadn't heard of it either. In nearby Pyinmana, residents knew something was up when throngs of Chinese engineers began showing up at local restaurants. At Insein, we heard rumours while eavesdropping on indiscreet guards. New inmates who'd worked on the project told them it cost four billion US dollars to build — this in a country which, at the time, spent less than two per cent of its GDP on health care.

Entire villages had been wiped out to make room for this new capital. Countless workers had perished after endless rounds of sixteen-hour shifts, a necessity to finish the project on time. Most civil servants had moved there during a mass evacuation in which the entire apparatus of government — except for Defence, which moved there a few months earlier — was expelled from Rangoon with two days' notice. On the day of the big move, a giant convoy of military vehicles transported everyone — the remaining ministries and their staff, civil servants, and their families — on the five-hour journey north. Now that I'm going there, I look forward to my first glimpse of Naypyidaw. And I'm grateful to Hein Zaw, the AAPP's lawyer, for joining me at the last minute. He wants to fly, but I insist that we drive; I want to experience my first glimpse of the city from the ground like those civil servants did in 2005. Hein Zaw picks me up in a rented van, and we hit the road a couple of hours after the Ministry's phone call.

Toward the end of the journey, we are well into the country's dry zone when the van turns east off the main highway, the hypnotic hum of its tires switching abruptly from rugged asphalt to what must be the smoothest pavement in the country. Seen from the van's tinted windows, a ten-lane highway stretches out before us like an airstrip. Unlike most highways in Burma where serious money is never spent, this one has enough street lights going up it to power all the villages wiped out to make way for it. Within city limits, the boulevards are gigantic but there's no traffic; the blocks seem half a mile long and the buildings a football field apart. Pedestrians are nowhere to be seen. I am reminded of a Western blogger's account I read on Khine Kyaw's laptop before we left. "Like the plague-emptied metropolis of Charlton Heston's *The Omega Man*," it said, "there's a kind of dystopian, post-apocalyptic vibe here; a stench of evil hinting at the lives that must have been sacrificed to the cause of the city's construction ..." I look up "dystopian" and "post-apocalyptic," and remind myself to look up that film.

As we drive through Naypyidaw, I am struck by the mind-numbing sameness of it all. The empty highways, the porcelain flower-festooned traffic circles, and what the Western blogger called the city's "block after block of soul-dulling, Soviet-giantist-meets-North-Korean-brutalist architecture." Naypyidaw, or "Seat of Kings," was named for the last dictator Than Shwe's three favourite monarchs: Anawrahta, Bayinnaung, and Alaungpaya. From the city's main parade grounds, off limits to the public but visible in the distance from our van, the iconic status of these three kings is reflected in the ghostly presence of their ten-metre-high statues, which must tower over Tatmadaw soldiers while they march. A city conceived by military men — strong on regimentation but weak on aesthetics — the "Seat of Kings" is divided with strategic precision into functional zones: military, ministries, diplomatic — five acres of land set aside for foreign embassies and UN missions, still mostly unused, I've read — residential, hotels, shopping, recreation, and landmarks. No wonder Khine Kyaw hates this place so much, I think, as we enter the hotel zone and find our government-approved lodgings for the night.

The next morning, I'm awoken at seven by a phone call. An official from Home Affairs, apologizing, says that our meeting at the ministry has been postponed until the next day. Hein Zaw and I groan. What does one do with a full day to spend in Naypyidaw? Within minutes of leaving the hotel after breakfast, we are confronted by the dullness. There are several private golf courses in the new capital, but neither of us golfs and wouldn't be allowed on these courses. Going for a walk would be nice, but there's nowhere to walk and no public park of any sort. There are exhibition halls for precious stones, but we can't afford to buy any. We'd visit an art gallery, but there are none — nor any spaces for working artists. Between meals at empty restaurants, we spend the day driving around and looking at Naypyidaw's "attractions."

Double Karma

Our final stop is Uppatasanti Pagoda, a Shwedagon replica. We laugh at the irony: "Uppatasanti" means "protection from calamity," but this whole city seems a calamity. The name is from a 16th-century Sutra recited in times of crisis, especially in the event of foreign invasion. Never mind the pagoda, I tell Hein Zaw, Than Shwe must have had those three kings' statues put there to watch over the city. Maybe their eyes have cameras. The lawyer says he wouldn't be surprised; the city is filled with hidden cameras, so the entire population must be under surveillance.

According to the Western blogger, Than Shwe's vision was to build a city with the splendour and magnificence of an ancient Aztec or Egyptian metropolis. But such pretense is laughable, he wrote:

> The great cities Naypyidaw was meant to emulate are historically significant. They were cities that prioritized a healthy public sphere with prominent gathering places like the Zócalo in Mexico City or Tahrir Square in Cairo; cities designed to engage the citizenry, with the infrastructure to maximize such engagement; cities that spawned civilizations whose lessons live on for eternity. Naypyidaw, a postmodern, totalitarian Disneyland, offers nothing but meaningless distractions and no place for civic engagement, which its founders see as dangerous ...

Civic engagement? In Naypyidaw? There isn't even public transit here once you step off the train from Rangoon. Nowhere to gather and plot an uprising. Naypyidaw is impossible to love, and no one would choose to live here. But since we are here on business, I suppose I can stand one more day. That said, there is still a whole evening ahead of us. What shall we do? The sidewalks roll up at six o'clock, so there isn't much entertainment on offer apart from hotel karaoke or prostitutes. With so few options, Hein Zaw and I decide to check out the light show at Naypyidaw Water Fountain Park. Passing through the entrance gates, we walk over a suspension bridge glowing with green neon and wander through the crowds of ministry employees, Tatmadaw personnel, and their families. Between the fountains, I spot a couple of young boys engaged in a plastic sword fight, chasing each other around with their rainbow-lit blades. On this night such innocence, such youthful spontaneity, is the best show in town.

In the morning, we report to the Ministry of Home Affairs. Staff lead us through one layer of security after another until we reach a small chamber outside the minister's office. Up to now we've assumed that our meeting will be with the minister himself: Lt. Gen. Ko Ko, former Chief of the Bureau of Special Operations-3, a high-level field unit of military operations that covers a massive portion of Burma stretching from the Bay of Bengal to the Irrawaddy Delta and the central plains region surrounding Rangoon. I'm curious to meet such a man in a lobbying context, since he and his colleagues have spent the past twenty-five years demonizing me as an enemy of the state. Much to our dismay, however, a secretary informs us that our meeting will not be with the minister but with one of his assistants.

After a short wait, we are escorted into an adjoining office from the minister's where we are greeted by a cheerful staffer in his thirties who introduces himself as Kyaw Myint.

"It is so very good to meet you, Daw Thandar," he says, using the "auntie" honorific to remind me of my senior status. He is a little too flattering, treating me like some kind of celebrity while all but ignoring the AAPP lawyer accompanying me. Offering coffee and making small talk, he asks how life on the outside feels after twenty-five years. I give him a quick answer before changing the subject by introducing Hein Zaw, which reminds the junior staffer that we are here on business. Directing us to sit in front of his desk, Kyaw Myint sits behind it and picks up a folder. Opening it, he pulls out the list we sent to President Thein Sein. The minister has reviewed our requests, he says, and sees no reason not to grant some of them. But the overall list does present problems.

When Hein Zaw asks him to be more specific, Kyaw Myint reviews the list and starts talking about one of the prisoners without naming him, forcing us to lean in from the other side of his desk to look for it. This prisoner, he says, was only admitted a few weeks ago. We're asking for his release, but Kyaw Myint says he's afraid that is impossible. The government has determined that he is a member of the Karen National Liberation Army whose connection to that bombing in Yangon has been clearly established.

No, it hasn't, Hein Zaw interjects. With all due respect, he tells Kyaw Myint, the evidence was circumstantial, and the man was sentenced without trial. Regardless of what the authorities claim to have established about his KNLA connection, his culpability in the crime was not proven in court. And now this fellow is facing twenty years at Insein despite new evidence suggesting he is innocent.

Kyaw Myint replies abruptly that he knows the evidence of which we speak. Special Branch is not convinced, he says, and neither is the minister.

Then he runs a finger down the list and stops at another name, assuring us that this is someone the minister will agree to help, including hospitalization and early release. He is talking about a man arrested for staging a solitary demonstration in Rangoon without a permit. His offence was protesting a land grab that had cost him his farm and his livelihood.

I note, pre-empting Hein Zaw, that the man was sentenced to five years and has been on a hunger strike. His family is very worried.

Kyaw Myint replies that he has spoken with the minister about this case. The man is not a risk to reoffend, he assures us, so there's a good possibility that the Ministry can issue an order approving a reduced sentence and hospital treatment. He can be released as early as tomorrow.

Kyaw Myint then looks at his watch and, apparently needing to be elsewhere, quickly runs through every name on the list — about 20 people. They're all prisoners of conscience, so we are seeking outright release in every case. Being realistic, we know the best we can hope for is reduced sentence, medical assistance, or transfer to minimum security. But Kyaw Myint says no to every one of our remaining requests. By the time we review the entire list, it's clear that the minister only arranged this meeting because I'm a celebrity ex-prisoner whose release has received high publicity. By throwing us a bone or two, then telling *The New Light of Myanmar* about it, Kyaw Myint's boss thinks the government will come off looking good. The bastard.

I am stewing in this thought, exchanging glances with Hein Zaw, when a secretary peeks in and asks to speak with Kyaw Myint. Turning to us, he excuses himself to join her outside. Five minutes later, he returns and sits down.

"It seems that there is new business," he says, looking me directly in the eye.

What does he mean? I ask, afraid of the answer.

What can I tell the government, he asks, about an American citizen named Benjamin Malcolm?

My lawyer looks at me and shrugs. He doesn't know about Min.

"It's okay, Hein Zaw," I tell him. I can answer this.

27

Min:

The undercover cops who busted me for saving the life of an old Muslim man they were trying to kill tie my hands behind my back before leading me, at gunpoint, to the police station. There they bring me downstairs and lock me up in a tiny cell that reeks of piss and shit. An hour later, a guard arrives to march me down a dimly lit cement corridor to an interrogation room. Back and forth between my cell and this room they take me for the next two days, doing their best to break down my resistance. Every few hours they try to punch, kick, or whip me into obedience. By the end of day two, the local captain has lost patience.

What am I really doing in Meiktila? he asks, kicking me in the shin. He tells me my business card is a fake and that I must have been sent by Al Jazeera. Then he punches me in the face, cutting my cheek. Another police officer enters the room, interrupting the beating. Handing his superior a note, he tells him there is news about the prisoner.

As he reads the note, the captain's face lights up with a sadistic grin. Well, well, he informs the room, it seems the local Meiktila constabulary has the honour of hosting a very important prisoner.

Then he turns to me and welcomes me back to Myanmar, addressing me as "Min Lin — or should that be Aung Win?"

My heart sinks as Captain Sarcastic reveals how I've been exposed. After taking me to the station, his officers dug through my camera bag and found my passport. After making a copy, they sent it to the Special Branch of Myanmar Police Forces, the new intelligence service, where it was circulated among senior staff. Before long, some ace investigator not only discovered my identity but also my whereabouts between March 27, 1989, and August of 1990. As a result, the national hero Aung Win — unjustly accused of desertion twenty-three years ago — has been posthumously rehabilitated as a tragic war casualty, his reputation restored. Meanwhile, his imposter, apprehended by a local police force in Meiktila, awaits justice. A lucky break for the New Myanmar. Not so much for me. Soon I will be returned to Rangoon and delivered to the Special Branch, whose agents will be intrigued by my fortuitous landing in their laps — and at the very moment the New Myanmar is presenting itself to the world as a nation in transition.

At the Mingaladon airport, two suited men from the Special Branch await my plane on the tarmac. One of them handcuffs me the moment I finish descending the staircase from the plane. He welcomes me back to his country with a sneer, addressing me as "Captain" and adding that the Special Branch didn't expect to see me back here again. Then he and his partner lead me to a white van. After all the years Thandar spent in that place, it must be my destiny to land at Insein Prison. As a prize catch for the Special Branch, I do not expect to be treated well there. Thanks to my escape in 1990, in which I effortlessly ghosted my way out of the country, heads must have rolled at Military Intelligence. Today's top brass are unlikely to be compassionate now that their elusive prey is finally in their grip. They will have their way with me, at last.

At the prison gates, my escorts hand me over to a couple of guards who lead me inside. From registration, they bring me straight to the solitary confinement wing. Oh no, the dog cells! They can't put me in here. They mustn't! Designed, quite literally, for military canines, the dog cells at Insein are reserved for a special kind of political prisoner. During the 1990s, a select group of inmates including NLD co-founder Win Tin had been locked up in these cages. Today, under quasi-civilian rule, hunger strikers and other political prisoners still receive this form of punishment. A quarter century removed from the events that might have landed me at this prison with Thandar, it's my turn for the treatment.

My cell is ten feet long by seven feet wide, windowless, and soundproof. There is no toilet, bed, or even a floor mat. It is filled with maggots and smells like a sewer. What will happen to me here? I have returned to Burma on an approved journalist's permit, using my legal name, not imagining there was any chance I could be imprisoned for political activity, much less exposed as Aung Win's long-forgotten imposter. Now that both have occurred, it's anyone's guess what will happen next. How will I get out of this mess? How will Robert find out where I am? And how will Dad react when Robert tells him? Having finally been revealed as Min Lin, accused of returning to the country to cause mischief by supporting Muslims, I have now been charged with trespass and obstruction of justice.

It is hard to be optimistic. Will President Thein Sein want the hassle of a trial, knowing it will attract Western media coverage and international pressure? Probably not. I'm sure some of his men would just as soon put me in front of a firing squad. But the more likely temptation, I'm sure, is to lock me up, throw away the key, and deny any knowledge of my existence. If that happens, who will even know I'm here? If Thandar finds out — and she likely will, given her connections with the prisoners' association — what is she going to do about it? Can I expect someone who has just been released from the same prison after twenty-five years, who has found out that I worked for the SLORC while she was there, to put aside her personal feelings, disregard my support of the Rohingyas, and rally to my cause? The more I think about it, the more likely it seems that I'm destined for disappearance. For real this time.

In the middle of my first night, I wake up shivering. A guard has taken away my blanket, giving it to someone else. Then I hear music: a traditional Burmese love song, with a repetitive upbeat melody, wafting through the PA system. "Sar-Eu" is beautiful, its first verse almost soothing to hear. But as the song continues, it is suddenly accompanied by the screams of a prisoner being beaten. Later I hear the song again, followed by another prisoner being beaten. Then I understand: the broadcast of "Sar-Eu" is Insein's way of terrorizing inmates, first by waking us up in the middle of the night and then by reminding us that excruciating pain is about to be inflicted on a yet-to-be-determined victim. Sometimes, the prisoner's cries continue for the duration of the song, other times until long after its final verse. For the next few days, I cower in my cell whenever I hear "Sar-Eu," wondering if I'm next.

I am dangling upside down, my feet tied to a meat hook in the ceiling. Blood rushes to my head. I hear the mocking laughter of my tormentors as I fail to obey them. In this position, I am supposed to keep my back straight at ninety degrees while fully extending my arms to forty-five degrees, maintaining the pose until our "interview" is over. But my arms are tired, so I let them drop a little, to relax. And then, for relief from that rush of blood to the head, I try to bend upwards. When I do this, they thrash me with a bamboo whip until I resume the position. Holy shit, does that ever hurt! A young investigator bends on one knee and leans toward me, our faces inches apart. "Who is paying you? Why do you support the *kalar*? Why are you a terrorist?" His spittle rains down on my face, his bad breath triggering a gag reflex.

Growing dizzy from hanging upside down, I am still nauseous and cannot speak. He grips the elbow of my straight left arm and yanks it like a propeller blade, turning my body into a spinning rotor. The room revolves. Ah, so this is why they call it "The Helicopter." Only a matter of time before they gave me this treatment, having already put me through "The Motorcycle," where I was forced to make engine noises while balancing on the balls of my feet with pins beneath my toes, and "Walking on the Beach," where I had to crawl on my stomach across sharp stones, glass, metal, and gravel. There must be a manual on torture for this place, they have so many methods for breaking our spirits. And it doesn't end back in our cells between torture sessions, either. Whenever a senior prison official drops by the ward and happens to ask my real name, I have to respond with "Ma" — a female prefix for younger women — before "Min Lin," or the guards will whack me with a bamboo stick. If the conversation continues and I fail to finish every sentence with "Shint," a suffix for politeness used by females — rather than "Bya" used by males — they'll beat me for that too. They think this will humiliate me.

Here in the interrogation room, they just want me to talk. And that's a tall order right now because the rope is fully coiled from the spinning, and I'm getting very dizzy; after my torturer begins twirling me in the opposite direction, I can't utter a single word even if I want to. The young investigator, stubbing out his cigarette on the back of my neck, asks for the hundredth time why I'm here and why have I come back to Myanmar. When I say nothing, he leans over and whispers in my ear: "Listen, you little shit. No one is going to help you now — least of all Thandar Aye." When I turn to face him, indicating that he has my full attention, he says yes, it was Thandar Aye who turned me in, who gave me up to the police. Sold me down the river for a cup of tea. My tormentor, sounding like a bad Hollywood villain, suggests that it's "payback time" for Aung Win's imposter.

He's bluffing. I know Thandar wouldn't snitch on anyone, not even me. She hates the government too much to collude with it. But the mention of her name is upsetting. How do they know of our connection? My interrogator, deciding I've had enough for one day, hands me over to the guards who take me back to my cell. I roll over in pain, wincing from at least two broken ribs and bruises on my back and arms. Nothing offers relief from the cold cement floor until hours later when one of the guards, in a rare moment of compassion, slips a rattan mat into my cell. A nice gesture, but cold comfort given that my interrogators are likely not done with me yet. The higher-ups at Special Branch are frustrated by the failure to extract more information. And I am not sure how much more of their persuasion I can take. I am getting weaker.

Several days, maybe weeks, have passed. I have no idea how long I've been stuck in this shithole nor how long my captors intend to keep me here. Before throwing me into the dog cell, they said nothing about the charges against me and, of course, nothing about my rights. Nor was I granted access to a lawyer. This dog cell stinks to high heaven — an actual canine must have been its previous occupant — and I'm becoming more claustrophobic. This space is not much larger than a coffin, a thought that sends me into a panic; could I actually die here? My pain is becoming unbearable. My back, hips, and knees ache terribly. I find it nearly impossible to walk when the guards pull me out for my daily thrashings, the only relief from that cell.

I could easily go crazy here. The prospect of dying in this place is bad enough, but I could also go mad with self-loathing because of the wilful stupidity that landed me here. I can hear Robert now, giving me hell for risking it all at my age. He's right, of course, but I thought my biggest risk was in Arakan State. I was sure I'd dodged the bullet when I flew out of Sittwe, that my great run of good luck would pull me through the rest of my return visit to Burma. Fuck. I should not have stepped out of that taxi in Meiktila; I should have listened to the driver. But here I go again, falling into that self-blame cycle of woulda-coulda-shouldas. To avoid going crazy, I will need to think about happier things. So I think of Robert, of how much I miss him right now ... But then my thoughts go dark again ... He must be mad at me and think he's right that I shouldn't have made this trip ... Is he fucking around on me with someone else — right now, at this moment — while I'm stuck here?... No! Don't go there, Min ... Instead, think of music ...

An old song creeps its way back into my brain and stays there, a real earworm. An earnest piece of anthemic rock 'n' roll that reminds me of being right here, stuck in this place. It's a U2 song about Burma, the one dedicated to Aung San Suu Kyi and the NLD. The one that talks of darkness and daylight, of being strong, of singing birds and open cages, of flying for freedom. Back in 2001 the junta banned that song, and the album it came from, because of the Suu Kyi dedication. But the lyrics have not aged well: one verse talks about how precious home is, especially if you've never had one. Today, that sounds like a *cri de coeur* for the Rohingyas. Given Suu Kyi's abandonment of these people to their fate, Bono and the boys must be feeling a tad embarrassed about that dedication now.

There was a story I'd read somewhere, perhaps urban myth, from the year that album came out. It was about a family in Karen State who one day received a visit from some young American backpackers. Among the gifts the foreigners left behind for their hosts was the Irish supergroup's new CD. As the tourists continued merrily on their way, the father paid for that gift with seven years of hard labour. And what was the album called again? Oh yeah, *All That You Can't Leave Behind*. Sounds like a hint those backpackers didn't take. The end of the song, calling up the album title, is an invocation to leave behind all that causes us pain. I laugh as I recall those words from Dr. Jules during our long-ago sessions; he wanted me to leave behind my baggage from Burma. Now I think about that singing bird, like the peacock of democracy, and its open cage. My "cage" is this very closed dog cell. I shut my eyes so I can't see what's around me. I try not to smell anything or hear the cries of other prisoners. Or think of what's happening to me right here, right now, in Burma. Must. Think. Of another. Song.

28

Thandar:

The young Home Affairs staffer, Kyaw Myint, has caught me off guard with that question about "Benjamin Malcolm." My instinct is to not say anything about Min. Why get both of us in trouble? On the other hand, I can't really afford to be evasive with a government that has just granted me early release from Insein. Hein Zaw looks at me warily as I prepare to talk, the AAPP's lawyer clearly preferring that I keep my mouth shut.

Benjamin Malcolm is someone I used to know many years ago, I begin, choosing my words carefully. I tell Kyaw Myint that he visited the country during the demonstrations in 1988, that he is back here on business and wanted to see me again after my release. Kyaw Myint says nothing, waiting for me to go on. I've got a feeling that something bad has happened to Min, so I hesitate. Back in '88, I recall, my former fiancé came to Burma naively unprepared for the events that overtook us. But now, post-dictatorship, I could see from our visit that he doesn't have a clue of the potential dangers that still exist. Not having set foot here in twenty-three years, he didn't appreciate how much more volatile the country has become, despite the new freedoms. The adventurous side I so loved about Min when we were young — the openness to new experience, the willingness to learn from mistakes — might have been a form of recklessness I didn't see at the time; a disregard for consequences, a stubborn failure to think things through. That certainly seems true of his crusade on behalf of the Bengalis. Now, without knowing what has befallen him, I feel compromised by his actions. Part of me would like nothing more than for my ex to learn a hard lesson, a reality check for his simplistic idealism. But if Min has been arrested and thrown into a Burmese prison, especially Insein, I cannot turn my back on him out of spite. I must help him.

I tell Kyaw Myint that I assume someone informed the minister that Benjamin Malcolm contacted me through the Assistance Association. I am about to ask this junior official how he knows of our connection when he interrupts.

The authorities know much more than that, says Kyaw Myint. They know that Benjamin Malcolm is another name for Min Lin, the spy, the American imposter who spent sixteen months pretending to be the war hero Aung Win before fleeing Myanmar twenty-three years ago. But perhaps I knew that already, he says.

Uh-oh. It's worse than I thought. Hein Zaw turns to me with concern in his eyes, imploring me to say nothing more until we've had a chance to discuss the issue. But I cannot give this minor official, this USDP hack, the satisfaction of criminalizing me again. So I tell Kyaw Myint that, yes, I do know of Min's background. But if he's trying to imply anything illegal, he should understand that, as a prisoner of the state, I was not aware of Min Lin's time as an imposter until he shared it with me when we met recently. As I'm sure he can imagine, I was shocked — shocked that Min would —

He interrupts by informing me that my brothers have confirmed that Min and I were dating while he was living illegally in our country.

Oh, shit. They got to my siblings. Okay, fine, I say. It's true. So why are they telling me this?

Kyaw Myint pauses until he has both of our attention and then informs us that Min Lin was arrested in Meiktila last week after an altercation with the police. He was flown back to Yangon and sent to Insein, where his American status will not be grounds for leniency.

Hein Zaw and I look at each other, stunned by this news. What happened? I ask Kyaw Myint. Have they provided details?

Not much, Kyaw Myint replies, only that Min tried to intervene when local police were about to arrest a suspected terrorist. The report from Meiktila says he has been charged with trespass and obstruction of justice.

Hein Zaw speaks up, asking the Ministry staffer to add Min's name to our list. We will investigate his case once we are back in Yangon. When we do, he says, he is fairly confident that Min will stay on the list until he is freed. Kyaw Myint agrees, while adding that Min's being a foreigner will complicate matters. After promising to forward our request to the minister, he asks us to keep Min's situation out of the media. There are back channels, he says, for dealing with such a unique case. The government will keep us informed of further developments. And with that, Kyaw Myint rises from his desk and sees us out the door.

The next day back in Rangoon, I'm at the Assistance Association office, volunteering at reception, when Khine Kyaw forwards an email that's been sitting in his junk folder for nearly two weeks. The message was sent to the AAPP admin address with the subject heading "Attn: Thandar Aye – meeting follow-up," but Khine Kyaw only noticed it now while checking his junk folder before trashing its contents. The sender is Min. He must have sent the email right before his trip to Meiktila. Inside is a brief message, saying nothing about our meeting but noting that I will want to see the results of his latest work. Before signing off, he provides a link to something called "Dropbox," which appears to be an Internet program for photo storage. He advises me not to forget to open it, as the link will no longer be available after two weeks.

When I click on the link it still works, leading to a folder entitled "Arakan." Inside is a large gallery of photos, all taken during his visit there. There must be two hundred images, every one of them high quality. I go through them, stopping occasionally to study a photograph carefully. I see a Bengali man on his knees, begging Rakhine police. The police whip him. A photograph of an elderly woman, crying for who-knows-what, her arms in the air. A group of Bengali men, a dozen or so, posed together, half standing, staring at the camera — almost proudly it seems — their faces a portrait in collective stoicism, endurance, and survival. A large group of Bengalis behind barbed wire, crowded together. They're all skinny, complete bone racks. The children are severely malnourished and stare blankly at the camera. *Help us. Do something. Get us out of here.* Then, in one of the few photos without people in it, I see a neighbourhood in ashes. An entire block of houses, shops, and what must have been mosques, reduced to black dust, the charcoaled remnants of community.

Despite my better instinct, which is to close the file, I go back to the photo of the starving people behind barbed wire. Sure enough, it makes me feel nauseous. It is not so much the condition of the people in this picture that makes me feel this way, but the photo's very existence. For I know that such images — such glaring evidence of profound human suffering — would not be published in Burmese newspapers. Nor would those group photos of the

Double Karma

Bengali men, whose collective pride suggests they are respectable, decent human beings who are active in their community, providers for their families, and completely at home in their environment. These photos say far too much.

All of this has me pondering the *taingyintha*, the national races ideology. A way of thinking that attributes cultural and psychological traits to ethnicities, which are assigned to geographical territory within the Union. *Taingyintha*, or "sons of the soil," is an ideology based on Bamar Buddhist assumptions about who should belong where — or if they belong at all. It is meant to separate ethnicities deemed worthy of citizenship from those who ought to be considered outsiders. There is no science to *taingyintha*, no proof of its legitimacy. It is based on the same logic of racial prejudice that has existed everywhere from the beginning of time. But in the land that became Burma, it was the British who codified the dividing and categorizing of ethnicities according to existing judgements about character traits, geography, and religion. During the colonial period, such a system enabled the British to control the population and promote national unity. Since independence — especially since the first military coup — our national army has taken this concept and run with it, perfecting the codification of race and ethnicity to an extent our colonizers could not have dreamed possible. Yes, the British-hating Tatmadaw have turned racist British ways of classifying us into an art form.

Looking at these photos, I feel sick. I have subscribed to the *taingyintha* without realizing it; I have swallowed its assumptions unquestioningly. Growing up, I belonged to the Bamar majority, the most privileged ethnic group in Burma. We don't deny injustice against the Karen, Shan, Mon, Chin, or Kachin peoples, but only because we've written them into the national race equation. And we're usually the last to know about atrocities in the ethnic border areas, the last to insist that the Tatmadaw put a stop to them. We're too busy fighting for civilian rule. As for the Bengalis? We've been taught our whole lives not to bother thinking about them.

I know that Min did not visit Rakhine State until the latest round of violence was over. There are no photos here of people being slaughtered. But the residue of trauma is etched in all of these faces, in every person caught in his lens. It's there, as well, in the photos without people: in the images of smouldering neighbourhoods, of makeshift graves behind ruined mosques, indicated by multiple rows of mounds of dirt and of discarded items of clothing and flip-flops, in the street. There has been murder here. Buddhists did this, people who share my religion. It is indefensible. I don't care how long these people have been in Burma or how long they claim to have been here. What I see in these photos is people who have been cut off and deprived of services and resources that all Burmese citizens take for granted. They have been turned into the alien "Other" by successive governments determined to make us avert our eyes from their poor management of the country, directing our attention instead towards an enemy that does not exist. And we are falling for this racist propaganda.

After two hours of reviewing these photos, I look up from my computer. Everyone else has left for the day, except of course my boyfriend, who's been waiting patiently for me, cleaning up the office. Khine Kyaw, finally having my attention, says he's hungry and needs to eat. So we leave the office to go get some food. In the car, I direct him to Tamwe district, north of Shwedagon. On U Chit Maung Road, we park in front of a chicken biryani restaurant. The place is filled with people of Indian descent, people my people refer to as *kalars*. I've ordered chicken biryani for takeout many times but have yet to sit down for a meal in one of these restaurants which have dotted the city for as long as I can recall. Khine Kyaw is not opposed to the idea of chicken biryani in Tamwe, but he is intrigued by my choice to eat in. Opening the door for me, he asks why here and now? I remind him that I've been in prison for the past twenty-five years and that my world needs to expand.

After we're seated near the window, a young *kalar* woman takes our order and leaves. Then I start telling Khine Kyaw about Min's photos. The email wasn't addressed to him, so he did not open the Dropbox folder. I describe the photos and my reaction to them. Khine Kyaw listens intently, without responding. It's clear he hasn't thought much about ethnic and religious violence in Rakhine State, as he doesn't seem particularly moved by the issues one way or another. But he does seem intrigued by my revelation about *taingy-intha*, by my fresh conviction that Bengalis deserve human rights.

As I'm telling him all this, I find myself drawn to a Bengali man circulating busily about the restaurant. I first spotted him inside the door when we arrived. I thought he was a customer and noticed him later, sitting alone at a table. But then, distracted by something he sees in another part of the restaurant, he rises to speak with a waiter. Taking the young man gently by the arm, he leads him to the kitchen and points at the chef before turning to speak with other waiters. Okay, so he's not a customer, but he's more than an employee. He must be the manager of this place, possibly its owner. Despite giving orders all around he has the respect of his staff, who listen carefully and nod dutifully before turning to their tasks. He is in no way intimidating or overbearing, on the contrary speaking so softly that he can't be heard above the din of this busy establishment. Once satisfied that everything is in order, he returns to his table, picks up a newspaper, and starts reading.

I don't know why I'm so drawn to him, as I've never paid much attention to *kalars*. But this one, in his early forties if that, is uncommonly handsome. Apart from the middle-age paunch, he looks like a movie star. Thick, shiny black hair and such a dazzling smile. Beautiful teeth. A young waiter approaches, interrupting his reading. He calls his boss by name ("Sayed. Sayed!") and asks if he wants anything from the store. Only cigarettes, he replies, without looking up from his paper. When the waiter asks him what kind, he tells him Red Ruby and sighs, as if the kid should know his boss's favourite brand by now. Then he slaps the lad's bottom to send him on his way. As he does this, the man named Sayed looks up to see me staring at him and gives me that dazzling smile with a wink. My heart skips a beat.

That's when Khine Kyaw, still waiting to hear more about my new understanding of *taingyintha*, waves a hand in front of my face to get my attention, reminding me that we're here in this restaurant together.

I tell my boyfriend that maybe it's time for we Bamar Buddhists to take a look in the mirror. Long ago, I risked my life for the sake of freedom and democracy. At the time, I didn't think there was any greater burden to bear than being a Burmese citizen under the yoke of the Tatmadaw. Now I know otherwise.

"Is this Mister Robert Malcolm?" I ask, flipping over Min's business card to make sure I got the name right. The long-distance phone line crackles, but I hear nothing at the other end. A few seconds later, there's a voice: "Yes."

"Please excuse. My English, it is not so good. My name is Thandar Aye. I am sure that Min, I mean Benjamin, has told you about me, no?"

I don't know how else to do this. I am sure I have caused heart palpitations for this poor man. For mine is the voice of a woman who, but for the whims of dictatorship, might have become his spouse's wife. He must know that a phone call from me could only portend bad news about Min, so I get to the point.

"I am sorry to tell you, Mister Robert, but Benjamin has been arrested by Myanmar Police and sent to Insein Prison."

"Oh my God ..."

I can hear the horror in his voice, so I let him absorb the news before I continue. In effect, I am telling the husband of my would-be husband that Min and I have basically traded places after twenty-five years. I tell Mister Robert that I'm doing everything I can to secure Min's release. I tell him about the political prisoners group I'm part of, that we have a lawyer who's working hard on the case as we speak. Mister Robert thanks me for the call and congratulates me on my own release. While the news about Min is terrible, it also comes as a relief.

"I stopped receiving emails and Skype calls from him a couple of weeks ago," he says. "Now at least I know why."

"He is still okay, as far as we know. But Insein can be a tough place."

"It must have been very hard for you to make this call, especially after all the years you spent there. What can I do to help?"

We don't know how long it will take to free Min, I tell him. But having his family show up in Burma would make a big difference. It would put pressure on the government, which would definitely help. Together we could fight for Min's release and also use the media if necessary. So, I tell him, the sooner he can come the better. He thanks me and promises to come as soon as he can.

"Please let me know when you will arrive. I can meet you at the airport."

"You are so very kind to be doing this."

I tell him to never mind, that I understand how hard it must be to learn this news, perhaps especially from me. But what happened before is in the past. Min was another person, and so was I. After spending twenty-five years at Insein, I do not wish for Min to suffer the same. Pausing a moment, I then ask Mister Robert if he is on speaking terms with Min's father. He says he is, but that Ko Lin Tun is eighty-eight now and quite frail. This news will upset him. I tell him I understand but ask to bring him if he's healthy enough. It will help for Min's release.

"Yes, I think you're right," he replies. "Ko Lin Tun hasn't been to Burma since 1962. But I can't think of a better reason to go back now than to free his only child from that prison."

29

Min:

In the dog cell, I am forced to learn new ways of falling asleep, if only to spend as few hours as possible in the conscious present. When I'm awake, the pain, boredom, and depression are constant. It is like slow death in here, my hope and optimism evaporating by the day. As hard as I try to think good thoughts, I struggle against self-loathing. I keep hearing Dad and Robert berating me for coming to Burma. I keep seeing Thandar, her arms crossed with that knowing look, not surprised at all that I have ended up in such deep trouble. The best distraction from such thoughts is to think about my photo projects. I mean all my subjects, dating back to the start of my career: the kind of shoots involved, the locations, and where they ended up being published or displayed. After a while, floating in all these images and memories, I can lose consciousness. I can fall and stay asleep, regardless of the cockroaches crawling around me. Every minute, every hour not conscious in this shithole is a blessing.

After a month in the dog cell, there is good news: my jailers are transferring me to a standard cell. No one tells me why, so I don't bother asking, for I am glad not to have to spend another minute in that cage, braying like an animal from the agony of an aching back, hips, and knees — or from a growing sense of despair. Compared to the dog cell, this cell is a luxury. It has a squat toilet hole, a wooden platform for sleeping, and more room — at least enough for me to move again. Enough to stretch the muscles. Enough to stand up and do small exercises. For these most basic of human needs, the first couple of days in my new quarters lift my spirits.

But then the guards come calling, and it's time for more interrogation. I am not sure what they hope to achieve by putting me through any more of this. They already know the full story about my Aung Win episode. They know about Thandar and me. I have answered all their questions about us, and multiple times, so there is nowhere else for them to go. Or so I think.

What did I tell the US government? they ask. Wow. They still care about intel from 1990.

When I reply that I told the US government how much I couldn't wait to get the hell out of Burma, one of my interrogators gives me a whack on the knee with a lead pipe.

There are more of these questions, repeated in two or three sessions after this one, and more abuse. I am losing faith that I will ever see the outside again. Meanwhile, that month in the dog cell has taken its toll; I am too thin after losing my appetite for the thin gruel of rice, garlic, and fish sauce they serve every day. Struggling with diarrhea for about two weeks now. The beatings haven't helped. Have I earned this suffering? Perhaps I deserve it. Perhaps this is my karma, my long-delayed comeuppance for having served as a SLORC minion. And what does my suffering mean, compared to that of the Rohingyas? Any comparison is obscene. Unlike theirs, my situation is entirely the result of self-agency and privilege. Unlike them, I have the citizenship, wealth, and connections to find my way out of the mess I'm in. At least, I should be able to get out of Insein, once those acting on my behalf make all the right contacts. The Rohingyas have no such luck, and far fewer options, in their collective prison of daily existence.

A few days later, the Special Branch interrogations become gentler. The beatings stop. I wonder if there's been contact with the US Embassy. Is Thandar working on my case now? Has she been able to reach Dad and Robert? In the meantime, there is fresh relief from the boredom in my ward. A new inmate has been brought to the cell next to mine, a farmer in his mid-fifties named Sai Latt. When he asks what I'm in for, I tell him I was busted during the riots in Meiktila. He wants to know what I actually did to deserve ending up here, so I tell him that I tried to stop two policemen from killing someone, an old Muslim man. I add that my case is complicated because I'm an American and a journalist. When I ask what he's in for, he says he was arrested for organizing a protest at the Letpadaung Copper Mine. This is his second visit to Insein after another demonstration a few months ago.

I know about this. The copper mine is a hot issue for residents in Sagaing Division. As with so many other megaprojects in Burma, this one calls for the eviction of farmers from their lands to make way for development that's deemed to be in "the national interest." The tension has been rising since the subsidiary company for a Chinese arms manufacturer took over the project and began ramping up evictions without compensating the farmers. Aung San Suu Kyi, as Opposition leader, has led a commission to study the project. She now agrees with its conclusion that the development is necessary. On a recent visit to the area to hear from villagers, she did not receive a warm welcome.

The Lady did not come to listen, says Sai Latt, but to give the villagers a lecture. And they were not in the mood for a lecture.

They were offered six hundred dollars each to lease entire rice paddy fields for a massive industrial project. The villagers were threatened with jail if they refused. Sai Latt refused, he says, so they sent him down to Insein for a month. Now he is back again for exercising his human rights. He does have a right to his liveli- hood, does he not?

When I express surprise at the hostile reception Suu Kyi received in Sagaing, Sai Latt tells me that the people there have long since given up on the Nobel laureate as any kind of advocate to defend their rights. Sure, she will probably win the election in 2015, he says, but who cares? She is not a true democrat but an elitist; an upper-class politician who's out of touch with the people and doesn't care about the peasantry. She sees herself as the indispens- able leader who should be able to tell the little people what to do. Does this sound familiar?

It's been a long time since I have truly embraced Buddhism. Probably as far back as the two and a half years I spent in this country. In 1988, I thought of myself as a true believer. But back then, my belief — my religious piety — was only skin deep. I was no different from any other Western dilettante with a New Age sensi- bility and vocabulary. Despite my early education, once I landed in Rangoon I could only see the Buddha through the rose-tinted glasses of a tourist: bedazzled by the glitter and gold of the city's finest temples, mystified by the inscrutable wisdom of its senior monks. Under the spell of my father, a deeply conservative man who took the precepts seriously, I was credulous as a child because Buddhism seemed the most benign of all the religions; apart from self-discipline, it made so few demands of me. At a time when I was still in the closet, Buddhism also relativized the whole thorny question of sexuality out of existence. Besides which, it seemed more a philosophy than a religion.

But as Thandar and I grew closer and I began to experience more of Burmese culture, a more nuanced perspective took root. The more temples we visited and the more conversations I had with Burmese men, the more I picked up on a Brahmin-informed, caste mentality. As practiced in Burma, Theravada Buddhism could be every bit as socially backward and politically reactionary as any other religion. Burman Buddhism was not only susceptible to ethno-nationalist racism. In many ways, it was also sexist. Nuns, seen as incapable of reaching nirvana, were forbidden from performing religious rites and excluded from certain areas of the temple. A bit like the Catholics. Today, with feminist literature circulating throughout Burma's public sphere, Buddhist shrines still feature crude artistic renderings of woman as temptress, woman as devious manipulator, woman as shameful object of scorn. And yet here was Thandar, in our debate at Junction Square, defending her religion. Shrugging off the misogyny, I suppose, as a quaint anachronism of the faith hardly worth fretting about.

Fuck religion, anyway. Fuck all of it. I am rotting to death in this place, and guess what? I am an atheist in a foxhole. If my family doesn't save me, no God is going to. I refuse to be one of those cowards who, at his dying breath, clutches pathetically for some non-existent deity. If I can't get out of here alive, then all I want is for the pain to stop. Preferably forever. Is God going to show up right now with a morphine injection? Or a nice, thick mattress?

30

Naypyidaw
May 2013

The "back channels" of which Home Affairs Ministry staffer Kyaw Myint spoke in his meeting with Thandar Aye and the AAPP lawyer are still working on the case of Benjamin Malcolm, a.k.a Min Lin. For starters, they have recruited an old SLORC legend to help them out of a potentially awkward situation: Khin Nyunt, the former Military Intelligence chief who, in 1989, presented Aung Win's imposter with a medal for bravery before getting him a job at the Ministry of Information. After a long time out of the spotlight, the old spy chief is on a comeback of sorts, recovering from an ignominious fall from grace in September 2004. At the time, Khin Nyunt had been serving as prime minister for about a year when he was suddenly deposed. Arrested and jailed for corruption, he was accused of importing luxury cars for personal use without paying the proper duties. His actual crime was a power struggle with then-dictator Than Shwe.

The fallen junta bigwig was sentenced to forty-four years in prison, later converted to house arrest. But eight years later, with Than Shwe comfortably retired and a military moderate, former general Thein Sein, at the helm of a new quasi-civilian government, all was forgiven. Thein Sein cancelled Khin Nyunt's house arrest by presidential decree in January 2012, reducing his sentence by thirty-seven years. Since then, Khin Nyunt has wasted no time reconnecting with old friends from the intelligence community. It is during one such call, in late March 2013, that the case of Min Lin first comes up.

An official from Special Branch asks for Khin Nyunt's help in finding more information about an ethnic Burman foreigner who has just been arrested in Meiktila on terrorism charges. Khin Nyunt agrees to assist and, after going online, digs up enough information to embarrass the new government — and, by implication, himself. A simple Google search in English turns up a few hits for "Benjamin Malcolm," including a photo studio called Karma Communications, which then leads to its date of incorporation as 1991 and the name of its founder and sole proprietor as Min Lin. From there, it isn't long before Khin Nyunt opens another link to a photo from 1995, published in a newspaper called *L.A. Weekly*. In the photo, taken at a Hollywood fundraiser, the actress Elizabeth Taylor is seen onstage, standing beside the spitting image of Aung Win. The caption reads: "ARTS FOR LIFE — Some of LA's hottest artists auctioned off their works at an amfAR event Saturday to support programs for people living with HIV/AIDS ..." The man standing next to Miss Taylor is identified as Min Lin.

The day after Khin Nyunt informs his Special Branch contact of this troubling discovery, the official has called him back, asking him to attend a meeting with President Thein Sein to discuss the Benjamin Malcolm/Min Lin case. Presidential Spokesman Ye Htut, Tatmadaw Senior General Min Aung Hlaing, and Foreign Minister Wunna Maung Lwin will also be in attendance. The Special Branch contact, a younger man, understands that the former spy chief is a civilian now. But he notes that Thein Sein would appreciate Khin Nyunt's sage advice, adding — unnecessarily — that the president knows how grateful he is "for last year."

At the President's Office in Naypyidaw, Thein Sein paces the room. The Listener-in-Chief, having listened a great deal, has heard enough. The situation is most vexing to Thein Sein. To make sense of it all in order to come up with a plan, he sums up what has transpired so far: the wrong person being taken off the Maw Pokay battlefield in 1989, then receiving a medal before being appointed to a job requiring full security clearance; that mistake being drawn out for another year and half, allowing this person to infiltrate the SLORC and, once it suited him, escape before anyone noticed; and, finally, the latest episode, which presents more of a problem. How on earth, the president wants to know, did this person get past customs at Yangon International Airport?

"Min Lin legally changed his name and had credentials with the Associated Press," says Wunna Maung Lwin.

Thein Sein, grimacing, thanks the minister for stating the obvious. But he was hoping there were other red flags that might have identified this man as Min Lin. The problem is that the US is aware of his presence in Myanmar because he is here on a legitimate journalist's permit. If the story comes out that Min Lin was a spy for the US, which he must have been, and that he has been arrested here twenty-three years after escaping the first time, there will be no end to the media circus, says the president.

Min Aung Hlaing, shifting uncomfortably in his chair without saying a word up to now, finally speaks up. "We cannot just release him," says the Tatmadaw senior general. "He's a terrorist. Special Branch has traced his movements since he landed here. We know he was in Rakhine, where he was found to be supporting the Bengalis. In Meiktila, he interfered with a police investigation while defending a Muslim."

Thein Sein asks Min Aung Hlaing if he has any suggested course of action. "Yes," the senior general replies, "Foreign Affairs should contact the US Embassy and tell them what we know. Tell them about their spy and propose a deal of some sort. Either that, or don't tell the US anything. Instead, we could arrange for some kind of 'accident' at Insein. Problem solved."

The president tut-tuts his supreme army commander. "There's no need to get carried away here," he says. "After all, there is my diplomatic mission to think about."

The room falls silent. The president is referring to his upcoming trip to the United States, an official visit to be highlighted by a meeting at the White House with Barack Obama. Foreign Affairs has been working hard to ensure a successful trip. Thein Sein will be the first leader from this country since Ne Win, half a century ago, to hold bilateral meetings on US soil.

Wunna Maung Lwin, again stating the obvious, reminds the men what an embarrassment it would be if reporters bring up the issue of Min Lin while U Thein Sein is joining President Obama at a press briefing. "We would be the laughingstock of the international intelligence community," he says. "Our position within the Association of Southeast Asian Nations would be weakened — and only a few months before we assume the chairmanship. Imagine how this could be used against us!"

Khin Nyunt shakes his head as the foreign minister is speaking. Then he interjects, looking Wunna Maung Lwin in the eye. "Reporters in Washington are not going to bring up the issue of Min Lin during our bilateral meetings," he says. "As long as the media doesn't catch wind of this story — and they haven't yet — US reporters need not find out he was here until he has already left. And that is because you, Minister, will reach a deal with their Secretary of State."

Wunna Maung Lwin furrows his brow. "And what deal is that?" he asks.

Khin Nyunt sighs impatiently. "Myanmar will release Benjamin Malcolm from Insein and then deport him. We'll put him on a plane to Los Angeles the moment U Thein Sein boards his own plane in Washington for the return flight to Myanmar — that is, after he meets President Obama. Benjamin Malcolm's release will be subject to the Americans' agreement not to announce it until he is on US soil. All things considered, Mrs. Clinton and the State Department should have no difficulty agreeing to this request."

Wunna Maung Lwin turns to the president, shrugging. Thein Sein turns to Khin Nyunt. He understands the logic, he says, but is intrigued by the former spymaster's confidence in such a plan. What makes him think this turn-the-other-cheek approach is the right way to go? Khin Nyunt pauses before asking: "U Thein Sein, could we have a word in private?"

The two confer in another room. When they return ten minutes later, the president looks like he has seen a ghost.

31

May 22, 2013

Min:

I wake up. A rat scampering across the floor has broken the silence. I struggle to sit up, then notice that the guards have brought me breakfast: a cold serving of congee with fish sauce. My appetite is back, but I have to force myself to eat this meal; it's been sitting there a couple of hours already, so the maggots are having their way with it. Taking a deep sigh, I pick them out with disgust. I feel ten years older than when I was brought here, and that was two months ago. Since then, I've received word through the warden that Thandar is working on my case and relatives will soon be coming to Burma to help secure my release. That lifted my spirits, but the news came a couple of weeks ago. Since then, I've heard nothing more than short messages of encouragement from Robert and Dad, relayed by Thandar and the AAPP.

When will I be free? As I am fretting, two guards arrive and pull my crumpled body off the floor. "Come on, Min. Start walking," says one, who has taken to using my real name. Together they drag me out, hanging from their shoulders, and take me down the hall. As we pass the interrogation room and keep going, my panic returns ... Oh no, they're taking me to the warden's office for "special treatment" ... No, it's ... Admissions? A door opens. I'm led to the same desk from day one. Someone passes me a clipboard with an official release form. I sign it. Then a door to the visitor's gallery opens. In walks a young, well-dressed American who looks like a lawyer.

"Benjamin Malcolm? Min Lin?" he asks, extending his hand. "My name is Randall Carson. I'm with the US Embassy. You are being released on condition of deportation. Don't worry, everything will be fine. You are now under protection of the US government."

Then he turns to another Embassy official, who has followed him in with an empty wheelchair, and directs him to me. I sigh with pain and relief as I lower myself onto it.

I am not going to die.

Déjà vu. I am waking up in a hospital bed in Rangoon. But this time from a restful sleep, not a coma; this time in a civilian hospital, not a military one. This time there's no surprise visit from a SLORC big shot, no press conference turning me into someone else. On the bedside table is a large fruit basket, a gift from the taxi driver who brought me to Meiktila. It comes with a note apologizing for his failure to prevent me from leaving his car during the riots — unnecessary, since I was the one whose actions put us both in danger. There's also a wad of cash that probably amounts to half a month's salary for him. This by far overcompensates for the return trip to Rangoon I didn't take. I will make sure it's returned to him.

The door opens. Randall Carson, the American lawyer who sprung me from Insein, approaches my bedside and hands me a copy of *The International Herald Tribune*. There on the front page, above the fold, is a photo of Thein Sein at the White House with

Barack Obama, the two men shaking hands before sitting down for the first bilateral meetings on US soil in half a century.

"Your timing is good," says Carson. "The doctors say you have recovered nicely here over the past few days, so you can be released today. And that's good news for us; we're supposed to ship you out of the country by midnight. I've asked some of our staff to help you get your things together. But first, you have visitors." Carson winks at me before leaving.

When the door opens again, an old man with a cane who's neatly dressed in a sharp black suit and fedora shuffles in. It's Dad. When he looks up to reveal his face, I see a much older Ko Lin Tun than I recall from only months ago. He is frail and seems to be in pain. Dad is followed by Robert, also dressed in a fine suit. Robert moves forward and supports my father's arm as he leads him toward my bed. They, in turn, are followed by Thandar, who is casually dressed in jeans and a light blouse. The three of them surround me, Dad at my feet and Thandar to my left as Robert walks up from the right and plants a kiss on my forehead. I turn to Thandar.

"I guess there's no need for introductions here, right?"

"Not at all," she smiles. "U Lin Tun and I are well acquainted. And your Robert is very charming." Robert blushes.

"Dad was hoping for you instead of Robert," I reply. No one laughs. "But thanks for your help getting me out of Insein. You work much faster than I did — and with much better results." That does draw a laugh, except from Dad, who hasn't said a word while he stares at me. This is his first visit to Burma since he fled in 1962, which means he's been away from his native land for more than half a century — minus a day, as long as I've been alive. I motion for Robert to bring him closer. Dad shuffles up to my right, gripping the side rail with both hands.

"So," he says at last, "you finally found a way to get me back here." Tears stream down his face and then mine, and we all laugh. Except for Thandar. Her reaction is barely audible as she regards me intently. I think I know what's on her mind. She wants me to fess up already.

"Dad, come closer. There's something I need to tell you. Robert, you too."

They both look at me expectantly. I begin, "About that time I was reported missing, um ... I didn't go to Thailand — at least, not when I said I did." Then I repeat what I shared with Thandar at Junction Square. My father and spouse say nothing as I unload my big secret, obviously needing time to absorb it all, never mind consider what it reveals about my relationships with them. Both men — especially Dad — seem on the edge of anger as they receive the details. But the longer I speak, the more they relax. It's as if the gravity of my deception, the sting of betrayal, is outweighed by necessity. But they are still perplexed. Robert understands why I would hide my true identity from the SLORC, but not why I'd keep the secret once I was free. Dad asks me what I was afraid of. Did I think my father or husband would turn me in?

"I lied to the US Embassy in Bangkok, Dad. That's a pretty serious offence," I reply. "So no, I don't plan on unburdening myself to the world about it, regardless of how much time has passed. What I have told you here should remain between the four of us." Robert looks toward the door, behind which Randall Carson is waiting. Everyone nods silently.

Apart from the legal issues, I continue, there was also shame: I could not forgive myself for having accepted a salary from the SLORC while Thandar was locked up at Insein. And I felt that other aspects of my story — especially how I met Aung Win — would have seemed too far-fetched. The notion of escaping to Thailand

and living a life of hedonism for sixteen months was easier to justify than working for a military regime. Certainly an easier sell for family and friends.

Back at The Strand, where Dad and Robert have also been staying, Thandar and I wait in the bar while they settle accounts. When the waiter leaves after taking our drink orders, I turn to my former fiancée and lower my voice. "We didn't finish that conversation at Junction Square," I say. When I first contacted her after her release, I was afraid she wouldn't answer, that she would not want to see or speak to me again because I had abandoned her so long ago. When she agreed to a meeting, I was hopeful that we would get along. I expected her to be angry that I'd worked for the SLORC, perhaps disappointed that I'd turned out gay. But instead, it was my position on Arakan State that upset her the most. I still cannot fathom why she hates the Rohingyas, I tell Thandar. She is far too intelligent to be an ethno-nationalist.

But then she surprises me again. She doesn't really hate them, she says. How could she? She doesn't actually know any of their people. She confesses to her own ignorance and, yes, racism. Her response to me at Junction Square that day was a kind of lashing out. She was also irritated because so many foreign do-gooders come to Burma and go straight to Arakan when there are so many problems in other parts of the country that need international help. This country has a hundred and thirty-five ethnic groups, she says. I do remember that, right?

Yes, I reply. And eight major racial groups to contain them. Excluding the Rohingyas.

Thandar goes on to explain how Bamars have a long, sorry legacy of oppressing the Karen, Shan, Mon, Chin, and Kachin peoples — pretty much any ethnic minority that threatens central control by the Bamar Buddhist-led national army. Over the years, the Tatmadaw have killed hundreds of thousands of ethnic minority villagers along the border areas. Perhaps a million. I tell her I know this — that I have read about the infamous "Four Cuts" policy, in which the Army blocked rebel groups' access to food, funds, intelligence, and popular support for independence while terrorizing the people. The policy is decades old, but they're still using it. In Kachin State, I've heard, Christian churches and villages are routinely destroyed, and the people slaughtered, raped, or left homeless, all for the crime of not subscribing to Buddhism.

Thandar nods. Yes, she tells me, but it was unfair of her to give me a hard time for focusing on the Rohingyas. The police and the Tatmadaw have been terrible in most border areas, she adds, but they are not doing anything close to what's happening in Rakhine. Nowhere near on the same scale. She thinks the signs are there for possible genocide.

Given the vehemence of her anti-Rohingya stance not that long ago, I am surprised to hear this coming from her. What made her reach this conclusion?

It began with my photos from Arakan, she tells me, and then she did some more research, not being so quick to dismiss international NGOs and other Western sources. Speaking of my photos, she adds, it's a good thing I uploaded them to Dropbox and shared them with her and others before I left for Meiktila; after my arrest, Special Branch confiscated my MacBook. I tell her that I saw far worse things in Meiktila, and the photos I took there were in my camera when I was arrested, so they're gone forever. But at least I still have the Arakan images.

Those images don't lie, says Thandar. They are excellent photos, but shocking. Burmese media — state-controlled or independent — would not publish anything like that because they don't want the Burmese people to know the truth. Then she congratulates me, saying I was right about the Rohingyas. I have convinced her. She clinks my glass, and we laugh.

I wasn't out to win an argument, I say, but wait — she just said "Rohingya"!

Well, yes, Thandar replies, but outside this room they are still Bengalis, okay? She tells me that she deleted the Dropbox folder as soon as she finished looking at my photos. She is starting to like this thing called freedom, she adds, so she doesn't need any more trouble from the police. Besides, she is only one person. She will never change people's minds about what's going on in Arakan.

I can't help laughing at that; Thandar would not have said such a thing in 1988.

Well, she smiled sadly, 1988 is over now, isn't it?

I couldn't agree more. We clink glasses again.

When Dad and Robert arrive at the bar, Thandar leaves my side to join Dad while Robert sits down with me. After a few minutes of enduring my hubby's predictable admonishment for my reckless behaviour, I have to beg his pardon. I cannot resist eavesdropping on Dad and his would-be daughter-in-law; the former major general and the ex-political prisoner are getting quite animated in Burmese, discussing the thorny topic of social justice and the Tatmadaw.

The Burma Campaign UK and other international NGOs have been trying to secure the generals' conviction for genocide and other crimes against humanity, Thandar is telling Dad. But the Tatmadaw take no responsibility for their many atrocities over the past half-century. They insist that all their actions have been legitimate responses to threats against national unity — that is, in defence of the Union. What does U Lin Tun think? Dad, leaning back on the sofa, takes a swig of his cocktail and exhales. He thinks that both sides — the Tatmadaw on one, and the United Nations, NGOs, and ethnic minorities, including the Rohingyas, on the other — should agree to a trade, endorsed by the Security Council.

A trade? Thandar is confused. What does he mean?

All the generals, including the retired Than Shwe, replies Dad, would receive total immunity from prosecution for human rights abuses. No charges at all. Like the constitution says.

Thandar is beside herself, wondering what he's going on about with this crazy idea. What's the other part of the trade?

Dad smiles. The generals would agree to the dissolution of the Union of Myanmar by an order of Parliament, he says. All the ethnic minority leaders would be invited to Naypyidaw to witness the historic re-signing of the Panglong Agreement of 1947 — but under revised terms. With the stroke of a pen, Shan, Kachin, and Chin states, along with Karen, Karenni, and Arakan states, would secede from the Union and become independent republics. Burma — Myanmar — would be reduced to the divisions in between, from Sagaing in the north to the Tenasserim in the south, with Mon State remaining to unite them. Sort of like how Russia was carved out of the dissolved Soviet Union in 1991. Dad, pleased with himself, gulps down the rest of his cocktail and smiles. "Good idea, no?" he says to me in English. "Just thought of it now."

Thandar ponders it for a moment before pronouncing her verdict on the trade: it's a nice fantasy, but it could never happen because the Tatmadaw would not allow it. Everything's been working fine for them up to now, and the generals hold all the cards. Besides which, she adds, independent statehood would not solve all the problems for the non-Bamar states, especially Rakhine.

It's time to go. Thandar and I look at each other and open our arms to embrace. She holds on to me for a long time, then pulls away. The Burmese are not really big hug people, she laughs. But she understands that hugs are part of my Western culture. The funny thing is, we did not have much physical contact when we were dating. But now that she understands why, she seems to want to hug me all the more. She is going to miss me again, in a different way this time, she admits. For I am going back to the world I came from, the world I left her to go back to all those years ago, and it's a world she will probably never see.

When I object to that last comment — telling Thandar that she could come to the US any time, and we would be happy to fly her over — she tells me it's not that simple. She doesn't want to go anywhere else until things are better in her own country. There is too much work to do.

Come on, I tell her, give yourself a break. You are free now. There are others to do this work, not just you. And don't you think Suu Kyi will win the 2015 election?

Sure, she will, and maybe the next one, too, Thandar replies. But what difference will that make? Parliamentary democracy guarantees nothing. The Tatmadaw will not allow Daw Suu to change the constitution. Even if she supports their policy in Rakhine, all it will take is one decision they don't like, and they can launch another coup at any time. And if that happens, all her work — all that struggle and sacrifice since 1988 — will have been for nothing.

There's an awkward silence. What can I say to that? We stand there, staring at each other and saying nothing more, when I suddenly remember: we must have another photo together. Special Branch has kept the one from Mandalay, which I was going to give Thandar before the argument at Junction Square. I still have the negative and can send her another print later. But we need a new one, so I enlist Robert to do the honours. Thandar wraps an arm around my shoulder while my husband pulls out his iPhone. She gooses me, just as she did in 1988, the moment Robert takes the shot. Then it's time for goodbyes.

"Until we meet again," I say, giving Thandar the folded-hand greeting of respect.

"I hope so," she smiles faintly, returning the gesture.

32

On the drive to the airport with Dad and Robert, Randall Carson tells us there has been a request to make one stop along the way: Khin Nyunt, the former head of Military Intelligence, has asked to see Ko Lin Tun before we leave. There are no details about the reason for this meeting, says Carson, only that the infamous spy catcher wants to pay his respects to a former Tatmadaw officer. If Dad agrees, we are to stop at an art gallery on the northeast end of Inya Lake, where Khin Nyunt will be waiting. Dad shrugs. He cannot imagine why Khin Nyunt wants to see him, since they have never met. I convince him not to worry; we are still under Embassy protection. Besides, it's not every day that you get a chance to meet a former SLORC bigwig who's now a civilian. And, I must admit, I am somewhat intrigued by the prospect of my own reunion with this man who once pinned a medal on me thinking I was someone else.

Since my return to Burma, I've been catching up on Khin Nyunt's life from reading foreign news reports. Despite having spent seven years under house arrest, he seems to have done pretty well for himself. For starters, he owns a mansion in General's Village, an exclusive Rangoon neighbourhood for the military elite where driveways are filled with German luxury cars. The mansion earns him more than $80,000 a month from the USAID-funded global development firm that rents it from him. Khin Nyunt owns other lucrative properties, too, but he seeks publicity only for an art gallery that he opened recently beside his home near Inya Lake. That's where we're going right now.

Turning into a densely forested driveway, our limo follows a path to the gated compound of Khin Nyunt's mansion, a one-level postmodern complex painted yellow ochre. Parking in front of a smaller building beside it, Carson directs us to the art gallery gift shop, where he says we'll find the former secret police chief. While he waits in the car, Robert and I help Dad out of the rear seat, escorting him into the gallery. There's not much to see in the unremarkable collection adorning its walls, mostly folk art typical of the tourist shops that have sprung up all over Rangoon: painted renderings of pastoral scenes with lush green rice fields, pristine lakes, peace-loving monks, and humble villagers. Or still lifes of mangoes and jackfruit.

In the gift shop, a framed photo on the wall shows Khin Nyunt and his wife holding white doves. Part of the former spy chief's image makeover, I suppose, as a cultured man of peace. I announce our presence to staff. The cashier asks us to wait while she goes to find the owner. Robert and I wander through the store, browsing while Dad stands at the cashier's till. When the cashier returns, the Big Man himself is right behind her. Khin Nyunt is dressed in a casual grey T-shirt and khaki trousers. The cashier introduces her boss. When he steps forward to greet Dad, the two men's eyes meet. Khin Nyunt smiles, shoots up his right arm, and salutes my father. Dad does not return the salute but begins to tremble, literally shaking in his boots.

"*Kgyi-gan myat see!*" he gasps in Burmese. "Little Crow Eye!"

"Greetings, Major General. So wonderful to see you again. It has been a very long time, has it not?"

It takes me a moment to put two and two together: that Khin Nyunt was the young soldier my father had mentioned in his journal, the one who helped our family escape from Burma on the night I was born, the night of the 1962 coup. The one with the strange nickname, the one whose real name Dad could not recall because he regarded him as a yes-man whose career path would never interest him and because of his own estrangement from Burma since he fled the country. Dad knows the name "Khin Nyunt" from news reports since 1988. But he has not seen the man's photo, so he has not made the connection until now: the notorious Khin Nyunt is Little Crow Eye, his one-time subordinate and saviour. Dad looks like he's going to faint.

Khin Nyunt turns to me and grins, addressing me with my real name as if he had never mistaken me for a dead soldier. "Your father and I used to work together," he boasts. "I was the one who helped him and the rest of your family leave the country on the night you were born."

Dad, staring at Khin Nyunt, struggles for words as he tries to reconcile the young soldier from 1962 with the SLORC monster who, during the late eighties and early nineties, presided over the arrest and detention of some four thousand people; a man whose misdeeds were well-known throughout the world. While Khin Nyunt makes small talk, his former superior takes a deep breath. When he speaks up, Dad continues addressing the former statesman, somewhat rudely, with his youthful nickname.

Why, my father wants to know, did *Kgyi-gan myat see* warn him of his arrest and allow his family to escape? He took a tremendous personal risk in doing so. He could have been executed.

Khin Nyunt smiles again. Sometimes, he replies, again addressing my father as "Major General," we are not who we appear to be. Your son — he turns to look at me — has proven this more than once. Khin Nyunt says he was a young man in early 1962: twenty-two years of age, his entire life ahead of him. Yes, he was a good soldier and loyal to superiors. But Ko Lin Tun was one of those superiors, too, and Khin Nyunt did not wish to see him or his family suffer.

Dad, dissatisfied with this answer, wants to know more. It never made sense, he says, Khin Nyunt's being at the hospital. How did he know about Min's birth?

"Well, Major General, that is why I have requested this meeting," he replies in English. "Can we speak alone for a few minutes?"

My father turns to me. I shrug my consent. He turns back to Khin Nyunt and slowly nods his agreement. The former SLORC number two then takes my father by the arm, leading him to a room behind the cashier and closing the door. Robert and I return to browsing while we wait for the two men to finish their conversation. They are gone for nearly fifteen minutes. We are both growing bored from the wait, and I am getting restless knowing that we need to be at the airport soon. When they return, Dad is visibly upset.

"Take me to the car, now!" he mutters. "We must be on our way." Walking ahead of Khin Nyunt, he proceeds out the gift shop door without turning around to say goodbye. Khin Nyunt has no reaction to this abrupt departure but stops at the cashier and puts his hands on his hips. He seems pleased with himself, despite having told my father something that has clearly upset him. At this I, too, dispense with good manners and leave without saying goodbye, running after Dad to prevent him from falling. Robert follows close behind.

"Dad, what happened? What did he say?" I ask once we're in the limo.

My father says nothing but shakes his head, tears rolling down his cheeks. He is fumbling with something in his pocket, an envelope Khin Nyunt has given him. Robert and I remain silent. So does Randall Carson, who pulls the car away from the parking lot and proceeds toward Kabar Aye Pagoda Road. I look out the rear window to see Khin Nyunt standing in the driveway, watching us leave. Then he walks to a path behind the gallery and disappears. On the road to the airport, no one speaks as the limo passes beyond city limits. Dad, still in shock from his unexpected encounter with Khin Nyunt and what they shared in private, is staring straight ahead, quietly weeping. On the plane, Robert takes the aisle seat while I sit between him and Dad, who has the window. I wait until after takeoff, when Robert has put on a pair of headphones for music, before turning to my father.

"Okay, Dad. Speak up. What happened with Khin Nyunt?" He turns to look at me for the first time.

"Such a cold, terrible man. So awful!"

"Yeah, Dad. That's kind of old news. 'Khin Nyunt bad' — got the memo."

"He was so proud of himself, so proud of his disgusting lie. He called it the moment when he secured his future by saving his own skin. As if that were somehow a virtue."

"What are you talking about?"

"The night of the coup! When he was there at the American Hospital. He said he had pledged to serve Senior General Ne Win in whatever capacity was required of him. He said he was loyal to me, but that only the Senior General could guarantee his future. So he took the path of least resistance. His every decision that night was based on whichever action would serve his own self-interest. And that meant betraying me."

"But how?"

"He said that Ne Win wanted to teach me a lesson for opposing the coup. He would do something cruel. He would take something away from me that was precious. Oh, it could have been you, my son! Thank heavens it wasn't. But still, such a terrible, terrible thing to do."

"Come on, Dad. I don't understand. What's in the envelope?"

"He was lucky, the little rat. *Kgyi-gan myat see.* Because of what happened in the delivery room, it all worked out nicely for him. I was late arriving at the hospital, so he could betray me without my knowing it. Your mother couldn't have known because she was unconscious, and Than Tun didn't know because he was down the hall in a waiting room. Even Ne Win was none the wiser! Yes, Khin Nyunt followed his orders and gave him what he wanted without the Senior General ever finding out he had pulled a fast one because he made sure we were already gone."

"Dad, I don't have a clue what you're talking about. What happened in the delivery room?"

Dad stares into space for a moment, shaking his head. "We had no idea. I could not have imagined … We didn't check for heartbeat. There was no ultrasound in Burma back then …"

"Are you talking about when I was born?"

"Not you, son."

"Well, then who?"

Dad looks at me sadly, shaking his head. Then he reaches into his pocket and pulls out the envelope, handing it to me. Inside is a double-folded, legal-size sheet of paper: a notarized birth certificate, dated March 1, 1962. Signed off by the medical superintendent at the American Hospital in Rangoon, it lists the father as Maj. Gen. Ko Lin Tun and the mother as Nu Nu Lin.

The baby's name is Aung Win.

"Your other brother," sighs Dad. "Your twin."

Note on Names

Key events in *Double Karma* occur in 1988. In May of the following year, the military junta renamed Burma and its then-capital city, Rangoon, as well as several other places. However, both the country and city are referred to throughout the text as "Burma" and "Rangoon" rather than "Myanmar" and "Yangon." Similarly, the state known as "Rakhine" is referred to as "Arakan," and "Kayin" as "Karen," while other places, including rivers ("Ayeyarwady" becomes "Irrawaddy") appear with their pre-1989 names. There are exceptions: citizens of the country who are residents, for example, use the new names, while "Rakhine," which also refers to a specific Buddhist group from Arakan state, is used in that context.

At the time the changes were announced, the Bamar Buddhist-dominated military junta claimed that the country's new name incorporated all Indigenous peoples. This is false. As one historian has noted, the SLORC administration "was moving in a nativist direction and looking for easy wins to burnish its ethno-nationalist credentials."[1] Many human rights activists, civil society organizations, and public intellectuals thus continue using "Burma" as a rebuke of the country's military dictatorships: from Ne Win in 1962, the State Law and Order Restoration Council in 1988, and

1 Thant Myint-U, *The Hidden History of Burma: Race, Capitalism, and the Crisis of Democracy in the 21st Century* (Norton, 2020), p. XXI.

the State Peace and Development Council in 1997 to the current regime of Senior General Min Aung Hlaing, which deposed the elected government of State Counsellor Aung San Suu Kyi and the National League for Democracy with a coup on February 1, 2021.

Acknowledgements

As a work of fiction, *Double Karma* encompasses actual events and real persons, both living and dead at the time of writing. Because the story is set during a period ending in 2013, many events were still fresh as some of the research for this novel took place. A personal interest in Burma had already led me to hundreds of newspaper articles, academic papers, and NGO reports — and several dozen books — before I even began. *Double Karma* was thus influenced by many writers who have contributed to the literature on Burma, some of whom I would like to acknowledge. For general historical background, I am indebted to the works of Thant Myint-U; for the events of 1988, to the works of Bertil Lintner, especially *Outrage: Burma's Struggle for Democracy* (White Lotus, 1990); for the dictatorial mindset, to Benedict Rogers' *Than Shwe: Unmasking Burma's Tyrant* (Silkworm Books, 2010); and, for women's experience as political prisoners, to Ma Thanegi's *Nor Iron Bars a Cage* (Things Asian Press, 2013). Among recent works about the Rohingyas, Carlos Sardiña Galache's *The Burmese Labyrinth: A History of the Rohingya Tragedy* (Verso, 2020) and Francis Wade's *Myanmar's Enemy Within: Buddhist Violence and the Making of a Muslim 'Other'* (Zed Books, 2019 edition) were most helpful.

In the decade it took to produce this book, I relied on the good will and generosity of many people. My first debt of gratitude is to the Pacific Burma Roundtable (a.k.a. Vancouver Burma

Roundtable), whose commitment to the people of Burma inspired my earliest efforts for this book. I am especially grateful to Rod Germaine for his kindness and support over the years — not least for reading several drafts of the manuscript and even solving my search for a title. Thanks as well to Mike Orders, Joie Warnock, Brenda Belak, Maung Tin, Soe Naing, and PBR's Burmese readers of the *Double Karma* manuscript: Tony Aung, Maria Hla Tin, and Margaret Nutt. I am also grateful to the late Helen Lee and another Burmese Canadian I interviewed who asked not to be named. Many thanks as well, to those who assisted my spouse and I in various ways while we lived in Rangoon for several months in 2013–14: Pana Janviroj, Daniel Collins, Benoit Trudel, Jerry Peerson and Kamil Pawlowski, and a group of Burmese friends, colleagues, and relatives whose kindness and generosity we'll never forget but, for their own safety, are not named here. Special thanks to my employer, the Canadian Union of Public Employees, for granting me the leave of absence that allowed our sojourn in Burma.

Back home, I am grateful to many people for their assistance during the manuscript stage. The biggest thanks go to a couple of writer comrades, Carellin Brooks and Brett Josef Grubisic, for their endurance of multiple drafts. Thanks as well to fellow scribe Dennis E. Bolen and to Soressa Gardner, Don Larventz, Jeff Mildner, Erin Mullan, Walter Quan, and Luci Standley. Further character development and helpful input came from Brenna Bezanson, Rob Jandric, Jemmy Peng, and Kira Yee, and others who assisted with a different version of a major character. Thanks as well to family members, friends, and colleagues I haven't mentioned who shared articles that kept me up to speed on Burma, sat through readings of excerpts, or otherwise expressed interest in this novel and waited patiently for its release.

I am most fortunate to have met Marc Côté at this stage of my writing life. My deepest thanks to Marc, not only for believing in *Double Karma* and having the faith I could pull off a novel but also for his guiding hand as editor, in advising me on the narrative approach and helping to bring the manuscript to the finish line. And thanks to the fabulous team at Cormorant Books — Sarah Cooper, Marijke Friesen, Angel Guerra, Sarah Jensen, Barry Jowett, Luckshika Rajaratnam, and Tiana Trudell — for their fine work.

Double Karma is in memory of my father, Paul Gawthrop, who I miss dearly.

It is dedicated to the people of Burma, whose yoke under military dictatorship has been interrupted by only a single decade since 1962. Atrocities inside the country have continued since the February 1, 2021 military coup, so please donate to one or more of the organizations assisting Burmese residents and refugees, including those aiding the Rohingyas.

Finally, *Double Karma* is for my spouse. Saw Aung Htwe Nyunt Lay — renamed Aung Htwe Nyunt Saw when he became a Canadian citizen, but better known as Lune — showed much patience and fortitude through the countless hours that I worked on this book. I thank him for his love and devotion, as always, but also for his help on the project: from the indispensable roles of guide, translator, and personal assistant while we lived in Rangoon to the photo he took at Inle Lake that graces the cover. Lune would never have come into my life had it not been for the scourge of military dictatorship in his homeland. More than anyone, this book is for him.

Daniel Gawthrop
New Westminster, Canada
December 2022

We acknowledge the sacred land on which Cormorant Books operates. It has been a site of human activity for 15,000 years. This land is the territory of the Huron-Wendat and Petun First Nations, the Seneca, and most recently, the Mississaugas of the Credit River. The territory was the subject of the Dish With One Spoon Wampum Belt Covenant, an agreement between the Iroquois Confederacy and Confederacy of the Ojibway and allied nations to peaceably share and steward the resources around the Great Lakes. Today, the meeting place of Toronto is still home to many Indigenous people from across Turtle Island. We are grateful to have the opportunity to work in the community, on this territory.

We are also mindful of broken covenants and the need to strive to make right with all our relations.